Taken to the Grave

Taken to the Grave

By

Craig Godfrey

www.penmorepress.com

Dedication

For my parents, Dorothy and Ken, forever encouraging.

Introduction

In 1804, due to fears of French occupation, Lieutenant David Collins, was sent to the fledgling colony of Van Diemen's Land. In February of that year he set up camp in Sullivans Cove. Sullivans Cove is now bustling with tourists as is the whole of Hobart's waterfront. Lieutenant John Bowen had raised the British flag on the opposite side of the river in swampland four months earlier. From the beginning law and order was an issue. Times were tough in this open-air prison and discipline essential to its success.

Crime in old Hobart Town met with swift 'justice', where short trials often ended with the prisoner at the end of a rope.

A decade later free settlers started arriving, attracted by land grants, the chance of a fruitful future and the government's offer of free convict labour to build the growing colony. As convicts completed their sentences more and more destitute souls roamed the streets. Crime was widespread. Summary corporal punishment in the streets was common and even dished out to the free settlers who transgressed. With a shortage of volunteers due to poor pay and conditions, police constables were recruited from ex-convicts. Corruption was rife.

When Lieutenant-Governor George Arthur, of Port Arthur fame, governed Van Diemen's Land from 1824 to 1836, he controlled the colony as an autocrat, creating a powerful police presence. However this was resented by many citizens as a number of ex-convict constables abused their authority for personal gain.

By the time Sir John Franklin took the reins in 1837, the British Government refused to fund the police force, ordering Franklin to finance the police force from local taxes and funds. This had a further detrimental effect on law and order.

In 1842 the British Government introduced a probation system. Convicts of good behaviour were offered tickets-of-leave firstly, and eventually a conditional pardon allowed them into society as free employees. Some built up businesses and became wealthy citizens.

With this system being moderately successful the British Government, in all its wisdom, sent large numbers of prisoners to the island, including convicts from New South Wales, where transportation had ceased after 1840.

But the police force took a downturn in 1843 during an economic depression under governorship of Sir John Eardley-Wilmot. The pardoned convicts found it difficult to find work, crime increased and bushrangers, who had been suppressed under Arthur, were now roaming free in the countryside.

By 1847 the population of Van Diemen's Land was 70,164 with 517 police constables. The discovery of gold at Ballarat in Victoria in 1851 changed everything. Police constables retired in droves and headed for the *rush*.

The life and adventures of Caspian Hunter from Birmingham is fiction. However it is easy to imagine a small group of men, along with trusty Holly, couped up in a small dank office hidden behind barrels of salted meat at the prisoners' barracks storehouse, solving the more serious crimes.

Prologue

From the Diaries of Caspian Hunter Esquire

My name is Caspian Hunter. I am enjoying the third decade of my life, having grown up in Birmingham where I was educated at Grammar School at the expense of my god-father, Albert Hunter, a reclusive gentleman with no children of his own and a passion for books. He had made wise investments within the merchant trade. I discovered I had the mind of a sleuth seven years ago now, when I solved the mystery of the Birmingham Fair Murders, where four young women in a travelling circus were murdered. Not only did I single-handedly arrest the perpetrator, but I also collated enough evidence to ensure the villain's hanging. With *the world is my oyster enthusiasm* I sailed from my home in Birmingham to Van Diemen's Land, on the other side of the globe, to take up the position of second-in-charge of the newly formed crime detecting agency in the fledgling colony. It was 1855, the twenty-second year of the reign of Her Majesty Queen Victoria. Little could I have suspected how my life would change from the moment I sailed up the mighty River Derwent towards Hobart Town.

An abandoned ship drifting at sea was but the beginning of a mystery that would lead me after villains the likes of which were rare, even in Old London Town. Within ten days of sailing into Sullivans Cove I had solved three major crimes and made a name for myself – rather unexpectedly I must confess. Life in Hobart Town for a bachelor lawman was good – the ladies accommodating, the fare toothsome and the ales made from the fresh mountain water was as good as any I had sampled anywhere.

We made a great team, my colleagues and I. We were enthusiastic; we watched each other's back. Our commission was dangerous, dare I say adventurous and my records meticulous …

This is my story.

But first, my partners in crime:

Heading the office is Mr Fabian Winter. What can I say about Fabian? Well, to begin with, he is a rake; a likeable scoundrel I guess one would say. He will reach his thirty-sixth year this year, god willing. Certainly, he has an ego to match his prowess, after all who would name the police sloop *Fabian*, after himself. Fabian enjoys the company of beautiful women, delights in the pleasures of an inn beverage or two and a fine meal. Fabian has a charismatic charm women find irresistible. I imagine personable would be a suitable description. He cuts a stylish figure with his usual smart dress of tartan trousers, waist jacket, frock coat and boater hat. He has the large brown eyes of a Labrador and keeps his hazel hair neat, with a pencil thin moustache in a straight line across his upper lip. Oh yes, the man *is* a stylish rake.

Fabian is married, yes. At least he tells us so. Although no one in our circle has ever met the good lady. Sally I believe her name is. But the woman is shrouded in mystery. 'Sally is understanding,' Fabian would crow with a quart of porter in one hand, and the other comfortably resting on the derriere of some inn wench. 'It don't matter where I get me appetite, she tells me. So as long as I eat at 'ome.' All very well I say, but I have known the man to dine out on more than one occasion.

Under Fabian's and my authority – did I mention I am second in charge? – Fabian and I command four constables. Jasper is the youngest at twenty. An apparently undernourished lad who had been taught the basics in life at Ragged School in Wapping. But Jasper is by all means a likeable character with his hooded eyes and slow speech, naïve yes, but blessed with unquestionable courage, a dedication to the service and a hunger to learn. He married young; some say there was no choice in the matter, to protect the virtue of his sixteen-year-old lover who was with child. However, he vehemently denies this.

Billings is more dignified. A twenty-eight-year-old gentleman of fine proportions and pleasant appearance. Billings is my age and the only one educated to my standard. He sports thick mutton chops that do not quite meet beneath the chin, but has no moustache; appearing more like a Bow Street Runner in his top hat and wielding his truncheon. Billings shares a dry sense of humour with a neatness of dress about him becoming of the quintessential lawman.

Holly Villan is no fair maiden. Holly is a sharp-witted, green-eyed, red haired Irish girl who grew up with six brothers. Six brothers who treated her ... well, like a brother. She is a robust, strapping young lass; the word 'fear', I swear, is not in her vocabulary. Holly is short, four eleven maybe, with the build of a sawyer. She dresses like a farmhand from the country, with a smock coat to protect her undergarments, a simple smock of cotton requiring few seamstress skills. The britches carry on up towards the ribcage to keep her lower back warm; fastened with gaiters wrapped around the lower leg and tied with one piece of string. As I said: fair maiden Holly is not. Holly prefers to keep her hair short-cropped; kept short *so it was easy for bestin' the villains,* she liked to say. And tackle villains she would. Holly sported a leathered scar across her brow that proved this statement. A blade wound of some description. But under her no-nonsense façade Holly concealed a heart of gold.

The latest member to join our ranks is Lantern Jaw Lincoln. No one knows his given name so we simply call him Lincoln. Six foot six Lincoln has, well, a square jaw reminiscent of a lantern. He grew up as a mudlark on the Thames before ending up in the colonies. Lincoln has a lasting musty smell about him, like the atmosphere of a damp cabin. But there is a comfort in this lingering musty scent. A sense of security accompanies the man with his towering presence and pugilist's jaw.

Then there is me, Caspian Hunter. A little fish in a huge pond; one lawman in a sea of villains. I work hard and yes, I confess, I play hard. The truth is hunting scoundrels and rogues is a stressful career. Certainly I have brushed shoulders with many an innkeeper, fille de joie, felon and malefactor, and have been known to partake of life's many pleasures. But I have also dined with magistrates, taken brandy with the governor and shared company with the gentlemen and fair ladies of the colony.

However chasing criminals is my priority and I like to think I do not take fools easily. But I will let you, the reader, be the judge of that ...

Chapter One

Day One – Hobart Town, Tasmania, Winter 1857

It would start as it ended. Unpleasantly …

Self-proclaimed evangelist Ashley Andrus Alcock barked his misguided beliefs before an outdoor congregation of Hobart Town's less-fortunate; gullible, ignorant souls desperate to believe in his hypocritical views of god almighty and his personal convictions against the fairer sex. 'Humanity's greatest threat,' Alcock shrieked in his piercing falsetto, 'is when women are allowed to make decisions.'

''e's got that bit right,' I heard a some toothless ex-convict mutter to anyone who would listen. And he was not short of sympathisers. Uneducated dullards the lot of them I noted. Alcock burst into a tirade against the sins festering in the colony. All because of women. Apparently.

'Gin, tobacco, inns, music … all sins dear people, sins!' he squealed. He leered down at one hapless Hobartian. 'And I trust you sir … you are aware that bathing in warm water leads to masturbation, consumption and all sorts of evils.' The grubby recipient returned a salacious toothless grin. Even the temptation of sweetmeats came under his self-righteous broadside. Apparently sweetmeats were weapons of seduction and in this man's mind they should be banned. Sweetmeats for Christ's sake. Blasphemous I say. And people, he suggested, were indulging in sex for pleasure and not procreation.

'For pleasure!' the man raved, his salivating spittle spraying the gathering with a mist promoting chaste abstinence.

Forty-year-old Ashley Andrus Alcock was a short, portly individual with a receding hairline circling his pate. From each side of his chubby cheeks, manicured mutton chops gathered, sweeping to the base of his generous jowls. Here they united beneath his nose – itself a fine representation of a ripe William's pear – standing sentry above a waxed and coiffured moustache of magnificent proportions and architecture.

'And literature,' the corpulent orator singled out the printed word. 'Let me explain the evils of uncensored literature.' I shoved rather clumsily to the front of the rabble, the better to hear this god-fearing clod. I should divulge here, for anyone reading this memoir, that I had only this moment egressed through the threshold of the Sailor's Rest Inn. The Sailor's Rest belonging to my good friend, now retired whore, Bonnie Nettle. But more of my friend and the popular inn later. Suffice to say I had spent the afternoon in celebration after solving the gruesome murder of the butcher's wife; a most unfortunate soul whose husband saw fit to kill the poor woman so as to replace her with a younger version – all too often a fool's errand. But it was the method of disposal that shocked us all. The man boiled her in a vat of acid. And he would have gotten away with the dastardly crime had I not discovered the woman's wedding ring in the bottom of the vat. The ring and part of an ankle bone being the two pieces of evidence not dissolved by the acid.

'Yes. Literature,' Alcock prattled on after waiting for the murmurs to subside, murmurs aimed at my graceless intrusion. 'A good friend of mine had the misfortune to read *The*

Lustful Turk.' The man's voice rose in volume while tittering and chortles were barely suppressed by turning heads and craning necks as the peasants struggled to glean his every word. '*The Lustful Turk* good people, I am ashamed to repeat such a lewd title for any book that I have ever encountered. And my good friend read this licentious manuscript and was overcome with lascivious thoughts. These desires lead him to seek out a whorehouse.' This word was greeted by sharp inhaled gasps and a variety of subdued giggles. 'A house of ill-repute ladies and gentleman. A place where the good Lord has been abandoned.' Alcock timed a pause for maximum effect.

'Wha' 'appened next then?' some impatient wit demanded.

The sober abolitionist teetered on the edge of the empty ale keg that doubled as his podium. 'He procured syphilis,' Alcock spat, his eyes bulging to the size of boiled eggs. 'Syphilis, people. A flesh-rotting parasite that plagued him for years. He eventually went mad and finally plunged down to hell and into the fiery pits of Hades.'

'Devil's blood!' I muttered aloud before thinking.

'Devil's blood indeed sir,' the sanctimonious preacher fixed me in his sights as I listed to starboard on heavy wine-laden legs. 'You are a man of sober habits I take it,' he shot at me. My audible hic-cup could not have been better rehearsed. Laughs from the more corrupt amongst us fuelled the pious pulpiteer further.

'Shame sir!' he roared down at me. 'You are under the influence of evil drink.'

'Sh-shame?' I was affronted. 'How can you sh-tand there and accuse me of ... of being under the influence of drink when you sh-tand on your big fat barrel and shlander the virtues of women?'

''ear 'ear.' a few, faithful to my cause, chirped.

Alcock's vitriol was almost palpable. 'You step from a whorehouse, taken with liquor, and dare challenge my views sir.'

Now *I* was riled. 'Yes, I do. Women are the sholt of the earth, our flowers of procreation, without them we would be ex-extinct.' I surprised myself with my choice of prose. Immediately I was aware that colleagues Holly and Lantern Jaw Lincoln had joined me, one each side like gateposts. In fact we were all in need of each other's support, literally.

'Oh,' Alcock gripped the lapels of his coat and pushed his chest out like some prize cock. 'And I was of the opinion that men are also required in the procedure of procreation,' he sneered sarcastically at the increasing crowd.

'Aye,' the man at my side piped up. 'It takes two ter tangle.' Salacious laughter echoed around the waterfront at this comment. Holly cheered.

'And that it does dear sir,' Alcock's face reddened. 'But only when sanctioned by god almighty should these liaisons occur and only under the roof of those married in the eyes of the Lord and only for the purpose of procreation.'

'Humbug!' The word spilt from my lips as naturally as taking a breath.

''ear 'ear.' Holly belched.

'I hate to say this Caspian sar,' Lantern Jaw Lincoln said matter-of-factly, 'but he does have a point.'

'What?' I scrunched my face in disgust.

'Gettin' married first like,' Lincoln said. 'No man wants a bastard.'

'Oh please,' I dribbled. 'Do not tell me you believe all the fallacious mullock vomiting from the mouth of this holier-than-thou, priggish, goody-two-shoes?'

The preacher stiffened. 'Excuse me! Sir.'

Bugger. He heard me.

'Hobart Town needs cleansing. Van Diemen's Land needs cleansing ...' Alcock raised his head and hands to the heavens and hollered. 'The entire world needs cleansing.'

'H-Have you ever married?' I asked as I managed to synchronise two images of the man shifting into one like a three-dimensional photographic image seen through a stereoscope.

'I don't see that is any of your business sir,' Alcock hissed with a double measure of venom.

'Ansher the question if you please?' I persisted, lips pinched, shaking my head and shrugging my shoulders to my ever-more-captivated audience. The mob all around me was united. They wanted answers.

'I ... ah ... I ... well if you must ask. I was once betrothed.' Alcock's little fat feet shifted on the barrel. He wanted to be elsewhere.

'Betrothed ... huh?' I asked with a sense of victory. 'And why, I am certain all these fine people would like to know, why did you not follow through with this commitment of betrothal?'

'Now you are being too bold sir.'

I was starting to enjoy myself. I felt like the cross examiner in the courtroom. 'Well?' I insisted, pushing my chest out with thumbs under my lapels.

The crowd jeered for a response.

'No!' Alcock stood erect. 'I will tolerate this inquisition no further. For that's what it is, an inquisition.'

'Answer the man,' someone bawled out.

'Absolutely not … that is certainly none of your business …'

'She run off with Captain Maypole from the barracks,' another inebriate yelled.

'Who?'

''is betrothed. I remember 'er well I do … 'twas back in '46 weren't it?'

'Aye,' an old woman cackled. 'She were a doxy if'n my memory serves me correct.

'No bloody wonder she left,' another cried out. ''e's got the charisma of a slop bucket.'

Suddenly the preacher's arrogance faded and if I did not know any better I was certain I saw a tear moisten the preacher's cheek.

'Lynch 'im!' a voice cried out from the perimeter of the discourteous onlookers. Two or three yelled in agreement. I really do not believe they knew what lynching meant. 'Lynch 'im I say.'

'This isn't the dark ages.' I managed to cry out before being shoved aside. I stumbled three steps to port before bracing my fall in an abrupt judder against a brick wall. Holly, in her state of befuddlement reached out to aid my stability only to trip over Lantern Jaw Lincoln's clown-sized boots and ram the said wall like a forward in a rugby match … head first.

Holly crumbled semi-conscious onto the wharf as her devoted friend Lincoln dived on top of Holly to save her from the rabble charging the man of god.

Now I know, reader of my memoir, what you are thinking. This self-proclaimed apostle did not deserve a lynching.

We are talking about a man having his arms and legs wrenched from his torso by a frantic, angry and lawless mob. But in my opinion he at least needed dismounting from off his high horse. Well, on this occasion his high barrel.

Suddenly the crowd dispersed in a panicked stampede. I heard the unmistakable cracking of skulls accompanied by screams in pain as thugs brought lead-lined coshes to bear on the spectators nearest to Alcock. In truth, I now realised, the man had little faith in his god and more reliance on his hired ruffians. Four seafaring brutes wielding their short but effective clubs soon cleared a path for the not so reverend Alcock. In the pandemonium the man was hustled past me.

'You villain,' he scowled in passing. 'You are the devil incarnate ... you ... you whoreson!' He screamed out, 'We will meet again.'

'I'll drink to that,' Holly rose to her feet, albeit unsteadily.

'Whoreson?' I yelled back, snatching the man's coattail. 'I'll have you know ...'

My words were cut short by the glancing blow of a sailor's cosh on the side of my head. Orbs of light darted before me.

They say you see stars.

Urgent hands the size of shovel blades hooked under my armpits and I felt myself lifted crudely into the upright. Lincoln had my back. God bless his woollen socks.

'I hate to say this Caspian sar,' Lincoln felt compelled to say, 'but you caused a right kerfuffle you did.'

Immediately Fabian appeared with Jasper and Billings at his side and clenched fists matched the coshes, blow for blow. Man to man. Brutes against brawn and brawn against brain. A wild exchange of fisticuffs, all part of the daily life of a colonial waterfront.

And it was Sunday!

From the corner of my eye I saw Bonnie Nettle step from the Sailor's Rest armed with a broom and shouting, 'There'll be no fightin' outside my inn!'

Bonnie immediately laid into all and sundry within her range; be they fighters or innocent bystanders. Black Gavin, her six-foot-six Negro watchman, a former Yankee whaler, stepped into the fray snatching punters by their collar and tossing them aside like rag dolls.

'Caspian!' Bonnie singled me out, while Lincoln propped Holly against the wall, Holly's eyes crossing and having difficulty focussing. 'Caspian,' Bonnie shouted over the cursing brawling rabble. 'You lot get back to the inn, go through to the parlour. Smartly now.'

Black Gavin found Fabian, Jasper and Billings in a tight knot, cornered by two of the reverend's henchmen and four other gin-fuelled compatriots bent on venting their anger on the Hobart Town lawmen. Black Gavin snatched the closest pair, cracking their heads together in a sickening crunch. The others saw the error in their choice of foe and dispersed while the hired thugs joined the preacher and finally spirited him to a waiting coach.

Meanwhile, us exhausted, overworked, underpaid and inebriated lawmen were herded back into the inn by a vexed innkeeper. I should mention here that the Sailor's Rest is a well-operated inn at New Wharf on Hobart Town's busy waterfront. An inn of fine repute, although the haunt of several filles de joie who accommodated the needs of seaman. My good friend Bonnie Nettle was at the helm, a feisty lass many years older than I, who had traded French hosiery for modest pantaloons years ago. We became good friends – platonic, I hasten to add – when I stayed at her inn for some months, on arriving in the colony in '55.

As news travelled of the outdoor skirmish, Black Gavin escorted us through the taproom and away from further temptation where encouraging hoots and whistles followed us into the rear parlour. Bonnie ordered several pots of steaming black coffee and closed the parlour door before turning to me.

'I heard you started that Caspian.' She was displeased.

'I ... ah ...' I rubbed the side of my head where I had been clubbed and looked at my hand; there was blood but not enough to worry about. Bonnie on the other hand was seeking blood.

'Well?'

'He was slandering women Bonnie,' I said in my defence. 'Pity help mankind if women are allowed to endure what he preached.'

'Bastard,' Bonnie said. 'I warned his minders he was not to preach outside my inn.' Bonnie ran an eye over my colleagues and back to me.

'You know as well as I do my licence will be revoked if there's brawlin' inside or out.'

'Sorry Bonnie,' Fabian spoke up as our supreme leader. 'But they were beltin' Caspy and us lads stick together.'

'Very commendable of you Fabian,' Bonnie had us in her palm. 'But do you know who that preacher is?'

'Ashley Andrus Alcock ...'

'Smallcock more like,' Holly coughed a laugh before holding her aching head.

'Hah!' Bonnie spat, fanning her hand before her nose as the fug of Holly's last rum assaulted her senses. 'You can laugh.'

Bonnie certainly wasn't laughing. She placed her hands on her hips, her brow wrinkled in an intense scour and her gorgeous big blue eyes narrowed as she singled out yours truly once more. 'That man, I'll have you know, is no other than ...'

Two things instantly killed the conversation.

The parlour door flew open with a bang against the wall and two Redcoats barged into the room, followed closely by Black Gavin carrying a tray with pewter coffee pots, cups and accoutrements. I gathered that if the Negro did not have his hands full he would have manhandled the soldiers back out of the parlour.

'Sorry madam, they just beat me to the door,' Gavin looked about desperately for somewhere to place the tray.

Bonnie turned on the soldiers. 'What's the meaning of this?'

'I beg your pardon Miss Nettle,' the corporal tipped his shako to Fabian who was desperately trying to wipe blood from his tartan trousers. 'But we 'ave been sent to find Mr Fabian Winter there ... and his entourage,' he added looking at the rest of us.

Entourage? I thought. *I suppose I've been called worse.*

'Haven't you been taught to knock?'

'As I said miss, I beg your pardon like, but this 'ere Negro gentleman was ...'

'No excuse.'

'Aye miss.'

'Wha ...' Fabian started to talk but his parched throat temporarily strangled him. He cleared his throat loudly. 'What do you want corporal?'

'There's been an unlawful killin' sar.'

'Jesus, it's the Sabbath fer Christ's sake.'

I should mention here that the colony had been murder free the past week. We had become blasé of late, let our guard down and took the liberty of celebrating our last success with a well-earned sojourn at The Sailor's Rest. Now, while we were at our most vulnerable ...

'A murder yer say?'

'Aye sar.'

'One hour,' Bonnie told the soldiers.

'Madam?'

'They'll be one hour.'

'But ...'

'Are you deaf man? I said they'll be one hour. They're not on duty 'til they drink them pots of coffee.'

The corporal looked at his colleague and fidgeted anxiously.

'The victim *is* dead I assume,' Bonnie was adamant. 'So another hour won't matter, now bugger off.'

God bless you Bonnie.

Holly, Lantern Jaw Lincoln and my good self found the small vertical board cottage on Cascade Road in South Hobart Town, a sobering hour or two later. Two soldiers watched over the scene of the crime, relaxed and jovial while sharing a pipe. Although the soldiers had opened all the cottage windows and doors the horrendous stench of burnt human flesh assaulted our senses immediately. Sickly, almost sweet. Like a burnt suckling pig on the spit but with its innards intact. Holly vomited. Lincoln consoled his friend while I took in the scene inside.

Edwin Piketon, the victim, lay spread-eagled face down on the flagstones in front of the smouldering stove. He had been bludgeoned to death and left where he had fallen – backwards over the fuel stovetop. There was no way of knowing exactly how long he had lain there but the area of his body over the hot plates had cooked his body and his cadaver still smouldered where it lay, having been dragged onto the floor by the neighbour first on the scene. To the back of the stove an iron pot of blackened burnt stew cooled where it had been pushed aside, presumably by the neighbour who found the man. On the small pine kitchen table a large doughy mass was forming a crust. Bread or damper? It appeared the victim was in the throes of preparing a meal. I held my handkerchief to my nose as the neighbour, a man in his seventies and of gnome-like proportions, appeared from the shadows, quite startling me.

'Don't smell too good eh sir?' he said in a loud voice.

'You can say that again.'

'I said 'e don't smell too good sar.'

'Yes, yes,' I realised the man was holding an ear horn in one hand. He stared back at me with tiny black eyes peering from an unruly circle of chalk white hair, hair covering every inch of his face bar his nose. He had rosy red cheeks and lips.

'You are the neighbour first on the scene, yes?' I asked.

'What?'

'I said you are the neighbour that found this man?'

He stood staring at me blankly. I nodded to his ear horn, which he dutifully twisted into position in his left ear.

'You are the neighbour that found this man are you not?'

'Aye.' The man nodded curtly towards his smouldering former neighbour. 'Edwin Piketon be 'is name. He's a gravedigger for St Mary's.' He looked at the body a moment. 'Or at least 'e was. I live four cottages down the 'ill sar, but I also knew 'im from the Grey'ound. Me an 'im would play cards on euchre nights. But still I didn't know 'im all that well.'

'What were you doing here?'

'Eh?'

'I said what were you doing here at Mr Piketon's cottage?'

'Oh, I was lookin' for a missin' chicken. Bastard slipped the coop, when I seen smoke comin' under the front door like, so I looked in the windows an' seen 'im over the stove and smoulderin' like a side of beef.'

'Hmm. Married?'

'What?'

'I said was he married?'

'No sar, my wife died some years back.'

'Not you ... I meant Mr Piketon here.'

'Oh ... I thought you said ...'

'Never mind. Does anyone else live in this cottage?'

'Not that I know of. No sir.'

I poked the doughy mass on the table.

'That's damper sar. 'e was preparin' 'is midday meal, poor beggar.'

'And your name is?'

'What?'

I pointed to the ear horn, encouraging its continued use. 'What is your name sir?'

'Oh, Fred.'

The neighbour stepped into the late afternoon sun, which was now low on the horizon shining beams of light that accentuated the lingering smoke. It was then I noted the orange ring of nicotine staining the gnome's beard, common with bearded pipe smokers. 'Fred Finlay,' he reiterated. 'But most people call me Freddy.' I noted his eyes darting about as if he was in search of something.

'Oh Jaysuz!' Holly walked into the kitchen, took one look at the body, turned face about and made her exit to the sound of further retching. Lincoln watched her hurry back outside. He stroked that substantial lantern shaped chin of his for a moment and finally looked down at me as he bent under the low beams.

'I hate to tell yer this but there's a bad smell in 'ere.'

'Lincoln,' I said, ignoring the obvious.

'Sar?'

'Please fetch a bucket of water and douse the victim's wound. He smoulders still and yes, it is a most unpleasant odour.'

'Aye Caspian sar.'

I was starting to wish I could join Holly in the garden myself. 'And make haste man, if you please.'

As I could feel my stomach churning from my breakfast of black pudding and bread fried in lard, chased closely by several hours of drinking cheap Burgundy. I ordered Lincoln to roll the cadaver onto its back, the better for me to look for the cause of death.

'Oh!' The victim's deathblow was now clear for all to see. On the upper left side of his face and down his cheek to the jaw was the imprint in the perfect shape of a flat iron; and a hot one at that for the church window shaped wound was a darker shade of purple.

'Flat iron,' I said. 'It's been slammed with some force into his head.'

'Thart's gotta hurt,' Fred Finlay said almost cheerily from the bedroom doorway, his eyes darting about like a wary lizard.

'And on a more sinister note,' I observed, 'I think Mr Piketon was still alive, but unconscious, when he fell onto the stove.'

'Are you tryin' to say ...'

'He was insentient.'

'What?'

'Insentient. Senseless, yes. And his internals grilled while he was stupefied.' I saw a look of horror cross Lincoln's face. 'Oh, he would not have felt a thing,' I added. 'Like dying in your sleep.'

'Oh, thart's alright then.'

'Well, maybe.'

Fred Finlay rattled a whalebone ditty box on the sideboard. I started to suspect the man was looking for something in particular. 'Mr Finlay.'

'Freddy sar. Call me Freddy. Everyone does.'

'Freddy ... then. Ah ... what are you looking for?'

'What was that?'

'I said ...' I stabbed a finger at his ear horn in frustration. He acted on my recommendation and jabbed the infernal contraption in his ear. 'I said what are you looking for?'

'Nothing squire. What makes yer think that?'

'You are fossicking sir. Handling the deceased man's property.'

'Was I?'

'Yes you were.' My head was starting to ache as the earlier celebrations wore off and I longed for a spoonful of Weaver's Fluid Magnesia. 'A crime has been committed here,' I went on. 'You could be tampering with vital clues sir. Kindly do not touch anything.'

I was answered with a grumpy harrumph, when Holly returned from the garden looking positively pale.

'You alright Hol'.' Lincoln put an arm about her shoulder.

'It's not the drink Lincoln,' Holly said through watery red eyes. It's the cursed smell. It's ... it's ...' Holly heaved involuntarily. 'It's like the smell at the abattoir mixed with burning guinea pigs.'

Lincoln considered Holly's words a moment. 'Can't say I ever smelt a burning guinea pig Hol'.'

'Oh, I nearly forgot Caspian sar,' Holly wiped her sullied mouth with Lincoln's bandanna. 'One o' them soldiers outside told me Piketon here ...' and she nudged the smouldering cadaver with the toe of her boot. 'The dead'en *is* Mr Piketon I take it?'

'Yes.'

'Well Mr Piketon here was accused of being in possession of a huge diamond once looted some years ago from a palace in India.'

'What? How?'

'Apparently it was purloined from some Indian king or whatever and it was never found. The thief ...'

'Who, Piketon?'

'No sar, not Piketon, another lag what Piketon was involved with, who was court-martialled in India and ended up transported here to 'obart Town.'

'Oh.'

'Rumours have it that he...'

'The other lag?'

'Aye ... it was this other lag what smuggled the diamond with 'im when he was transported here to the colonies from India, where he finally died, but not before informing his friend Mr Piketon there who in turn hid the diamond somewhere. No one knows where.'

I looked back at the neighbour Fred Finlay whose wandering eye darted this way and that and guessed there was a fair chance this diamond was why the neighbour was poking about.

Lincoln rubbed his hands together. 'Motive for murder I'd say Caspian sar.'

'The guard outside told you this?' I asked Holly, thinking the story preposterous.

'Aye.'

'Fetch the man if you please.' Holly marched off with purpose at last. Another clumsy tinkering near the kitchen dresser drew me back to Fred Finlay the nosey neighbour. 'Were you aware of this?' I asked.

'What's that?'

'This diamond, Mr Finlay? Were you aware of a stolen diamond?'

He looked like a rabbit with one paw in the trap. 'Oh ... ah ... I may have heard stories years back. But they was only stories.'

'Is that right?' My personal thoughts about Mr Finlay were interrupted by the young soldier stooping low under the lintel yet still managing to knock his shako to the floor. It was then I noted tufts of hair missing. The man was a head scratcher and hair puller; an unfortunate casualty similar to a face twitcher or a nail-biter, except it left red patches of baldness on one's scalp like a rabid dog.

'Wilbur Barn, Anglesea Barracks, at your service sir,' the soldier was in the earlier years of his third decade.

'You told my colleague Miss Villan a story about a stolen diamond.'

'Aye sir. The Salmon Princess.'

'Salmon what?'

''Twas a rare diamond, salmon pink and that's why the Maharaja named it the Salmon Princess.'

'Interesting. Then please enlighten me if you will.'

'Well I don't know an awful lot Mr Hunter, suffice to say old Piketon there was recently a lag at Port Arthur.'

'You mean a prisoner?'

'Aye. And while there he befriended the likes of Corporal Hannibal Comstock, late of the British Foot Soldiers stationed in India some time back in the forties. This Hannibal Comstock was there in the Punjab when the Sikh kingdom fell into disorder after Ranjit Singh died.'

'My, your knowledge of foreign names is a credit to you Wilbur.'

'Aye sir. I've always had a thing for the British Empire and in particular India.'

'How commendable. Please continue.'

'Well in all the turmoil the palace was looted of fine art, gold and jewels. But the army caught most of the culprits and the loot was returned to the Maharaja, however a rare pink diamond was missing.'

Holly. 'The Salmon Princess?'

'Aye.'

'How would they ever know that one diamond was missing?' Lincoln wanted to know.

'Ranjit Singh's illegitimate son Kharak Singh, although deposed soon after he took power, had an old inventory of the more precious stones.'

'And the pink diamond was missing.'

'Aye.'

'So where does our deceased Mr Piketon fit into all this?'

'Hannibal Comstock was seen by a rival soldier pocketing the gemstone ... in India that is. And this man reported the incident to the army. Comstock was arrested, flogged and left in solitary for weeks. But he always claimed he was innocent. He was finally court martialled, dismissed from the Indian infantry and given seven years transportation for good measure.'

'To Van Diemen's Land?'

'Aye, and following another crime, robbery I believe, he was sent to Port Arthur.'

'And that's where he met our Mr Piketon here,' Holly kicked the cadaver once again as if half expecting the man to sit up and defend his reputation.

'Mr Piketon,' the soldier continued, 'was a small time criminal, a re-offender who was sent to Port Arthur in 1845 for larceny. The two met on a road gang and became close. Then after three years, as the story goes, Comstock caught the liver disease and it was on his deathbed that he told his friend about the pink diamond and where he had hidden it.'

'If this was true Piketon would surely have retrieved it after he was released from servitude.' I looked about the cottage. The dwelling was modest by all means and there certainly was no sign of overindulgence.

'Why would he live in this hovel?' I asked myself aloud.

'Excuse me,' Mr Finlay the neighbour was affronted. 'This 'ere hovel as yer call it is better than mine. We can't all afford a maid to sweep, cook and clean.'

'Yes. Quite.' I seemed to open my mouth to change feet frequently these days. 'What I meant to say Mr Finlay is this does not appear the abode of a man in the possession of a diamond worth a fortune.'

We stood about silently a moment contemplating the thought of such riches.

'How credible is this information Wilbur?' I finally asked the soldier. 'I mean if it is the truth then it is a possible motive for murder. Where did you hear this story?'

'My uncle sir, Humphrey Llewellyn, were a guard at Port Arthur.'

'Then I would like to meet your uncle, talk with him.'

'Trifle difficult sir.'

'Why?'

'He's dead.'

'Oh. I am sorry.'

'Don't be Mr Hunter. He was a genuine bastard.' The soldier took a long lock of hair and twisted it through his fingers. 'Tell you what though.'

'What?'

'Auntie Shirley's still alive, Shirley Llewellyn, his wife. And I know she knows more than me sir.'

'Wonderful. Give your auntie's address to Holly here and I require you to return to your barracks and requisition a cart to have this body removed to St Mary's Hospital. Also bring timber, hammer and nails. You will secure these premises once the body is removed. Understand?'

'Yes sir.' The soldier stood silently a moment, as if contemplating something important. 'There's one other thing sir,' he said.

'Oh?'

'Aye. There's been a couple o' housebreakings in the neighbourhood around 'ere as well.'

'Has there now?'

'Aye. A big olive-skinned cove was seen hereabouts an' at least two other cottages were entered when their owners were away, but nothin' serious stolen like.'

'Hmm,' I knew burglaries were common in these parts. 'Thank you Wilbur, I will take note.'

I slipped my watch from my waistcoat pocket. It was half the hour past two in the afternoon. 'But do not return until five o'clock. Do you understand?'

'Five sir.'

'Yes. And not a minute earlier. And send your colleague ...'

'Thomas Green.'

'Yes, Green, to fetch Mrs Rowley from her Collins Street photographic studio. She is to come here immediately ... immediately, do you hear me?'

'Aye sir.'

'And bring with her, her equipment to make images of the body and crime scene for the courts.'

The stalk thin soldier bowed once more beneath the sill and went off dutifully with his orders. I heard Mr Finlay fiddling in the shadows.

'Mr Finlay.'

'Yes sir.'

'Why are you still here?'

'I ... I ...'

'Kindly vacate these premises. I have told you once already this is the scene of a crime and I cannot have you tampering with what could be vital clues.'

The old neighbour grunted something, something derogatory I am certain, before dragging himself lazily out the back door.

'Oh Finlay,' I called after him. He turned to face me. 'We will be needing a statement from you in the next day or two. I would appreciate it if you could call at the prisoners' barracks in Campbell Street at your earliest convenience.'

'The b-barracks sir?'

'Yes. Do we have a problem?'

'No sar. Not at all.'

I don't know why, but I was starting to dislike this man.

'Holly.'

'Sar.'

'As you are feeling off, maybe you can search the yards outside for any clues. A sharp eye if you please. You know what to look for.'

'Aye Caspian sar.'

I looked to Lincoln who was stooped like an old man. At six foot six he was finding the six-foot beams a challenge. 'You can help me inside Lincoln. Start with the bedroom.'

'Aye sar.' The lanky man turned to negotiate the entrance to the bedroom only to crack his head on the lintel. 'Jaysuz Christ!' he cursed, falling hard against the bedroom door. The door slammed against the wall and we both heard a tinker as the lower brass door hinge fell from the doorjamb onto the bare floorboards. Lincoln spun back to me to apologise. 'Excuse the blasphemy Caspian sar, but Christ that hurt.'

He leant over picking the hinge up from the floor, when something caught his eye. In dislodging the hinge, the door now listed at an angle placing more strain on the upper hinge. And where the door was prised from the jamb Lincoln noticed an anomaly. 'What's this then?' he muttered.

'What's what?'

Lincoln answered with a question. 'Can you hold this door straight a moment sar?'

He fetched a round-ended dining knife from the dresser drawer and unscrewed the remaining hinges while I took the weight of the door. Moments later the door was free and together we leant it against the wall. 'Will yer look at thart sar!'

Where the bottom hinge had been was now a cavity, a small enclosure.

'A neat hidey hole for a diamond maybe?' Lincoln grinned. 'But it's empty!'

'By Jove Lincoln. I think you are right. How ingenious. The door must have been loosened or the hinge not screwed tightly back in place.' This discovery seemed to give some credibility to the diamond story. Suddenly a knock on a windowpane startled me. It was Holly and she held up a large kitchen knife.

'It's got blood on the point sar,' Holly said through the open window.

'Blood? But our Mr Piketon has no stab wounds,' I said.

Lincoln stood stooped, a wave of sage thoughts wrinkling his brow. 'Maybe Mr Piketon stabbed his attacker.'

'Or attackers,' Holly suggested.

'What do you mean? Attackers, Holly?'

'Well there are distinctly two sets of footprints in the garden bed here sar. Like someone was spying on Mr Piketon from out here.'

'Oh.' I hurried outside. Indeed there were clearly different boot sizes. Recent rains had rendered the earth clayey and the prints were distinct, although one was a heel only.

'And I spoke to the nearest neighbour,' Holly said. 'She told me she did see a stranger here on Piketon's property early this morning.'

'Excellent. Did she get a good look at him?'

'No. But she said 'e were a dark gentleman and big to boot.'

'Dark? Like a Negro?'

'No sar, like an Arab or someone from the Mediterranean.'

I made hurried notes. 'What is the knife doing outside? More questions than answers as always,' I said. 'Right, I want this cottage and surrounds searched thoroughly. Lincoln.'

'Yes sar?'

'Seal off that garden,' I pointed to the footprints. 'Then get some plaster of Paris and make casts of those two foot prints.'

Mrs Rowley. Oh how the name fuelled the fire burning within my furnace of love. Nay, I exaggerate. Lust. Aye. My furnace of lust. Known as Royle to her closest acquaintances; albeit yours truly. But *Mrs* Royle Rowley to the likes of you, dear reader of my memoir. I felt myself flush when I mentioned her name to the soldier earlier. My palms moistened. My loins tightened to attention.

'Fetch Mrs Rowley from her Collins Street photographic studio,' I ordered the man. 'She is to come here immediately ... immediately do you hear me?'

Take deep breaths Caspian. You've an hour to kill before she arrives.

Nothing gained, nothing lost. Meanwhile Holly, Lincoln and myself searched the cottage. There were very few clues. Two separate footsteps in the flower garden but little else. However I knew our victim had been struck with a red-hot clothes iron. The missing diamond was an intriguing fact we would have to confirm, but the cleverly hand-carved recess disguised in the bedroom door hinted at the possibility ...

The Salmon Princess? Maybe it did exist.

I heard carriage wheels crumbling over the gravelled road at the front of the cottage.

Royle!

I flipped open my pocket watch. Little hand on 1V, big hand on V. *She's cutting it fine.* I raced to meet her as the Hanson cab pulled up to the gatepost, threw my hands under her arms and heaved the dainty wench from her perch with the brawn of a randy seafarer and the elegance of a tannery apprentice.

'Ooh Caspian,' she giggled.

The driver fetched me a stare. 'That'll be five bob.'

'Fi ... five bob!'

Daylight robber.

'Five bob on account o' all that equipment in the back,' he muttered.

I fished a heavy silver crown from my purse and sent good Queen Vic into a spin where the driver plucked the coin mid-air like a lizard might snatch a fly.

'There's your crown.' And I tossed him an additional florin. 'Be a good chap and put the equipment inside the door.' The man was not averse to hard work, especially for the two extra shillings. 'And there's another crown here,' I tapped my purse, 'if you'll then make yourself scarce and return for said equipment and Mrs Rowley quarter the hour after five of the clock.'

'Aye sar. I can manage that.'

'Good man.' I turned hard on my heels in time to see Royle's sweeping petticoats gather about her ankles as she disappeared over the cottage threshold.

I should mention here my relationship with this most attractive forty-something widow. Mrs Rowley arrived in Hobart Town with the scientific equipment to start her own photographic studio some three or four years ago. You see her husband Lieutenant William Rowley was killed by a stray cannon ball at Balaklava at Crimea. (At least that is what I thought. He actually survived the wound and had recently turned up in Hobart Town searching for his estranged wife. All hell broke loose but he has since returned to England in irons, accused of treason, but that is another story.) At my instigation, after my own experiences in Birmingham, where I trained as a lawman, I convinced the court to hire Mrs

Rowley to make exact and irrefutable images of crime scenes with her photographic equipment, to use in the investigations and in the courtroom. Unbeknown to me at that time, Royle found crime scenes seductive. The hot-blooded woman of outstanding talent turned into a raving nymph and, as our liaisons were inevitably at crime scenes when we were alone, we sated ourselves in the most bizarre of locations, attempting situations that would make any reader of the Kama Sutra blush.

But let's be clear. I am an unattached man. Royle is a widow – well sort of. I promise, until recently I thought her estranged husband nothing but a ghost.

So, lucky me. And Royle only ever knew half of it.

'Oh Royle,' I gasped taking short breaths to catch up, while the woman surveyed the crime scene, hunched over the dead body.

'Oh Caspian.'

'Oh Royle.'

'Caspian ... there's no blood.'

'Oh ... ah ... no. He was bludgeoned with a flat iron but although the skull appears fractured there is no blood. So yes. You are correct. Come here you little munchkin.'

'Oh Caspian, you wicked, wicked boy.'

'I was a man last time I looked.' And to prove a point I allowed my britches to hit the deck ready for action. Royle stared at my manly evidence taking short sharp breathes like a hungry fat woman in a patisserie. I shuffled forward, careful not to trip on my attire encompassing my ankles. Royle's head disappeared momentarily as her frock and petticoats were hoisted aloft. 'Oh dear,' she whispered. 'I seem to have forgotten my pantaloons.'

'How forgetful,' I rasped. This foreplay was wearing thin and my voice was breaking. *In fairness the clock was ticking.* I hoisted the woman from the floorboards and lumbered to the kitchen table where I landed my catch – buttocks first – in the clump of uncooked dough.

I will leave the rest to your imagination, suffice to say … try it sometime.

Sometime later Royle managed two wet plate photographic images before the sun deserted behind the hills to the township's west. One image of the body and one of the cottage kitchen. While she developed the plates in her portable dark tent outside, the soldiers returned with a cart to remove the body to the morgue. I took it upon myself to nail up the windows and the two entrances, when the annoying and nosy neighbour Mr Finlay reappeared at the rear door.

'Now what, Mr Finlay?' I said abruptly.

'Say what?'

I pointed to the ear horn hanging loose in his hand. 'I said, now what?'

'Oh. I just had a thought sir,' he said.

'Oh. What?'

He looked beyond me to the damper dough flattened on the table. 'Well I was thinkin' like …'

'Yes.'

'Well thart damper there what Edwin left uncooked …'

Oh god! I looked over my shoulder and although the dough was rising once more it was clearly in the moulded shape of Royle's derriere. I stepped to the table smartly and folded the culprit in half. 'What of it?' I said rather bluntly.

'Well it occurred to me, sir, thart it'll go to waste like, and thart seems such a pity. So I was thinkin' ... well ... maybe I could bake it for me evening meal.'

This was totally unexpected. 'I ... I ... ah ... I don't know Mr Finlay. I ...'

'It's not like it's evidence, eh Mr 'unter?'

Evidence of what?

I felt caught between a rock and a hard place when suddenly I had a wicked thought. 'No. No of course it's not evidence. Fill your boots Freddy. It's all yours.'

'Why thankee sar.' His face exploded with appreciation 'It'll be much appreciated.'

Fred Finlay wrapped the uncooked dough into a square of cheesecloth he had brought with him in anticipation, and with the most satisfying grin he bid me farewell and pushed past Royle in the doorway.

'Ma'am.' he tipped his head in greeting and hurried away. Royle recognised the bundle under the man's arm and looked me in the eye.

'Is that what I think it is?' she asked.

'Do not ask,' I replied.

Blue Whale Cottage. Cromwell Street. Battery Hill.

I found the front door key hidden under leaves beside the sandstone sundial in the front garden of my neat little cottage where my housekeeper, Mrs Rumball had left it. My cottage being a leased dwelling, once belonging to a sea captain whose murder I solved nearly two years earlier. His distraught wife was only too happy to let me have the property at a modest rent as she could no longer bear to live there.

The bluestone cottage had three rooms downstairs and two attic bedrooms with large windows and wooden shutters. It was on a long narrow grant of land, with its own well at the rear and a moderate stable; not that I could afford the luxury of a horse. The neighbourhood was pleasantly quiet except for the constant clack clack of the cogs of Cowgill's flourmill opposite.

I had purchased a pine dresser from Rodney Burns, the used furniture merchant of Murray Street, and also invested in my very own set of dinnerware, namely blue and white crockery known as the willow pattern. With the plates displayed on the dresser shelves, along with teacups and pewter tankards hanging from hooks and a handsome soup tureen at its centrepiece. I felt quite the squire whenever I received a visitor.

My housekeeper, Mrs Emma Rumball, whom I could afford only four hours a day three days a week had left me a parakeet pie in the meat safe, a loaf of freshly baked bread under the protection of a muslin cloth and a rather worrying note.

My Dear Caspian,

It is with regret that I must inform you I could not wait for your return. I fear for the safety of my sister Hyacinth and her two wee daughters, who as you know works a farm with her husband Samuel on a small grant of land at Broadmarsh. And I have heard this day, from a friend at the barracks that the Port Arthur escapee Erasmus Peck maybe hiding out in the area. He has hitherto caused mis-

chief of a violent nature and I fear for their safety. Hyacinth is a gentle soul and needs me by her side.
Please accept my sincere apologies.
Your humble servant
Emma Rumball.

I sat alone. Alone with my repast of parakeet pie and the company of a lone candle, its flame dancing the occasional jig to a frisky draught blowing in off the mountain. I made a mental note to purchase a draught sausage for the door from Susman and Co. Haberdashers. The stopper remained in the decanter. Water was my companion this night. And my thoughts drifted to Emma Rumball. What could she do against a wanted felon like Erasmus Peck? But as the exhaustion from my eventful day incapacitated me with fatigue, I retired to my attic bedchamber where I was smartly borne away into a heavy sleep. Soon thereafter I dreamt my sturdy housekeeper, with the strength of a carthorse, could quite possibly be a challenge to the likes of the escaped villain Erasmus Peck.

Chapter Two

Day Two – Monday morning

Clack-clack-clacketty clack

I woke with a start at six in the morning. Cowgill's Windmill sails had been unleashed to the morning breeze fresh in off the River Derwent, propelling the infernal sails into perpetual rotation; well for the next twelve hours any-way. All the same I felt refreshed after a good night's sleep. I washed in my basin, dressed, breakfasted and marched off across the docks towards the prisoners' barracks in Campbell Street with a spring in my step and whistling a ditty when ...

'Mr 'unter ... Mr 'unter. Wait up sar.'

It was Jiemba, a ten-year-old aboriginal lad who often ran errands for my innkeeper friend Bonnie Nettle. 'What is it Jiemba?'

'Bonnie wants yer.'

'Oh?'

'Aye,' Jiemba danced in front of me. 'Bonnie says ter me, Jiemba, go tell 'em Mr 'unter ter get 'is arse to the Sailor's Rest quick now 'cos I wanna see 'im.'

'Did she say anything else?'

'Aye.' The four-foot-two scrawny bag of skin and bones was fast to answer. 'She said 'e's got a crown fer yer.'

'Nice try Jiemba.' I hoist my purse free from my waistcoat pocket, loosened the strings and rummaged through my coins for the standard remuneration for a ten-year-old messenger, a threepence.

'A threepence sar! Yer too kind.' This was his standard sarcasm.

'And don't spend it all at once,' was my standard reply.

Sailor's Rest. New Wharf west of the cove. Quarter the hour before eight.

Bonnie Nettle sat by the window in the empty inn parlour. Her shapely profile was silhouetted somewhat by the warm morning light. Just beyond the panes of glass three masted whale ships were docked, and the busy wharves absorbed in commerce. On the table before Bonnie lay an open box and standing over her was a rather handsome man of middle age; mixed race by all appearances, English Bengalese if I was to hazard a guess, with his long hair fastened within a turban. Bonnie caught sight of me from the corner of her eye. 'Caspian, you received my message?'

'That I did Bonnie, rather urgent I gather.'

'Yes. Please join us. I'd like you to be acquainted with Benjamin Raj.'

The Hindu traveller fixed me with a confident stare. His eyes were large and chocolate brown, complimenting the lighter fawn skin of the half-caste. He finally smiled, displaying the most perfect white teeth. We shook hands. His grip was rather weak. 'Mr Hunter, it is a pleasure to make your acquaintance.'

I nodded but my attention was drawn to the display box on the table. It was neatly laid out with male contraceptives.

Bonnie caught me looking. 'Benjamin is a merchant Caspian.'

'Hardly a merchant Madam,' Raj interrupted. 'I would prefer to think of myself as a travelling salesman.'

'Selling the latest in rubbers I see,' I said. Raj proffered a wide smile. 'Then you have come to the right place sir.'

'Oh yes. I visit all the bordellos.'

'And do a roaring trade no doubt.'

'Absolutely. These are the latest vulcanised rubbers made from Indian rubber.'

'Volcanized?'

'Yes. It's a process where the rubber is heated with sulphur. It softens the device. Please have a feel.'

I must have hesitated longer than I thought. 'Go on Caspian,' Bonnie grinned. 'You can feel the darn thing. It ain't been used.'

'Thank you for your assurance Bonnie.' I plucked a rather long specimen from the box.

'That's ten inches of India's finest rubber,' the salesman pitched.

'You'd need something with more generous proportions wouldn't ya Caspian,' Bonnie maybe the retired madam but she still enjoyed the wit of a whore.

'You'll never know Bonnie.' I teased, and then quickly changed the vulgar direction of our conversation. 'It certainly is soft, much softer than the sheep intestines most brothels use.'

'Oh please,' Bonnie feigned indignation at the 'B' word. Fact is we all call a spade a spade.

'The sheep intestine contraceptive is more to prevent syphilis than pregnancy,' Benjamin Raj noted in all seriousness. 'And they have to be soaked in water to soften them before use, precipitating a long wait for the impatient customer.'

'At least they can be washed for reuse,' Bonnie said in their defence.

'True.' Raj was quite at home with this rather personal conversation. 'You know women can use these also without the man's knowledge.'

'How's that?' I asked.

'By positioning them discreetly prior to penetration.'

Sorry I asked.

I felt a slight flush and thought it innocent to ask about the ribbon dangling agreeably from the open end. 'And the ribbon?'

'That, Caspian dear, is to fasten the contraption to the base of your John Thomas.'

'Oh. Of course.' Now I was fidgeting. 'So why did you want to see me Bonnie, business I trust?'

'Pink Diamond Caspian,' Bonnie said matter-of-factly. 'Do them two words mean anything to you?'

I looked at Raj immediately. 'I ... I ... ah ...' I floundered. 'Why do you ask Bonnie?'

'Well do they or do they not?'

'P-pink Diamond ... I ...'

'Yes or no?'

I felt uncomfortable having this thrust upon me in the company of a stranger. 'Well there is a rumour going about,' I said. 'And it is only a rumour mind, that a diamond could have been the motive for a recent murder.'

'Huh! I knew it.'

'Knew what?' I asked.

Bonnie jammed tobacco into her favourite churchwarden; a twelve-inch long clay pipe, compacting it with a whalebone tobacco plugger carved in the shape of a women's naked leg, complete with garter. She lit the bowl from a wax-headed match and drew hard, until she had an even smoke cooling through the long pipe stem before inhaling.

'Benjamin 'ere,' Bonnie exhaled. 'Who I've known awhiles by 'n' by, arrived last evening on the clipper *Calcutta* and we supped together. Caught up on all manner o' news. And eventually we got around to discussin' 'obart Town, its virtues and bad points. One thing led to another then I told 'im about a pink diamond, the size of a quail egg they say, what's supposed to have been the motive for a recent killin'. *Pink Diamond* says Benjamin. *Do you know how rare they are?* No says I. But then I tell 'im that the diamond was supposed to have come from India and that's when his little brown ears did prick up.'

'Oh?'

'Brown ears?' Benjamin repeated to me, his face close to mine. 'I prefer to think of them as light tan.'

'No Benjamin, they're brown,' Bonnie had that cheeky look she wore from time to time. 'Trust me,' she said, her words escaping through a drifting ring of smoke.

Raj looked about the room for his reflection. Nothing. 'I have got a mirror in my luggage you know,' he said with a cheeky grin.

'This diamond,' I smartly went on, not wishing to enter into a debate about the man's colour. 'This so-called pink diamond was possibly a motive for the murder of Mr Piketon but we have no proof it exists, or even if it ever did. And besides we searched his property with a fine toothcomb. It could be anywhere. A diamond is an easy thing to hide you know. It would be like searching for a needle in a haystack.' I decided to keep the hidey-hole Lincoln had uncovered a secret.

'The fact remains Mr Hunter,' Raj said in his heavily accented English, 'that the pink diamond *did* exist. It was stolen, it disappeared and the word in India amongst those in the know is that it did come to Van Diemen's Land and it is presumed here still.'

'Nice to meet you Mr Raj,' I said and made to leave.

'Call me Benjamin, please. Ah, can I call you Caspian?'

'Of course.'

'Then Caspian. If this diamond does turn up you may like my advice on how to … ah … well deal with it.'

'It would be evidence to a crime, Benjamin. The queen's evidence.'

'Yes. Quite.' But the smirk of the entrepreneur unmasked his true thoughts. 'All the same,' he persisted. 'It is worth a small fortune.'

Campbell Street Prisoners' Barracks. Half the hour past seven.

Her Majesty's Gaol, already thirty years old, was a stone fortress built between Brisbane Street and Bathurst Street. It housed one thousand two hundred felons. So cramped were the lockups that even ceiling cavities held prisoners. Five years prior to my arrival in Hobart Town a chapel and criminal law courts were added at the northern end of the prison, along with the most modern contraption for the executioner – a gallows complete with a trapdoor. A villain could be imprisoned, tried, executed, given a perfunctory few words from a man of god and then dumped into an unmarked grave on site. How civilised.

I stood a moment before the prison gates, better to catch my breath before taking on the challenges of another day. The massive gates of wood and iron were painted a dark green that I found quite pleasing, and were surrounded by fifteen-foot-high brick walls. Square stone pillars either side of the gate supported an ornate cast iron arch that in turn supported a large oil lamp at it centre. An iron door within the gate on the right side boasted a large brass doorknocker, which I recognised from my past studies of ancient Greece, as an image of Dionysus, the god of wine, ritual and madness. I wondered about this choice of entry for a prison full of villains as I put it to service with a thunderous knock.

The elderly keeper of the gate, Sergeant Richard Clincher, waddled to the prison gate like a man with one leg four inches shorter than the other. Leaning his Brown Bess musket against the wall he struggled with the iron pedestrian door within the main gate. As it slowly squealed on oil-starved hinges, I couldn't help but wonder what the man's response would be should a dozen prisoners escape the courtyard and rush the gateway at this very moment.

'Top o' the mornin' to yer Mr 'unter,' he cheered, through his painful arthritis and gout. He stood half to attention in his soiled red coat, stitched blue britches with a black leather shako balanced on his head, looking much the worse for wear. But for all his tardiness he was salt of the earth type. A man to have on one's side when in need.

'And a good morning to you Richard,' I replied.

'You don't sound like yer be wantin' Weaver's Fluid Magnesia this mornin' then sar,' he grinned, revealing a devil-may-care grin exposing a missing front tooth. For more often than I care to confess the man had come to my rescue with his cure-all for overindulgence after a night at the inn.

'No Richard, my mind is clear and I'm keen to catch a villain or two.'

I stepped onto prison property while Clincher made his cursory glance up and down Campbell Street. He made to close the gate once more, when urgent voices called out to him.

'Well if it ain't Holly god bless 'er,' Clincher kept the door ajar. The old guard had taken a shine to Holly, but then, who couldn't help like the brazen rascal.

Minutes later I stood staring at our workroom wall ...

Black Gavin, Bonnie Nettle's Negro watchman, a Yankee sailor at the Sailor's Rest who had jumped ship, gave me the idea. He had watched with some interest as I made extensive notes about crime scenes on several sheets of paper and suggested I paint a large board with black paint mixed with fine grit and secure it to the wall of our moderate office at the Prisoners' Barracks.

'All dem schools in America's usin' 'em,' he said. 'Blackboards they's called.' Then, as he suggested, I could display my notes written with chalk and link the clues and information, all the more convenient to study, when written up on a wall so to speak. And he was right. I purchased a cane swagger stick and hooked it beside the board to use as a pointer and assumed the role of tutor with Holly, Jasper, Lincoln and Billings, my obedient students.

Our leader, Fabian, on the other hand, had been vague of late. Secretive even. I had found him increasingly distant, pre-occupied with some matter he certainly did not wish to share with the rest of us. While the others concentrated with a keen ear and listened to the evidence analysed on the new blackboard, Fabian lent a shoulder against the door frame and puffed at his pipe, ever more distant, while we analysed what information we had in regards to the latest killing.

'Hannibal Comstock was transported to Van Diemen's Land from India in '45,' I ran my swagger across the board connecting the snippets of information, 'where he befriended Edwin Piketon ...'

'The dead'en',' Holly shifted proudly on her chair fishing for credit.

'The deceased. Yes Holly. Now it was always rumoured that the pink diamond accompanied him.'

'How?' Billings questioned. 'I mean, if the army suspected him, surely they would have searched him thoroughly before he was transported from India.'

'I am thinking he carved a small pod from wood,' I said. 'A capsule with a tight-fitting lid and inserted it in his rectum.' Twitches and winces followed this announcement. 'This,' I continued, 'is also how he managed to hide the gemstone for years at Port Arthur. Whenever he was moved cell to cell for instance.'

'But how can you be certain Caspian sar?' Jasper asked.

'I can't be certain. But I have spoken to old lags and more than one suggested this method of concealment.'

'Oh.'

'Then eventually he met Edwin Piketon.' I tapped the point of the swagger stick at the name. 'The two men met on a labour gang and over the next few years they became close friends and allies. But in 1851 thereabouts Hannibal Comstock contracted a liver tumour. He was confined to the infirmary where after some weeks passed he asked the matron at the Port Arthur hospital to allow his good friend Piketon to come to his bedside to say his farewells.'

'On compassionate grounds.'

'Exactly. And as Piketon was a model prisoner, he was allowed to the infirmary. Here he was given fifteen minutes to bid farewell to his old friend. Now on his deathbed Comstock told Edwin Piketon everything, and about the diamond and where he had hidden it.'

'Really?'

'This is my theory only Jasper.'

'Oh, Aye.'

Holly. 'Is it back in 'is arse?'

'For use of a better word, yes Holly. But this is awkward for Piketon. Can you imagine Piketon fidgeting about with the sick man's nether regions while he's dying and the matron is nearby?

'Shudder to think sar.'

'However he is successful and Piketon manages to smuggle the diamond back to his own cell. All the while his time alone with his dying friend has not gone unnoticed by other inmates aware of the rumour about the pink diamond. But the matron at Port Arthur, impressed with Piketon's bedside manner and compassion to a dying friend, puts in a good word for Piketon ...'

'Little did she know.'

'Yes well ... and soon after, Piketon is granted his ticket of leave and he moved to Hobart Town.'

Billings. 'This still your theory sir?'

'No, Billings, this bit is fact. The matron also wrote Piketon letters of introduction to the St Mary's Hospital here in Hobart Town and he was given the position of sexton at the Davey Street cemetery near the hospital. He was noted as an ex-prisoner of sober character and was seen daily, except for the Sabbath, walking the two miles from his cottage to his place of employment and back. Nothing untoward. No nefarious activities recorded. Now this.' I tapped the point of the swagger stick on the board again, underlying the name Piketon. 'This. The victim of foul play.'

'So, what happened?'

'I am thinking, yes, he had the diamond and kept it well hidden.'

'In his arse?'

'No Holly. He had found somewhere much more stable by now and I am certain I know where, but more about that later. He told no one, naturally. And it was still early days and far too valuable to try and sell, especially here in the colony. It would attract immediate attention from the law and Piketon would spend the rest of his days back in servitude. What I am suggesting is that he was keeping it for his old age.'

'I hate to tell yer this Caspian sar,' Lantern Jaw Lincoln said with disquiet, 'but Piketon were already old.'

'Maybe, but he probably did not think so. Maybe he thought he had a few years left digging graves at the cemetery yet. By the time he finally retired he would have had a full pardon and would be able to leave the colony, return to

England even. He probably thought he could fence the diamond in Sydney Town maybe.'

Billings. 'And live happy ever after.'

'Exactly. But,' I continued, 'now this is my thoughts only, one of the lags at Port Arthur has been finally released and has paid Piketon a visit. He threatens the man with death if he doesn't divulge where the diamond is hidden. Under torture Piketon has capitulated and the diamond is exposed from its hiding place ...'

'In the door cavity.'

'Yes Lincoln. In the cavity *you* so smartly discovered.'

'So why did he wind up dead sar?' Jasper asked.

'Well I am thinking that at some stage, probably while his attacker was retrieving the diamond from the cavity, Piketon has taken his kitchen knife and stabbed the lag. But he only wounded the man. The attacker fetched the flat iron off the stove and struck Piketon one deadly blow to the head. A blow that knocked him unconscious and he collapsed onto the stove top.'

'And this 'ere lag made his escape with the diamond.'

'Yes.' I chalked my thoughts onto my blackboard. 'But then we have the second boot print. Was this an accomplice?' I tapped the cane swagger stick on the plaster moulds taken from the footprints in the garden. 'Good work by the way Lincoln, perfect casts.'

'Thankee sar.'

'Do we have any idea what the diamond's worth?' Billings asked.

'I have been assured by a certain knowledgeable gentleman it would fetch upwards of eight thousand pounds in London.'

Whistles all round.

'So now where do we go?'

'We go to Port Arthur and interview some likely prisoners who may give us information.'

'We?'

'Yes ...'

Fabian finally interrupted. 'You can have Holly an' Lincoln. I want to get our filing system better situated. Jasper an' Billings, stay 'ere and arrange the cabinets.'

Fabian was right of course – our filing system was a shambles and the prison department had handed down to us two old filing cabinets.

'Then it is Holly and Lincoln who join me,' I said. 'We'll sail on *Cygnet* to Norfolk Bay on Tasman Peninsula in the morning,' I said of the official convict department supply brig. 'And then take the railway from there to Port Arthur.'

'Railway? On the peninsula?'

'Yes Holly. You're in for a treat.'

Chapter Three

Day three

We arrived at the penal settlement of Norfolk Bay on Tasman Peninsula aboard the government brig *Cygnet* – a 125-ton Royal Navy ship of 87 feet, 21 feet in the beam – mooring off shore some hundred yards from the convict station. The convict station was a rectangular construction eighty feet long and thirty wide with a shingled roof over attic rooms on the upper floor. A veranda enclosed the front and northern end of the building where a tall flagpole proudly displayed the Union Jack. Smaller prisoner huts were situated further into the cleared bushland a hundred or so yards up the hill. But most of the men required to operate this high maintenance, man-powered railway – and we are talking man power – were housed at the halfway point where, like coach horses, they could be watered and rested. It required fifty prisoners of good behaviour – in other words men that would not attempt to abscond – to operate the commandant's human-powered railway. In reality this railway was more a tramway, with wooden rails supporting small carriages pushed by convicts to Port Arthur, eight kilometres distant. This tramway, I was assured, avoided having to sail through the treacherous Storm Bay around the Tasman

Peninsula and into Port Arthur, where Antarctic swells and westerly winds often made for perilous voyages.

Almost akin to an omen, the weather deteriorated as we anchored in the bay. A chilly westerly harassed the giant gum trees surrounding the station and with dark black clouds gathering overhead a moonless sky threatened a dark and squally night. Holly, Lincoln and myself stepped onto the thwarts of the second tender rowing us *Cygnet* passengers ashore.

'Mister 'unter?' I heard my name before I saw the caller. The owner of the voice was a plump, squat, middle-aged man who tottered unsteadily down the embankment to greet me.

'You are correct sir,' I said formally, being acutely aware that I had alighted onto Her Majesty's prison property. 'Pray tell, how did you know my name?'

'One o' them coves in the first boat tell me you was he. Said important police business.'

Christ! Can't one keep anything secret on the island?

'Oh I see ... and you are?'

'Cook sir.'

'Great,' Holly piped up. 'I could eat the crutch out of a low flying duck. What's fer vittles?'

'I ain't the cook matey,' the man said rather indignantly. 'Robert Cook's the name.'

'Let's get somethin' straight,' Holly stood unrepentant, legs planted firmly apart and hands on hips. 'I ain't yer matey, right.'

'I hate to tell yer this Mr Cook,' Lantern Jaw Lincoln said defusing the situation. 'But this 'ere is *Miss* Holly Villan.'

'Oh, of course,' the soldier stood corrected. But in his defence Holly appeared, at times, more male than female.

'And,' Lincoln went on, 'I'm Mr Lincoln. We are both with Mr Hunter and the police department.'

'Quite right sirs ... madam ...ah ... miss. So where were we? Ah yes. Lieutenant Fribbens sent me to fetch yer to his quarters. I'm 'is steward, 'is right'and man yer might say, and he asked me to prepare your rooms and cordially invite yer to join 'im for dinner.'

'Great,' Holly said without thought. 'Food. And when might that be, Mr Cook?'

I shot Holly a look. 'Well I ... just askin' that's all,' she added shamelessly.

'Seven Miss.'

Holly fetched a pocket watch from her waistcoat pocket without any sign of subtlety. 'Seven huh?' she harrumphed.

'That is kind of Lieutenant Fribbens Mr Cook,' I said. 'But I was rather hoping we would be railing to Port Arthur this hour.'

Cook stiffened. 'Oh no sir.' As the black clouds burst their seams overhead, behind us the *Cygnet* tugged at her anchor on a rising swell, the great eucalyptus trees surrounding the bay shook from the sudden squall and a deluge chased us under the roof of the convict station veranda.

'Goodness,' I said, grateful I was wearing oilskins. 'That was sudden.'

'Aye sir,' Cook said lighting outdoor lanterns as late afternoon seemed to turn to evening in the blink of an eye. ''Tis the way o' the Peninsula. There's a wild Southern Ocean just yonder and the weather 'ere sir is most unpredictable. That's why the rail ain't operatin' until the morning Mr 'unter. May I suggest a navy rum to warm yer cockles.'

Holly was about to answer for the three of us but I shot her a look.

'That would be appreciated Mr Cook,' I said.

'Robert, Mr 'unter. We are most informal 'ere on the frontier.'

Robert shuffled through the front door into a dark foyer; a hallway leading through to a rear door with doors left and right.

'In there Miss Villan, Mr Lincoln,' Robert pointed to the right portal. 'That's the mess an' young Timmy there will serve yer refreshment.' Holly was first through the door. 'An' if'n you'll follow me sir,' Robert told me. 'Lieutenant Fribbens would like a word.'

'Of course.' My rum would have to wait. Robert led me off to the left through a communal room, a space, I imagined for reading and relaxation. Finally he knocked on the third door and a rather effeminate voice sang out, 'Enter.'

Lieutenant Fribbens reposed in a tin bath unabashed and as happy as a pig in its muck. I stood in his quarters startled at the man's candour. Robert left me alone and closed the door with a thud snapping me to attention.

'Come in, come in,' the lieutenant said. 'Hunter isn't it?'

The lieutenant looked a little older than me, thirty-five maybe, with high cheekbones and a pointed chin. His complexion was pale and with his long black hair I surmised he would pass for a woman should he be wearing a bonnet.

'Yes lieutenant,' I acknowledged. 'Caspian Hunter.'

'From the police department I was told,' he rolled his eyes at me, head to toe.

'That is correct.'

'Take a seat,' he splashed a wet finger towards a chair resting precariously close to the bath. 'Sit.'

I pushed the seat back a yard and sat.

'So it is my duty to ask you Caspian, what is your business with the prison?'

'I have papers here signed by Fabian Winter, head of my department,' I tapped my frock coat pocket, 'to interview prisoners about a murder committed in Hobart Town about which we believe certain prisoners may be of assistance.'

'Hmm. Good luck old chap,' he rolled his eyes as if knowing my mission was near impossible and started looking about at my feet. 'Ah, there you are,' he spoke to a square of soap the size and colour of a large piece of cheddar cheese. 'Be a good chap and pass me the soap.'

I handed the man his soap.

'So pray tell, Caspian.'

'Lieutenant?'

'Call me Sedgwick.'

'Sedgwick. Pray tell what?'

'Why have you journeyed thus far to interview felons at the notorious prison?'

As the man had the right to ask I told him everything. And as he was blatantly relaxed bathing himself before me, I made my speech short while he sipped at a balloon of French brandy.

'Aha,' he finally acknowledged.

'So if you will excuse me lieutenant ...'

'Sedgwick.'

'Sedgwick. If you will excuse me I will take leave and see to my colleagues.' I stood to leave. So did the lieutenant. He stood naked as the day he was born, contentedly exposing himself before me without a shame in the world. 'Pass me the towel, there's a good chap.' I handed him his towel and made haste to the door. 'Oh Caspian,' he called out.

'Lieutenant?'

'We're having a dinner to honour yourself and your colleagues. Cook's roasting some kangaroos and I have a very prolific vegetable garden. Not to mention a fine cellar.'

'Oh that is not necessary,' I lied. Truth was I was famished.

'Actually, we have banquets here every night,' he giggled and toasted me with his brandy balloon. 'There's naught much else to do in this godforsaken place.'

I joined Holly and Lincoln in the mess where they were partaking indulgently of the proffered Navy rum from a tall black bottle stamped with the British Empire's broad arrow. Oh well, I thought, it is at the government's expense. At the table with them was Captain Claiborne of *Cygnet* with two of his mates Hilbert Kipp and Richard Steer. The rest of the ship's complement was ordered to stay on board the brig, for fear they should fraternise with the convicts.

Robert Cook hurried to the table as I sat, passing me a rather grubby empty glass. 'How was it sir?' the steward asked me.

'How was what?' I asked, pre-occupied with the soiled vessel.

'Your audience with His Excellency?'

'His Excellency?'

'Only jokin' Mr 'unter. But the lieutenant does like to act high and mighty. Bit of a dandy I suppose you'd say.'

'Yes, quite.' I was not to be drawn into criticising the commanding officer at this convict station, and behind his back to boot. Even if I did think the man was a Molly.

'His daddy bought him a commission,' he whispered under his breath. 'So they say.'

'Hmm ... Do you think I could have a clean glass please Robert?'

Robert looked at the glass like a spider crawled over my hand. 'Dear me. Goodness gracious. Wait 'til I see that little bastard. Excuse the French sir.'

He walked away and I could only assume the *little bastard* was the scullery *maid*, probably a male convict.

The chatter at the table was convivial and the rum appreciated. Outside had turned ugly with a storm sweeping across the bay, but inside the mess Robert had a log fire radiating heat throughout, and with the candlelit table and two lanterns – one each end of the room – the atmosphere was warm and inviting.

Almost an hour had passed when the door behind me opened. The conversation stalled and the men stood to attention, their gaze fixed on whoever had just entered. I turned to see the most beautiful woman. Early twenties, five foot nine and pleasantly rounded but not overly. She wore an ankle-length, yellow silk dress of muslin, complimented by a deep green cashmere shawl; a flowing mantle fell back from her shoulders exposing her chalk white skin. Her long red hair was tied back in a tight chignon with an ivory hairpiece locking it in place. I could see her bright youthful eyes were a beautiful green and I found myself in awe, like the other men at the table.

In awe!

Steady Caspian. Not so obvious.

I pushed my chair back noisily to stand and was the first to speak.

'Caspian Hunter at your service.'

The steward was directly on her heels.

'Ah gentlemen, Holly, this 'ere is Mrs Fribbens, the lieutenant's wife.'

'The lieutenant's wife?' I nearly cried out.

'Mr Hunter,' she addressed me. This magnificent specimen of womanhood offered me her hand, hidden beneath a white kidskin glove. I took it gently and kissed the back of it. 'Enchanté,' I purred with a Birmingham French accent.

Enchanté! Really?

'Call me Caspian madam, please.'

'Then you shall call me Petula.'

'Petula,' I crooned. And nearly said, *'What a most befitting name for a most beautiful woman.'* But wisely left it there.

The others introduced themselves – and I must admit rather clumsily from where they stood to attention – while Robert settled Petula into the seat directly opposite me. Sedgwick Fribbens, the commander and lieutenant of questionable sexuality entered moments later. He had finally dressed, and now wore a pelisse on his left shoulder. He sat alongside his beautiful wife but showed little interest in the woman.

Outside, the wind had died but the rain persisted. Inside we did not have a care in the world. Sedgwick Fribben's eccentric attire and mannerisms were soon of little regard as the evening progressed. The kangaroo was an hour late, undercooked and almost inedible. Lascivious eyes danced across the table as the seamen present stole glances at the lieutenant's wife whenever they thought the commandant's attention was diverted.

However I suspect the lieutenant did not care. If anyone should be aware it was the second mate Richard Steer, for as the burgundy flowed freely the lieutenant found Steer particularly interesting. I wondered if it was the second mate's wooden leg that fascinated Sedgwick or some other attraction.

Without warning I felt the gentle caress of a woman's foot against my thigh. Naïvely I thought it an accident, but when it occurred a third time and more persistently, I dared to look across the table. Petula and I locked eyes for what seemed a dangerously long moment. Petula smiled. Petula ever so subtly licked her bottom lip. I felt my heart skip a beat.

'Caspian. Caspian sar.' It was Holly.

'What?' I said more abruptly than intended.

'Could yer pass the salt cellar ... please?'

It was midnight by the time Robert showed us to our attic rooms. It had been a long day and an even longer night. Now I felt the inebriating effects of rum, wine and brandy. Robert had lit the fire grate in my room and my cot was made up with cotton sheets. I was impressed. Tiredness imprisoned me like an opiate; I disrobed and pulled my blanket over my head to be immediately devoured by the world of dreams and nightmares ... *the world of dreams and nightmares.*

Never before had I had such an erotic dream. I lay alone on a feather-down quilt deep within my realms of fantasy. The room was warm, too warm. I discarded my blanket. A moment passed when my single sheet lifted free exposing my nakedness. But I felt secure. Safe in this room of warmth and well-being, floating on a cloud of passion. I felt aroused, my unconscious thoughts possessed by desire. I was caressed, stroked, taken to the brink and brought back again. Lust overcame me. My ardour turned to carnality. I thrust myself upon the beauty beneath me, burying my passion deeply within the siren of my dreams. She stifled screams. She clawed my back, craving for me. We writhed and wrestled, two sweat-soaked bodies ravishing each other like wild dogs. Our licentious crescendo peaked. We exploded.

'Caspian,' she gasped and clamped her teeth onto my ear.

'Petula,' I wheezed.

PETULA!

'Jesus Christ what have I done?' I blabbed.

'Shush my sweet,' she whispered through the moonlight. 'You'll wake the household.'

'Petula?' I hissed. 'What? How? Where did you come from?'

'Oh darling, you were so sound asleep when I snuggled under the sheet. Then you became a lion, a tiger ... you were like Stephenson's Rocket ...'

'Stephenson's Rocket?'

'Yes darling man. Choof, choof, choof. There was no stopping you.'

'Oh Christ.'

'Do not worry so.'

'But Lieutenant Fribbens, your husband ...'

'Fear not. We have an arrangement.'

'An arrangement?' My voice notched up a few octaves.

'Yes. I know you already guessed my husband prefers the company of other men.'

'I ... well ... ah yes. It did cross my mind.'

'Amputees in fact.'

'Amputees?'

'Yes I know. It's a bizarre trait of my husbands. Ever since he returned from the Crimea he has had this fetish for amputees.'

My immediate thoughts went to the *Cygnet's* second mate Richard Steer whom only had one leg, the other being amputated at the hip after poisoning in his blood nearly killed him back in the forties.

'So there you have it dear Caspian. As long as I am discreet in front of the men working at the station he closes a blind eye.'

'How ... how convenient,' I smiled. Petula smiled.

I now realised the woman was completely naked except for her white cotton gloves. In the soft blue hue of a new moon her smile was infectious. My situation suddenly felt fortuitous and I immediately felt arousal whet my carnal appetite once more. The temptress needed no prompting.

'My, my,' she groaned excitedly and forced me onto my back mounting me with haste. 'All aboard the Rocket,' she giggled. And helped herself to a first-class seat.

Day Four

Breakfast. One hour later. I was at once sated and drained. Weak from exhaustion yet I felt like the winner of ten rounds in the ring against bare-knuckle boxer Tom Sayers. Yes. I was at the top of my game.

Lieutenant Sedgwick Fribbens was amicable enough, but he knew. I just knew he knew. Although his wife had her own bedroom adjoining his, he knew.

'I trust you slept well Mr Hunter,' he said at the breakfast table.

'Fine thank you,' I stifled a yawn.

'Quite. So today you must venture into the dark side.'

'The dark side?'

'Port Arthur my dear chap. Where villains and felons are gathered aplenty.'

'Oh. Yes.'

Holly entered. 'Good morning Caspian sar,'

Thank god, now I am not trapped alone with the lieutenant. 'Morning Holly.'

Lantern Jaw Lincoln followed close behind, looking rather sheepish.

'Lincoln,' I smiled warmly.

'Good morning sar.'

'Sleep well?'

'Pardon?'

'I said did you sleep well?'

'Oh, aye ... yes sar. Slept like a log I did.' Holly's grin said otherwise. *My god, had they been at it as well? It must be the country air.*

With full bellies we were shown to the railway, built I was told, at the behest of Commandant Charles O'Hara Booth back in the thirties. Already I felt mixed emotions leaving Petula behind in such a god-awful place.

We would be travelling over hills where a slight humidity set low clouds in our path. I took one last look behind me, back to the convict station and Norfolk Bay. We listened as the bosun's pipe echoed across the water from the brig *Cygnet*, already sails unfurled and she drifting lazily on the tide, searching for a breeze. Our return journey to Hobart Town would be aboard another government cutter, *Seagull*, no doubt already sailing from Sullivans Cove for the peninsula, with a cargo of stationery and medical supplies for the penal settlement I am informed.

Lieutenant Fribbens sat cross-legged on a veranda chair smoking a cheroot and watching us with some interest. Then I saw her! Petula appeared at the window. She was some distance away but her red hair was tied back in a ponytail and I noted her smile. A sad smile. She waved ever so subtly and I allowed a subtle wave back, for I knew the lieutenant had his eye on me.

'On you hop then squire,' the convict overseer was bright this early hour. He stood with the side door of the small wooden carriage un-hitched, so I could slide across onto the single seat of the four-man-powered rail cart. The cart was some eight-foot long and five wide. A bench in front of the passenger seat was for two of the prisoners to ride when coasting downhill. Two prisoners at the rear had to mount a wooden step, when not shoving the craft uphill. The carriages sat upon wooden rails made from two pieces of quartering fastened together, which were nailed to log sleepers. Genius.

Holly and Lincoln mounted the carriage behind mine while the overseer pushed his backside alongside me, and gave the order to 'shove orf.'

'Nice mornin' for it squire,' the overseer spoke slowly and deliberately. He was a good behaviour convict, given liberties and responsibility – a round-faced, jolly man about my age with the paunch of a prisoner with access to extra rations. I noticed he had lost his left arm at the shoulder, hence his employment as overseer I imagined.

'It is indeed a nice morning,' I agreed. 'Caspian Hunter,' I introduced myself.

'Aye, I know. Police business.'

Of course he knew.

Two guards watched us with lackadaisical interest from a sentry post next to the rails. They were more interested in mugs of steaming hot tea and warm crusty bread brought to them from the kitchen and I had the impression, as only prisoners of good behaviour were permitted on the railway, that their duties were less than onerous.

'Come on you blokes,' the overseer ordered the prisoners, who I noted were trim athletic specimens, as one would expect, pushing these carriages day in day out. 'Let's get a move on,' he called out. 'Mr 'unter 'ere has important police business to conduct in Port Arthur. Move it lads.'

We slowly shoved off on the gentle rise towards the first hill, the four prisoners pushing from behind, all in step and picking up momentum quite briskly.

'I'm Bowyer sir,' the overseer acquainted himself.

'Bowyer?'

'Aye. Just Bowyer. An' before you ask, yes I'm a ticket man what's stayed on 'cos Lieutenant Fribbens treats me proper an' as yer can see I only got one wing and ain't much good for anythin' back in 'obart Town.'

'Amputee eh?' I said. 'What happened if you do not mind me asking?'

''Twas near on eight year ago now Mr 'unter. I escaped a work gang at Stewarts Bay near the settlement ...'

'Port Arthur?'

'Aye. Me an' little Timmy Carron. We rid ourselves of our irons and bolted overland to Eagle'awk Neck where we was told we could escape to the mainland o'er an isthmus there. They's got dogs there guarding this narrow spit so we decided to swim for it pushing out into the surf.' Bowyer stopped a moment, the memory became painful. Finally. 'No one told us there was sharks there. Jesus Christ! Excuse me sar ...'

'That's alright.'

'Big bastard it were. It tore Little Timmy ter shreds right near me. I was terrified, swimmin' crazy like in deep water not knowing when it was my turn to be ripped in two by a monster from beneath me. Terrifying.'

'I could only imagine. Dear me.'

'With Timmy gone I swum frantic back towards the shore, towards them waves crashing on the beach. But then I see it. Its great fin pokin' up out o' the water like a jib. It came right at me. I fought and splashed but it hit me like a runaway carriage sar. BAM! Took me by me arm and tore it clean off it did. It circled an' came back to finish me when I seen Little Timmy's leg float to the surface right next to me. The shark charged. I can see its jaw open right before me as we speak. It rolled on its side to attack, I seen its black eyes closing like they do at the last moment. I squealed. Squealed, sar. Terrified, I snatched Timmy's leg and shoved it in the damned thing's jaw. It took the leg and slammed me aside like I was a rag doll. By then I was in the surf. Waves were washin' me ashore and I seen soldiers, redcoats on the beach, waitin' for me. I never thought I would be so pleased to be recaptured. Lucky for me there was a sawbones stationed at The Neck. He stopped the bleedin', amputated what was left to the shoulder and cauterised the wound. Six weeks I spent in the infirmary then they gave me sixty days in solitary. And I got another two years on me sentence. But I lived to tell the tale sar and that's exactly what the commandant wanted. Live to tell the tale and deter others what may try an' bolt.'

'Well Bowyer, that's some story.'

'Aye. Thart it is.'

'But Port Arthur had a successful escape recently did it not?' I said.

'Aye. Erasmus Peck. Mad bastard. He be a cruel sod sar. An' I mean sod in the true sense of the word. Sodomite 'e be, and a vicious bugger at that.'

I was curious to know more. 'How did he escape?'

'Huh!' Bowyer laughed in my face. 'You ain't heard?'

'No. Kindly enlighten me.'

'He feigned a sprained ankle and got light duties at the settlement slaughter yard, just temporary like. So then when a dray-load o' mutton carcasses were ready to be carted to the Saltwater River coal mine station seventeen mile away 'e hid under the carcasses. 'e would've been covered in blood that's for certain, underneath a dozen butchered sheep. I doubt 'e tried swimmin' in shark-infested waters like that sir. Like I say, Erasmus Peck is a mad bastard. They say 'e must have had an accomplice at the slaughter yard. But if'n 'e did 'e's never been caught.'

I looked over my shoulder beyond the prisoners propelling us forward, to Holly and Lincoln, comfortable in each other's company in the following carriage. Then I became aware that we were at the peak of the first hill. We levelled out when the four prisoners propelling my carriage pushed that little harder over the rise before jumping on board, rewarding themselves with satisfied smiles for the downhill ride. And what a ride it was.

'Hold on to yer hats,' Bowyer yelled back at the second carriage. I heard a whoop from Holly as we picked up speed and a nervous groan from Lincoln holding his top hat with one hand and gripping the handrail with the other. All prisoners were now on board. Suddenly Lincoln turned pale and I turned to face ahead ...

And face downwards!

Down into a steep gully some three hundred yards distant. Somehow the wheels managed to stay on track as we were propelled by gravity faster and faster towards a narrow fresh water spring surrounded by man ferns. The clacketty-clack of the wheels was loud and resonant in the valley. Birds in treetops scattered. The further we dropped the faster we sped along. I looked to wide-eyed Bowyer whose mouth had formed a perfect circle. He held his hat to his chest and yelled back, 'Thirty miles an hour they estimate.'

'Th-thirty?' I repeated, astounded, our voices jittering comically. Bushes and trees either side whipped by at extraordinary speed. We approached the spring. The prisoners prepared to jump from their perches and push us once more uphill. But we were still racing at high speed when I heard a meld of screams and shouts. I dared turn about, at the very moment the following carriage de-railed. Lincoln, in all his six-foot-six, cartwheeled by me thrown free from his truck and discarded like detritus into the ferns. Holly flew in the other direction while their prisoners dived to safety. Clearly they had done so before. While the overturned cart slid on its side into the bushes our cart trundled across a short bridge and started up the other side. Twenty feet on it stopped with the aid of our pushers.

'Jaysuz Christ!' I heard Holly stomp from the undergrowth with cuts and bruises. Two of the convicts helped Lantern Jaw Lincoln dislodge his lanky carcass from the soft trunk of the man ferns that had saved him from ruin. He brushed himself down and located his squashed hat, punching it back into shape. 'I hate to say this Caspian sar, but I ain't too keen on climbin' aboard that contraption any time soon.'

Less than an hour later we coasted into Long Bay at the northern end of the settlement of Port Arthur. As protocol demanded that the commandant be briefed of our visit, a dispatch ran ahead to the commandant's house. Meanwhile we were afforded a wash bucket and soap at a guardhouse to tidy ourselves after the hair-raising eight-mile journey.

Passing by the settlement's largest building, the granary, we were led beneath the stone arch with its iron gate to the commandant's residence with its magnificent vista over the bay. Originally built as a simple wooden cottage in 1833 the guard told us, it was now a handsome brick affair, each commandant adding his own touches and extensions. And the current commandant, Mr James Boyd who took charge just three years ago in '53, was no exception, separating the kitchen, adding servants' quarters and building the porch overlooking the water at the front of the residence.

'Mr Boyd even rendered the front of the house to make it look like it was built of stone Mr Hunter,' the guard said proudly. 'And he planted them there sweet smelling shrubberies,' he added with a sigh, pleased to be on light duties sniffing plants rather than bawling orders at unruly convicts. 'This one here, Mr Hunter, I am told is a sweet wattle,' he caressed the yellow flower with reverence, unusual for a man in soldier's uniform with a Brown Bess musket slung over his shoulder. 'The seeds were brought down from New South Wales by some botanist back in '06 I do believe.'

'Thank you Mr Bacon,' a commanding voice boomed, 'but Mr Hunter hasn't all day to listen to your notes of importance regarding my flower beds.'

It was the commandant, James Boyd. He leant over the rail peering down at our small party looking a trifle impatient.

'No indeed sir, Mr Boyd sir.' The guard who I now knew as Mr Bacon touched his shako and made a hasty retreat.

'Come on up Mr Hunter. We can talk in my office.'

The commandant was a tall slender man of impeccable dress and appearance. His hair receded well back from off his forehead culminating in neat curls above each ear with a dominant waxed curl on top and to the right of a part. His coiffure appeared well greased and immaculate. Prominent eyebrows were like lintels over sunken small serious eyes that yet had a kindness about them. His nose was long and dominant above a well-manicured moustache reaching beyond the corners of his mouth and terminating in pointed waxed twists. He wore the latest in frock coats over a dark waistcoat with light coloured woollen britches. His boots were valet shiny.

I left Holly and Lincoln to walk the nearby foreshore whilst I conducted the formalities and met the commandant at the top of the steep front steps.

'What do you think of my porch?' the commandant asked. 'I had it recently added on.'

'Jolly nice sir, a pleasant place to sit and read I should imagine.'

'That it is Mr Hunter.' He opened the door for me and waved a hand down the passageway. 'Please. First door on your left.'

The office was dark, even though the sun shone brightly outside. James Boyd lifted his coat tails and sat at his desk offering me one of two armless chairs that appeared to me to have be made in the colonies from cedar. They were upholstered with leather and brass studs over horsehair.

'Thank you for your audience sir,' I started.

'Well I must vet all visitors here, after all it is a prison.'

'And run most proficiently I am assured sir. Your underlings speak highly of you.'

'Do they now. Well that is reassuring. I have been commandant here near on three years now and it has not been easy. But I have made changes for the better. We are in the process of closing the area around the Cascades to the east of the peninsula, as it is almost depleted of useful timber. We will remove the sawmills to the grounds next to the penitentiary and build sawmills in the hills around Port Arthur.'

'Wonderful.'

'Yes, quite. Also now we have log-slides ...'

'Log slides?'

'Yes. Long log-lined channels that allow timber to be slid down hill saving the centipede gangs that in the past have had to carry the logs by hand. Laborious business that.'

'I'm certain it is sir.'

'Five years ago steam engines were introduced to run the sawmills, which has improved efficiency. This was a godsend, as since the *Cessation of Transportation Act* was passed in '53 we now receive fewer prisoners and as the old lags here are aging they can no longer work as well in the bushlands.'

'The wonders of the industrial age eh,' I said enthusiastically, and immediately wondered why.

'Yes, well. I have also recently ordered cultivation to begin in the surrounding lands and the granary you passed on the way here is to be converted into a penitentiary where we hope to house workshops and another steam driven mill, a blacksmith and forge and carpentry workshop and teach the prisoners skills for when they are released.'

'Wonderful sir. I can see why the men speak highly of you.'

'Thank you. So what police business brings you to Port Arthur, Mr Hunter?'

'Edwin Piketon, Mr Boyd. Do you remember a prisoner with that name?'

'No. You must understand thousands of men pass through here.'

'Of course, sir. But this man Piketon had befriended another prisoner whose name you may recall, as he was a Queen's soldier in India. Corporal Hannibal Comstock.'

'The pink diamond affair,' Boyd huffed. 'Now that is a name I *do* recall.' Boyd searched the walls of his office racking his brain for retention. 'But he died here.'

'That is correct. But not long after he died here his good friend Piketon was released on a ticket and settled in Hobart Town. This man, sir, was murdered only days ago and I have good reason to believe he had acquired the diamond from Comstock when Comstock died here in the infirmary, eventually hiding it in his cottage.'

I quickly explained the murder scene and the information passed on from Humphrey Llewellyn, the Port Arthur guard, including the hiding place of the alleged gemstone; at the prison and at the cottage.

'So how can I assist you Mr Hunter?'

'I need to interview lags that were close to either men. Prisoners who may shed light on who would have known about the diamond. For I suspect the diamond was the motivation for the murder.'

'Hmm. Everyone knew the rumours.'

'Yes, I understand. But I would like a list of men given their ticket or pardoned since Comstock's death and then, if the guards can assist, the names of the men who were their confidants.'

'It seems a little futile to me.'

'If you would be so kind as to humour me sir.'

'Naturally I will do all in my power to assist you. I suggest you refresh yourselves at the officers' mess, one of the guards will direct you, and give me one hour.'

Prison warder Carvel Dwight, a thickset man with large bushy eyebrows and unusually red lips, ran a bony finger down the short list. 'Eight likely coves 'ere Mr 'unter,' he said. 'All men what was close to Piketon, after Comstock kicked the bucket.' He looked to his colleague, a hairy-fisted man with a nervous twitch. 'Isn't that right Oswin?'

'Aye Carvel. But two 'ave flown the coop.'

'Flown the coop?' Holly asked. 'What, escaped?'

'No miss ... got their ticket. They's in 'obart Town on probation.'

'Right.'

I sat opposite in his prison office, which felt more like a dungeon, with bare stonewalls and a tiny barred window well above head height. Holly and Lincoln sat with me at a pine dining table doubling as a desk, ready with notebooks and lead pencils.

'Kindly read them to me Mr Dwight,' I asked. 'Can I have the names of the two who have their tickets first please?'

'Calhoun Nyle, fourteen years for uttering false promissory notes and Phineas Nibley, seven years for larceny. Nyle, I do believe, has found a situation at a quarry near the Cascades in 'obart Town. At the base of Mount Wellington. But Nibley I would not know. However both men would have had to register at the Hobart Town watch house the day they arrived.'

'Holly.'

'Caspian sar.'

'Make note if you please. Now, the men still imprisoned are ...?

'William Shipley ...'

'Dead,' Oswin interrupted.

'Oh yes. Came here without a pot to piss in and died potless.' Both men laughed.

'Gordon Nash,' Dwight continued. 'Seven years for sheep stealin'.'

'Oh aye, he loved 'is mutton did our Gordon.'

More hysterics. I snapped a false smile. The warder put on his serious face while pinching and stroking a tuft of hair beneath his bottom lip where assumedly a beard should have been. 'Edward Smith. Assault. Fourteen years. Henry Cooper ...'

'Dead!' Oswin cut in again.

'That's right, a month ago.'

'Senile decay,' Oswin said matter-of-factly.

'He were near sixty Mr 'unter. Couldn't hurt a fly no how.' Dwight checked the list. 'Thomas Derwood, seven years for housebreaking. And last but not least Erasmus Peck.'

'Erasmus Peck!' I declared. 'The escapee.'

'Aye. But 'e bolted a few days back,' Dwight looked wide-eyed. 'There's yer man.'

'And do you know how 'e escaped Mr Hunter?' Oswin asked me.

'Yes I heard. He hid amongst sheep carcasses.'

'A desperate man indeed.'

'Another man fond of mutton.'

'Aye.'

'It seems we have come all this way for naught,' Holly sighed.

'Maybe Holly. But I still wish to interview the three men on that list still in servitude. Mr Dwight.'

'Aye.'

'Who are the two on probation in Hobart Town again?'

The warder consulted his list. 'Calhoun Nyle and Phineas Nibley.'

'I hate to say this Caspian sar,' Lincoln started. 'But it *does* look like Erasmus Peck's our man ... don't it?'

'Never look a gift horse in the mouth,' was my answer.

'Don't yer mean Don't tell a book by its cover,' Holly said.

'Something like that. Now.' I faced Carvel Dwight who was looking confused. 'Mr Dwight.'

'Sar.'

'Where can we interview these felons?'

'Ah. Come with me sar. We will catch 'em at the mess. Tis dinnertime so the men you seek will be together.'

'They'll be right 'appy, them ones yer want to talk to,' Oswin said while another guard unlocked the door to the prisoner's mess. 'Cos they'll miss an hour o' field work.'

This dinner of beef stew and bread was the prisoners' main meal for the day. Many prisoners, I was told, saved some of the bread for the evening. We waited while the men completed their meal and were herded back out to the fields and mills and work gangs. The three men I wished to interview were separated and taken aside where one by one I was presented with each man.

Edward Smith, fourteen years for assault, was looking down the barrel at another seven years for attacking a guard. He was a most unfortunate and unpleasant fellow and I could sympathise why. He was handcuffed in our company and, although he appeared remorseful, we were warned not to get too close. However he was co-operative enough; my guess was that he enjoyed the limelight, no matter how short it be.

'Aye. I knew Comstock well,' he said to my first question. 'We got on good like. And 'is best mate Edwin Piketon ...'

'Who is dead, Smith,' the warden said.

'Wha'?'

'You heard. Dead. Murdered.'

'Oh,' he looked genuinely upset. 'I liked Edwin. Worked in the bakehouse with him.'

'Bakehouse?' Holly asked.

'Aye. We make ship biscuit here for the Navy.'

'So you say you were friendly with Edwin Piketon,' I said. 'What did you talk about? I mean did you ever discuss what you would do when pardoned for example?'

'O' course. All lags do.'

'And?'

'Well Edwin always talked about getting' his full pardon and returning to England.'

'Well he ain't goin' there now,' Holly said without an ounce of tact.

I fished for any sign of a hidden agenda. Nothing. If anything the man was vague and thought only of his own sorry affair, when I had a thought.

'Erasmus Peck,' I said aloud. I watched the blood drain from his face.

'What of 'im?'

'You were acquaintances were you not?'

'Acquaintances yes. Friends no.' Smith eyes narrowed. ''e escaped last week, but you know that don't yer?'

'Yes. What can you tell me about the man?'

'He's a bad apple that'n. You mark me words. A bad apple.'

'Pray tell.'

Edward Smith looked to the warder Dwight, then Oswin. 'They'll tell yer. Can I go now?'

Dwight lifted the man from his seat by the lapel of his canary yellow and black prison jacket. 'Bugger off,' he spat. Smith was shown out the door.

'What was that all about? Tell me what?' I demanded to know.

'Smith said 'e were assaulted by Peck. About two months ago.'

'Assaulted? You mean beaten?'

'No Mr Hunter. 'e were buggered.'

Holly poised with her pencil. 'You mean …'

'Buggered miss. But Peck denied it and the superintendent let it be. The next day Smith is assaulted again. But this time, beaten first and buggered again. He's a piece o' work is that Erasmus Peck.'

The second prisoner was unrestrained but suspicious of our presence, aware and alert. 'Gordon Nash. Seven years for stealin' a sheep,' Warder Dwight added when he introduced the man after shoving him backwards into a chair.

'Aye, an' only one year to go,' Nash muttered sourly.

'If'n yer behave yourself Nash,' and Dwight made to poke the prisoner in the ribs with his truncheon, but thought twice when I shot him a stare. Nash glared at the warder but held his tongue, there was certainly no love lost between them.

Nash turned his head slowly to look up at me. Prison life was taking its toll on the man. He was hard and I imagined him an intimidator in the yard.

'So did yer find the diamond?' he said out of nowhere.

'Di … diamond?' I showed surprise.

'Aye. The pink firker … '

'Watch yer mouth Nash!' Dwight tightened his grip on the truncheon but refrained from swinging it.

'What do you know about a diamond?' I asked.

'The one from India, nicked from some emperor or king or whatever.'

'What about it?'

'Everyone knows about it. Bastard hid it somewhere. Even this lot sniffed about for it,' he jerked his head at Dwight who reddened with anger. 'But it could never be found could it Mr Dwight?'

'You were friends with Edwin Piketon were you not?' I asked the prisoner.

'We was acquainted, yes. But I wouldn't say we was the best of friends.'

'What about Hannibal Comstock?'

'What about 'im?'

'You were on friendly terms with him were you not?'

'Well when coves spend days and weeks on a treadmill together yer tend to bond somewhat,' he answered, with a hint of derision.

'So you *were* friends?'

'I suppose.'

'Did he talk of a diamond?'

'The diamond? No. It were only rumoured after Piketon became matey with 'im and then Comstock died in the infirmary. Very convenient I thought ...'

'He died o' liver disease Nash.'

Nash shrugged, *whatever*. 'Piketon's the lag yer want ter be talkin' to.'

The warden said, on cue. ''e's dead.'

'Piketon? Dead? What about the diamond then?'

'You don't sound too surprised,' I said.

'What?'

'That Piketon is dead?'

'No. Doesn't surprise me at all. Stupid bastard couldn't keep 'is trap shut. I even heard he talked about it in 'is sleep. Jesus, a rare diamond worth a king's ransom and a dullard lag with a ticket. No, I am not surprised he's dead. I assume it was murder?'

Standing behind the seated prisoner I looked to Oswin the warder and tipped my head towards the door.

'Take leave Mr Nash,' I said. 'If I want you for further questioning I know where I can find you.'

Nash stood and turned to face me. 'One year left,' he seethed. 'One firkin' year.'

Thomas Derwood sat nervously with his hands clasped together and pushed through his knees.

'Derwood,' Oswin introduced the prisoner. 'Thomas Derwood, seven years for housebreaking.'

'I'll not waste your's or my time Mr Derwood,' I started. 'You were an associate of Hannibal Comstock and Edwin Piketon I am informed.'

'Why do you ask?'

Warden Dwight hooked the end of his truncheon under the prisoner's chin and lifted, forcing him to look me in the eye. 'Answer the question.'

'I suppose we was friends.'

'You either were or you were not,' I insisted.

'We got together sometimes, aye. But Hannibal's passed.'

'That's right. And so has Mr Piketon.'

Suddenly the man looked shocked. 'Piketon! Dead sir?'

'That is what I said.'

'How?'

'Murdered.'

'Jesus! He only got his ticket not that long ago. He was so dead keen to settle down back at the camp,' Derwood spoke of Hobart Town, still called 'the camp' by some older lags. 'He told me he had a situation as a gravedigger.'

'That is correct. But he was murdered only days ago.' I went on to question the prisoner about the diamond and received the same answers. Everyone, it seemed, knew about the stolen gemstone.

I sat on the corner of the table with my arms crossed before me to look Thomas Derwood in the eye.

'Erasmus Peck,' I said.

Derwood's left eye twitched slightly. 'What of him?'

'Were you friends of his?'

'Not likely. He escaped last week.'

'That he did. But I have been led to believe Peck was a friend of Piketon. Is that correct?'

'I suppose. They messed together. We all messed together.'

'In your opinion, Mr Derwood, is Erasmus Peck capable of murder? Would he in your opinion take another man's life for ... say, a diamond worth a king's ransom?'

Thomas Derwood grew fidgety and nervous. 'I ... I ...'

Warder Dwight stabbed the truncheon into the prisoner's side.

'Answer the question!'

'Mr Dwight,' I grew angry. 'I wish to speak to the prisoner alone.'

'Oh I can't condone that Mr 'unter.'

'Alone,' I reiterated. Dwight looked at Holly and Lincoln who had been quietly taking notes at the table. Lincoln stood his six-foot-six and crossed the room in two steps opening the door wide for the warder. Dwight sighed and capitulating unhappily, he made his exit. 'You too,' I ordered Oswin. Lincoln closed the door behind them and twisted the key.

'Erasmus Peck Mr Derwood?'

'He's a tough bastard sir and that ain't the half of it.'

'Do you mean he is a standover man?'

'Aye. He's a mean son of a whore. He is also a ...' Derwood seemed to be suffering from fear of retribution and had second thoughts. 'A ... ah ...'

'Speak to me. The man has escaped and when he is recaptured he will be doing two years hard labour in chains on the road gangs and nowhere near you. Now then?'

'He's a damned sodomite sir. He's a tough bastard, a fearless, fearful man who takes liberties with the weak.'

'Sounds most unpleasant,' Holly said.

'Sorry to curse before you miss, but that's the only way I could describe him. He's possessed by the devil he is, a bastard sodomite and yes ... yes. I would not put it past him to commit murder.'

'Thank you.'

'I hate to say I told yer so Caspian sar,' Lincoln stated. 'But I told yer so.'

I was starting to agree.

Derwood suddenly sat upright with the most serious expression and fixed me a stare.

'There is something.'

'What?'

'I remember one night when me and Peck were together, alone like ...'

Holly. 'Alone?'

'Oh not like that miss. Me and Peck had latrine duties and I think it was the buckets of muck that give him the idea.'

I was hesitant to ask. 'What idea pray tell?'

Peck said if he was in possession of, say, a rare gemstone, and the troopers were after him, he'd swallow it.'

'Hmm. Makes sense.'

'He said something else.'

'Oh?'

'Aye. He said he'd never surrender and that he would shoot it out to the death.'

Early afternoon

Lantern Jaw Lincoln flatly refused to be railed back to the convict station where we were to rendezvous at Norfolk Bay with the Navy transport *Seagull*, a fast cutter. Lincoln walked the eight-mile track instead. More fool he, Holly and I agreed as we gave him a three-hour head start. Holly and I, on the other hand, partook of Reverend Musk's hospitality of luncheon at his refectory. Cold cuts of roasted mutton, boiled potatoes, boiled eggs, crusty bread, beetroot relish, Stilton cheese and Madeira wine.

'Scrumptious,' Holly garbled through a full mouth. And I had to agree.

Mid-afternoon

Holly and I disembarked the rickety rail full of verve and liquor with our sated appetites rendering our moods jolly. I stood erect and stretched my weary bones.

Ah ... this is the life ...

When ...

Petula rushed to greet me from the convict station and threw her arms about my neck. I was bereft of speech. Such a public display of familiarity after our all-night tryst frightened the devil out of me. I sobered. 'Petula! What are you doing?'

'Caspian, you must take me with you.'

'What?'

'He knows.'

Close behind me Holly belched and I distinctly heard her choke a laugh.

'Who?' I panicked. 'I mean what does he know? How?'

'Sedgwick knows about us Caspian. Oh Caspian I must sail with you.'

'Jesus! Sorry ... I ah ... I mean ... I thought you said you had an arrangement. You and the lieutenant. You had an arrangement you said and he closed a blind eye.' I was confused. Startled. 'He likes amputees you said.'

'Amputees?'

'Petula. What are you saying?'

'I lied.'

'You lied about the amputees?'

'I said nothing about amputees ...'

'But ...'

'I lied. I lied about the arrangement.'

'CASPIAN HUNTER!' My name reverberated about the settlement like someone was yelling through a speaking horn. 'Caspian Hunter you despicable excuse for a human being.'

'He's behind me isn't he?' I whispered and Petula nodded, clinging to me firmly.

'Turn and face me like a man,' he cried out.

I sensed the hint of a lisp so turned to face him like a man. 'I can explain,' I said rather weakly.

'Explain! Explain! You bed my wife like some whore and you want to explain.'

'It wasn't what you think ...'

'Oh. Then what was it then, a wee cuddle?'

Petula found courage and called back. 'I'm leaving you Sedgwick. I cannot go on any longer with this loveless marriage.'

'Whore!'

'Now steady on man,' I asserted.

'Whore!' He stepped unsteadily off the porch and I realised he too had had a long lunch. 'Whore!'

'Stop that,' I demanded.

'Whore!' The lieutenant was wound like the spring in a bell tower clock. He marched towards me shouting profanities, his face exploding with anger, his eyes bulging and red and finally I caught his breath reeking like spillage at a distillery. He threw a punch. I ducked, taking up a pugilist's stance with my fists before me.

'Stand shtill you coward,' he slurred, throwing another pathetic punch a foot to my left.

'You don't want to do this,' I was becoming angry. Another feeble attempt missed my right cheek. I decided against fighting, of lowering myself to his level. I stepped away. He lurched forward and swung a left hook into thin air. Soldiers had now gathered to watch their commander's pathetic performance. The lieutenant was making an absolute fool of himself. I decided to walk away and took Petula by the arm. We moved towards the bay when the overwrought drunkard pounded the side of my head with a haymaker. I felt my head spin. I saw white orbs of semi-consciousness before me. I staggered seeking balance.

'Coward!' he yelled. 'Whore!'

He had overstepped his mark. Gaining my footing, with adrenalin shooting through my arteries, I danced before him, my clenched fists seeking a clear shot. 'Shit!' he cried out as my right knuckles crushed his nose. Blood spiralled. I swear I saw a tooth loosen. I followed with a powerful left hook that cracked him on the chin. Two punches were all it took. Sedgwick staggered backwards, tripped and collapsed in a pool of mud in front of a dozen soldiers and twice as many prisoners. For a moment I thought he was unconscious. But then I realised he simply was not prepared to climb back to his feet. I offered him my hand but he looked at me and sobbed. It was too pitiful to witness. Petula picked up a carpetbag with her meagre possessions. 'Goodbye Sedgwick,' she said quietly. 'I'm leaving for Moreton Bay.'

'Go,' he spat. His eyes raw and weeping.

Soldiers immediately surrounded me.

'Come on yer mongrels,' Holly stepped between them and myself. 'That was a fair fight and you lot bloody well know it.'

'The largest of the redcoats, a man I had met the day before named Melville, turned his back to his commander and looked me square in the eye. 'I'd be off now sir if'n I was you. Mum's the word eh?'

'Aye,' Holly answered for me. 'Mum's the word.'

All the above happened within four minutes. *Coward. Whore. Punch. Mum's the word* ... just like that. Four short minutes. By the time the crew of *Seagull* alerted Lincoln, already on board, we were being rowed out to the cutter by its crew. I sat in the stern of the tender with my arm unashamedly around the shoulders of Petula. The young woman was an emotional wreck. I was an emotional wreck.

'Two punches and he went down like a sack o' manure,' Holly grinned. 'Nice work Caspian sar.'

'I'd rather not talk about it Holly.'

'What was that about amputees anyways?'

'I said I'd rather not talk about it.'

Seagull's headsail trapped a late sea breeze and we soon sailed away from Norfolk Bay, rounding South Arm and into the Derwent Estuary. The wind picked up considerably and the streamlined cutter made pleasing haste.

'My husband can be a dangerous man,' Petula said as we sailed towards the setting sun.

'So can I,' I answered instantly and hoped my gallbladder did not fail me as I swallowed the lie.

'He has friends, acquaintances in high positions. Commandant Boyd for one.'

'I spoke with the commandant. He seems a straight shooter. I actually got along fine with him.'

'Wonderful. Then you may need him one day. But Sedgwick loves to wine and dine, socialise. He even has the warders eating out of his palm. Carvel Dwight the warden for one.'

'I met Dwight, an irritating man.'

'The man is a fiend when he consumes too much wine.'

'Oh?'

'Yes. Only recently he was travelling through the station and he tried to take liberties with me.'

'Well who would not?' I grinned, but Petula chose to ignore the statement. 'Moreton Bay?' I finally asked Petula as she snuggled closer to me – we had found some privacy seated behind the sail lockers – avoiding the spray from the bow.

'Pardon?'

'You told your husband you were travelling to Moreton Bay.'

'Yes. I have a brother stationed there. You need not fear Caspian Hunter, I will not burden you with my presence.'

'Burden?' I remarked, sensing future pleasures. 'Why, Moreton Bay is a long way away,' I said artfully. 'You will need somewhere to stay until you get back on your feet, somewhere to rest your weary body before your journey.'

'Oh.' Petula snuggled closer, unashamed of her damaged reputation. She had made one mistake in marriage, but now the world was her oyster. 'Somewhere to rest you say,' she looked up to me with her huge green eyes. 'I don't suppose you know of anywhere?'

'Hmm,' I teased. 'I might.' And I kissed her full on the lips.

By the time we disembarked at Waterman's Dock it was early evening.

'Are you partaking of refreshment Caspian sar?' Holly asked as I stretched on the wharf. 'Maybe Custom's 'ouse?'

'I ... ah ... maybe I'll meet you there Hol. I've just some police business to attend to first.'

'Police business,' Holly nodded sagely to Lincoln then fixed Petula with a knowing stare. 'Good-o then. Maybe we'll see you there.'

'Ah Hol,' I had a thought.

'Aye.'

'First thing in the morning I would like you to concentrate on this Calhoun Nyle. You heard the warder, he's working as a quarrier near the mountain so it should not be too difficult.'

'Aye sar.'

'But just confirm he is in their employ, do not let him know you are enquiring. Savvy?'

'Savvy. What about the other cove, Nibley?'

'Yes. Lincoln, maybe you can make enquires around the township about Phineas Nibley. You noted his description and he is a recent ticket man, someone will know him.'

'Aye Caspian sar. Leave it to me.'

I watched Holly and Lincoln cross the docks and enter the tavern and promptly flagged the first fly carriage trotting by. Ten minutes later we were at Blue Whale Cottage. The tall-case clock, I had named Long Tom, struck seven as we walked through the door. Bypassing the kitchen and downstairs rooms we hurried up the stairs to my bedroom, the room that Petula was eager to inspect. The minx had no qualms about disrobing immediately while I stood awestruck and intoxicated by her presence. Stripped naked she dropped to her knees before me, loosened my britches and went to work like a seamstress on a mannequin.

Fifteen minutes passed. I knew it was fifteen because Long Tom informed me. Petula threw her legs over the side of the bed. 'I'm famished,' she said.

'I'll say.'

'No silly. I'm hungry. What's to eat?'

'Nothing I'm afraid.'

'Nothing!'

'Sorry but my housekeeper has deserted me temporarily. There is naught here to eat, not even stale bread.'

'Dear me. Typical bachelor.' Petula leapt from the bed and began dressing. I watched, captivated. She was a curvaceous young lady but with balanced proportions and it was as sensuous watching her dress as it was undress. 'Well come on then,' she demanded.

'Come on what?'

'Come on. Let's eat.'

'Eat?'

'I seem to recall the Derwent Chop House does a delicious roast beef,' she said. 'And serves it with gravy and Yorkshire pudding.'

I had to admit the day's events – the sea air and the dalliance – had given me the appetite of a Tongan king. The Derwent Chop House did itself proud. The roast beef, the porter, we even managed a bottle of Burgundy wine. But there appeared to be more to Petula Fribbens than met the eye of a gullible police investigator – that being me. For a start she was a helpless flirt. She insisted on retiring from the dining room to the taproom where she unashamedly danced to the fiddler's tune. I grew irritable, I was exhausted and wanted to retire. More than once she conversed with other men. One I recognised as the first mate on *Cerberus*, a regular passenger ship between Hobart Town and Sydney. Finally I managed to draw her away from the inn where we retreated to Blue Whale Cottage. It was late, after midnight. We coupled once more but it was mechanical lust and I collapsed into a deep dreamless sleep to be woken by the clacking of the windmill, its sails unrestrained once more right on six.

There was no sign of Petula.

The woman and her carpetbag had gone. Later I learned that indeed the *Cerberus* sailed at dawn, and I could only imagine that Petula had secured a passage with the first mate, in his cabin.

Good luck to them both I say.

Chapter four

Day Four – St Mary's Hospital Morgue, Davey Street

Any thoughts of Petula quickly faded as Fabian and Jasper met me at the prisoners' barracks' main gate. 'You're late,' Fabian said. He looked stressed and out of breath. 'Everyone's late,' he muttered out of character.

'I sent Holly and Lincoln on a search for two suspects on the Piketon murder,' I said.

'Oh.'

I explained what we had gleaned from Port Arthur, omitting any reference to Petula of course.

'Right. The journey was not fruitless then.'

'On the contrary,' I said.

Fabian. 'Well, me and Jasper were just on our way to fetch you.'

'Oh?'

'Aye. There's been another killin'.'

'Little girl,' Jasper said.

'No!' My heart sank and we three turned for St Mary's.

One never becomes accustomed to the morgue. Especially this poorly vented and lit underground dungeon entered by a spiral stone stair with only two sconces pinned to the wall to usher the unwary into the pit of death.

Fabian, Jasper and myself had made haste to St Mary's Hospital morgue to view a new arrival. The victim had been dredged from the River Derwent twenty miles north of Hobart Town at the small rural township of New Norfolk – now a food bowl for the colony. She was seven years old. And now a month-old missing persons investigation had been confirmed as a murder.

We stood about respectfully inspecting the tiny cadaver of someone's treasured child. She lay on her side on the coroner's sandstone slab, her body *frozen* in a foetal position with her knees up to her chin. Her shape was bloated from decomposition gases and her once adorable and innocent face now a macabre image one might see in a demonic engraving. The smell of formaldehyde and cheap scent combatting putrefaction was horrific. Thankfully she was clothed in her mauve frock; at least she had the benefit of modesty in these darkest of times.

I always said that any man whose prime interest in life is death has to be a little peculiar. Doctor Ernest Crawley was no exception. He was tall and slim, slovenly in his dress although clean in hygiene with mutton chop sideburns joined by a moustache but no beard. Long silky strands of snow-white hair were combed lazily over his bald pate in an attempt to deduct a few years from his appearance. Nevertheless he was seventy-one and looked it.

'Was this a rape Doctor Crawley?' Fabian asked.

Crawley was painfully hard at hearing but it was as though he anticipated this first question. 'No, I don't believe it was Mr Winter. But what I *can* tell you is the cause of death was asphyxiation.'

'Asphyxiation?' I had to clear my throat from pent up emotions to repeat the word.

'Yes Mr Hunter.' He pointed to dark marks around her neck. 'The wee lass was strangled.'

'Who would do that?' Jasper asked angrily.

'Well son,' Crawley answered impatiently. 'If we knew that you wouldn't be here.'

'Yes ... but ...'

I stopped Jasper there. 'She was found by the local ferry-man I believe.'

'That's correct,' Crawley said. 'You've a copy of my notes right there.' He nodded to papers soiled with split formalde-hyde at one end of the slab. 'The thing is Mr Hunter, that lass disappeared over a month ago but she was tethered in the foetal position meaning she was murdered elsewhere and tied later.'

'How's that?'

What I'm suggesting is that she was killed elsewhere and only weighted and thrown into the river recently. The ferry-man has loosened the weights, probably rocks, when he was pushing away from the shore using his oar.'

'Like a Cambridge boatman?'

'Exactly. And there would have been existing gases in the body to aid buoyancy.'

'I wonder if it was a kidnapping gone wrong?' I said to Fabian who now dragged heavily on his clay pipe pervading the putrid morgue atmosphere with the more pleasant aroma of burning tobacco. 'And the parents were under pressure from the kidnappers not to go to the police.'

'Possibly. The parents are well heeled I do believe.'

I fetched up Crawley's notes shaking drips of toxic formaldehyde from the damp corners. 'Gilbert and Nell Noble,' I read aloud. 'Hop growers and sheep farming their primary source of income. Settled on 400 acres of land granted them by Governor George Arthur in 1835. The Noble homestead is a six-bedroom, two-storey timber dwelling named Wynald House overlooking the River Derwent one mile south of the New Norfolk township.' I shook the papers afresh and turned to the coroner. 'Who gave you this information sir?'

'The constables who delivered the body.'

'Surely these constables are responsible for solving the crimes in their own district,' Fabian said.

'Yes, well, Mr Winter,' Crawley tipped his head to look over his pince-nez at Fabian. 'That's a matter for you to take up with the governor.'

'Sir Henry Fox Young?'

'Yes. Tis he, you must understand, who has ordered your office investigate this dastardly crime. It appears he knows the Nobles well and wants this crime solved post haste.'

I read on. 'Gilbert Noble 58, Nell Noble 49. Six children of which Violet, seven, was the youngest.' I felt a chill up my spine. Suddenly the body had a name. 'Violet,' I said once more. 'Seven years old.' I looked at Fabian. 'I will leave for New Norfolk immediately.'

'I'll come with yer,' Jasper volunteered.

'No,' Fabian puffed at his pipe. 'You're needed back at the barracks. You be right to do the preliminaries alone Caspy?' he asked me. 'As yer know we've been put under the pump. We've got felons to arrest, namely the two who got their ticket in Port Arthur, and now they are on the loose in the colony. Either one o' them could 'ave murdered Piketon and stole the diamond.'

Of course Fabian was right. 'I am only too happy to go it alone,' I said. The truth is the sail up the river would clear my head and give me time to think.

Wynald House, New Norfolk

Skipper Ben Swain met me at Waterman's Dock on Hobart Town's waterfront where our official police sloop named *Fabian* – by Fabian – was docked, always at the ready for police business. Swain headed out of Sullivans Cove and a westerly breeze smartly stiffened our sail. We made good speed up river – around five knots, finally sailing into the beautiful Derwent Valley, picturesque as any landscape painted by Turner or Constable. It was mid-afternoon. To the north, Mount Dromedary gathered dark clouds at its peaks while an overcast chilled the air reminding me of why I was here. It was uncanny, but I sensed the lost spirit of little Violet.

Wynald House loomed from behind thirty-year-old oaks and willows. Neither tree being indigenous to the colony. The house itself was a statement of wealth, already twenty years old with a Gothic tower added more recently. South of the homestead I could make out hop kilns and acres of hop vines in full bloom. We sailed silently up river in front of the property, there was no sign of life but I had a sense that we were being watched.

'Leave me at the jetty,' I told the skipper who dropped the sail and we coasted up to the modest landing. He lassoed a post and I jumped ashore, ordering Ben to meet me at the

Township upriver in an hour. The jetty was short and I noted the bank dropped away deeply close to the shoreline where I followed a neat gravel path towards Wynald House. As I marched the hundred yards up an incline towards the house my mind was awash with questions. I touched my frock coat pocket to be certain I had my notebook and lead pencil, when the prettiest young girl I had seen for some time stopped me dead in my tracks. She seemed about twelve years old and wore an elegant grey ankle length dress with a paisley pattern blouse and long rippled brown hair falling half way down her back from under a grey bonnet style cap.

'Who are you?' she said sternly without the hint of any welcome.

I was caught unawares. 'Me?'

'Yes you. Who else would I be talking to?'

'Oh me. Yes. Sorry.' I stiffened. 'I am Mr Hunter from the Hobart Town Prisoners' Barracks.'

'What? Did you escape then?'

'No, no. I am a police investigator. Are you perchance the daughter of Henry Noble?'

'Yes.' Then without hesitation, 'What do you want?'

'I am here to talk to your father ... and mother.'

Instantly an attractive woman appeared from behind a bend in the pathway. 'Georgina,' she called to the girl. 'Inside if you please.'

'This man is here to talk to papa.'

'Inside this instant.'

Georgina dutifully obeyed and turned to depart but not before flashing me one last scowl.

'Mrs Noble?'

'And you are?'

I introduced myself and stated the purpose of my visit.

'You best come inside then,' she answered and it was then I noted how exhausted the woman appeared. The loss of her daughter must have been an incredible strain. She walked briskly. I followed her to the veranda steps where she hitched her skirts hurrying up the treads. A maid met us at the front door.

'Fetch Mr Noble please,' she ordered the servant before ushering me into the hallway and to the first room on the left. 'Wait in the drawing room ... Hunter was it not?'

'Yes madam.'

The drawing room bore all the trappings of moderate wealth; from chandelier – which I imagined to be crystal – to the Persian carpets that I felt a little intimidated to be walking upon in my police issue boots. A large mahogany lounge with embroidered cushions had before it a sofa table, mahogany with four matching chairs. Carved oak corner chairs were pushed into ... well the corners. I imagined these to be occupied by chaperones whilst young gentlemen entertained the young ladies of the house. The main wall displayed a French tapestry, last century I guessed, and gilt framed portraits filled the other walls. The latest imported knick-knacks required by those with expendable wealth filled cabinets, the mantelpiece and sideboards. I clapped my hands behind my back and studied an oil painting of a lady on a horse with a Great Dane sitting on its haunches and looking up at the rider with adoring eyes.

'Mr Hunter.' My reverie was interrupted. I jerked involuntarily. 'My apologies, I did not mean to startle you,' he said.

I turned to meet Gilbert Noble to be immediately taken by his handsome features. For a man in his fifty-eighth year he appeared forty-eight. His hair was curled and cropped short, enough to hold his beaver fur top hat in place I fancied – should he be outdoors. He was clean-shaven with perfect and neat sideburns of fashionable length and 'L' shaped to the lower jaw. His eyes were blue, his nose petite yet manly and he possessed a smallish mouth over a dimpled chin.

'My wife informs me that you are from the police department,' he said. 'Here to ask questions about Violet.'

'Yes sir. If you will, forgive me for arriving unannounced.'

I was aware Mrs Noble lingered in the hallway but she chose not to reveal herself.

'Come Mr Hunter,' Noble stepped aside from the drawing room portal motioning me to step into the hall once more. 'If you don't mind I would prefer to discuss this delicate matter outside. I find the house claustrophobic since ... since Violet passed ... and I crave the open air.'

I stepped onto the veranda and again the melancholy sky caught my attention.

'Looks like rain is on the way,' I said before realising how hollow the remark sounded. I twisted about as Noble closed the front door behind him, to briefly see Mrs Noble backing into the dark recess of a doorway down the hall. She looked miserable and appeared to be weeping.

'Rain!' Noble answered. He looked pained. 'Hopefully. We need the rain Mr Hunter. Look, these are painful memories, can we make this brief?'

'Certainly.' I opened my notebook and poised with my pencil trying to look as professional as possible. 'Did you have any enemies sir?'

'No. Not that I know of.'

'You haven't recently upset anyone, disgruntled employee maybe.'

'No.'

'You are a wealthy man are you not Mr Noble?'

'What's this have to do with my daughter's death?'

'I'm sorry sir. It is pertinent to the inquiry. Please answer the question.'

'Then yes. We have a successful property here. The hops have been exceptional and the price of wool has continued to rise year after year of late.'

'So you *are* a wealthy man?'

'Yes.'

'Then please forgive the next question but it must be asked sir.'

Noble turned his gaze from the river to me and looked fixedly into my eyes. 'Well?'

'You are not perchance hiding a kidnap threat are you Mr Noble? I mean a kidnapping demand that was not met for reasons unknown and the kidnappers then murdered you child.'

'Jesus Christ man. Do you think I would not have informed the police should that have been the case?'

'Quite. As I warned sir, it was a question I had to ask.' We faced off for seconds that felt like minutes. If he was hiding something he was a damned good liar. 'So here lies the problem Mr Noble. If Violet was not kidnapped or the victim of some deranged persons wishing you harm what did happen to her?' I took a moment to pause and choose my next words carefully. 'And it appears Violet was not the object of a predator.'

'Predator?'

'A deviant sir who may have ...'

'Oh Jesus no!'

'The coroner, Ernest Crawley, is confident your daughter was not interfered with.'

'Then what *do* you know?' Noble asked with a measure of sarcasm.

'Violet was asphyxiated. But her body was left where she was murdered for one month, and then later moved to be placed with weights into the river.'

'No!' Suddenly the strain of our conversation crept up on the landowner, like a malicious spectre siphoning all his energy. 'I was informed yesterday of her discovery but the full details ... these facts ... are new to me.'

'I am so sorry to be the one to tell you this sir, but yes, her body was hidden and then transported to the river.'

Tears welled in the man's eyes and he fell heavily into a veranda chair.

'Your daughter was found by a ferryman,' I continued. 'New Norfolk is a small community, would you perchance know where he can be found?'

The devastated father was lost in his own dark thoughts for some time and I could only imagine his anguish.

'Mr Noble ... sir.'

'There are two,' he said in a weak broken voice. 'They work from the town jetty. Make your way there and I will send my maid to advise one or the other to meet you.'

The mile walk into town cleared my thoughts once more. I sensed there was no guilt on the part of either of Violet's parents, I was leaving behind me nothing but sorrow and misery. Mary the chambermaid hurried ahead to arrange a meeting with one or both ferryman and met up with me on the riverbank path on her return. I was to rendezvous at the pier she told me in passing.

I avoided the New Norfolk township and kept to the river bank until I came to the pier where Ben Swain had tied our sloop and where I was to meet the ferryman. There was no sign of my skipper.

'You Caspian 'unter?' a young boy, one of two, called out.

'Who wants to know?'

'Walter.'

'Oh. Then yes Walter, I am Caspian Hunter.'

'Yer skipper Ben's gone into the township. 'e said 'e'd be back within the hour.'

'Oh, and how long ago did he tell you that?'

'I dunno. I ain't a timekeeper.'

With time on my side I watched these two young tykes near the end of the pier. They had time on their hands and pockets full of rocks. Each lad sported his own shang-eye or slingshot as they say in some parts; the fork of a sturdy bush cut down to size with a handle and a crude rubber strap fastened to catapult the projectiles forth at speed. They lined up pottery ginger beer bottles balanced on the pier pylons and took orderly turns in target practice. And they were good, rarely missing the solid stoneware bottles that shattered or were flung sideways into the river.

'Who's the better marksman?' I asked.

'Me.' The lad fast to answer was maybe eight, and now I guessed the other, possibly ten years old, was his brother.

'Bollocks,' the older boy said. 'I just got three in a row.'

'Do you mind if I attempt a shot?' I asked.

'Sure.' The ten-year-old looked me up and down as the entrepreneurial cogs in his brain went to work. 'I've got an 'alfpenny what says yer can't hit the target in three shots.'

'Halfpenny? Is that what my skipper paid you?'

'Maybe.' He dug deep into his three-quarter britches and presented proof of his wager.

'Hmm,' I said. 'Alright then. It can't be that difficult.' The fact that they had made it look simple had not dawned on me.

'Show us yer coin sir, if'n yer please.'

'Smart boy.' I took out my purse to a pleasing rattle. Satisfied, the lad passed me his slingshot and three rocks. He then took a stoneware bottle from a hessian sack where I read the impressed label. *W. Cutts. Black Snake Inn.* 'That's the Black Snake Inn down river is it not?'

'Aye.'

'Well would not the innkeeper reimburse you some pennies should you return his bottles?'

'No sar.'

'And why would that be?'

'Mr Cutts carked it years ago.'

'Oh'

My first shot was wide. No, worse than wide. It shot off towards the distant shore. Less cocksure I took more care with my second rock and was rewarded with a near miss. Yes indeed, *it can't be that difficult.* I drew back the rubber strap a third time, this last rock was smooth and round as a marble. I closed my left eye, made certain the sling was taut and the bottle lined up and ...

'Mr 'unter.' Right on queue. *Damn and blast.* The rock sizzled over the river and skipped on the surface before sinking. The ferryman, whom the maid told me was named Hatch, trundled heavily towards me on the timber planks of the jetty.

'Mr 'unter?'

'Yes.' I turned to greet the man when it struck me *he* was a *she*. What I am trying to say is the ferryman was a woman. A sturdy woman at that, dressed in sailor calicos and a blouse strung at the breasts. 'Ah, you must be Hatch.'

'Aye.' She stopped dead in her tracks fastening her eyes on mine with hands planted on hips like some fishwife. 'Say it then.'

'Say what?'

'You're a woman.'

'Oh. Ah yes. You're a woman.'

'Ferryman is not a title exclusive to men yer know. Ferryman, ferrywoman just sounds a little dull-witted. Ferryperson! Firk! Why should I give a rat's arse?'

'Quite. Hear, hear.'

'But you do give a rat's don't yer Mr 'unter? I makes yer feel uncomfortable eh? What's a woman doin' rowin' folk across this 'ere river. She must 'ave the arms of a sawyer and tits like rocks.'

'No,' I *was* feeling uncomfortable but not for the reason *she* was a woman. 'You miss understand madam ...'

'Madam! Firk! Hatch'll do just fine, savvy?'

'Savvy. I mean yes. Yes of course ... Hatch.' I needed to steer our conversation to business. Fast. 'Tell me, is there much call for a ferry ... *man* ... on the river with the bridge yonder?' I nodded to the fifteen-year-old bridge further up river.

'Well for some it's easier if'n I collect 'em at their farms on the river's edge and take 'em across with their produce for market. Saves a longer walk like.'

'Fair enough.'

'An' some get snaky about the bridge toll.'

'Oh. So could you kindly explain how you discovered the body?'

'Aye. I was takin' old Ma Brewer 'cross the river to 'er farm yonder,' and Hatch waved a wayward finger across the river some two hundred yards away. 'She'd been to the market all day an' then spent 'alf 'er yield at the Bush Inn by the smell o' her. Well I pushed off from the shallows yonder, where I moor *Rub-a-dub-dub*.'

'Rub-a-dub-dub?'

'Aye, That's the name o' me wherry. You know 'ow the nursery rhyme goes ...

> *Rub-a-dub-dub,*
> *Three men in a tub,*
> *And who do you think they be?*
> *The butcher, the baker, the candlestick maker.*
> *And all o' 'em out to sea.*

Hatch snapped off a laughing cough, cleared her throat and spat sideways. Now I was starting to think Hatch had spent the day in the Bush Inn also. She looked at me incredulous. 'Ain't yer heard the rhyme?'

'Yes but I ... oh never mind.'

'What?'

'Please continue.'

'Well I just shoved away from the riverbank with Ma Brewer, her hound Harry and a half bottle o' Geneva when me oar dragged on somethin'. It caught like. So cursin' and tuggin' I finally loosed it when bugger me if that little'n didn't burst to the surface, bubblin' and fartin' rotten gasses. It were awful. I could see she'd been dead a while. The stink was horrendous an' then Ma Brewer starts fetchin' up in me boat. Jaysuz it was a firkin' nightmare.'

'Where exactly?' I asked.

'Yonder thirty feet.' Hatch pointed to a muddy river ledge where a huge willow tree at the water's edge offered good anchorage for a small boat. Now I could make out the thirteen-foot clinker *Rub-a-dub-dub* hidden by the sweeping willow. I started to follow Hatch when the ten-year-old lad stood by waiting for his wager.

'Oi, where do yer think you're goin'?' He nodded to his open palm reaching towards me and I dropped a lone half-penny into his grubby paw.

It can't be that difficult. Bollocks.

Hatch and I negotiated the water's edge where few positions allowed a safe landing. I followed closely in the ferryperson's footsteps, for the River Derwent this far inland flowed briskly and was mostly very deep. Hatch led me down log steps she had built herself into the embankment. At the landing, tree roots strengthened the ground beneath us but it dropped away several feet in relative calm water for another two yards, before dropping off into much deeper water into the fast-flowing river.

'There.' Hatch flicked a finger towards the shallower water, dark with tannin and mud and a knotted maze of drowned tree roots. 'She came to the surface there, about ten feet out.'

'How deep is it there?'

'Well I ain't never swum there matey. But going by the length o' me oar I'd say no more than eight feet. That is of course until you get to deeper water a further twenty feet out. It can be a bastard rowing across sometimes, specially when the snow melts up in them mountains.'

The wind had died completely and skipper Ben Swain prepared to settle the night. I on the other hand walked back into the village where I caught the last coach back to Hobart Town. But not before posting notices about the settlement for any persons with information, any persons who may have seen anything strange, on the dates I had estimated, to come forward to the local constabulary. It was the least I could do.

......

Prisoners' Barracks. Campbell Street.

I arrived back at the prisoners' barracks late afternoon with more questions than answers and was staring blankly at the blackboard when Holly bowled into our workspace with the eyes of a startled deer. 'God almighty Caspian sar!'

'What is it Holly?'

'Jaysuz. Come see for yourself sar.'

And she twisted on her boot heels and hob-nailed back down the stairs as if chased by the banshee itself. Lincoln, Billings. Jasper and myself dutifully followed; for it was clear from past experience we would not hear the end of it until we did. We caught up with Holly mingling with a dozen soldiers before the superintendent's house within the main prison yard. All watched a strange woman, followed closely by Charlie Griff of the afternoon guard on the main gate, who had abandoned his musket for the ever-handy halberd, which the man wielded with menace.

'Best to prod a woman rather than shoot 'er, eh sar?' Jasper said, noting Charlie's anxious stance brandishing the halberd.

The woman stood five-foot-eight-inches with her thick brown hair cut short in a military style, which I thought a shame as she had such attractive feminine features and visage. She wore a thick woollen coat of kangaroo skins over a calico blouse strung at the front over pert breasts with a tattered ankle length skirt barely exposing men's boots. I guessed her age at twenty-five but what caught my immediate attention was the aroma. The woman had clearly hiked some distance and was accompanied by a rather unpleasant odour. At least at first I thought it was her, and yet a hint of lavender oil lingered like cheap perfume.

'What's happening?' I asked.

'That's Annie Eddington,' Holly said. 'The word is she's a bounty 'unter.'

'Look at the bag she's carrying!'

'Oh!' I then realised the sack the woman slung from one arm had left a trail of blood and gore from the gate. It was also harassed by large black flies and the stink of decay.

'She gone an' captured One Ear Kearney,' someone cheered.

'Kearney?'

'Aye. The bushranger what killed them soldiers in Ross Town.'

'She did?'

'Aye.'

'An' that's the bastard's head she's got in the sack.'

'She's 'ere for the 'undred quid reward.'

One Ear Kearney was a murderous rogue, a thorn in the side for our northern brethren. He bludgeoned a fellow prisoner to death and wounded the overseer before escaping a road gang near Port Dalrymple. For five or maybe six weeks he terrorised settlers in the north. But then we heard stories he was causing havoc in the central highlands. He was almost captured at Ross but killed two soldiers single-handedly before escaping once more.

And why was the head in the bag my readers back in England might ask? Well here in the colonies they do not dilly-dally. When a villain has a price on his head it means just that ... *a price on their head.* Which also equates to decapitating the corpse to deliver the head to the authorities for proof. It cannot be simpler than that.

'Mr Mead,' Annie Eddington roared for the prison superintendent, and the woman had a voice to match her strength.

Simeon Mead, the prisoners' barracks superintendent, stepped onto his veranda with his thumbs hooked behind his lapels and puffing on a cigar, which made me wonder if the foul breeze was blowing his way. The sixty-two-year-old superintendent and myself go back aways and I preferred to avoid crossing his path, since starting off on a bad foot two years earlier when I arrived in Hobart Town. My dalliance with his nineteen-year-old-year-old daughter Elizabeth had caused some grievance. But that was all forgotten about, or so I thought.

'Mr Mead,' Annie Eddington yelled across the superintendent's rose garden to the man larger than life standing on his porch. 'I am here to claim one hundred pounds if'n yer please.' Annie dropped the sack with a sickening thud – we now knew what it contained. She tugged on a slipknot, the bag loosened and she upended it, disturbing a horde of flies as One Ear Kearney's severed head rolled across the flagstones.

'She's done that before,' I heard some cove say. This bravado was rewarded with collective gasps of admiration. Simeon Mead kept his distance and puffed his cigar. He looked at Private Charlie Griff who stepped up and poked the trophy with his halberd. Flies circled Charlie. The crowd grew silent.

'Well?' Mead called out to the guard.

'It's a cove's head all right sir,' the guard answered, slapping at the winged pests.

'I think we can all see that. And you madam?' Mead asked Annie who stood defiant, hands on hips. Where did you ... ah ... obtain this?'

'I separated it from the beggar's shoulders meself, after I shot him through the heart. You see, sir, he tried to rob me. Me! Annie Eddington. In me own camp. But I was too quick for him. Shot him once with me pistol.'

'You mean you set a trap for him?' someone called out.

Annie turned slowly to glare at the man who had asked. 'An' what if'n I did.'

'Where, pray tell?' the superintendent called out.

'Green Ponds sir. When can I get me reward?'

'You will be rewarded madam as soon as we verify it is the outlaw Kearney.

Charlie.'

'Aye sir.'

'Get that ... that thing to the morgue,' Mead said of the blood-soaked head. 'I want the coroner to confirm it. And take down that woman's details for the record.'

I stood in the shadows watching the superintendent a moment. Every time I saw the man I thought of his daughter Elizabeth. She was a bewitching, charming nineteen-year-old when we met on my arrival in Hobart Town nearly two years earlier. I will never forget her, dressed in blue, an ankle-length dress with a pink and blue bodice and a sky-blue bonnet with her long blonde hair curling in spirals down her back. She wore kid gloves and her curvaceous ankles were hugged with brown leather boots buttoned up at the side. She had the most extraordinary smile showing off her almond shaped azure eyes.

Elizabeth!

Like an apparition, a wish come true, she materialised on the upper balcony. Following our dalliance back in '55, and the fact that Mrs Mead had died and left Elizabeth motherless, Simeon Mead sent his daughter to finishing school in London. Now here she was. And she presented herself more stunning than ever.

I had forgotten Elizabeth's interest in the macabre and clearly the severed head was an attraction to the minx. I say minx, for Elizabeth seduced *me* when her father left her alone in the residence while he travelled to Oatlands on business. Returning early the man was not amused to find me with his daughter. Shortly thereafter Elizabeth was kidnapped and I was accused of her murder, until I cleared my name by rescuing Elizabeth from her captors. But that was all forgotten about ... Or was it?

Simeon Mead was a man of acute awareness, although unaware his daughter was on the balcony above. Before I realised, as mesmerised as I was with Elizabeth, Mead had me in his sights.

'Mr Hunter,' he called out across the yard.

Bugger.

'A moment of your time.'

He sounded amicable enough. I crossed the courtyard and entered the superintendent's residence via an iron gate within a head-high stone wall. The man met me on the steps to his veranda. Clearly he was not inviting me into his lodgings and I can't say I blame him. I snatched a glance skywards. Elizabeth had stepped to the bannisters and watched my approach briefly before delivering a playful smile and then shrinking away.

Once the minx, always the minx. That is what I say.

Mead cleared his throat. 'Mr Winter has been given furlough on unforeseen grounds,' he said with a contemptuous scowl that reminded me why I had avoided the man the past two years.

'Fabian?' I said, insisting on informality.

'Yes, Fabian Winter.'

'But I was with him only this morning, he mentioned nothing ...'

'Mr Hunter,' he interrupted.

'Unforeseen grounds? May I ask what?'

'No. you may not,' he spat. 'It is for personal reasons only he and I need to know. Captain Maddox will be taking Mr Winter's position until he is fit to resume his duties.'

I knew Captain Maddox from the prison guard; a most obnoxious and egotistic man. 'Bradley Maddox?'

'Captain Maddox to you Mr Hunter. Do not lose all sense of propriety.'

'But Mr Mead, I am second in charge, surely I should be responsible in Fabian's stead.'

'There you go again.' Mead's eyes narrowed and he glared at me with his beady black eyes. 'Show some respect Mr Hunter. Captain Maddox, who is a war hero no less, is replacing Mr Winter.'

War hero?

It seemed Mead read my mind. 'Captain Maddox led soldiers against those rebels at Ballarat – the Eureka Stockade – the newspapers are full of accounts of that terrible event.'

So what? I pained to answer but thought better of it.

'And he was wounded no less, one of a hundred and twenty I am told. Six soldiers were killed and twenty or so rebels. Captain Maddox was in the thick of it. So I trust you will afford the man all assistance. Now, good day to you ...'

'But sir, this is ...'

Simeon Mead craned over me from his perch on the upper veranda steps and fixed me a stare like an eagle might before pecking the eyes from its prey. Mead was a stubborn man with a personal grudge. And he was my superior.

Best I leave it there, I thought.

I was too annoyed to brief the others before we returned from the prison yard. We ascended the stairs back to our office where Captain Bradley Maddox was already seated at Fabian's desk. He was a sly-faced man, with a thin head and wiry build with ginger hair and pale skin, which was not enhanced by his face pockmarked from smallpox in his youth.

Holly was first in the room. 'Who are you?' she spat at Maddox, the words spilling from her mouth without hesitation.

Maddox was incredulous. 'Pardon?'

'Are yer deaf or what. I said ...'

'Let me introduce you all to Captain Maddox.' I cut Holly short before she made matters worse. 'Captain Maddox is replacing Fabian. Temporarily.'

Mouths opened. Maddox picked the dirt from under his nails with a miniature sword letter-opener, a birthday gift from Fabian's aunt that he kept on his desk. He fixed his eye on Holly to study her reaction, which I tempered by putting my hand on her shoulder and squeezed. 'This is Holly,' I said, before turning to the others. 'And Jasper, Billings and Lincoln.'

Maddox remained slouched at Fabian's desk. He swung back in the chair and hooked one boot over the other on the desk.

'Right then. As Mr Hunter announced, I am in charge of this office now. I've read the notes and memorandums given me by Superintendent Mead and I see we have two unsolved murders to attend to at this moment. I do not suffer fools lightly. I will not stand for failure.'

'I assume you have studied our track record Mr Maddox,' I said curtly. 'And noted we have a high success rate.'

'If you'll let me finish Hunter.' The atmosphere was uncomfortably sour already. 'I would like you and Billings on the Piketon killing as you are the seniors. We all know what is at stake here.'

'The diamond,' Jasper said brightly.

'Yes. There is no doubt Piketon was in possession of the missing diamond and that the killer found it. Good work Lincoln,' Maddox tapped the paperwork detailing how Lincoln discovered the hiding place, albeit by accident. 'If that is not motive to kill someone I don't know what is. Holly and Jasper will continue with the Noble murder, Hunter, you are to brief them on your recent visit to New Norfolk.'

'As a matter o' fact me and Lincoln was on a stake out this mornin',' Holly said.

'Oh?'

'Yes,' I said. 'I ordered them to track down Calhoun Nyle.' I hastily explained the Nyle and Nibley suspects and possible connections. 'By the way Holly, did you locate the man?'

'Aye, I did. He's a quarrier all right, works at the quarries behind De Graves Brewery.'

'An' I hate to tell yer this Caspian sar,' Lincoln added. 'But he's a big devil an' all.'

'Aye,' Holly cut in. 'If'n yer was ever goin' to arrest the bastard ... sorry cap'n, excuse me French ... if'n you was ever wantin' to arrest the beggar I'd put a musket ball in his kneecap first. 'e's built like a brick shithouse.'

'Fine.' Captain Maddox stood, his lean figure neat in almost military order; white duck trousers, knee high boots with civilian frock coat and swagger stick. 'But now you and Lincoln will continue with the Noble case. Hunter, I want you and Billings to solve this damned diamond business.'

Jasper looked dejected. 'And me Captain?'

'For the moment you will sort out the filing system here. It's a shambles.'

'Aye.' Jasper looked to me, I shrugged. *Best do as you are ordered lad.*

'Now,' Maddox said. 'The clock reads seven, you are all dismissed and I will see you here in the morning. Eight o'clock sharp.'

My colleagues, still nonplussed by the turn of events, gathered themselves together and left without a word, although Lincoln shot me an encouraging wink.

'Hunter,' Maddox stabbed his swagger stick between the exit and myself. 'A word.' He waited until we were alone. I drew breath; this man was proving himself tiring. 'Lieutenant Fribbens of the Norfolk Bay Convict Station,' he said with his chin in the air and a look of contempt and superiority. He allowed the name to linger in the air like bad intestinal gases.

'Fribbens,' I finally answered, knowing exactly what he was about to say. 'What of the man?'

'You should know that Lieutenant Fribbens is an acquaintance of mine. He is a good man, a friend even and you sullied his name.'

'The man struck me first captain, and in a most cowardly manner.'

'You struck the commander of one of Her Majesty's Prison stations Hunter. If you had been in the army you would be flogged.'

Christ! The audacity of this impudent dullard.

'Well I am not in the army, captain. And your friend is lucky I did not do him more harm.'

'Why you insolent bastard.'

'Bastard? I don't think so. *I* know who my father and mother are. May I remind you, captain, that I am here in the colony on a five-year contract between Birmingham and Tasmania. I have a track record and an excellent rapport with His Excellency Sir Henry Young, the governor. My skills are in demand here. You sir, on the other hand, have no experience in police work. How you were given the position is beyond me. You are also in a temporary position so unless you want anarchy on your hands I suggest you treat the team here with civility. Now if you will kindly stand aside I'm off to an inn.'

I hurried down the stairs and through the prison gates seething. The man had no real jurisdiction over me. *I* should be filling Fabian's boots whilst he is on furlough. Especially as it was only temporary.

Angry, I crossed the prison yard and was about to slip through the security gate leading to the gatekeeper and main entrance when I heard a soft voice hiss my name. 'Caspian.' Always alert within the prison grounds, I twisted about to catch the figure of a woman in the shadows. She was calling to me from the direction of the chapel. 'Caspian Hunter. Over here.'

'Elizabeth!' It was the superintendent's daughter Elizabeth Mead. She remained in the shadows. Although nightfall was still some time away it was dusk and the prison lamps were yet to be lit. I looked about, no one near the chapel, and hurried to her.

'Oh dear god how I've missed you Caspian Hunter, you gorgeous man you.' She took my hands outstretched and looked me up and down. I was aware I had put on a pound or two in weight but, hell, I am after all in my third decade damn it.

'I've put on a little weight,' I said lamely.

'Oh, but it suits you.' Elizabeth pulled me towards her, threw her arms about my neck and kissed me full on the lips. I must say I was a little stiff lipped and she sensed my disconnection.

'I ... ah ... I did not expect to see you,' I said. 'Not so soon that is. When did you return from London?'

'Three days ago. Daddy secured me a berth on HMS *Garrison*.'

'Oh yes.' I remembered watching the Royal Navy frigate docking recently. 'Well well,' I tried to relax. 'Look at you. All grown up.'

'Yes. I'm twenty-one now.'

'Look Elizabeth, I have my colleagues waiting for me. My sincere apologies but I must skedaddle.'

Instantly Elizabeth's face stiffened. 'We need to talk,' there was almost a hint of desperation in her voice.

'T-Talk?'

Laughter spilled from the guardhouse and three red-coated soldiers appeared. They were clearly off duty. It was time for the change of the guard. The men gathered down the southern end of the prison yard near the entrance to the mess. Soon they would walk in our direction. Suddenly I was propelled backwards by my collar. 'Come,' Elizabeth whispered. 'Follow me.'

'What? Ah pardon ... what are you doing?'

'Quickly now or we'll be seen.'

'Eliz ...'

'Hurry.'

Like the fool I am I followed the siren by the chapel to a side door at the northern end of the Separate Apartment building, a two-storey lockup where all the prisoners were already in lockdown for the night.

'But my colleagues await me,' I whispered pathetically. My voice lacked authority, none whatsoever.

'It won't take a jiffy. Promise.'

'What won't?'

'I have something important to tell you.' Elizabeth gripped the brass knob of a side door to the chapel.

'Tell me here,' I said.

'Can't,' she said rattling the door handle.

'Why?' I asked, before mentioning, 'The doors locked. All the doors are locked. This is a prison remember.'

I heard the rattle before I saw the ring of keys appear from inside her jacket. She fumbled about.

'What's that?' I asked dumbfounded.

'Keys silly.'

'I can see they are keys but ...' a key turned in the lock. She opened the door and we slipped into the darkness. 'Where did you get those? Oh do not tell me. I do not want to know.'

'Daddy has spares to every lock in the prison, except the cell doors that is.' Elizabeth closed the door, quietly re-locking it. 'Follow me.'

She took my hand and as familiar as I was with the prison layout the darkness bothered me. The darkness and the fact I was once again in the company of the superintendent's daughter. We stumbled along a narrow passageway. Not too far away I could hear the sounds of misery, the sobs, the snores, the curses of the men in solitary. Which also meant we were close to the solitary guards. Elizabeth had stopped at the end of the passage and turned to face me in the pitch darkness. 'Shush my dearest,' she whispered and I felt her warm sweet breath on my face. She placed a finger to my lips, and her command was heeded. Another door opened silently in the dark. I followed Elizabeth blind into the cold dankness. Immediately the room had a distinct smell I was familiar with. Stockholm tar, the same sealant used aboard ships on the decks and on rigging.

We were in the gallows!

Elizabeth struck a flint on a tinderbox and sparked a candle. Yes. We were in the gallows.

'Jesus Elizabeth!'

'Hush my sweet.' She threw her arms about me kissing me once more with moist soft lips. I weakened, returning the intimacy only to be rewarded with the woman's tongue exploring the inside of my mouth. I pulled back for air.

'My,' I said, unaware I was panting. 'Where did you learn that?'

'Never you mind.' Elizabeth had the most seductive look on her face. Nay ... mischievous was the word. And she too was breathing heavily like a miner carting a sack of coal, uphill.

I had no illusion where this was headed. 'But in here?' I said.

'There is nowhere else this private my dearest.' We kissed once more. A brief and lustful kiss while Elizabeth fumbled artfully with the buttons on my britches. In the candlelight she looked striking in her cream skirts, with yellow blouse and light brown bodice and matching jacket but I must say, dear reader, Elizabeth looked even more magnificent stripped out of them.

Oh Jesus Lord save me from evil!

Naked as the moment she appeared from her mother's womb, Elizabeth stepped off the flagstones and hurried up the stairs to the scaffold. I followed. A lamb to the slaughter. Throwing herself across the trap door I joined her in the vague candlelight from below. It was a stolen moment of passion. And a brief one at that. Yet the act was euphoric ... And on the scaffold. Who would ever guess?

Elizabeth fetched our clothing and we shared a quiet giggle. She lit a cheroot on the candle flame, puffing away like an innkeeper.

'You smoke?' I said incredulously. 'Something else you picked up in London?'

She shot me a disarming smile, finally passing the cigar to me. I do not smoke but felt mischievous. I drew on the cheroot while Elizabeth sat opposite, sitting upright and hugging her knees to her chin, when she said, 'I have a baby!'

I sucked the smoke into my lungs and thought it my last breath. Coughing violently, the pain tormenting my chest and throat I managed to wheeze. 'What?'

'I have a baby. Caspian. A baby boy. he is thirteen months old and he is yours.'

'Christ's blood Elizabeth, what are you saying?'

'I am announcing to you my dearest, you are a father to a beautiful baby boy.'

'But Elizabeth I ... we ... ah ... we ...'

'What, what are you trying to tell me dearest?'

'Stop calling me that.'

'What? Dearest?'

'Look Elizabeth, we may have lain together that day two years previous but we ... your father came home early, surprising us remember?'

'Oh you silly boy. You do know how babies are made do you not?'

I grew angry, jumping to my feet and hopping about like a madman whilst trying to pull up my britches. 'Our liaison ended prematurely, remember?'

'Is that what you think?' Elspeth bottom lip dropped. 'Is that really what you think? Oh Caspian my dearest ...'

'Stop calling me that.'

'You don't have to shout.'

I took a deep breath in. This was not happening, surely. I recollected the event clearly; surely I could not have ... well ... impregnated this woman with my child. I had a sudden and horrid thought. 'What is he called anyway ... this child of yours?'

'Our child. His name is Caspian.'

'Argh!'

'What's the matter dear... Caspian.'

'How could you?'

'And I thought you would be so excited.' Now Elizabeth put on the tears. And they were real. She bawled and I felt a right scoundrel. What I wanted to ask next was, *are you certain the boy is mine?* But I felt I had done enough damage for the time being.

'Does your father know?'

'Of course he knows,' she managed between sobs. 'How could I keep a wee bairn secret from daddy?'

'I meant does your father think ... ah know it's mine?'

'Not yet.'

'I heard nothing of your child mentioned around the prison. I mean the gossips and nags would have field day if they knew.'

'That's because baby Caspian is with a wet nurse at Austin's Ferry.'

'A wet nurse?'

'Yes Caspian. He is well looked after. Daddy was ... well ... furious when he discovered the news. Thankfully I wrote him a letter over a year past and I was not here to face the music so to speak.'

'How is he now?'

'Daddy is very upset, he barely talks to me, called me awful names, said I was scandalous and a wanton woman of low esteem.' Elizabeth's eyes welled up again. I finished dressing and felt less vulnerable.

Finally I took a stern stance and asked, 'What is it you want from me Elizabeth?'

'Why would you even ask such a thing,' she sobbed.

Jesus Christ!

'Well?' I demanded.

'A gentleman would ask daddy for my hand in marriage.'

'M-Marriage!' I needed to sit down and sat at the edge of the scaffold dangling my feet over the edge.

Suddenly the gallows seemed an option.

'I need time to think,' I lied. More like I need time to escape. Elizabeth shuffled over to sit beside me, on the edge of eternity – well edge of eternity for many villains that is. She placed an arm about my shoulder.

'Caspian dearest. I love you. I have always loved you and always will.' I said nothing. 'You were my first love,' she added to try and seal the deal.

First!

I had to hold my tongue on that one. Like this evening, she seduced me two years ago also. *I* just took advantage of a weak moment.

'I must go,' I said shuffling to my feet. 'My friends are waiting.'

We made our exit in silence into the evening of the moonless night. Old Jack Spencer the lamplighter was doing the rounds of the prison yard, otherwise the yard was eerily quiet. I bid Elizabeth goodnight outside the chapel and, head bowed, hurried to the gatehouse.

Gate keeper Charlie Griff pushed the heavy iron gate open and I stepped onto Campbell Street, my mind scrambling with angry thoughts of Captain Maddox and now, apparently, I was a father. I could hear the words of my own dear father – deceased – calling to me from the heavens, *I told you boy, one day your womanising would catch up with you.*

Thank you father.

I looked about for any sign of the others. Charlie noticed. 'Oh,' he said. 'I near forgot sar. Holly and the others said to tell yer theys gone for refreshment at the Good Woman.'

There is something decidedly homely about a colonial inn, and the Good Woman, a few hundred yards north of the prison, is as homely as one could hope for. I stooped below the main entrance sill, a beam of iron-hard eucalypt where a thousand skulls had unwittingly tested its strength, and stepped into the fug of grog and burning tobacco. The taproom was full, standing room only and I jostled a path between the jolly imbibers to the bar, where Holly noticed me first. Shouting to the bar wench she demanded a quart of porter for me. I watched her silver shilling spin in a puddle of ale on the counter and Holly shoved a tankard towards me. 'To Fabian,' Holly cried out.

'To Fabian,' we cheered, and the five of us gulped our porters in one draft.

'Well then?' Lincoln asked me.

'Well then what?'

'Cap'n Maddox sar, *a word if'n yer please* 'e said to yer as we were leavin'.'

'Aye Caspian sar,' Holly said. 'Spill the beans.'

'Oh that.' My mind was still awash with Elizabeth and her news. I told my colleagues of my altercation with Maddox.

''e's a right bastard, that Maddox,' Jasper agreed. ''e's got a reputation and a half around the prison.'

I was lost once more in my thoughts when a familiar aroma caught my attention. Even over the crowded bar of unwashed bodies, over the rumpus of noisy drinkers, I detected an essence only recently whiffed in the prison yard; a not too unpleasant aroma of sweat doused with lavender oil. Annie Eddington the bounty hunter. She stood alone, one elbow on the corner of the bar with her hat pulled over her brow to hide her face. She appeared to ponder, her thoughts lost in a quart of ale. I stared a moment, she really was a wild colonial woman. But there was a sensuality about her, a *je ne sais quoi*. Like the trapper she was, she sensed my presence and tipped her head back enough to catch my eye. The wryest of smiles curled the corner of her mouth. I nodded a polite greeting. Immediately she moved towards me, shoving hardened drinkers aside.

'You're with the police department aren't yer?' she asked.

'Ah ...' I was caught totally unawares and yes, lavender was prominent. 'Ah, yes,' I answered. 'I was there when you delivered One Ear Kearney to the superintendent.'

'You mean his head,' she corrected and treated me to a full smile. She really was a most attractive woman. I introduced myself.

'Caspian Hunter.'

'Annie Eddington,' she answered. There was an awkward silent moment. 'Sorry if'n I'm a little ... ah, fragrant,' she admitted.

Fragrant? Redolent more like, I wanted to say.

'But I've been in the wilds hunting that murderin' Kearney.'

'And what a task you completed. I must congratulate you, miss.'

'Mrs.'

'Oh, pardon me.'

'That's all right. Call me Annie. Mr Eddington left for the goldfields months ago.'

'Oh.'

'Yes. We lived in Port of Maryborough in Queensland for a year or two. My estranged husband is of Greek descent you see, and prefers the warmer climate.'

'Oh.'

'Yes. At the moment he is working the goldfields at Ballarat, on his way back north. Me, I like cooler weather and a little more adventure. Kearney is my third capture you know. I caught two others in New South Wales.'

'So you *are* a bounty hunter.'

'Aye. That I am.'

'You said your husband was Greek.'

'Greek father, English mother actually.'

'Oh. But ...'

'Eddington is not a Greek name you ask? My husband's father's name is Manis. However after that business of Greece sympathising with the Russian forces against the Ottomans he chose to take his mother's name, here in the British Colonies.'

I understood immediately. The orthodox Greeks sympathised with the orthodox Russians in the Crimea kafuffle and King Otto of Greece took the opportunity to invade the Ottoman areas of Thessaly and Epirus. Britain acted swiftly, blocking Greece's main port Piraeus, effectively grounding Greece's navy. It was a failure that cost the Greek king his throne and Greece lost face with Britain.

The woman looked at me a moment, unsure of my motive for so many questions.

'But in all appearances he looks more English than Greek,' she said. 'Is that what you were thinking?'

'My apologies. I am inquisitive by nature,' I said.

Holly's arm squeezed between us with four empty tankards. 'The lads was just wonderin' if'n you're ... well ...' she tipped her head to the empties. Subtle as ever. I fetched a coin from my purse.

'Another?' I asked Annie.

'Aye, if'n you're paying.'

The barmaid slopped six pewter vessels of the inn's finest porter on the counter and moved on. Annie lifted hers and drank like a woodchopper.

'Erasmus Peck,' she finally said, wiping froth on her sleeve and looking me straight in the eye. My response spoke of recognition. 'When will *his* reward be posted?' she asked.

'What do you know of Erasmus Peck?' I asked.

'He's a villain and absconder from Port Arthur.'

'That's correct.' It appeared that is all she knew.

'So, when and what price?' she asked. 'A hundred guineas I'm guessing.'

'I really cannot say Annie. Where did you hear of this man?'

'Hobart Town's a small place Mr Hunter. I visit the inns. I listen.'

Moments later the woman thanked me for the porter and bid me farewell.

'Well it's good to come in out of the bushlands occasionally,' she said in parting and drew a phial from her pocket. 'Lavender oil,' she smiled. 'Never fear Mr Hunter, I'll visit the bathhouse before retiring for the night.'

And I watched her leave the inn.

'What was that all about?' Holly asked.

'Not certain,' I lied. 'But I am thinking we have not seen the end of that woman.'

As conversations between colleagues have a tendency to centre on business, Fabian's situation was raised.

'What's wrong with Fabian anyhow?' Billings asked.

'Yes,' Jasper said. ''e was fine this morning.'

'I honestly don't know,' I said. 'Mead was most insistent it was not our business.'

'All the same,' Holly said, 'it's you what should be fillin' 'is boots Caspian sar.'

'Aye.'

'I think I remember something about the head position requiring a married man,' Billings said.

'True,' I answered. 'But Maddox *is* only temporary.'

'Thank god.'

'And he does have a wife and three children in Melbourne,' I said, adding. '*And* he's a hero no less.'

'Pardon?'

I told the others about his apparent heroics at the Ballarat Rebellion.

Chapter Five
Day five

If nothing else Captain Bradley Maddox was punctual. He was, after all, an army man. Jasper, Holly, Lincoln and Billings were also early, and looking suitably busy as I entered; ten minutes past the eighth hour, and deliberate I might add. Maddox hooked his turnip watch free from his waistcoat pocket and flipped open the cover, making a show of reading the time. He said nothing, but scowled. Jasper was already standing at a table where he had hundreds of files before him, struggling to put them in alphabetical order. The fuel stove had not been lit. There was no hot coffee. *Dire* I thought. *Dire times indeed.*

'Well Billings,' I attempted some cheer. 'Let us go catch some villains.'

Outside, the warm sun in a clear blue sky gave us some joy.

'What is it with that man?' Billings asked me as we put distance between the prison and us. 'He is so ... what's the word I am thinking? Churlish. Yes that's it. Churlish.'

'I could think of a better name for him,' I half smiled. 'But I think he's missing his mother,' I jeered, leaping into a passing fly carriage.

We found the quarry Holly spoke of, where we hoped to question Calhoun Nyle, in the foothills of the great sphinx-like Mount Wellington. Our carriage left us at a gate to a narrow, overgrown driveway that led into the bushland. Although this was a private quarry there were still ticket men labouring here for an emolument. I counted twenty men before we were noticed by the overseer who demanded to know why we were there. I produced my brass badge and his attitude mellowed.

'Calhoun Nyle,' I said. 'I believe he plies his trade in this quarry.'

The overseer pointed to four men broaching a large step at the base of the quarry face. ''e's the big cove with 'is shirt off. He ain't done nothin' wrong 'as he?'

'Well we will see.'

'Argh,' he looked at us suspiciously. 'Cos he's a hard workin' cove an' I don't wanna loose him.'

Billings and myself stopped at the base of the stepped ledge where the broachers pounded the huge sandstone blocks apart with sledgehammer and wedges. The roughed stone blocks were *rocked out* by two men using a timber stretcher and carried to the dressing benches, known as bankers, where stonemasons dressed the blocks ready for carting to building sites nearby. Nyle, the only shirtless labourer in his group, was well over six foot with arms like hams. On both lower inner arms he wore fading tattoos of what looked like beehives.

'Mr Nyle,' I called out over the pummelling sound of iron on iron.

Nyle turned sharply and I felt a mist of fine sweat splash my face. He had grown his hair long and perspired like a workhorse. And he was indeed built like a brick shithouse, as Holly so eloquently put it. 'Mr Nyle?'

'Who wants to know?'

I introduced us both and presented my badge. He was not impressed. 'What d' yer want?'

'Edwin Piketon,' I started.

'Look mate. I had nothing to do with 'im.'

'You knew him then.'

'O' course, we was at Arthur together.'

'So you know that he was murdered?'

'Aye.'

'And my guess is you knew about a diamond allegedly in his possession.'

'Look, I done nuthin' wrong. I got me ticket and all I want is me life back, so don't try pinning Piketon's killin' on me, alright?'

'That's all very well,' Billings said. 'But we will need an alibi. Where were you Sunday last?'

Nyle leant forward on his sledgehammer handle, leering down at us from the advantage of the three-foot high step. 'Last Sunday?'

'Yes.'

'In church,' he said with a chuckle. 'Where else would I be?'

In church. Not likely I thought, but said, 'All day?'

'Aye.'

'Can you name witnesses?' Instantly he realised the church ruse was a mistake. Of course plenty of people should have seen him there … *should* he have been there. He looked vague.

'Mr Nyle, can you prove you were in church for *any* time at all last Sunday?' Stubborn silence. 'No,' I answered for him. 'Look we can order you to be taken to the watch house for further questioning. May I remind you this is a murder investigation.'

'A hanging matter,' Billings added.

Nyle's brow furrowed. 'I was at Jane Bell's,' he said with a sigh. The men within earshot waiting for him to re-join them laughed.

'Jane Bell's, at King's Road?' I asked, aware of a disorderly house I knew that operated in Sandy Bay, south of Battery Point near the public baths.

'Aye.'

'When?' Billings asked. 'In the evening, afternoon? An hour in the morning maybe?'

'All day.'

'All day!' I looked at Billings and back to Nyle. 'All day in a whorehouse?'

'Aye.'

'My. You are certainly making up for your time incarcerated at Port Arthur.'

'Miss Bell and me go back-a-ways, to Manchester like.'

'For fear of asking the obvious Mr Nyle,' Billings said, 'surely you were not fornicating the entire Sunday?'

'Huh!' The man's laugh was infectious. And god only knows I needed a good laugh. 'Miss Bell and me is friends. It wouldn't seem right to bed her.'

'And you will be vouched for, should we seek your alibi.'

'Aye. I'm helpin' Miss Bell build a scullery at the back of 'er premises. I spent Sunday layin' flagstones.' The smile returned. 'Mind you little Jessie English fixed me right proper when I finished. She bathed me, we drank, we supped and we …'

'Yes, I've got the picture. Well good day to you Mr Nyle and be assured we will be checking your alibi and no doubt will have more questions in the near future.'

'Fine.'

'What of Phineas Nibley?" Billings reminded me of the second ticket man we were looking for.

'Yes indeed.' I twisted back to Nyle, poised to strike a fresh blow. 'Phineas Nibley Mr Nyle. You two earned your tickets at the same time. I do believe he returned to Hobart Town the same time you did.'

'What of him?'

'Do you know where we can find him?'

'Aye. He's taken up as a feather man and resides in Wapping where he collects feathers from the poultry slaughter yards for mattresses and pillows like. Most days you'll find 'im along Old Wharf selling feathers and plumes to outgoin' vessels or whoever tickles 'is fancy.'

Cheap laughs, I thought, retreating from the quarry.

'He's a real wit that one sir,' Billings said when we were out of earshot. 'Did you notice the tattoos on his arms?'

'Yes I did. The beehive – it's a Manc seaman's thing.'

'Yes. He *did* say he's from Manchester.'

The beehive I knew was a common tattoo amongst sailors from Manchester.

'And it is also a Masonic sign,' I told Billings. 'But I doubt Calhoun Nyle is a Mason.'

Whilst I could garner some respect for Nyle, I found I had an instant dislike for Phineas Nibley. He was a short grubby little man; grubby with greedy eyes closely spaced, which phrenologists are quick to point out is a sign of cunning. Billings and I found the man sitting with an equally grubby woman, a fish fag I was told by those who knew her. Some would say a fishwife, but it would be difficult to imagine the woman partnered with anyone. She had eyes skewwhiff, one ahead and one to port, not unlike a Chinese pug dog. But her hearing was acute and she was the first to turn her head from where the two dangled their legs over the wharf's edge, taking a rest from their mornings hawking, I imagined. She grunted and I noted her mouth void of any teeth. Nibley turned and shifted nervously. If he had not been seated I had the feeling he would have bolted.

'Phineas Nibley?'

'Maybe,' he mumbled.

The fish fag stood unsteadily and, head bowed, made her exit hurrying off towards the Steam Packet Tavern across the wharf, leaving behind an unpleasant odour of stale fish and neglected sanitation.

'Well are you or aren't you Phineas Nibley?' Billings asked the creature with undisguised contempt.

'Aye. Who are you?' We presented credentials. 'Why can't youse leave a cove be? I got me ticket.' And he pulled a dog-eared document from his pocket with blackened hands imbedded with grime. The ticket was signed by Commandant Boyd himself. 'I done no wrong since I left Port Arthur. I ...'

'Keep your shirt on Nibley,' Billings said. 'We just want to ask you a few questions and if you've been a good lad then you've naught to worry about.'

Nibley's eyes narrowed. He had difficulty looking either of us in the eye. If one was ever to judge a book by its cover, this was your man.

'Sunday last. Where were you, what were your movements?'

'This is about that fool Piketon ain't it?' he asked and his mouth remained open with his tongue sitting on his bottom lip, like he was the sagacious defendant in the witness box nailing the answer to the prosecutor's guileful question.

'Piketon, yes it is,' I humoured the ex-prisoner.

Billings was less patient. 'So answer the question.'

'I was with Rose.' And he nodded to the fish fag disappearing into the tavern taproom.

'Rose?' Billings also followed Nibley's eye line. 'I must say she didn't smell like a Rose,' he whispered to me.

I studied Phineas Nibley a moment longer. He certainly didn't seem capable of tackling another man let alone crushing someone's skull with an iron.

'You wanna catch Piketon's killer?' Nibley murmured. 'Go find Erasmus Peck. 'e absconded last week an' 'e always said 'e'd find that diamond.'

Billings. 'What diamond?'

'Don't treat me like a dullard. Everyone knows about the Salmon Princess, worth twenty thousand guineas they say.'

'More like eight, but that's still worth killing for isn't it Phineas?'

'Like I said. Don't look at me. I 'ad nuthin' to do with Piketon gettin' cooked.'

'Cooked? What do you mean, cooked?'

''e died on 'is stove didn't 'e?'

'And how would you know that?' I asked. 'It has not been made public.'

'Jaysuz every cove knows. This 'ere is 'obart Town. Yer can't keep a secret 'ere.'

And there was truth in that.

It was early afternoon by the time we returned to the barracks. We immediately made our way to the guards' mess, hoping the midday meal was still being served, only to be confronted by shouts and disarray. I collared one guard hurrying by with backpack and Brown Bess in hand. 'What's happening?'

'We have a lead on the Port Arthur escapee Erasmus Peck, the mongrel's hiding out in the Dromedary Mountains. There are caves on the foothills near Broadmarsh and his camp has been under surveillance.'

'Oh!' Immediately I remembered my housemaid Emma Rumball's letter mentioning the possibility of the escapee hiding in the area. Now it made sense.

'The Anglesea lads have got a delegation together,' the guard went on, 'but as they are undermanned with troops spread out at Eagle Hawk Neck, Oatlands and Launceston, they're calling for troops from here as well.'

I knew the Imperial 99th Foot soldiers were being thinned out in Van Diemen's Land. Or I should say 'Tasmania', as the colony is now being touted, to dampen the stigma of transportation. With less than four hundred soldiers now stationed here on the island the prison guards are in greater demand.

'Good, then we shall ride with you. Who's in charge?'

'Captain Philbrick sir.'

Captain Philbrick I knew. A tall man of slender build, he had a rounded and pronounced belly from the good things in life. Fond of a challenging game of chess, Philbrick was also an excellent soldier who transferred to Hobart Town when Norfolk Island was closed for the second time as a penal colony last May.

'I'm told you're joining us Hunter,' Captain Philbrick appeared from the direction of the officers' kitchen with a napkin still tucked into his tunic. Well at least *he* had eaten.

'With your permission captain.'

'Absolutely dear chap.'

'I believe the escapee you seek is also the villain we wish to question about a recent murder.'

'So I believe,' Captain Philbrick's valet appeared. He tugged the serviette free from the captain's tunic and subtly drew Philbrick's attention to what appeared like egg yolk on his chin. The captain looked vague so the valet wiped it for him only to have the cloth snatched away.

'Good heavens Manly,' he snapped at his manservant. 'I'm not a child.'

Our small caravan comprised five vehicles; the soldiers and guards seated on three four-wheel prison wagons pulled by two horses a piece. The higher-ranking personnel and myself rode in a coach followed by the notorious prisoner's lockup wagon. This wooden and iron contraption was a prison cell on wheels; totally enclosed except for a barred grate at the rear. Holly caught up with me rushing from the mess as we rode through the main gate onto Campbell Street.

''ere ya go Caspian sar,' she threw me a small cloth parcel. 'Cheese and pickles,' she barely managed coherency with her own mouth full of food. 'No bread I'm sorry to say but I scavenged a ship biscuit.'
God bless the woman.

Our route followed the course of the River Derwent on its western bank. We left Roseneath Ferry to the east before passing the dubiously named Black Snake with its single inn, eleven miles from Hobart Town. Here we made for the crossing at Granton a further half mile distant where gravelly hills hung precipitously over the river.

The darkness of night met our party at the Granton watch house on the western side of the River Derwent. Here the Bridgewater causeway would take us cross-river; a crossing of some two hundred and fifty yards at this point. Twenty years old now, the causeway was built from mudstone quarried nearby and wheeled out across the water by prisoners, little by little to form the foundation on river silt and clay. Known for some time as the Bridgewater folly by those two hundred and eighty men in chains who slaved here, battling for years to fill a massive soft mud hole.

We were billeted at the watch house, a sturdy rectangular sandstone building built parallel with the river, fifty yards away. Here the soldiers had been housed for the causeway's construction. Now it would accommodate us for the night.

Day six

I woke to an unfamiliar sound. I was in the company of dozens of men relieving themselves, cursing, clearing throats and demanding food. Ah food. That was the other predominant thing assaulting my senses. I rose from my narrow iron bed feeling an old man. My back ached; every muscle pained me for I had only my folded britches for a pillow and a single blanket for a mattress, wrapped also around my body.

'Wakey wakey ol' chap,' Captain Philbrick was cheerful. My guess was that success was in the air, and the captain *was* due for a promotion.

'What time is it?' I asked, for the morning was still gloomy.

'It has passed five o'clock. Hungry? Cook's prepared a fine stew.'

Indeed I was hungry, the cheese and pickles of the night before had done little to sate my hunger.

Outside I realised why it was so gloomy. The fog that ambles lazily down the River Derwent, known as the Bridgewater Jerry, was meandering by like the spectre of some monstrous dragon. As thick as any pea souper I had witnessed in London, the Bridgewater Jerry, named by the lags building the causeway, was a local phenomenon. It passed over the causeway, where only the yellow orbs of lantern light on the far shoreline, shining through the fog, acknowledged the existence of the eastern shore. By quarter of the hour before six we were underway once more; our caravan trundling over the gravel road of the causeway through the tail of the mighty dragon. Almost as if by the hand of some almighty magician we were welcomed by sunlight on reaching the eastern shore, at a place named Herdsmen's Cove. Here straggling farms were scattered, each with cultivated patches of produce crudely fenced against the wallabies and other animals determined to exchange their indigenous diets with English vegetables. Most notably though, these settlers enjoyed magnificent views across the huge river from their rich soil land grants.

We climbed steadily up the slopes following Dromedary Creek, where true to the unpredictable weather of this island, light snow showers began to fall and dark clouds gathered about the hills.

'Bush fires last year cleared much of this land,' Captain Philbrick told me as we pushed ahead. The summit of Mount Dromedary itself was only a mile distant, when we made our rendezvous with Corporal Simon Tinker. Tinker had been observing Erasmus Peck hiding out in a cave. As much as Tinker could use the reward money, he valued his life too much to tackle the escapee on his own.

'Half a mile captain,' the corporal told Philbrick. 'Livin' up there like he ain't got a trouble in the world.'

'You've done well corporal.' Captain Philbrick looked back down the slopes we had traversed. The breeze was minimal and blowing from the mountain. 'We have the wind on our side,' he said quietly. He addressed his troopers. 'Listen up men. Our man is half a mile distant near the summit. We must proceed with all caution. He is armed and dangerous. There will be no talking, no smoking. Do I make myself clear?' Collective nods all around. The soldiers were anxious and the thoughts of success palpable.

We followed the corporal, passing a clearing where he had been observing the absconder the past day and night, behind an embankment. From here the captain and myself crawled to the edge and peered over the top where banksia bushes camouflaged our presence. Two hundred yards distant up the slope towards the pinnacle we saw a cave entrance. It was only small but no doubt quite deep inside. The slightest of smoke spiralled away from the cave roof and without this sign there was little else to denote the existence of a campsite. There was no sign of our man.

'Where is he?' Captain Philbrick hissed at me in a whisper.

'Asleep inside I should imagine,' I said. 'That will make our capture easier. I trust your men's arms are loaded.'

Philbrick looked at me as if I had just failed elementary mathematics. Then, without warning, the breeze changed direction and picked up slightly. The low cloud lifted. If Erasmus Peck had a keen nose he would smell twenty sweaty bodies.

'We must move immediately,' Captain Philbrick whispered. He signalled the sergeant as pre-arranged ... split up the men, spread out and advance.

I took my ever-faithful, twin-barrelled pistol from my frock coat pocket and pulled back the hammers, muffling any sound with my sleeve. While the soldiers spread out over a fifty-yard radius – covering left and right flanks – I joined the captain and three of the prison guards for the direct approach.

It was too easy. I heard at least half a dozen dried branches crack and snap, dead giveaway for any felon that foe approached. There was not a sound from the cave. Finally, in desperation as our advance had been so obvious, Captain Philbrick prompted me to the right of the cave entrance while he rushed to the left.

'Erasmus Peck,' he yelled into the cavernous gloom. 'Erasmus Peck. You are trapped man. Come out with your hands clear where we can see them.'

No answer.

He yelled again.

Nothing.

Not a sound.

I dropped to my knees. Pistol in hand, both barrels cocked, I crawled on my belly into the cave. Behind me the captain called out once more to distract the prisoner. I inched further and further into the darkness. The cave proved to be smaller than I had imagined. In the centre a small campfire smouldered. My eyes adjusted. The cave seemed empty. When I was certain there was nowhere for a man to hide I leapt to my feet and made a hasty survey. The cave *was* empty. There were no supplies.

The absconder had absconded.

'Corporal Tinker!' Captain Philbrick shouted. The man skulked forward with his tail between his legs. 'How the hell did our prisoner slip away? Were you sleeping on duty? Jesus man!'

'Captain,' Tinker pleaded. 'He was there at first light. I watched him fetch sticks for his fire. I watched him pissing sir.'

'Then he must have been aware you were there you clumsy oaf.' Captain Philbrick, understandably angry, fished for answers. 'He must have bolted when you came to meet up with us. Damn it man.'

'I think I know what happened captain,' I told Philbrick.

'You do?'

'Yes.' I held up a swatch of kangaroo fur caught on a branch of a large bush at the entrance. It had stitches through the middle and smelt strongly of lavender oil. I explained my thoughts to the captain on the beautiful bounty hunter Annie Eddington.

'How on earth did she know? How on earth did she arrive here before us?'

'She must have ridden ahead through the night while we billeted at Granton,' I suggested. I studied the ground more closely. 'I feel there has been a struggle.'

I pointed out disturbed boot marks in the soil and explained what I had once learnt from an aboriginal tracker, whilst chasing another villain near Oatlands.

'You think Peck's had an altercation?' the captain frowned in amazement. 'With a woman?'

'I am certain of it,' I said, handing the captain the swatch of fur. 'But she is no ordinary woman.'

We stood a moment studying the sweeping view down the mountain. This cave site was a model lookout for someone hiding from the law. From here we had a perfect view of the Derwent Valley, the River Derwent and to the northeast. Broadmarsh.

'Broadmarsh!' I suddenly cried out.

'What of it?'

'Well that is where my house servant Emma Rumball has taken leave, to keep her sister company.'

'Your servant?' Captain Philbrick looked incredulous.

'Yes, but only four hours a day three days a week,' I felt compelled to explain. 'Her sister has a small farm there you see and she was concerned, for she heard rumours that the escapee, Erasmus Peck was indeed in this area and she feared for her sister's safety.'

'This housemaid of yours, you say she knew the absconder was hiding here?'

'It was only a rumour.'

'A rumour we should have taken heed about earlier by all accounts.'

Hmm. I stand corrected.

Philbrick planted his hands on his hips. 'And what is a woman servant going to do in such a situation pray tell?'

'Oh you don't know Mrs Emma Rumball, captain.'

We grouped a moment, the soldiers, guards, Captain Philbrick, myself and failed Corporal Tinker, observing the valley and flatlands of Broadmarsh. In the distance we noted small farming grants dotted about, fingers of smoke barely visible escaping from the stone chimneys of timbered farmhouses and larger estates of sandstone with multiple barns and outbuildings.

'I suggest he has headed in that direction,' Captain Philbrick finally said. 'There's some wealthy landowners thereabouts and the pickings would be ripe for a bushranger.'

'What are your orders captain?' the sergeant asked.

'We'll return to the wagons and take a look at the Broadmarsh area,' he ordered.

It was midday by the time we pushed through dense bushland and followed the creek leading us to the first property. Although settlers here had cleared land for cultivating and grazing, much of the forest was the way it had been for thousands of years. Captain Philbrick told me soldiers and prisoners were stationed here since the early '30's, mainly to maintain roads in and out of the area leading to Bagdad and Brighton. 'But they left ten years ago,' Philbrick said. 'And it is my guess the escapee knows that.'

'If Annie Eddington disturbed the man I suggest he does not know about us,' I said.

'Then we still have the element of surprise.'

'Maybe.'

One young soldier fidgeted like a schoolboy eager to help. 'Permission to speak captain?'

'Granted.'

'What if she's already killed 'im sir, cut 'is head off like and is on 'er way to 'obart Town with it in a bag ... as we speak like.'

'Doubtful.'

'Oh?'

'For starters we would have heard a shot ...'

'Not if'n she stabbed 'im.'

'There would have been blood, a lot of blood at the cave site. Especially if she cut off his head.'

Our party's advance was suddenly halted by the sound of a gunshot.

'That sounded close.'

'Hunters?'

'Maybe.' Captain Philbrick leapt from the coach and drew his pistol, signalling to the men. 'Dismount. Spread out. If my hearing hasn't failed me it came from that direction.' And he pointed his pistol east towards the closest homestead. I agreed. Immediately a second shot and then a third confirmed our suspicion. 'That's no hunter.'

I joined the charge. Now on foot we rushed the creek bed, the captain leading the charge with the zeal of a light horseman. Instantly I heard a shot. It sounded nearby. Close. Captain Philbrick let out a shriek and fell face first into the creek.

'Jesus no!' someone screamed out.

I ran to the captain's side while soldiers spread out disappearing into foliage on the other side of the stream looking for the sniper. Captain Philbrick skewed about to face me and winced with pain.

'Where are you hit?' I asked.

'Hit? I'm not hit man … just twisted my bloody ankle.'

'But I heard a shot.' It was then I realised Philbrick's own pistol had discharged the moment he twisted his ankle on slippery river rocks. 'Oh,' I mouthed and offered the man a hand lifting him to his feet. He hobbled. 'Put your arm around my shoulder,' I said helping him from the creek bed. We rested a brief moment and listened to his troopers thrashing through the bushland searching for a sniper who did not exist. He hopped one legged and I helped him up the embankment.

'Mum's the word old chap, eh,' he said awkwardly, ramming a fresh measure of powder and ball down the barrel of his pistol.

'Mum's the word.'

Moments later we joined the soldiers at a clearing in front of the Invercarron homestead.

'Couldn't see the blighter captain,' the sergeant said, sporting a desperately serious face. 'Are you wounded captain?'

'Sprained ankle.'

Immediately a man's voice hailed us. 'Is that Philbrick? Captain Philbrick?' The voice belonged to a well-padded gentleman wearing only britches and shirt. He stood in the doorway of the handsome, one-storey sandstone homestead.

'Wingy?' Captain Philbrick called back. It was then that I noticed the voice belonged to a gentleman settler with one arm.

'Yes,' Wingy yelled. 'It's about time you chaps showed up. Take cover man. The villain is afoot.'

Instantly I felt a musket ball whip by my ear the moment I heard the explosion. The shooter was in the barn, fifty yards from the west wing of the homestead. I was clearly the target. I shoved Philbrick unceremoniously to the ground and dived behind a stone sundial. Peering around the pedestal I took a wild shot towards the sniper's position. The shooter took cover, giving the soldiers a chance to race across the manicured lawns to the safety of the homestead. One guard ran to the corner of the house and fired another shot affording myself cover. I hoisted the crippled captain aloft and limped unsteadily to the veranda.

Philbrick looked to Wingy who I now realised was also barefoot. 'How many?' he asked.

'One. Send your men around the back Philbrick, cut the mongrel off.'

'Yes. Quite so ... sergeant.'

'Aye cap'n.'

'Send half the men to the rear of the homestead and the others to spread out in the bushland. Smartly now. He's in the barn. We've jolly well got the man surrounded.'

'It's the Port Arthur absconder is it not?' the landowner Wingy asked the captain.

'Yes. Erasmus Peck.'

'Well he's wounded Jim Davey my manservant. Shot him through the window and wounded one of the nearby neigh-bours. The scoundrel has had us bailed up in the drawing room for quarter of an hour. From what I can ascertain he has three or more guns and one's a six-barrel pepperbox.' Wingy finally acknowledged me. 'You a lawman?'

'Yes. Caspian Hunter at your service.'

'Caspian Hunter? Where have I heard that name before?'

'I ... ah ...'

'He nearly shot you did he not.'

'Yes sir,' I said, still shaken.

'This is Magistrate Gunn,' Philbrick told me of the landowner. 'We go back aways, eh, old chap.' Gunn nodded. 'Hunter's from the police department at the barracks Wingy, I mean William.'

The magistrate and I exchanged cordial nods, but the blue-eyed puffy cheeked one-armed landowner was understandably anxious.

'Well we've got him cornered now I should imagine,' Philbrick said.

'I think he's wounded also,' Gunn said.

'Oh, how's that?'

'Well he limps awkwardly.'

'Oh.'

'Come through the house,' Gunn said. 'We can see the barn clearly from the drawing room.'

I aided the captain and as he limped down the corridor he whispered to me, 'We call him Wingy on account he lost his right arm in a shoot-out with Mathew Brady and his gang back in '25. He was a police lieutenant then. Now he's a magistrate and successful landowner. He was once the superintendent at the Prisoners' Barracks too I'll have you know.'

We followed Gunn into his drawing room where a group of people were already huddled in the dim light from the closed shutters. Children were crying. Others prayed.

'Caspian!' someone cried out.

'Mrs Rumball ... Emma.' I was amazed to see my housemaid huddled with the others. She rushed to meet me and ignoring all decorum she hugged me like a long-lost son. 'Dear boy. What are you doing here?'

I quickly explained. 'And you?' I asked. 'What brings you to Invercarron?'

'We were attacked, Caspian, at Hyacinth's cottage, half a mile from here,' Emma told of her sister's farm. 'It was frightful. The savage came without warning, kicked the door down and shot Samuel.' Emma alluded to the wounded man with his wife and children.

'Your sister's husband?'

'Yes.'

I looked to the group huddled in one corner away from the window. Gunn's manservant Jim Davey sat in a gentleman's chair looking ghostly white with a bandaged midriff. Emma Rumball's brother in law, Samuel, nodded a shaky greeting with his crudely bandaged arm held high while his wife, Hyacinth, hugged their two young daughters. Gunn's wife and three other servants consoled their four children, all huddled on the floor.

'Well fear not Emma,' I said, feeling rather chuffed that I was still in the land of the living while the absconder was in the throes of capture. 'We have the villain trapped in the barn.'

Philbrick, leaning against the wall for support, tugged at my coattail to grab my attention. I looked him in the eye. He jerked his head to Emma while she looked the other way. Was this a subtle hint?

'Oh Emma,' I said. 'Please excuse my bad manners. This is Captain Philbrick.'

'Enchanté Madame,' the captain swooned, pushing himself from the wall to try and stand to attention only to wobble. He groaned in pain.

'Oh you are wounded,' Emma stepped forward.

'Wounded? Hardly madam, it is merely a sprained ankle.'

'Let me be the judge of that.' Emma had bandages from William Gunn's medical chest at the ready. She pulled the captain's boot free and massaged his foot gently before wrapping it tightly.

'You've done that before,' Philbrick said. 'Have you studied nursing?'

'No. Only what I have learnt as a humble housekeeper.'

'Then your husband is a most fortunate man indeed, madam.'

Your husband? Is the captain fishing here?

'Please, feel free to call me Emma. And my husband passed some years back Captain Philbrick.'

'Seabert,' Philbrick whispered, barely audible.

'Seabert?'

'Yes.' The captain looked positively embarrassed. 'That is the name my parents bestowed upon me.'

'Well Seabert,' Emma put on her officious tone once more. 'Compression will slow the swelling.' She juggled his boot back into position. 'But you will need to rest this foot.'

'Rest! I cannot rest.'

'Well at least use a cane for support. Mr Gunn sir,' Emma asked the magistrate, 'would you perchance have a stick you could lend this gentleman?'

Gunn paced the room nervously. *What on earth* he wanted to say. *There's a war on for god's sake.* Instead he nodded to a parasol holder with various canes and sticks poking out at every which angle. 'Help yourself.'

'There.' Emma passed Seabert a whalebone stick with a carved Turk's Head handgrip. Philbrick took the instrument gratefully and their hands touched briefly. Suddenly I realised the old soldier was keen on my housekeeper. He, tall and slender with a potbelly, and Emma a fine sturdy example of colonial womanhood. They appeared to have something to offer each other and Emma Rumball was not holding back on the charm herself.

At that very moment several shots rang out. I heard a blood-curdling scream and rushed to the window where I opened the shutters enough to allow a narrow slit. I saw the barn clearly. Suddenly flames exploded through the shingled roof, clawing at the sky.

'He's trapped?' Emma queried. 'In the barn you said.'

Staring at the fireball I called over my shoulder. 'Apparently.' Barely had I said this when Erasmus Peck galloped from the burning barn on a fine black stallion. Wild musket shots detonated. But the soldiers were ill-prepared for this unexpected breakout and their aim was sporadic to say the least.

'Ali Baba!' Gunn cried out throwing the shutters wide with his one arm. 'My horse. My favourite stallion,' he screamed out after his Arabian thoroughbred which, I was to discover, had direct lineage to none other than Hector, the

Duke of Wellington's Arabian, imported from Calcutta to Sydney Town in 1806.

Erasmus Peck would not have had a clue.

Neither would he have cared. He was an experienced enough horseman to manage the animal at a gallop back along Black Brush Road towards the River Derwent ... once again a free man.

And unfortunately for our party *our* horses were harnessed to the wagons and carriages of our caravan, back at the creek. Instead, the soldiers tackled the fire.

Captain Philbrick was the first to speak. 'Lucky no one was killed,' he said.

'Ali Baba cost me eight hundred guineas,' Gunn wept. 'Eight hundred.'

'We'll catch him,' I said to the magistrate rather lamely. 'We'll fetch old Ali Baba back for you sir.'

The fifty-six-year-old landowner was not convinced. He stood looking blankly at his burning barn, running his only hand through his coiffured hair greased and combed in ducktails across his brow, as was the current fashion.

Meanwhile the troopers did their best to fight the barn fire. Some men managed to free the remaining three horses while others doused the homestead nearest the fire, should it spread. But for all their efforts the barn was lost.

'I'll hang the bastard,' Magistrate Gunn vowed, before excusing his language in front of the women and children. 'You hear me Philbrick? I'll hang him myself if I have the chance.'

'Well hang, he must, Wingy,' Philbrick said sternly, catching Emma's eye. 'But I suggest you leave it to Solomon Blay.' He spoke of Hobart Town's notorious hangman.

The sergeant-at-arms rounded the west wing, his face and hands black from fighting the fire, and rushed down the hallway. 'The barn's lost but the fire's under control captain. Shall I rally the men to take pursuit?'

'Yes. And fetch a map of the area.'

A government map was unfolded onto the veranda and we knelt to study its detail. Suddenly my boast to recapture Ali Baba seemed premature.

'He's headed along Black Brush,' I said running a finger along the inked track. 'That leads to Brighton.'

'But he knows there are soldiers stationed from Brighton to Pontville,' the captain offered. 'If I were him I would follow the river north. He might even make New Norfolk.'

'And with Ali Baba between his legs he could just as easily ride to Port Dalrymple,' I muttered, immediately feeling incompetent. 'I will need to return to the barracks I am afraid.'

Convinced that our escapee would head upriver I bid Captain Philbrick farewell, for I had not the luxury of time on my side to pursue one villain. I parted company with the caravan back at Granton. Here I hired a one-horse trap and driver to take me back to Hobart Town only to be met by Jasper at the peak of the hill adjacent to the Queen's Domain and overlooking the township. He was the passenger of a one-horse fly. 'Caspian sar, what a pleasant surprise. I was on my way up river to fetch you, urgent like.'

'Oh?'

Jasper dismounted and jerked his head to a grassed area out of earshot of our drivers. I paid my driver the ten shillings promised and he about turned and rode north once more.

Jasper watched him depart. 'Billings was most insistent I come to fetch you sar.'

'Billings?'

'There's been a brutal killin' at the Sea o' Graves Inn.'

'Oh?' The Sea o' Graves Inn at Browns River, a good four-hour sail down the River Derwent, was owned by a rather colourful character called Lynch Savage; a man I was well acquainted with and whom I had formed a close working re-lationship. 'What has happened?'

'Well Billings has been in pains to keep this incident hush hush sar.'

'Hush hush?'

'Aye. Savage is desperate to solve this problem without involving the law.'

This I understood. And as for Savage; well he was a man of shrewd habits who I knew sailed close to the wind occa-sionally, especially on the legalities of some of his numerous business enterprises.

'Well it's a little late to not involve the law,' I groaned. 'We are the law.'

'Aye sar. But you know what I'm sayin'. Mum's the word an' all that.'

'Mum's the word! I've been hearing that a bit latterly.'

'Yes ... well.' Jasper waited for another carriage to pass by. 'So with Captain Bradley Maddox prowling about, peerin' over shoulders and interferin' in this an' that, Billings sug-gested I catch up with you and divert you direct to Browns River for as far as Maddox knows you're busy upriver.'

'What has happened at the inn pray tell?'

'I really don't know sar. Best you journey to the inn and find out for yourself, if'n you don't mind me sayin'.'

Taken to the Grave

The Sea o' Graves Inn, Browns River

With the aid of a decent wind in the sail the inn is usually a three to four-hour sail down the Derwent estuary. We sailed around Browns River headland in our police sloop *Fabian* into a scene of industry; a beach busy with vendors or those procuring, all haggling for a bargain or seeking a handsome profit. Jasper sat in the stern sheets at my side. I had taken him along to give him respite from Maddox, whose new situation as captain of the police department was corrupting his judgement of character.

The Sea o' Graves Inn was well appointed, and well named, being the heart of what looked like a ship graveyard. Sloops, cutters, tenders and every smaller craft imaginable lay moored or beached in various states of repair or desertion.

Innkeeper Lynch Savage operated a successful chandlery here also, a chandlery of pre-owned maritime equipment and fittings – a cover-up, so the word goes, for many other nefarious activities. The Inn itself, the remains of a whaling barque wrecked by a rogue whale in the Derwent Estuary several years earlier, was built into a steep embankment alongside Browns River. To a naïve traveller it looked like the abandoned wreckage of a tidal wave. The stern cabin had been rebuilt 'arse about,' as Fabian described it, so that the stern windows faced over the bow beneath it, looking back along the beach; one atop the other. The bow jutted over the river, its bowsprit snapped above the figurehead – the figurehead of a rampant wolf. The stern nameplate was nailed over the doorway, a low hatch at the port bow facing the River Derwent; it read *Sea Wolf*. But painted along her hull were the words 'Sea o' Graves.'

The Sea o' Graves was a gathering place for lawless rogues and villains, sealers, absconders, whalers, lost sailors and a trickle of law abiding citizens like myself. There was naught a vice a man could not find to pleasure him here, as long as he had coin in his pocket. And although Lynch Savage was an amiable host, I still felt compelled to wear a cutlass at my hip and my loaded Yale double barrel concealed within my frock coat pocket. Jasper too looked the lawman with cutlass and an issue Tower Pistol secured behind his britches' belt.

Our skipper Ben Swain sailed around headland and into the protected bay where the wide beach in front of the inn was a hive of activity. A dozen or so men of all ages, shapes and sizes, going about what I could only describe as a malfeasant trade masked by legitimacy. Abandoned craft at the end of their sea life were systematically broken down for parts. Marquees were set up for trade. Small craft from Hobart Town plied back and forth looking for a bargain while all along the beach steam hissed, tar smoked, smithies pounded anvils and the ever-present gulls circled overhead singing their song of the sea.

Fanny Peach, one of the inn's favorite filles de joie, hitched her skirts and ran across the sand to meet me, her bare feet squeaking in the soft dry sand. 'Caspian lovey, ain't you a sight for sore eyes.' Fanny threw herself into my arms hooking her hands around me and gave me a wet kiss on the lips. She had been drinking – no surprise there.

'You're in good spirits this fine afternoon,' I said.

'I have a new beau.'

'Oh, you are in love then?' I suppose even whores fell in love, why shouldn't they? 'And do I know the lucky gentleman Fanny?'

'Herbert Barker.'

'Now where have I heard that name before?'

'Isn't Herbert Barker the cove what worked at the gas works?' Jasper's memory was sharp. Now I remembered. He was a gasfitter working for the Hobart Gas Company who stole gas burners from his employer, selling one to a neighbor. But another employee happened upon the lamp, identifying it by a manufacturer's flaw on which he once cut his hand. This employee had a grudge to bear against Herbert Barker. Barker of course denied this saying he had purchased the gas burners in Launceston. Challenged, he presented receipts for the same; false receipts he had bribed a clerk to write for him. However on closer scrutiny the receipts were found to be dated on the 5th, a Sunday, when the business was closed. He was given two years' hard labour. That was only ten months ago. Jasper realized as well. 'Shouldn't he be in ...'

I stepped on Jasper's toe and cut him short. Jasper looked at me wide-eyed. Who are we to spoil Fanny's love?

'Lynch inside?' I asked Fanny.

We approached the inn, looming down upon us from its hillside perch, walking along a bridge of sorts; more a collection of slats roped together, which followed the river. Here the melted snow and water flowed off the distant mountain's south side and into the estuary.

'I'll wager yer thought this 'ere Browns River got its' name 'cos the water's brown, eh Caspian sar?' Jasper asked clattering along the boards in my tow.

'Never really gave it much thought Jasper.'

'Well it were named after the botanist Mr Brown what was the first one 'ere in 1804, when Governor Collins settled 'ere.'

'Fascinating,' I feigned interest.

'Aye, Robert I think 'e were named. Robert Brown.'

'And why would you have that information stored in your young head Jasper?'

'I learned it at ragged school. Always was interested in history sar.'

'Hmm. So why *is* the water brown anyway?'

'That's the tannin from the dead plants in the forest yonder.'

'Oh, of course.'

'Did you think it was because of the shit Caspian sar?'

To be honest it had crossed my mind. It was not of the most pleasant aroma and there were garderobes with their seats of ease protruding over the water from the stern bow adjoining the taproom.

Stepping across the gangplank from the embankment and into the inn was always fraught with danger; only three planks roped together side by side without a rail spanned the drop into the river below. And at low tide this was not a waterway one would want to fall into; not with stagnant spillage from the galley and the pre-mentioned conveniences. The dozen ducks, however, swimming happily, did not seem to mind and it was for this reason I avoided roast duck when it was offered at Lynch Savage's table. I bowed my head beneath the low sill of the arched doorway, cut into the port bow, and was greeted by the persistent fug of stale bodies and spilt ale and a blue haze of smoldering pipe tobacco.

Queenie Ruffle, a plump and rather comfortable woman was one of the older bar maids. She cried out over the noisy imbibers.

'Caspy. What a sight for sore eyes. What will it be love?' she asked, offering refreshment.

I pointed to a large stone jug where she had been pouring all the slops left over in the tankards.

'Well none of that thanks,' I said.

This brew, affectionately called sailor's trousers, sold for a fraction of the usual price and was popular with drunkards short of coin. I looked to Jasper who was temporarily distracted by Bernice, one of Lynch's new whores; tall with a curvaceous figure with a small waist; small enough to carry a child in its curve.

'Jasper,' I said. Nothing. 'Jasper!' I shouted over the din.

'Caspian sar, sorry ... I ... I was just ...'

'Would you like an ale?' I said.

'What was that?'

'I'm over here Jasper.' Finally he tore his eyes away from the new girl. 'Ale?' I reiterated. 'Would you like an ale to wet your whistle?'

'Oh, aye sar.' Jasper grinned like a hyena.

The past days had been rigorous and with another crime here to deal with I needed refreshment.

We refreshed ourselves smartly and were led to the innkeeper, patiently waiting our arrival at the crime scene.

Lynch Savage himself was an obese man; so fat in fact that he engaged four bearers to carry him in a sedan chair from one location to the next. The man was a legend. Born in England in 1795 he was now in his sixty-second year, and as generous as he was enormous. But he was a man of many talents, all of which made him a rich and envied. He also attracted enemies. Flamboyant in appearance and a hopelessly theatrical, drugged by the fancy of the stage, Savage insisted on attiring like Captain Henry Morgan, the 17th century pirate, complete with tricorn hat with ostrich feathers.

He liked nothing more than to entertain visitors at his table – a *hair-loom* as he called his ancestor's oak banquet table shipped all the way from Cornwall, and over two hundred years old. These feasts were always a sumptuous affair; served in the stern cabin they included shameless amounts of near extinct local game prepared by his *stolen* French cook, Jean Parton; bribed more like, from a visiting French merchantman. And fine wines and obliging women were also necessary accoutrements at the dinner table. Secretly I envied him.

And *my* relationship with Lunch Savage I hear you ask?

We had become friends over the twenty odd months I had known him. The man took a shine to me as an intelligent ally, albeit naïve, within the police force. Although I refused frequent offers of remuneration, usually in the form of employment within his situation, we remain friends. I imagine he respects me for this. However, I had been known in the past to reveal snippets of exclusive information for his use, in return for the assistance in catching a villain or two.

The Sea o' Graves victim lay twisted on the floor, his cranium sliced from the top of his skull with a cutlass. His body was slumped across his overturned chair in which he had been sitting when attacked. I knew the weapon to be a cutlass as a fine German silver-handled cutlass lay next to the body. The blow had been so severe the blade had been badly damaged. I will never fully obliterate the scene from memory; the man's brains spilt across the deck, like vanilla and strawberry custard. His mouth was locked wide open, the tongue hanging to one side, while his eyes – dull black orbs – bulged, frozen in the realization he was about to die a horrific death.

'They say the killer's image is etched in the eyeball of his victim,' Lynch Savage said dryly. 'If only you could have your confidante, Mrs Rowley with her photographic machine, develop that image, we would have an idea who the assassin was,' Lynch smiled.

While Jasper guarded the door outside, Lynch and I were alone in the dead man's cabin; one of four lodgings Lynch had recently build along the embankment next to the Sea o' Graves Inn. These he rented to weary travellers. I studied the severed cranium with a practical eye.

'It takes a strong man with honed swordsman's skills and a sharp blade to sever bone like that,' I said.

'Aye,' Savage agreed. 'Lopped it clean off like the top of a boiled egg.'

Hmm, the perfect analogy. 'Let us start with the obvious. Did he have any enemies?'

'Plenty.' Savage looked on philosophically from his perch where his minders and carriers had rested his huge body upon custom-made cushions the size of a stuffed ox.

'Who is he anyway?'

'He's a harpooner off *Aladdin,* well that's what he told the girls, but he don't 'ave the arms o' no harpooner in my book. Thirty-eight years old 'e told young Jude, what he took a likin' to. His name is Dan Wheeler and by all accounts he was a difficult bastard to get on with. But this is the first time anyone has been dispatched in the *Graves* and quite frankly, Caspian, I can't afford this to be made public.'

'I do not know Lynch. This will be a hard thing to cover up. I mean ...'

'You owe me Caspian. I've covered you on many an occasion, now I'm askin' you to find this 'ere cove's killer and bring the bugger to me.'

'And the body?'

'Don't ask. The lads'll take him out fishin' I should imagine.'

I dropped to my knees, careful not to kneel in gore, and rifled his pockets taking out a leather wallet with a coin purse, a tobacco pouch near empty, a fancy Meerschaum pipe carved in the shape of a naked woman's head and bust, and red coral rosary beads. *Lot of good they were,* I thought to myself. Amongst the silver in the purse were one sovereign and three half sovereigns. The wallet held five one-pound notes drawn on the Bank of England. A month's remuneration for me. And they were bloody. Although the crime scene was a gory mess, how could money in the dead man's pocket be bloody?

'Keep them,' Savage flicked his wrist nonchalantly. 'They're yours ...'

'You know I can't ...'

'Put them in your pocket man. For expenses.' I held them a moment, about to replace them when the door opened unannounced. Lynch motioned for me to be cautious and without hesitation I thrust the money into my pocket. Bayou, one of Savage's minders entered, looked at his master and shot me an inquisitive glance. Jasper followed. My face reddened, not being accustomed to dishonesty.

'The lads are ready,' Bayou told Lynch.

'Get on with it then.'

The door was opened wide and an empty hogshead with one end removed was pushed against the open portal. Harpooner Dan Wheeler's body was manhandled towards the waiting barrel, but in doing so his shirt shifted exposing his arms.

'Wait,' I cried out. 'That's interesting.'

'What is?'

'That tattoo.' Towards the crook of his left arm was a beehive tattoo.

'What of it?' Lynch shrugged, after all every second man in the *Graves* wore a tattoo.

'Well it's a beehive and this is the third I have encountered of late. One on a Port Arthur prisoner and another on a murder victim.'

'It a mark of Manchester,' one of the minders said.

'So I believe.' I nodded for the men to complete their macabre task.

The victim was folded over and shoved inside the barrel; his cranium and brains were shoveled in after him with a hearth pan and the lid nailed tight. Jasper said not a word. Oh, he had plenty of questions but to his credit he said naught; after all he was in felonious company.

Minutes later we watched the four minders roll the hogshead along the side of the river and onto the beach where lanterns were being lit for the convenience of the night revelers heading to the inn. It was growing dark, the merchants and chandlers had now retired from the beach marquees, and no doubt they entertained themselves in the taproom with the obliging wenches or maybe tried their luck with a wager in the cock-fighting pit. As we watched in silence a small sloop appeared around the headland to meet Lynch's men and I could not help but wonder, *indeed, Dan Wheeler the dead harpooner was going fishing.*

'Jasper,' I said.

'Aye Caspian sar?'

'A word if you please.'

I explained the situation to young Jasper who listened intently, although not entirely happy with the circumstances.

It was late evening when the police sloop jarred heavily against Waterman's Dock where I bid Jasper good night and sent him home to his forlorn wife. Custom's House Tavern, directly opposite, looked lively but I felt like female company; not a whore you understand, but my friend Bonnie Nettle at the Sailor's Rest. And possibly Bonnie could shed some light on the beehive tattoo. I looked across the wharves towards the Sailor's Rest where a dozen street lamps advertised the inns of New Wharf. The evening was pleasant enough with patrons and music spilling onto the docks. I crossed the quay and forced my way between cheerful revellers and sought out Bonnie who was changing barrels in a small store behind the taproom.

'Well hello stranger,' Bonnie was delighted to see me. 'I haven't seen you for ...'

'Three days Bonnie,' I answered. 'Since Sunday.'

'Oh ... Give us a hand 'ere Caspian.'

Amongst the aromas of malt and hops another fragrance caught my nose. 'What is that anyway?'

'This is a brown ale and it's taken on the flavor of the wood.'

'Do your patrons like it?'

'They love it. It's taken on an oak tang and they love it. What next I ask yer?'

With the keg tapped and the first ten drinkers served, Bonnie pulled me a quart and it was not all that bad. I found a corner of the bar to lean on and was about to ask Bonnie about the beehive tattoo when I recognized the prison warder from Port Arthur walking down the stairs from the rooms above; and looking rather pleased with himself I might add. He stopped near the bottom and straightened his attire.

'Bonnie.'

'Aye.'

'That man on the stair ...'

'I know 'im as Dwight. What of 'im?'

'Yes. Carvel Dwight. He's a warder stationed at Port Arthur. He's aways from home is he not?'

'Oh maybe so,' Bonnie said nonchalantly. 'But jus' between me and you, 'e gets' is fair share of punishment 'ere, that I can tell yer.'

'Oh?'

''e likes to get spanked if'n yer knows wha' I mean. 'e calls in 'ere every few months to see the girls, usually Sweet Pea when she's available.' I knew Sweet Pea as Lucy Norridge, released on a ticket from the women's prison at the Cascades last year.

Carvel Dwight made for the bar but I caught his eye. He looked directly at me, showed no recognition, about turned and hurried out onto the docks. I know we did not exactly see eye to eye at Port Arthur, but ignoring me like that, I thought, was downright rude.

......

Day seven, Next morning

Cowgill's windmill across the road woke me with its regular and dependable clacketty-clack. Damn the windmill. But where would the colony be without our staple, flour, to make bread? I lay in bed a moment, fighting sleep and preparing myself to tackle the day ahead. But my mind was clogged with questions. I wanted answers. Answers to Edwin Piketon burnt alive on his own stove. The diamond – did it exist and if so where was it? Erasmus Peck. Where did he fit in? The body in the barrel. The little Noble girl, Violet, and Annie Eddington. Ah yes, and Annie Eddington.

And then Elizabeth Mead. Was I really a father? My mind fogged.

However my morning scowl was replaced with a smile when I returned from the backyard privy and saw four eggs in a basket on my back doorstep from my neighbor Mrs Rust. God bless the woman. I teased alive the coals in my oven and cooked myself eggs, scrambled, just like mother had shown me; lightly beaten with salt and dropped into a pan with a knob of butter. Delicious over bread crusts fried in lard and accompanied with sweet black tea.

The morning was pleasantly sunny and, with a sated belly, I set off on my stroll through the docks and wharves towards the prisoners' barracks on the hill in Campbell Street. One never tires of Hobart Town's waterfront – Sullivans Cove. I enjoyed fond memories of arriving here near on two years ago. Today the harbour is more a port of trade, a mercantile hub, since the last convicted felons were transported here back in' 53. There is a huge trade here in whale oil although I believe that trade is waning these days. Riding at anchor in the harbor are a dozen ships, some Royal Navy, some merchants and others whalers, all serviced by wherries, punts and barges rowing back and forth from ship to shore. I heard the loud crack of canvas as a sail was reefed in a morning breeze and watched a moment as the sailors of a Navy frigate busied themselves aloft furling sails to the shrill orders of the bosun's pipe.

The Cove is well provided for with warehouses and bond stores both at Old wharf on Hunter Island and New Wharf, recently renamed Salamanca Place. Seagulls circle above chasing scraps thrown overboard. Convict work gangs repair and extend the wharves and at a more hospitable level many inns and bordellos line the streets around the docks. No, I never tire of strolling about the waterfront until ... I am accosted near Wapping.

The old lady, whom I was told was Margery Blowfield, recognized me from the barracks. Her tired old face was awash with tears. Her husband, the Wapping baker, was dead.

'Dead?'

'Come good sir, come see.'

For an old woman she set quite the pace. The bakery was at the east end of Sackville Street in Wapping, and, like its counterpart in London, Wapping was not the most savoury habitat in the colony. The door to the bakery was locked and she led me around the back. I saw the baker's legs lying on the flagstones before I saw the man; a large cove who had realized decades of sampling his own pies and pastries. I entered the store only to witness one of the more bizarre deaths I had ever seen. Charlie Blowfield, for that was his name, had collapsed head first into an upended barrel of flour and duly suffocated. Suffocated in the flour.

I felt for a pulse. Nothing.

Prisoners' Barracks.

Maddox un-leashed his turnip, flipped the lid with his thumbnail and made a show of checking the time. *So what if I was fifteen minutes late? What about all the extra hours I serve without remuneration?* I was finding the man irritating and made a mental note to find out what was wrong with Fabian.

Fabian. *Where are you man?*

Holly, Lincoln, Jasper and Billings all sat at their desks waiting for my reaction. Even stranger, they all had a tin mug of steaming coffee before them.

'Good morning to you all,' I said cheerily. Nods, Caspian sar, mornin' from all but Maddox. I looked to the potbelly stove, smouldering hot and with the copper coffee kettle in position. 'Lovely,' I said. 'Coffee.'

I gathered my handkerchief about the handle picked up the pot. Near empty. Brilliant. Everyone has a brew except me. I looked at Maddox. He smiled briefly, at my expense, before dissolving his grin, replacing it with a scowl.

'Did you not notice anything on your way through the yard,' he said in a caustic tone.

'In the yard?'

'In the yard,' he sighed, and nodded to the lone barred window of our ever-shrinking workspace. I peered out and down into the courtyard where I focussed on an incongruity. A halberd had been secured vertically between flagstones and I noted a grisly head skewered on its sharp end. Black bloodied hair was matted over the face yet one eye was exposed, staring back at me. I frowned.

'I hate to tell yer this Caspian sar,' Lincoln was the first to speak, 'but that there 'ead belongs to Erasmus Peck.'

'Or it did,' Holly snorted.

'Erasmus Peck,' I repeated astonished. 'How? I mean where did it come from?'

'Off his shoulders I'm guessin',' Holly croaked another laugh.

Whilst I returned from Granton and journeyed to Browns River the following situation had unfolded. It was as unexpected as it was brutal and none of my colleagues saw it coming. The following details were told to me later.

As I stated earlier, Erasmus Peck escaped from Invercarron estate on the stolen black stallion, Ali Baba, galloping along Black Brush Road. However his escape was fraught with disaster. One mile from the homestead the galloping horse rolled its hoof on a large stone. The leg twisted. Horse and rider fell and the stallion broke a leg. Erasmus escaped on foot, as painful as it was, for he was suffering a knife wound in the leg, we surmised from when Edwin Piketon, the man from whom he stole the diamond, had stabbed him during. Owner of the horse, Magistrate William Gunn, would find the horse hours later, whinnying in excruciating pain at the side of the road. He had to put down the pained animal. Gunn was understandably devastated.

Erasmus Peck continued on foot. Careful to avoid New Norfolk, he hiked into the hills to the town's northwest. Unbeknown to the absconder and the likes of Captain Philbrick and his troops, bounty hunter Annie Eddington had shadowed Peck in the forest surrounding Broadmarsh. She had seen everything unfold and waited her chance. She witnessed Peck's escape on the horse and silently cheered. Cutting cross-country Annie picked up Peck's trail after he deserted the horse.

Now, Erasmus Peck had a mortal fear. Spiders. And for a man hiding in Tasmania's wilderness amongst the devils, striped hyenas and snakes, this was a major problem. The indigenous huntsman spider is a fearful looking arachnid. With eight long legs, an unsegmented body composing fused head and thorax while sporting a rounded abdomen, the predator is often mistaken for a tarantula by those well-travelled, especially in the tropics.

The escapee's squeals should have been heard back at Port Arthur …

But I am progressing ahead of myself here. I should mention that Erasmus Peck, at some stage, became aware he was being followed and attempted to turn the tables on his pursuer. In doing so Erasmus Peck unfortunately experienced two traumas instantaneously. Whilst avoiding capture and spying on bounty hunter Annie Eddington tracking him along a dry creek bed, he walked into a cobweb. Now as any naturalist will tell you, huntsmen spiders do not have cobwebs, they stalk their prey. But the fine fibres of a lesser spider adhered to Peck's face and the man panicked, thrashing wildly. In the process he dislodged a gathering of huge huntsmen, which fell from the loose bark of the wattle tree behind which he lurked. Half a dozen of these large spiders scuttled over his body, through his hair; more than one disappeared down his shirt. Yes … the squeals should have been heard in Port Arthur.

I suspect the man was pleased Annie was there to rescue him; although unbeknown to Erasmus Peck his captor had no intention of taking him alive. Especially with a 100 Guinea reward on his head. He was starved, bedraggled, his hair wiry and knotted. His clothing was shredded and mostly discarded as he stood before Annie, his arms in the air and wearing only long johns from where he had thrown his britches aside in desperation to rid himself of his hairy eight-legged tormenters.

Annie would say later that she laughed. She could not contain herself. She laughed hard. The ruthless blackguard was incensed. Although his britches were missing he still wore a stolen hunting knife belted to his hip. He unsheathed the blade and charged at Annie. But his wounded leg slowed him somewhat and Annie had time to take careful aim and fire one barrel of her six-barrelled pepperbox. That was all it took. Annie Eddington had done it before. One shot, plugging the absconder in the heart with a half-ounce ball of lead.

I gazed at the lifeless head skewered on the halberd. Although Erasmus Peck's bloodied hair matted to his face I felt the villain stare me out.

'Annie Eddington,' I finally asked. Just saying her name aloud aroused me somewhat. The woman was a legend. 'Where is she now?'

'Why did you not report here before retiring last night?' Maddox asked sourly. 'On your return from Broadmarsh.'

'It was late,' I lied. 'This bounty hunter, Annie Eddington,' I persisted. 'When did she,' I nodded out the window, 'deliver that?'

'Last evening,' Maddox said. 'Had you been here you would have seen her grand performance. She was so determined Superintendent Mead gave her two promissory notes for 100 guineas each. One for One Ear Kearney the bushranger and one for Erasmus Peck. Then she left.'

'Promissory notes!' I declared. 'To be cashed at the treasury is that correct?'

'Yes.'

'Which opens at ...'

'Eight.' Maddox's smile returned as if to say, *and you are late once again.* 'What's the big deal Hunter? She captured the absconder and earned her reward.'

I spun on Maddox, my face flushed with anger. 'You do not get it do you?'

'Pardon?'

'The diamond! Erasmus Peck was in possession of the stolen Salmon Princess.'

'Oh!' Maddox unhitched his boots from Fabian's desk and sat upright, suddenly alert. The sarcastic grin vanished.

'I hate to tell yer this captain,' Lincoln said dryly to Maddox. 'But Peck's fellow inmates at Port Arthur said that he always said 'e would swallow the diamond if'n he was about to be caught.'

'That means ...'

'That means the diamond is in the headless corpse,' Holly's face was one of sheer amazement.

'Which is somewhere out in Tasmania's bushland,' Billings said. 'Probably in a shallow grave.'

Maddox fidgeted awkwardly.

'Annie Eddington did not know about the diamond,' I said. 'She was a bounty hunter after his head. His head only. And unless the diamond is lodged under the severed head's tongue, which I will wager it is not, we need to find the body.'

'Oh Jesus!'

'Yes. Oh Jesus!'

'The treasury ... opens at eight o'clock you said.'

Gus Fergus the cashier clerk at the treasury stood behind the teller's bars appearing mesmerised. The man looked eighty and sounded older; with unruly long grey hair and pince-nez held in place by a large wart on his nose. He slowly replaced his steel nibbed goose quill into a penny inkpot and looked at the five of us with trepidation – all panting from our haste.

'Eddington, you say?' he said.

'Yes, Annie.'

'Danny?'

'No, Annie. Five-foot-eight, short thick brown hair, quite attractive ...'

'Danny. Attractive?'

'Annie, you old goat,' Holly said impatiently. 'Not Danny.'

'She had with her two one hundred guinea promissory notes,' I pointed out. 'Signed by Superintendent Mead on behalf of the police department.'

'Oh that was a woman. She looked like a trapper and smelt of lavender.'

'So she *has* been here already.'

'Yes sir. She was here at eight on the dot.'

'And you honoured the reward money?'

'Of course I did. Why, shouldn't I have? It was signed by the superintendent himself after all.'

'Devil's blood,' Holly cried out.

'Why?' Fergus screwed up his face. 'Should I not have honoured the notes?'

'No!'

'He means yes but ...'

'No! I mean yes of course you should but have but ... Jesus! Did she happen to leave an address, the name of an inn perhaps?'

Gus Fergus scratched the back of his head in irritating contemplation. 'An address you say?'

'Yes.'

'No.'

We stood in a tight knot around the teller's counter, racking our brains for suggestions.

'We could door knock all the inns around the waterfront,' Billings offered.

'Yes, but it'll take forever.'

'We did see her drinking at the Good Woman Inn,' I said. 'Maybe we should start there.'

'I can't believe this is happening,' Maddox shook his head. 'What are the chances? We'll be the laughing stock of Hobart Town if this gets out.'

'Yes, the Good Woman Inn,' I said ignoring Maddox. 'I think she lodged there last time.'

'I suggest we urgently organise a door knock as Billings put it,' Maddox said.

'Fine,' I agreed. 'But we need more boots on the ground. Jasper.'

'Aye Caspian sar.'

'Hurry back to the barracks and ...'

Gus Fergus cleared his throat for attention. 'Ex ... excuse me a moment ...'

Lincoln aired his opinion. 'She's more likely to be around the docks I'm thinkin'.'

'Gentlemen,' the teller interrupted. 'Excuse me gent ...'

'Holly,' I said. 'Go see Bonnie at the Sailor's Rest, she might have seen ...'

'Will you all shut it?' Gus Fergus shouted.

'What?' Maddox spat vehemently.

The old man's eyes were popping. 'I said shut it.'

'But ...'

'You don't need to door knock inns,' the teller finally said. 'No sir.'

'And why not, pray tell?'

'Well she was in a hurry because she was sailing on the *Diligence*.'

'What do you mean she was sailing on the *Diligence*?'

'Like I said. She had a ticket for the *Diligence*, sailing to Melbourne.'

'When?'

The old cashier smacked his toothless gums and looked up at the bank wall clock behind us. 'About now I'm thinking.'

'Jesus Christ why didn't you tell us that in the first place?'

'No need to blaspheme sir.'

Police work is frequently charged with adrenalin, so it must have been a sight watching five lawmen and Holly sprinting down Murray Street hill to the waterfront.

'*Diligence,*' I yelled at the first watchman.

'Wha'?'

'*Diligence*. Schooner I believe. Where is she?'

'Dunno guv. Try the shipping office.' He tipped his head to a timber-boarded office wedged between the Customs House Hotel and a chandlery. A sign over the door read Ansell and Associates, Shipping Agents. A lackadaisical young cove enjoying his morning pipe stood leaning on the doorframe. He wore a boater with the name Ansell stencilled across the brow.

'We are looking for *Diligence*,' I said anxiously.

'Eh what?'

'*Diligence*,' I reiterated. 'Schooner I believe, leaving for Melbourne. Where is she docked?'

He was more concerned about his precious pipe, packing the tobacco in neatly with his thumb. '*Diligence* yer say?'

'Aye,' Holly pushed out her chest planting hands on her hips. 'Smartly now. This is urgent police business.'

'I'll ask me master,' he said in a slow lazy voice. ''ang about.'

He disappeared into the booking office while Lincoln hoisted Jasper onto a hogshead as lookout. But with the port hosting two dozen or more ships this day it was difficult to see.

'The schooner *Diligence* sir?' I asked a passing wherry-man.

'What of 'er?'

'Do you know if she is in port?'

'She's departed squire.' He narrowed his eyes down the river. 'Thar she be.'

We followed the direction of his gnarly finger and between two Royal Navy ships and a whaler moored mid harbour we could just make out *Diligence* under full sail in a strong wind beating out towards Storm Bay.

'Damn and blast,' I cursed.

The young cove returned with his master, the shipping agent. 'The *Diligence* departed at eight sar,' the older man said.

''Christ! We can see that.' Holly groaned.

Maddox rounded on me. 'This is your fault Hunter.'

'My fault ... I ...'

'Go pack a bag and report to the shipping agents. You're going to Melbourne,' Maddox shouted anxiously. 'You will track her down and find out where she buried Peck's body.'

These words grabbed the shipping agent's attention. 'Bring her back,' Maddox raved on. 'Under guard if you must.'

The shipping agent stood aghast. He finally broke into a smile. 'Melbourne sar?' he said to me. 'Will thart be a one-way ticket?'

Of course it made sense to follow Annie Eddington to Melbourne, and for my piece of mind I was certain she would head for Ballarat where she had previously told me her husband had left for the goldfields. So how hard could it be ... how hard indeed?

Chapter Six

Day eight. At Sea

Less than year ago I survived a shipwreck off Tasman Island (chronicled in a previous memoir) and I now found the horrors returning, as my transport to Melbourne, the 126-ton barque *Richmond Packet*, fought heavy seas in Bass Strait. Whilst foundering ships are rarities in these modern times they do, unfortunately, still occur. Struggling against adverse winds, the four-day voyage took six days. By the time I disembarked at Queen's Wharf in Melbourne I was disorientated and already anxious about my return trip.

Now, in 1857, I am pleased to announce Melbourne's infrastructure was at last improving since the so-called Gold Rush drew hoards to the goldfields of Bendigo, Ballarat and Beechworth. For those who don't know, gold was first found in Creswick's Creek at a place called Clunes, north of Ballarat, on the 1st of July 1851.

Now I had heard stories of shepherds and drovers deserting their charges and lawyers and merchants leaving their desks for the *Rush*. Other witnesses spoke of entire ship crews leaving their ships unmanned in the harbour, just like what happened in California ten years earlier. Even some captains were deserting their shipping contracts.

Melbourne suffered wretchedly. Locals spoke of Swanston and Elizabeth Streets running with sewage into the Yarra River, taking with it discarded garbage and the contents of overflowing privies. To make matters worse, thousands of successful miners were returning to Melbourne flush with money, desperate to celebrate, only to add to the town's woes. Accommodation was fully booked and tent towns appeared on the town's outskirts. These added to the squalor. And there were no tradespeople to mend the problem as all had left for the goldfields to seek their fortunes. Thus, on my second visit, Melbourne was not a pleasant place.

But now, as less fortunate miners returned as tradesmen, the infrastructure was improved. Prominent stone buildings were being erected, like the courthouse and a Town Hall, and plans were afoot for a Treasury building to house the immense wealth from the goldfields. And we are talking huge amounts of gold; two tons each week were flowing into the treasury. In later years a Treasury clerk told me there was so much gold pouring into Melbourne that it paid off all of Britain's foreign debt and helped her commercial expansion over the seas.

Day Fourteen

From Melbourne's Queen's Wharf I walked to Russell Street where the Police Watch House resides next to the courthouse. The courthouse's neighbour is the overcrowded Melbourne Gaol, a formidable and austere bluestone construction as sturdy as any I have seen in the colonies, and modelled after the Pentonville Prison in London. With my letters of introduction from Superintendent Mead in Hobart Town I was afforded assistance from police captain, Captain Broxam. But with the department stretched the way it was he could only assure me of transport on a police coach to the goldfields and warned me that once there, I would be on my own.

'The lure of gold,' Broxam told me in his deep baritone voice, 'and the possibilities of extreme wealth and greed have made lawmen wary, Mr Hunter. But the events leading to the Eureka Hill affair did however force our hand here in Melbourne and the Victoria Police was formed in '54, ostensibly to support the soldiers stationed at the goldfields. So keep this document on your person at all times sir,' and Broxam pushed a letter signed by his own hand over to me, 'to prove your bona fide position should the law in the area question you.'

Day fifteen

The next day, around midday, the four-horse coach rolled over the summit of an open forested hill on the outskirts of Buninyong, Ballarat's original entitlement.

'Named after the prominent mountain of Buninyong overlooking the goldfields,' a fellow passenger informed me. Under the circumstances the coach had made good time for the seventy-two-mile journey. As my destination approached my thoughts returned to the multitude following in our tracks. Hundreds of oxen pulled drays laden with miners and their paraphernalia, trundling along the muddy tracks at a few miles in an hour. Many walked also, all their belongings strapped to their backs. I sat up top with the coachman, a contented soul employed by the police department. He was a good ten years older than me and with an extra twenty pounds fleshed over his frame. He suffered from a stiff neck and turned bodily to face me when he spoke, which was often.

But up here with the driver I had a fine view of the tent encampment. Makeshift campsites stretched beyond Black Hill, with scattered parties up and down the Leigh and its tributaries. Here Golden Point – as the richest site was called – led to a running brook only four feet wide. Amongst the few trees were crammed tent after tent; from tiny one-man shelters to large tents with standing room for several people. Some dwellings had mud brick fireplaces and chimneys; others were made of stone and clad with bark. I saw timber-framed huts of semi-permanence and lean-tos of the short-term licensee; come to try their luck on a one-month stay. Conditions were abysmal. Sanitation poor. The coachman told me of the freezing and wet winters here, toiling in mud and slush, never to have dry clothing, always cold. And then the contrasts of summer with constant unshielded sun, the intense heat and threatening bushfires.

'Then yer got the pestilence and beasties,' the coachman said with a knowing twinkle in his eye. 'Mosquitoes, flies, rats and,' he turned bodily to face me for my reaction, 'and them damned snakes!'

After crossing Buninyong Gully, the coach took a snake-like path towards Old Poverty Hill and Red Hill where unproductive deserted holes either side of the road threatened the unwary, especially at night. Yet for all the pitfalls, new arrivals appeared daily.

'Are yer armed Mr 'unter?' the coachman asked me as we started down another hill.

'Yes I am.' I patted my coat pocket and felt comforted by my Yale double barrel pistol. And it was loaded.

'Good sir. I ain't sayin' yer'll need it but one can never be too careful. It can be a lawless place, although we 'ave a bigger police presence here since the horrors o' '54.'

We passed a hive of industry, a hive being the operative word to describe thousands of men accompanied by a handful of women, toiling energetically with riches in their sights.

Ah, a handful of women, I thought.

With the fairer sex in such short existence here, surely Annie Eddington will stand out like a sore thumb.

The coachman tried to read my thoughts as my head pivoted this way and that taking in a site rarely seen outside modern civilisation.

'There be two mile or more o' this sir,' he said as he kept his team on a narrow track.

Finally we arrived at a clearing where the diggings gave way to what some may call administration, dare I say civilisation. Here were bakeries, grocers, a blacksmith, boarding houses, cookhouses, a butcher, gold buyers' tents – where gold fetched 59 shillings per ounce I was informed – and an inn. All these were gathered around the police watch house. I even noted a bowling alley. I guess recreation during down time in this tent town was also vital.

The coach stopped before the watch house, a timber and shingled roof building of moderate proportions with a lockup at the rear.

'We keep a strong police presence here nowadays Mr Hunter,' a young recruit and fellow passenger informed me as he helped the coachman with the trunks strapped to the roof of the coach. 'And as you can see we're well armed,' he said with some pride.

I noted the immediate lawmen mingling in the area were all in neat uniforms with carbines, broad swords and holster pistols. 'Even since the skirmish of '54 we still have men try to work the diggings without purchasing the government license.'

'How much are the licences anyhow?' I asked.

'Thirty shillings a month sir.'

'Hmm. It sounds quite high.'

The young policeman looked at me as if I was conspiring with the miners and chose to leave me be. The coachman pointed to an inn, suitably named The Fat Nugget.

'You might wanna find a bed before you go about yer business squire,' he advised me. 'As beds can be 'ard to secure after dark.'

As he spoke the inn's front door slammed open against the wall and a rather intoxicated patron launched himself off the veranda before staggering away. I heard piano music and drunken singing. The coachman watched me.

'I'd be tryin' a boardin' house first Mr 'unter,' he suggested. 'Yer won't get no sleep at the inn.'

The Fat Nugget Inn

All the same I was parched after the long coach ride. I needed a quart of ale. And the Fat Nugget Inn, with its hollow piano tunes sounding like an echo from an empty room, was a distraction.

The inn was as rough on the inside as it was on the out. Built overnight by the look of it. But it was fiercely practical with its rafters exposed; without a ceiling. It had one long bar built parallel with, and close to, the rear wall. Un-glazed windows with single wooden shutters like gunports on a navy frigate let in light and flies. The piano player sat on a stool with his back to the patrons surrounded by half a dozen men who fancied themselves as songsters. On the opposite wall a huge mud brick fireplace smoked with an unattended iron cauldron of stew simmering over a low fire. Nearby two huge kangaroos hung by their hind legs, bleeding out into pans where hunting dogs slurped noisily. I guess this bleeding was conducted inside to keep the bush flies to a minimum. Four hams hung from a beam near a window and I fancy the smoke from the myriad of clay pipes added to the meat's preservation. Up-ended salted pork barrels served as tables. Chairs were few. Outback the cesspit trench off the west wing was under a tent, acceptable only when down-wind.

Next to the separate kitchen and scullery a large mutton carcass was turning on a roasting spit where a lunch crowd had gathered. Whether they were miners taking a break or men who had given up the search it was difficult to tell. The successful diggers on the other hand were easy to distinguish, surrounded by filles de joie and laughter, drunkenly splashing their wealth about.

The inn was built by an entrepreneur, in town for a fast profit I surmised. The ale was warm but wet and twice the price of its Hobart Town equivalent. And one old digger told me the whores were two day's wages of the average working cove.

'Suits me fine,' I answered him. 'I'm here on business'

'What kind of bus-i-ness?' he asked, his words in my ear fused together with beery spittle.

I thought a moment before realising this man could quite possibly know Annie Eddington. 'I am seeking a woman ...'

'I told yer lad, the price o' whores 'ere are up there with Paris.'

'No. Not a whore. I am looking for a woman called Annie Eddington. She is about five-foot-eight with short-cropped thick brown hair, quite attractive, about twenty-five.'

He stared off into his tankard a while. 'Annie yer say? Eddington?'

'Yes,' I sounded rather expectant.

He emptied his quart of ale and belched. 'Hmm, Annie Eddington ... you buyin'?' he nodded to his tankard and wiped his mouth with the back of his hand. I should have seen that coming. As a matter of goodwill I paid for another and made a mental note not to be caught like that again; not at those prices. The wily old veteran drew a lengthy gulp of ale and looked me in the eye. 'Annie Eddington?'

'Yes,' I said almost embarrassed at my gullibility.

'Can't say I 'ave heard the name lad. Annie Eddington ... nar.'

A bed in the nearest boarding house – Mrs Fothering-ham's Boarding House for single gentlemen – was five shillings the night. Clean sheets a shilling extra. There was a bathhouse on the outskirts of this bustling community, she informed me. Was that an insinuation the journey had made me fragrant?

I supped at the Fat Nugget; stewed goose and flour dumplings with mustard pickles. Later, as the sun set, I walked the goldfields. The diggers had retired for the night and now tested their cooking skills. Some men were lucky to be with wives or lovers, some with aboriginal companions, all of whom were darned better cooks than most men. The single men had to learn all housekeeping skills; sewing, washing, mending, baking and general hygiene.

The aromas of roasting kangaroos, pan cooked birds, baking damper, salt pork, ham, mutton and even frying snakes and lizards, permeated the acres of camping ground where the language was colourful and the characters eclectic. I was assured that recently fresh carrots, onions and cabbage were again available as market gardens, once deserted by the gardeners, were again operative. Interestingly pears and apples were imported from Van Diemen's Land – or Tasmania as the island is now officially called – and were fetching 6 pence apiece. For cooking purposes firewood was brought in from surrounding bushlands at 18 shillings a cartload.

Understandably kangaroos within miles of the goldfields were scarce and their meat alone fetched a shilling per pound. Many a large *roo*, as the locals called them, weighed in at 150 pounds so as one can imagine there was good money in supplying meat.

Cattle were herded in and corralled ready for the slaughtermen at the abattoir tents before they were sold to the butchers. Here, only the best cuts were prepared where the wealthier diggers were happy to pay top guinea. I noticed the local aborigines hanging about in small groups eager for the offal and refuse. This was in sharp contrast to the grocer merchant nearby with shelves displaying luxury items like Russian Caviar, English bloater paste, tins of sardines, lobster, anchovies and oysters, bottles of cognac, whiskey, wines, pickles or French glace fruits.

'Australia,' one merchant told me, 'was no longer an isolated country on the other side of the world. Clipper ships are sailing London to Melbourne in ten weeks now. Ten weeks I say!'

But I was here to search for Annie Eddington.

I began asking about, tent to tent, and it soon occurred to me that it was not going to be as simple as I anticipated. The police I spoke to estimated there were maybe twenty thousand transients on the fields. The night grew dark. Mosquitoes sent most people inside their tents. Others sat in close proximity to their smoking fires where the tiny winged pests could not reach them. Some men played harmonica, some the fiddle and other folk played tunes with the aid of none other than a gumleaf. Many drank, smoked and told yarns. No one had heard of Annie Eddington or, for that matter her husband whom I assumed went by the same surname.

It was late. After midnight. Back at the Fat Nugget Inn less than a dozen imbibers lingered; either drunk, unable to become drunk, or too drunk to find their way home. The fallboard on the piano was closed shut. A scullery boy raked straw over the dirt floor, two wenches washed pewter tankards in a bucket and the innkeeper leant on the bar smoking a fat cigar. He had had enough.

Me too.

I drank a large brandy and dragged my weary body back to my room on the ground floor near the back door of my two-storey boarding house. I stripped down to my long Johns, covering myself with a clean sheet – extra shilling – and thought of my day's travail. Fruitless. Outside a dog barked. Somewhere far off a couple quarrelled, while down the corridor I heard the incessant snores of lonely men. Finally I fell asleep to the tune of a mosquito menacing my right ear.

Soon I was in a heavy sleep, my snores no doubt in unison with one or another of my fellow lodgers. I dreamt of wealth, Lynch Savage, my mother and then diamonds. Pink diamonds, thousands of them trickling through my fingers like sparkles of fresh spring water. Royle Rowley appeared in my dream, we were naked dancing in an orchard. My nurse friend Millie appeared and then faceless whores with raised skirts and no pantaloons. My dreams aroused me, my sheet fell to the floor and I felt the weight of someone upon me. I was being manipulated, caressed, fondled. But then I felt a hand clasp firmly over my mouth and a sharp point at my throat. My eyes shot open …

'Annie!' my speech incoherent through her clamped fingers. 'Annie!' I could make her out clearly in the half moon, now shining through my open window from where she had entered. 'Annie Eddington?'

'Caspian Hunter?' The woman was as surprised as I was. 'What do you want with me?' she hissed. 'Why do you ask all about the camp for Annie Eddington?'

I mumbled something unintelligible. Annie repositioned herself upon me, a leg straggled either side where she sat on my groin.

'Keep your voice down,' she said seriously although her anger had subsided a little. She pressed the knifepoint harder into my throat. 'One false move, one call for help and I will skewer you. Got it?'

I nodded.

She relaxed the knifepoint and removed her hand from my mouth. I took two or three sharp breaths for I now realised she was almost suffocating me. 'Well?' she insisted.

'Well what?'

'Why are you here? You have followed me to Ballarat and you have been asking half the population about me. What's going on?'

Oh my god. She has got the most beautiful hazel eyes!

'Answer me Caspian Hunter.'

'Oh ... why am I here?'

'Yes curse you. Why are you following me?'

'Oh, I wasn't following you per se,' I tried to act relaxed, innocent. Truth was the gorgeous creature was sitting on my John Thomas ... and *John* was, well, handsomely aroused, both from the dream from which she awoke me and the proximity of her ... ahem ... womanly bits. 'I just wanted to ask you some questions that is all,' I said in a rather unconvincing tone.

'About what?'

'What?'

'What questions do you want to ask me?

If I was not mistaken Annie's breathing had become laboured and she too had to plan her words as if something else distracted her.

Something else?

'Oh Jesus,' I said involuntarily.

Annie shifted herself into position. She too was naked under her skirt. So it was not simply a dream. 'You want to ... ah ... ask me about ... Jesus,' she said.

'Do I?'

Annie threw the knife aside and lowered herself slowly onto me. 'Jesus,' she said, and closed her eyes. I reached for her breasts; they were well shaped and firm and her nipples like raspberry bon bons.

'Oh Jesus,' I reiterated. 'Jesus, Jesus, Jesus ...'

The siren fell forward. She smothered her wet lips on mine and we kissed passionately ...

Like famished nymphomaniacs. Her tongue sought mine. And as her groans turned to gasps I feared Mrs Fotheringham would be pounding on my door any moment. Annie rode me harder and harder. Our lust grew in crescendo. But we knew our passion must be brief. She broke into a gallop and I, Caspian bloody Hunter, galloped along with her all the way to the finishing post.

'Jesus Christ!' Annie sighed and dropped heavily beside me wriggling in close to share the narrow bed. 'I knew the day we met in the Good Woman Inn,' she purred, 'that you wanted me.'

What a nerve.

'I wanted you? *You* plundered *me*,' I panted, thinking to myself – *molested in my sleep twice in a fortnight, is not life grand?*

'Alright Don Juan, have it your way.'

'Why were you here?,' I asked. 'I mean you did not even know it was me until you ... ah ... woke me?' I wanted to say: you lush, you hussy, you were not even wearing knickerbockers. Do you always run about in the middle of the night like that?

'You ask questions around here, it is bound to reach me. Savvy? You were easy to locate, greenhorn.'

'Greenhorn!'

'So why are you chasing me?'

'Erasmus Peck,' I said sternly, attempting to regain some standing.

'What of him?'

'You killed him did you not?'

'Dead or alive the reward said. Don't tell me you're here to arrest me for killing a murderous outlaw with a price on his head.'

'No. No, not at all.'

'Good. Otherwise I would have to cut you.'

'And in that I do believe you would be more than capable.'

'Well then?'

'Where did you dispose of Peck's body?'

'In a shallow grave in the hills behind New Norfolk.'

'I need to know exactly where.'

'Why?'

I sat up and looked Annie in the eye. 'I need you to return to Hobart Town with me. It is imperative we locate the man's body.'

'Why?'

'I cannot say,' I said, before lying, 'I am under oath.'

'You cannot say ... then I cannot return.'

'I can subpoena you.'

'I'd like to see you try.'

Hmm. So would I.

'You will be outlawed if you do not return with me and show me where you buried the man's body. *You* will be the outlaw. Annie Eddington the bounty hunter. You will be hunted like a common criminal.'

'Why for Christ's sake? Tell me.'

'I am in a position to offer you one hundred guineas reward.'

'I have my reward.'

'No. Another one hundred guineas.'

'What, for the body? That's madness.'

'Let me be the judge of that.' I leant on one elbow and ran my hand through Annie's hair before leaning across to kiss her once more, when she sat bolt upright, shoving my hand aside and bouncing off the bed. 'Enough. I must leave.'

'Leave where.'

'Return to my husband.'

'Oh. I forgot. So you really *are* married? To an Anglo-Greek.'

'In an estranged way, yes.'

'How's that.'

'We are not close. But he needs me and I need him.'

'How is that poss ...'

'You don't need to know.' Annie Eddington sat on the window ledge.

'What does your husband do here? I asked around but no one seems to know an Eddington.'

'That's because he operates under an assumed name.'

'What? Another one. If he is not using the name Eddington or his Greek father's name Mandolos, what name does he answer to?'

'Can't say.'

'What does he do?'

Annie thought a moment as if struggling with the idea of divulging too much information. 'He's a boundary heavy weight.'

'A what?'

'A boundary heavy weight. If two miners dispute the boundary line of their staked claims, then he settles it for them.'

'What? With violence?'

'If need be.' Annie swung her legs outside the window.

'Wait!' I nearly called out. 'Wait. Please ...'

'I'll be in contact.'

'When?'

'Tomorrow.'

'Where?'

'I'll find you.' Annie dropped from the window three feet to the ground and disappeared from sight into the fading moonlight. She was gone and I had no idea if I would ever see her again. But one thing was certain. Annie Eddington knew nothing about the Salmon Princess.

Day sixteen

Mrs Fotheringham was not amused. She thumped on my door mid-morning. 'Rouse yourself Mr Hunter, unless you wish to pay for another night's board I must ask you to leave.'

I looked at my watch, open on top of my folded britches; it was almost nine in the morning. I had slept soundly after my late-night entertainment.

'I thank you Mrs Fotheringham,' I called through the flimsy door. 'I must have slept soundly in your most comfortable room.'

'Well?'

'Yes indeed Madam, I would like to keep this room one more night if you please. I have unfinished business in this town.'

'Then another crown Mr Hunter and your accommodations are secured until tomorrow morning.' And she added firmly, 'Until seven that is.' Silence followed. 'I assume you will not be requiring a new bed sheet.'

I ate at the inn; fried bread in dripping with lardons, one egg – which I think was from a chicken – and hot sweet tea, and considered what I would do. Wait for Annie to contact me? I was not all that certain she would oblige me with her presence. For all I knew she had met up with *Heavy-Weight* Eddington and left Ballarat, maybe for other goldfields at Bendigo or Beechworth.

I spent the morning and most of the afternoon walking the diggings, observing every campsite and goldmine I passed, clearing my thoughts and analysing my previous movements. There was no point asking questions, I knew that from yesterday's experience, as one person, out of the dozens I had questioned, had told me a lie, and then warned that agile minx, Annie.

Then I passed a butcher's shanty, the hand-painted sign out front read Wolfgang Schmitt. The man had his business on the wrong side of the Golden Point valley diggings, at Ballarat Flat. Here hundreds of campsites enviously overlooked their lucrative neighbours. Neighbours who were not about to share their licensed plots any time soon.

The guileful German butcher had a vertical timber hut with a shingle and bark roof sloping out a further five feet at the front to create a veranda providing at least some shelter from the sun and rain. As land space was at a premium he was afforded only six feet by six for a corral off to one side. Here five old sheep were crammed in misery. Butcher's hooks hung from the awning with various cuts of mutton bleeding onto the dirt. His cuts of meat for sale were advertised on a poster nailed to his hut, but prices were omitted. I guess purchase prices were negotiated. The multitude of flies however, simply helped themselves, as there was not a meat safe in sight. A faithful mongrel dog, sated with a belly full of offal, stared across the open mines towards me, where I had stopped to observe his master, Schmitt, sitting on a log reading a newspaper. As there were so many people about my presence went unnoticed.

I watched from some distance, observing the man. Call it a lawman's intuition, a sixth sense maybe, but there was something decidedly sly about him.

I sat in the shade of a eucalyptus tree half for an hour or more, despondent and lost in my thoughts of what I was going to do. I considered arresting Annie when, or if, I ever found her, and subpoenaing her to return to Hobart Town with me. In irons if necessary. The thought even excited me ... Annie Eddington in irons under my guard. I was lost in fantasy when movement caught my eye, off to the right a hundred yards distant. Two miners appeared from below ground, one a Chinaman and the other a huge man naked from the waist up with the toned body of a pugilist. His left arm was bandaged. He seemed to be sewn into tight britches belted at the waist with a silver buckle like I have heard American cowmen wear. An altercation began with the Chinaman, but petered out just as quickly. This miner, who I could only describe as a gorilla, strolled down the embankment to the creek where he washed the grime from his upper body. It was then that I noticed his hairy back. In fact I could see he was hairy all over.

The altercation, it appeared, stemmed from food. I surmised that the gorilla had exited his mine for a midday meal that was not forthcoming. I watched him stroll to Schmitt the butcher where their mutual intercourse was jovial and familiar.

Friend of Schmitt! Hairy back! Was this man Eddington the Greek?

It was imperative I manoeuvre closer. Taking the long way around I approached the rear of the butcher's shanty arousing the minimum of suspicion. At least I hoped so. Directly behind the butchers' I was accosted by the stink of the goldfield's detritus. Pickle bottles were piled amongst putrid offal, discarded gin bottles poked from rotting cabbages. I edged the perimeter, careful not to slip in the slimy pit of rat infested mess and managed to look suitably nonchalant within earshot of my target when I was accosted ...

'What are you doing here?'

'Annie!'

The woman grabbed my arm pulling me back from view and hissing once more, 'I said, what are you doing here?'

'Looking for you.'

'I can see that. But ... how did you find me?'

'I am a policeman remember.'

Annie pushed me further away before checking over her shoulder. Schmitt and Hairy Back had disappeared into the butcher's shop.

'That's your husband is it not?'

'What makes you say that?'

'Well I deduce same, because he himself is a foreigner he is tolerant of the Chinese and therefore employs a coolie to do his digging, for I notice he has a wounded arm.'

'Oh.'

'And he *does* look Greek, somewhat, he has a hairy back.'

'And you call that police work?'

'Well, yes. I do.'

Annie thought a moment before taking my arm once more. 'Come.'

We climbed a steep embankment and marched down the other side towards another tent town a hundred and fifty yards away. Stopping outside a two-man tent she looked about surreptitiously before pushing me inside. Annie pegged the flaps closed and turned on me. 'Why are you here?'

'Looking for you.'

'Yes, yes, you said that. But what is your purpose? You've come all this way to find me?'

'I told you that last night. It is imperative we locate the body of Erasmus Peck.'

Annie leant in close. 'What's so important about that man? Why would anyone need to find his body?'

'I told you I am under oath,' I lied lamely. 'I am not in a position to say.'

'Twaddle.'

'Twaddle?'

'Humbug.' Annie tried a friendlier approach. She became ravenous Jezebel. 'So Mr Policeman,' she purred holding me by the back of my head as she ran her tongue through my ear, whispering. 'Now you found me what are you planning to do with me?' And with that she forced her free hand down the front of my britches.

'What …' My throat was dry and my voice rasping. 'What am I planning you ask? But what about … ah … you know?'

'Alexander.'

'Alexander?'

'Yes. That is his name. Alexander. I told you we are estranged.' Annie's hand worked its magic. I was spellbound. We kissed passionately while she manipulated her bloomers down to her ankles, stepped from them, and kicked them aside.

She's done that before.

Without a wasted moment Annie popped the buttons on my britches. They also dropped to the ground rereleasing my truncheon. Exposed, so to speak, Annie hooked her left boot up onto a crate.

She'd practised that before an' all.

It is the story of my life, or so it appears. Stolen love. Swift and turbulent. Carnal lust has no boundaries. In those moments of blissful passion the outside world ceased to exist and at the very moment of our liberated tensions a voice boomed, 'Annie? You in there?'

Alexander!

As his giant hands clawed at the pegged tent flaps Annie and I sailed bodily backwards into the side of the tent. The small dwelling collapsed tearing a dozen pegs from their foundations and we crashed to the ground, shrouded in canvas.

'Annie!' the man roared. Alexander was angry. Very, very angry.

'Jesus,' I blabbed, struggling with my canvas shroud. The game was up. Our cover blown. Alexander Eddington, Hairy Back himself, hoisted the tent aside to reveal Annie in my embrace, both half naked. Some clown nearby laughed at our expense and soon spectators gathered.

'But you said you were estranged from your husband,' I said weakly, disentangling, re-dressing and backtracking at the same time.

Annie too tidied her person. 'I ... I ... well we are ... sort of.'

'Estranged!' Alexander bawled.

I managed to stand.

'Malakas!' he yelled at me, fetching a heavy two-foot branch from his wood heap and lurching towards me. But his wounded arm caused him pain and made him clumsy.

'Stop Alexander!' Annie screamed out, pointing a pistol at his head. 'Stop or so help me I'll shoot.'

Alexander froze. He knew she meant it. She was a bounty hunter after all. He said something in Greek I imagined to be derogatory. Annie signalled with the pistol for him to back away. He took several steps backwards, when I recognised the pistol. It was my double-barrel Yale. I patted my pocket. Empty. It must have fallen free when I fell. Or had the minx lightened my pocket when I was enamoured. With the gorilla so disposed, we backed away to hoots and whistles from our gathering audience.

'I'm leaving Alexander. Don't try and follow me,' Annie said calmly, staring the man in the eye with my pistol aimed at his chest. She gathered a few possessions into a carpetbag,

'I find you ... you bitch,' he said in his heavily accented English. 'I tell you true. I find you.'

'Well Mr Policeman,' Annie said as we made an urgent exit back to Mrs Fotheringham's boarding house. 'That was a turn up for the books. It looks like you got your way.'

'Pardon?'

'I am returning with you after all.'

'Oh.'

'You did say there was another hundred guineas in it for me, did you not?'

Now this reward, I might add, was not authorised by my superiors, not yet anyhow, so I trod carefully.

'Absolutely.' I said with confidence, excited by the company I was keeping.

'I hate the diggings anyway,' Annie confided. 'And I found your island prison full of opportunities, especially when your governor pays a hundred guineas every absconder.'

'Yes, well you cannot just wander about shooting people and cutting their heads off willy-nilly you know.'

Mrs Fotheringham was delighted. House rules, *no refunds*. So the god-fearing avaricious woman kept my silver crown and re-sold the bed. I collected my own meagre travelling possessions and walked to the police watch house. We were in luck, with Annie Eddington in my charge, we were given the last two seats available on the police coach to Melbourne and were leaving the goldfields behind us by mid-afternoon.

Melbourne early evening

From the Russell Street Police Watch house we walked to the recommended Mistletoe Hotel on Mackenzie Street. It looked promising. Recently opened by a Mr Charles Wright and paid for with gold from Bendigo. Mr Wright suspected his plot was dug dry and wisely moved to Melbourne with his gold and rheumatism – compliments of living through many winters in a tent – to invest in the hotel business. And did he make a wise decision? The three-storey bluestone building was a sturdy unadorned structure on the outside, but inside ... well no expense was spared, with marble floors, Persian carpets and French tapestries with massive urn cornucopias of fresh flowers for the foyer delivered daily. Yes indeed, Charles Wright had made a fortune and was not afraid to spend it.

I left Annie to order a bath of hot water to be brought to her room ... *Her room,* I hear you tut-tut. As much as I longed to share one bed, Annie was insistent we take two rooms and who was I to question her modesty or reputation. After all I was confident that hanky-panky was back on the menu this night, in one or another of our rooms; or maybe both.

I found the shipping office at Queen's Wharf open for late arrivals and was lucky enough to secure a berth to Hobart Town in a twin cabin by the saloon. I did however instruct the agent to record us in the passenger manifest as Mr and Mrs Hunter. He returned a knowing grin and did not refuse the ten-shilling inducement.

'Yer need to be at the docks at least an hour before squire, or three hours if'n yer got luggage to be stowed in the hold sar.'

'We have but one bag each sir, 'I answered, and made for the Mistletoe Hotel with thoughts of a delightful belle naked in her tub.

Annie was bathed and dressed on my return. Although her short, wet hair was uncombed she had dressed in a long skirt that showed off her delightful curves. The woman looked stunning. Annie sat on the seat of a bay window overlooking the street.

'I ordered the maid leave the water for you, it's still warm.'

'That was very thoughtful,' I said and stripped naked before her. As we had been intimate modesty had not entered my mind. Annie pulled her knees up to her chest and watched me bath.

'So Mr Policeman,' she started when I was at my most vulnerable; naked in the tub. 'What is so important about Erasmus Peck's body that I must show you where he lies?'

'I am not at liberty to say.'

'Nonsense. It must be very important if you came searching for me all this way.'

'Look Annie ... I ...'

'Come come. I'm here am I not? I'm returning to take you to his gravesite. What secrets lie with him?'

Sly minx. Did she know something?

'I told you ... I ...'

'I'm not at liberty to say,' she mimicked me. And her face darkened.

I made an executive decision. I would lie to keep her off my back ... and on hers.

'Do you promise to keep it secret?' I said with a rakish smile.

'Yes of course,' she answered far too quickly, swinging her legs over the seat and straining to hear my every word.

'Erasmus Peck stole important documents from Port Arthur when he escaped.'

'What sort of documents?'

'Ah ... maps.'

'Maps?'

'Yes maps of the Tasman Peninsula. Escape routes.'

'Escape routes?' Annie repeated incredulously, as if they were of no importance.' Is that all? Maps?'

'Yes.' I splashed water on my face to avoid her eye contact. Lying was not my forte.

'And they're on his person?' she fished. 'In his pocket like?'

'That is correct.'

'But he was only in Long Johns when he attacked me and I shot him dead with a single shot.'

'Yes, you told me that. But the maps would have been in his coat pocket where he threw it aside ... so you said. Before the spider incident.'

'But I searched his coat pockets before I buried him with it.'

'They would have been hidden.'

'Hidden?'

'Yes. Sewn into his coat lining.'

Annie grew annoyed. 'You lie!'

'Not at all. Why would you say that?'

'What could possibly be so important about maps that you had to track me to the diggings?'

'Alright, alright. There is one map drawn by the Royal Engineer surveyors that locates extensive coalmines on the peninsula. And the government do not desire these fall into private hands.'

'Coal?'

'Yes coal.'

'You expect me to believe that?'

'Of course. It is the truth Annie,' I lied pathetically.

Annie studied me a while as I lathered my chest with soap.

'Hurry and bath,' she said jumping to her feet. 'I am hungry and you are going to buy me a steak.'

'A steak?'

'Yes. I like it nice and bloody like the French eat it, and with fried potatoes and onions.'

'Onions with steak?'

'Of course. Haven't you ever tried it?'

'No,' I said, happy that the conversation had steered away from Erasmus Peck. 'But there is a first time for everything.'

'Then hurry. Dress. I will wait for you in the saloon bar.'

Now there is a liberated woman if I have ever met one.

Hotel owner Charles Wright was a married man with four children. But that did not stop him from exchanging niceties with Annie as she drank alone in the saloon bar of his grand hotel. Then again I do not blame the man; a woman drinking alone in a taproom is a rare sight. A rare sight indeed, which has a wicked effect on most men. My guess is that Mr Wright had already checked the guest list and found Mrs Eddington was accommodated alone.

'Ah Caspian,' Annie smiled as I joined them at a booth style table in an ill-lit corner. 'This is Charles. He owns this hotel.'

Charles. We are a little familiar already are we not?

'Charles,' I said glowing false charm. 'So nice to meet you.'

We shook hands although he was less than pleased to meet me.

'Caspian is a policeman,' Annie told the man.

'How nice.' Now he was even less pleased to meet me. He smiled falsely.

'Charles was just telling me he had a win at the races to-day,' Annie chatted away drinking her complimentary champagne. 'Two hundred pounds,' she said.

Charles boastful smile switched to embarrassment.

'Two hundred pounds,' I nearly whistled.

'Well ... it's not every day a man has a win like that,' Charles answered growing all coy and modest. 'Anyhow,' he added, standing. 'I must carry on with business. Nice to meet you Caspian.' And he left post-haste.

The beefsteaks at Harry's Chop House on Flinders' Street were superb. Expensive, but worth every penny. Besides my police allowance covered the tariff, even if I did have to tighten the belt for the remainder of my journey. Thankfully Annie was exhausted from our coach ride and we retired early to my room. Whilst our lovemaking was intense, if not mechanical and once again brief, Annie insisted on retiring to her room. She was a strange creature I thought, as I lay alone in my bed and my eyelids closed tight. *Yes, a strange creature indeed.*

Day seventeen

I awoke to pandemonium. Heavy footsteps on the landing outside my room ran past my door. I immediately realised it was the hotel owner, Charles Wright, doing the shouting. I dressed quickly and went to investigate.

'What has happened?' I asked a housemaid in the hallway.

'Oh it's Mr Wright sir. 'e's been robbed.'

'Robbed. Here?'

'Yes sir. Someone's broke into his quarters on the top floor while he was out. Made a terrible mess an' all.'

Another maidservant appeared looking flushed. 'Two hundred pounds,' she said. 'I heard him tellin' the constables he lost all the cash winnings from the race yesterday.'

'Two hundred,' the first maid repeated. 'Oh my.'

Two hundred I thought to myself. That will teach the bastard to boast to people like Annie.

Annie!

I hurried to her room five doors from mine and knocked. 'Annie,' I cried out. No answer. Not a stirring. Not a sound. I kept knocking when I had a horrid thought. I rushed back along the landing to the housemaid who had been watching me with some interest. 'I need you to open number 18.'

'Oh ... I ...'

'Look I am a policeman and I think my colleague in 18 might be in danger.'

The room was empty. The bedclothes skewwhiff, like it had been slept in by a mad drunkard. And her kit was gone. Annie Eddington had flown the coop, again.

Why do women have a habit of ravishing me in the middle of the night and absconding before sunup? Why?

'You're a policeman are you not?' Wright screeched down at me from over the bannister on the floor above where his abode was robbed. I nodded. 'Well come up here and see what you can make of this.'

I hurried up the stairs and into his luxurious apartment. Again no expense had been spared. There was a mahogany extension table set with the latest silverware from London. A pair of crystal lustres on the mantelpiece either side of the hotelier's commissioned portrait; by John Glover I was informed.

'The door has not been broached,' I noted as we entered. 'A window maybe?'

'Follow me,' the man growled. He was ropable, pushing two constables aside who had been summoned off the street. I followed him to the eastern end of the apartment where the morning sun poured through the windows; closed and locked windows I should add. Wright stabbed a finger towards the ceiling where several pine boards had been removed almost directly over his desk. Now I noted the sun pouring through the roof also. 'Oh!'

'Yes, oh!' he growled back.

Above the missing ceiling boards, above the attic, several slate tiles had been removed where the perpetrator had cleverly entered.

'And the money sir?' I asked. 'Gold or paper?'

'Bank of England, five and ten pound notes.'

'Where was the money?' I asked.

'Well here's the thing ... Mr Caspian isn't it?'

'Caspian Hunter. But please call me Caspian.'

'Here's the thing Caspian. I have three hundred and twenty-six pounds four shillings and threepence in that safe.'

He kicked an iron key-locked strongbox under his desk. 'Business proceeds you understand. Luckily that was locked away. However, I was distracted last night and my horse winnings were on the desk, under those papers. My apartment is as safe as a bank.' He looked back to the hole in the roof. 'Who would have thought?'

'How were you distracted Charles?' This question came from Mrs Wright, a robust middle-aged and firm bodied woman with a stern disposition. She stood in the doorway where she had been listening.

'Beatrice! Darling,' Wright's voice broke. 'You're back early my dear. I wasn't expecting you until tomorrow.'

'Clearly. Answer my question.'

'What was that my dear?'

'Why were you distracted?'

'Distracted?'

'Yes Charles,' she said coldly. 'You said you had been distracted. That is why you forgot to lock the winnings in the safe.'

'The hotel has been extremely busy in your absence my dear and ...'

'Do not *my dear* me Charles!'

One of the housemaids hurried from the main bedroom, feather duster in hand and looking red faced. Mrs Wright watched and waited until she was out of earshot before seething at her husband.

'Our bed was not slept in last night. Would you mind telling me why?'

Oh Christ, I thought. *I know why.*

'Mr Wright,' I interrupted.

'What?'

'I will return immediately,' I excused myself, keen to avoid the fray. 'I need some items from my kit,' I said. 'Police business you understand. To take down notes etcetera.'

And I left. Never to return.

Charles Wright was in more dung than the earlier settlers and I wanted nothing to do with it, especially as it appeared Annie Eddington was the culprit. Talk about *sleep with the enemy.* I settled the tariff at reception for Annie's and my room and stepped onto Mackenzie Street forlorn and feeling a failure, and looked for tearooms to find sustenance for my voyage. At least the morning was bright and sunny as I turned from Collins Street into Swanston Street where Susman's Tearooms had been recommended.

The tearoom was a respectable establishment opposite R. Potts the Importer and I was ushered to a window table where I watched the world go by over a fine meal. Over the road I watched R. Potts himself herding his employees into an orderly line in front of his premises. Standing in the middle of the street a photographic image-maker took advantage of the morning sun preparing to record their image for posterity. My thoughts went to Royle Rowley in her photographic studio in Hobart Town and I immediately felt alone and keen to return to my adopted home.

Chapter Seven

Day eighteen. Four days later. Prisoners' Barracks. Campbell Street. Hobart Town.

The news of my failure reached Captain Bradley Maddox before I could, which was probably a good thing and thankfully he was out of the office when I returned; fresh and relaxed from what turned out to be a most pleasant and brisk sail home.

Jasper fussed about, pouring me coffee, Billings shook my hand in greeting and Holly and Lincoln were full of cheer on my return. Apparently Maddox had been tiresomely annoying, only too willing to shoot Fabian and myself in the back with his verbal tirade whenever our names were mentioned.

'I hate to tell yer this Caspian sar,' Lincoln could not wait to tell me. 'But we have another killin' to solve since you've been in Victoria.'

'Oh?' I had enough on my mind without yet another murder and this news was the last I wanted to hear. 'Go ahead, is it anyone we know?'

'No. It was just some cove washed up in Kangaroo Bluff. An' the strange thing is 'e was washed up with the remains of a large barrel.'

'Large barrel?'

'Aye. It appeared 'e had been put inside the barrel, after' e was killed like, and the barrel was weighted with rocks. But apparently, Captain Maddox reckons, the lid popped off, the barrel's tipped and them rocks 'ave fallen out, floatin' the barrel and corpse to the surface again.'

'Jesus! Resurrected huh?' I tried to find humour in the situation until Holly continued,

'And he had the top of his head lopped off and all his brains had washed out.'

'Clean cut, by the stroke of a sword,' Billings said. 'So Captain Maddox suggested.'

Little did they know how right Captain bloody Maddox was. It appeared Lynch Savage's minders had done poorly when it came to the disposal of Dan Wheeler, *Aladdin's* harpooner.

'Here's the photographic image made by Mrs Rowley,' Holly said and pushed a sepia card across the desk for me to peruse.

It was Dan Wheeler all right, cranium missing and his skull empty and picked clean by crabs and surf.

'When did Mrs Rowley make this image?' I asked.

'Four days ago,' Jasper said. 'I fetched her on Captain Maddox's orders.'

'Did you now?' I asked with a twitch of jealousy.

'Aye. I helped Royle ... ah Mrs Rowley, set up her equipment for two images Caspian sar. One o' the dead'en and one o' the beach where he washed up.'

I studied Jasper a brief moment knowing he knew how and where Dan Wheeler's body originated from, after our recent visit to the Sea o' Graves Inn. He returned a knowing look and discreetly tapped the side of his nose. *Mum's the word, eh.* God bless his woollen socks.

'Where is Maddox anyway?' I enquired.

'Had an appointment with Governor Young.'

'Did he now. Do we know why?'

'Apparently the gov'nor wants progress reports on the latest investigations.'

'And has there been progress in my absence?'

'Nay sar.'

'But the filing system is the bees' knees.'

'Aye. And I hate to tell yer this,' Lincoln said, 'but the gov-'nor's impatient for answers on the missing diamond and he is a personal friend of Noble, what's daughter was killed in New Norfolk.'

'Bugger.'

'Aye sar ... Bugger!'

'What's the plan then?' Billings asked.

'Take a seat,' I told my assembly and, taking a long drink of my coffee, I brought them up to date with what had happened in Victoria, leaving out my romances. They were fascinated.

'Jesus, 'Holly cheered. 'Yer don't let the grass grow under yer feet do ya Caspian sar?'

'Hmm. I suppose not. Alright then,' I started. 'Since Maddox is not here I am the man in charge. All agreed?'

'Absolutely,' Billings said. 'We never doubted that.'

'Billings. I want you to get a dozen men together from the barracks and search the foothills behind New Norfolk. We have a rough idea of where the bounty hunter Annie Edding-ton buried Erasmus Peck, so do your best. Look for freshly dug ground. If it was a shallow grave, which I am certain it would be, maybe scrounging wildlife have unearthed it.'

'Yes sir.'

'Oh, and Billings. Have half the men in street clothes, not uniforms, and with small arms concealed.'

'No problem.'

'Now, Jasper.'

'Sar.'

'Did you interview Jane Bell the whore from King's Road in Sandy Bay, Calhoun Nyle's alibi? The one he was helping build a scullery?'

'Yes. And she swore on a stack of bibles he were with her all day.'

'I hate to say this,' Lincoln said, 'but she be a whore. Cos she would swear.'

'We will just have to take her word for it for the moment. Lincoln, Holly.'

'Sar.'

'You two walk the streets. I want everything you can find out about this beehive tattoo. We know it is a sign for Manchester but there has to be more. Edwin Piketon who was murdered, Erasmus Peck who was captured – now deceased – and Calhoun Nyle all have the tattoo and all were incarcerated at Port Arthur. There has to be a connection. Now our mystery man in the barrel, he too has a beehive tattoo.'

'Really. How do you know sir?' Billings looked surprised. *God*, I thought, I had let my guard down. I quickly inspected Royle's image on the desk.

'There!' I said relieved and pointed to the corpse's arm. There was the faintest hint of a beehive tattoo showing on his arm.

'Goodness me you have a keen eye Caspian sar,' Holly was impressed. So was I, the image was barely recognisable. In fact it was pushing the realms of imagination to their limit.

Billings picked up the image and began to study it with a magnifying glass mumbling his own thoughts.

'Billings,' I snapped, snatching the image from his grasp. 'Peck's gravesite if you please.'

'Certainly. But you *do* have excellent eyesight Caspian.'

'Yes I do, don't I ... now, New Norfolk. Time is not on our side.'

'Jasper.'

'Sar.'

'I want you in the taverns and waterside inns. Find what you can about this beehive tattoo.'

This was a strategic move on my part, Jasper could be trusted in the taprooms, Holly could not.

One hour later.

I had watched my loyal colleagues leave the office re-enthused with purpose, and sat a moment mulling over my thoughts, battling to make sense of the recent occurrences. Finally I decided I would pay a visit to Lynch Savage at the Sea o' Graves and demand to know why Dan Wheeler was not disposed of properly and ask more questions about the man, for I was certain he was acquainted with the other three men with beehive tattoos. It was too much of a coincidence.

Gatekeeper Sergeant Clincher at the prisoners' barracks saw me approach and lifted his backside from a barrel where he relaxed over a pipe of tobacco in the shade. He straightened his shako and wobbled towards me lazily. The old faithful was not growing any younger.

'Mr Hunter. On your way out sir, let me get the gate for yer.'

'Thank you Richard.'

'Be there in a jiffy,' he mumbled as he approached, his gammy leg giving more grief than usual. 'There now.' The heavy iron prison gate door squealed open on its rusty hinges. 'You'd think for a whalin' port we'd have some oil at the ready for squeaky gates, wouldn't yer Mr Hunter.'

I smiled and thought, *I wish I had a guinea for every time he had said that.* The door banged against the main gateway and instantly Holly ploughed through the portal from Campbell Street, as surprised to see me as I was to see her. Lincoln was directly behind her.

'Annie ...' Holly was struggling to catch her breath after running the mile uphill from the waterfront. 'Annie ... Edding ... ton.'

'Yes Hol'. What of her?'

'Annie Eddington, she's in 'obart Town!'

'What?'

'The bounty 'unter Annie Eddington,' Holly was wheezing. 'We just seen 'er.'

'And I hate to tell yer Caspian sar,' Lincoln too wheezed. 'But she's travellin' with that husband cove yer told us about.'

'Alexander the Greek!'

'If'n that's his name, well I'd say yes,' Holly said. 'Cos he's big an' hairy like yer told us.'

'So they have been in cahoots the entire time. They've come to fetch Erasmus Peck,' I deduced.

'But he's dead ain't 'e?' Clincher scratched his ear.

'No. No. They have come to fetch the body. They know something valuable lies with the corpse.'

Clincher's ears pricked.

'But they don't know about the Salmon Princess,' Holly panted. 'Surely not?'

'Salmon Princess?' Sergeant Clincher's brow furrowed.

'Maybe not.' I answered, paying no heed to Clincher. 'However if they asked specifically about Peck, in the inns and taverns for example, they would soon realise the truth. Billings did leave for New Norfolk already, did he not?'

'Aye,' Clincher said. 'He and a dozen come through 'ere a good hour ago now. What's the Salmon Princess sar?'

'Then,' I said, continuing to ignore Clincher, 'we need to get to Billings and his troops before they hit the hills around New Norfolk. They'll give the game away. We need to find them and stake out the bush land. Find high vantage points. If my guess is correct the Eddingtons will be on their way to New Norfolk as we speak.'

Clincher was swapping positions one foot for the other. 'Holly,' he grew more and more insistent. 'What's this 'ere Princess?'

'Holly,' I said.' Where were the Eddingtons when you saw them?'

'They was alightin' from the *Lady Rodney* steam packet from Melbourne.'

'Sounds right. Then we have the advantage of a head start, as brief as it is. Are you both armed?'

'Aye sar,' Holly's face brightened at the suggestion. 'Armed and dangerous.'

'Then hurry now.' I stepped out onto Campbell Street. 'Lincoln, hail a cab.'

Six-foot-six-inch Lincoln stood in the middle of the street waving frantically like a semaphore and caught the attention of a hansom carriage down yonder. I turned to Clincher. 'See that the prison-cell carriage is sent to the watch house in New Norfolk. We'll be needing it.'

'Aye.'

I fixed the old guard with a serious stare. 'Mum's the word old chap. Alright?'

'Alright sar,' Clincher fidgeted. 'Ah, what's the Salmon Prin ...'

'Later Richard,' I said running off to join the other two already in the cab. 'Later.'

The hansom cab driver was no novice at the helm of a carriage on urgent police business. And he charged a pound for the privilege. We caught up with Billings three miles beyond Granton on the west side of the River Derwent. Under my orders his charges split into four groups and continued at double pace. It was imperative we arrive in the township of New Norfolk and dissolve into the hills, attracting as little attention as possible. Holly, Lincoln and myself also continued post-haste.

Billings' troupe regrouped at the New Norfolk watch house before hiking into the hills. I ordered that two plain-clothed soldiers, disguised as surveyors, guard the only road into town.

I knew that once in the hills there would be no way of us communicating besides discharging two shots quickly in succession followed by one more four beats later. That would mean an arrest has been made. 'Three shots in succession,' I told them. 'Fifteen beats apart, means you have made contact, but they have escaped. Got that?' All agreed. Also under my brief, all parties were to observe and not engage until we knew where Erasmus Peck lay buried. I had a good feeling of success, and I could not wait to see Annie's face when I arrested her, the traitorous minx.

Holly, Lincoln and myself alighted from our carriage and stretched. We were near the New Norfolk lunatic asylum and invalid hospital. As instructed, the driver positioned our carriage out of sight alongside the south wall of the prison-like asylum. Over several acres of land there were a number of buildings within the rectangular stone and brick institution; with double-storey administration and staff accommodation buildings between the wards. Windows faced inwards only. It was a most depressing necessity. From here I could see to the hills and realised we had a steady hike ahead. I was starting to think I had not thought this through carefully when I heard a young voice.

'Oye! It's that policeman Mr 'unter ain't it?'

I turned to see ten-year-old Walter with his eight-year-old brother whom I had met on the jetty weeks earlier, standing confidently, legs apart, hands on hips, like two grown men. Only the shang-eyes hanging from their belts seemed out of place. 'Walter?' I acknowledged.

'Aye. What are you doin' back up 'ere in Norfolk then?'

'Keep it down Walter,' I said softly. 'We're here on police business, chasing villains.'

'Yer come fer Mad Percy Hachette huh?'

'And who is Percy Hachette?'

'The cooper Mr 'unter.'

'And why would I come for him?'

'On account 'e had somethin' to do with Violet Noble o' course.'

'Violet Noble.' The little seven-year-old who was found bound and gagged and dumped in the river a mile away. 'What do you mean Walter. What makes you say that?'

'Well Todd 'ere an' me seen Mad Percy Hachette with Violet the day she went missin'. My guess is 'e had somethin' to do with her disappearance.'

'Jesus Walter! Did you not tell someone about this?. Me for one, when we met two weeks ago.'

'No sar. Told no one.'

'Why for god's sake?'

'No one asked. You didn't ask.'

'Bloody hell Walter! Where does this cooper live?'

'At the cooperage outside the lunatic asylum.' I must have looked vague. 'There's a smithy there too and a carpenter.'

Walter jerked his head in an easterly direction following a two-storey brick wall. I was lost for words. Here I was on a breakthrough to capture Annie Eddington and finally secure the diamond when information was now forthcoming on another most horrific and unsolved murder. I was caught between a rock and a hard place ... when the two soldiers in civilian attire caught up with us, at the double.

'The-villain's-arrived-sar,' one said out of breath.

'Oh.'

'Aye,' the second soldier snatched breaths. 'Came in on a hansom jus' like you three sar.'

'Both parties? A male and a woman?'

'Aye sar.'

'Which way did they go?'

'They took to a track south-east.'

I turned back to Walter. 'Where can I find you, later this day?'

'Jus' ask for us squire, the locals will tell yer.'

'Not a word do you hear. Not a word about what you just told me. Not a word to a soul.'

'No sir.'

'On god's honour?'

'Aye. Mum's the word eh?'

'Yes. Mum's the word.'

Having earlier heard rumours of a lone bushman, a stranger seen in the area of the nearest hill north-west of the village some weeks earlier, we filed away from the town on foot. It was soon apparent that the apex-shaped hill afforded a good lookout, offering thick bushland, perfect within which to hide. Presently we picked up a trail of recently disturbed gravel. Silently we followed. The forest was overgrown and the path cut by sawyers narrowed until it vanished completely. We approached the summit and looked back at the township of New Norfolk nestled in its fertile valley. Under happier circumstances the view would have been pleasant. But a dark malevolence hung over the steep sided hill.

Suddenly Holly threw her arms out silently, like a bird. We all stopped. She whispered in my ear. 'Did you hear that?'

'Hear what?'

All I could hear were distant birds and a rustling of leaves with a gentle breeze as our sole companion.

Holly was barely audible to me. 'Listen.'

Lincoln heard the sound also and nodded silently. We stood motionless. I was beginning to think the two were imagining things when the stench of death drifted by, accompanied by the subtle, yet unmistakable sound of digging. The shovelling quickened, it was easy work as the ground had been dug before. And recently. The gentle wind confirmed our suspicions as the smell of decaying flesh drifted in our direction. Holly began retching, silently at first. I watched her body heave in surging convulsions as her stomach cramped, reminding me of her reaction to old Piketon burnt alive on his own stove top. Holly did not have a strong stomach for the odours of putrefaction.

'Holly!' I hissed urgently. 'Go back down the path.' Holly fought the urge to vomit. But it was a losing battle. 'Go, go ...' I said in a loud whisper waving my arm frantically back towards the path. Holly threw a hand over her mouth and hurried away, her body heaving in spasms.

'Jesus,' I muttered to Lincoln. There was no time to lose. I lead the way, creeping forward towards the sound of digging. Shortly we came to an exposed patch of button grass only a dozen feet square. We watched through dense foliage in silence. Annie had dropped to her knees and was frantically pulling at the decomposed remains of her victim. Fascinated by her determination and captivated by her beauty I signalled Lincoln to hold back a moment. True to her wild nature Annie drew her hunting knife and thrust it into Peck's bowels. The stench was unbearable. Undeterred Annie felt through the rotting intestine. Suddenly she felt an anomaly within the yards of gut. She slashed the colon and squeezed the lump free.

I was speechless.

The Salmon Princess!

Annie held the quail egg sized gem between forefinger and thumb and held it up to the light. She smiled to herself. The smile was infectious. I wanted to shout out. I could hardly believe our luck and, although I had no doubts, now we had proof.

The myth was true.

The treasure was a reality.

And Annie was my prisoner.

I waited while Annie poured water from her canteen over the diamond. She washed the gore from her hands and stood, looking extremely pleased with herself.

It was time for us to act.

Suddenly the unmistakable reverberation of Holly fetching up her last meal resounded through the trees.

Annie spun on her heels only to face me. I pushed forward through the bushes; my double-barrelled Yale cocked at the ready.

'Annie Eddington you scoundrel,' I called out, crushing dead bracken underfoot and stomping into the clearing. Lincoln followed. 'I am arresting you in the name of Her Majesty, Queen Victoria.'

'Caspian!' She was surprised to see me all right, but for a criminal caught red-handed she was overly confident. Maybe our intimacy accounted for her brazen attitude.

'Stand steady,' I cried out.

'Caspian. You ... what a surprise.'

'I'll say. You did not really think you could fool me, did you?'

'But ... but how?'

'Never mind.' I reached out for the diamond with open hand, my pistol in the other, levelled at Annie. 'I'll be having the diamond thank you.'

'Caspian,' she paused to study the rare diamond. So close yet so far. Annie's eyes were intoxicated with greed. 'This stone is enough to make us all very wealthy. Caspian ... we could share this. No one would ever be any the wiser. We could leave Tasmania together, go to England and live like royalty.'

'And there lies your answer Annie Eddington. I am loyal to my queen. Now I won't ask a third time. Pass me the diamond.'

There was no warning. Not even the snap of a twig. A shot rang out. A musket ball sizzled between Lincoln and myself drilling into a nearby tree.

'Get down!' I screamed at Lincoln.

We dived to the ground.

A second shot exposed Alexander Eddington. He stepped into a gap between two trees, Annie's six-barrelled pepperbox in hand.

Uh-ha, I thought. The pepperbox. They were never that accurate.

I rolled on my side and fired back but my short-barrelled pistol was also designed for close range. Alexander vanished back into thick bush and ... with Lincoln and myself lying on the ground, guarded ... Annie bolted.

'No!' I shouted.

Instantly Holly crashed through tea-tree bushes like a crazed bull. She crossed the clearing and galloped after Annie.

What just happened? It was all a blur. Seconds passed as Lincoln and I remained low, listening for Alexander. He was circling us. Stalking us like a trapper.

A shot rang out some distance away. 'Holly?' I hissed at Lincoln. I was confident it was Holly's Tower service pistol. I waited for a scream. A shout. Anything … but heard nothing.

I could see Lincoln thinking the worst. He stood to pursue Holly only to be confronted by Alexander.

'Look out!' I was about to jump to my feet when Alexander stepped into the clearing brandishing the six-barrel pepperbox. With at least four barrels still loaded, he had us covered.

'Drop your weapons,' The Greek's voice was laboured and I knew immediately the man was ill. Sweat from his brow trickled into his eyes and he shook his head like a dog might when wet. 'I have four shots to your one,' he went on. 'I tell you true … bas-tards … drop your weapons I say.'

And he had the advantage of point blank range.

'You do not want to be doing this Alexander,' I said. 'We are officers of the law, you will hang.'

'Ha!' he laughed. 'Me hang? Who's man with the gun isn't it bas-tard? Who's man with … '

Young Walter's shang-eye projectile smashed into Alexander's hand. The pepperbox spiralled to the ground and the Greek screeched out in shock. Alexander turned in Walter's direction, only to be slammed in the jaw with brother Todd's rock. The huge man crumbled to his knees and Lincoln pounced, securing the prisoner.

'Walter? Todd?' I was shocked. The two young boys stepped from their camouflage, flashing proud grins.

'Mr 'unter,' Walter touched the rim of his straw hat in salute.

'Nice shots both of you. But that was very foolish to follow us here. It was very dangerous, very dangerous indeed.'

Walter frowned. 'A thank you would nice gov'.'

'An' maybe a sov,' Todd quipped. 'Reward money like.'

Confident little sod, I told myself. 'All right, thank you to both of you.'

'An' the sov?'

'We'll see.'

'Caspian sar,' Lincoln had Eddington's wrists pulled together but the prisoner screamed with pain. It appeared his hand was broken.

'I hate to tell yer this,' Lincoln said, 'but we didn't bring no handcuffs.'

He was right of course. In all our haste we forgot the irons.

'Jaysuz,' Walter pulled a spare slingshot strap from his britches' pocket. 'Do I have to do everythin'? Here ya go matey.'

With a possible broken jaw and hand, the Greek put up no further resistance and now I could see he was ill with some other malady. Sick as a dog in fact.

'Alexander Eddington,' I said. 'I arrest you for the murder of Edwin Piketon.' Eddington said nothing.

With Alexander secure, Lincoln was about to go after Holly but the resilient lass appeared amongst trees some distance away.

'Holly!' Lincoln cried out.

By all appearances she looked in good health, accept for her spontaneous sickness. Holly doubled over, leaning her hands on her knees catching her breath. She was exhausted.

'That woman can run like a bloody jackrabbit,' Holly said between gulps of air.

I snatched up the pepperbox and fired a shot into the air, waited fifteen beats and fired again, before repeating the sequence once more, hopeful the others back near the village would hear the arranged signal and be vigilant. I turned to Holly who I realised was keeping her distance from the rotting cadaver.

'You all right Hol?'

'Aye. I'll not come no closer Caspian sar. No sar.'

'Get the prisoner on his feet,' I ordered Lincoln. 'We need to catch that slippery wife of his.'

We gathered once more at the village watch house where Alexander was locked in a cell until the prison cell cart arrived. I also arranged for a doctor to attend to the man's wounds and at least afford the villain a shot of laudanum, for he was in excruciating pain and I am, after all, an empathetic human being. Now we desperately needed to reach Hobart Town before Annie. 'Billings.'

'Yes sir.'

'Can you ride a horse?'

'A horse?'

'Yes dammit. A horse.'

'No. I can't'

I turned to the soldiers. 'Who can ride a horse?' Several hands were raised. 'Then we need to get word to the waterfront that our outlaw is on the run and will be looking to sail immediately. She must be stopped at all costs. Do we have access to any horses?'

'I could loan you my cousin's mare sir,' the guard of the watch house said helpfully. 'But she ain't the fastest equine transport on four legs.'

'Then fetch her immediately ... You,' I pointed to the slightest of soldiers whom I figured could ride fast. 'You know what to do. Raise the wharf guard and notify customs.'

Billings fetched a carriage and driver and followed as backup.

'Now,' I told Holly and Lincoln. 'One measure of bad luck can surely be retrieved with the solving of Violet's murder and the successful arrest of her killer.'

'Here, here.'

Walter and Todd waited patiently on the watch house veranda.

'Right lads,' I said. 'It is time we paid a visit to this cooper Percy Hachette.'

The local tykes led myself, Holly and Lincoln along a creek bed running parallel to the asylum; more a small-enclosed village really, there was even a private chapel. At the far end various tradespersons had set up business to service the asylum and the locals alike. The cooperage overlooked the creek but several healthy young willow trees, shooting up along the banks, masked our approach.

As unostentatious as our presence was in the township, I suspected the cooper had heard lawmen were in the area, for Percy Hachette was guarded and certainly did not seem surprised to see us. I have always tried not to let emotions interfere with an arrest or investigation. But when the crime involves an innocent seven-year-old lass it is difficult to remain distanced from such a horrific event.

We found the cooper in his cooperage pounding the interior of a large barrel with a wooden hammer. Aligning the staves I believe the action is called. He was a weaselling being, if I may describe a man like that. Short and gaunt, but fiercely strong. He would have to be brawny to manhandle large oak barrels the way he did. Percy Hachette was an unfortunately ugly man with a face I could only suggest was scrunched, in a permanent scowl. And his shaved head did nothing to help his unfortunate looks, with his large forehead and its gnarly lumps. He wore a calico blouse almost to his knees, tied with thin rope at the waist. His britches were filthy, worn and patched. The smell of his stale sweat cut through the fragrance of the searing oak where the half-completed barrel staves were set in position over small fires. He showed all the signs of a life of poverty, including yellowed teeth in dire need of medical attention and a weather-hardened complexion.

The barn-like cooperage was open to the elements at one end, which faced the creek. 'Mr Hachette,' I asked from the outside yard where half a dozen completed barrels awaited collection. 'Mr Percy Hachette?'

'Who wants ter know?' His voice was oddly high, almost effeminate.

'I am Mr Hunter from the police department at the prisoners' barracks.' I studied his reaction to the word *police*, but the man did not flinch. 'I would like to ask you some questions sir, if you will.'

His beady black eyes looked beyond me, scrutinising Holly and Lincoln who, for all appearances, did not appear to be law persons. 'Questions? What about?'

'Violet Noble, sir. The seven-year-old local girl whose body was found in the River Derwent a fortnight past. You were acquainted with her were you not?'

The cooper scratched his chin in a play of contemplation and I noted his hands; powerful clasp like claws, were black from soot with his long nails hard as flint.

'Violet who?'

'Noble.'

'No. Can't say I know 'er.'

'Oh? Are you certain Mr Hachette?'

'I know there's some Nobles what live down river,' he said, guarded and cunning. 'A wealthy squire on 'is grand estate so I 'ear.' There was a hint of bitterness in his voice, as envy was a common trait amongst any poor with rich living nearby. 'Can't say I've ever 'eard of a Violet Noble though.'

New Norfolk was a township of maybe five hundred people living in and around its surrounds and I was certain this cooper, who had worked here for decades, would know the Noble family in full.

'How long have you conducted your trade here sir?'

'It be more than twenty years now.'

'As I thought. And you do not know of the Noble's children, whom I am certain would walk the streets of New Norfolk as a family, say on a Sunday. To church maybe?'

'Wha' are you implyin'? Say wha' yer got on yer mind or bugger off.'

'It has come to our notice that you were seen with young Violet the day she disappeared.'

'Horse shit. Who told yer that?'

'I have two witnesses.' I omitted to say the witnesses were a ten and an eight-year-old. However young Walter was adamant he saw Violet walking along the side of the creek that fateful afternoon that she went missing, hand in hand with Percy Hachette.

The cooper twitched. It was only slight but I sensed his guilt.

'Witnesses?' he snapped. 'They're lyin'.'

Holly had had enough. 'You're the one lyin' yer mongrel,' Holly spread her legs and planting her boots firmly in the dirt she pushed back her un-buttoned smock coat to reveal her massive Tower pistol shoved behind her belt. Lantern Jaw Lincoln had her back.

'Now tell the firkin' truth,' Holly seethed. 'Yer was seen with little Violet, down the creek yonder.' And Holly jerked her head back down the embankment.

Hachette's demeanour instantly changed. 'Oh that little girl! Was that her name, Violet? Yes, I seen a little girl down the creek, cryin' she were. Lost. I had no idea that was the little girl what went missin'. She never told me 'er name like. She were lost an' I showed 'er the way back along the creek to town and to find her mammy.'

I was dumbfounded. I had no doubt this vile creature was Violet's killer.

'So you admit you were the last one to see Violet alive?'

'Now 'ang on a moment. Yer not fingerin' me for kidnappin' that little girl ...'

'Who said anything about kidnapping Mr Hachette?'

'What?'

'You said kidnapping. No one mentioned kidnapping ...'

'Bugger this,' Holly was ropable. There was no stopping her. 'Lincoln!' She grabbed Lincoln by the belt dragging him after her and marched up to Hachette, taking him by the collar.

'What are yer doin'?' The cooper struggled but Lincoln was on the case also. They frogmarched Hachette to a topless barrel and upended the man into the cask.

'You can't do this,' Hachette's voice was broken and high pitched, almost a squeal. 'Mr 'unter sar. Stop them.'

I thought of the consequences. 'Jesus Holly,' I hissed quietly. 'What if he is innocent?'

'I don't think so Caspian sar. And if'n yer don't mind me sayin', either do you.'

'You're right, what's the plan?'

'Just sit back and watch me sar.'

Mad Percy Hachette managed to jiggle his body into the upright position. *Christ* I thought, the man is a contortionist. He pushed his head free. 'Help!' he screamed out. But the nearest neighbour was the blacksmith twenty yards away pounding horseshoes on his anvil.

'Shut it,' Holly slammed the lid onto the barrel, but as it needed to be fitted properly – only when the head hoop was removed and the staves loosened – she drove four inch nails into the head instead. Hachette squealed in terror; trapped in a claustrophobic vat in darkness. They tipped the barrel onto its side and pushed it towards the creek. Hachette's finger protruded from the bunghole. 'Help me,' he pleaded. 'I know nothing of what happened to the little girl. Help ...'

Lincoln rolled the barrel over the bung crushing the cooper's finger. He screamed in pain. The barrel rolled again and when the bunghole was skywards once more Holly glared into the darkness. 'Well Hachette. Do you confess?'

'No! What are you talkin' about? I ...' Holly rammed a wooden bung into the hole and Hachette's pleas became a muffled babble.

'Well let's see how watertight yer barrel is, cooper.'

And together Lincoln and Holly rolled the cask to the embankment and let it loose. The forty-gallon vat escaped down the riverbank, picking up momentum until it hit the creek edge and soared a few feet into the air before splashing down in the water. It immediately began to sink. Mad Percy Hachette's terrified screams were muted within the oak coffin. We hurried down the embankment where Hachette was screeching hysterically. Water poured in through the ill-fitting barrelhead. But unbeknown to our prisoner the creek was only two feet deep at this point. I imagined his ugly face pushed up into an air pocket.

'Well?' Holly knocked on the barrel. 'Why did you do it?'

Hachette's petrified squeals continued.

'As long as he squeals we know he lives,' I said, and hoisted my boot onto the barrel urging it off the rock ledge on which it was wedged and into deeper water. The barrel sank completely under. The screams ceased. I counted to ten, and then nodded silently to Lincoln who jumped into the creek up to his waist rolling the cask into the shallows. I jabbed a small knife blade into the bung prising it free.

'Well?' I demanded.

Hachette gargled gasps for air, his foul lips sucking at the bunghole.

'Well?' I said. 'What have you got to say for yourself?'

'It's all lies Mr 'unter. I'm innocent I swear it.'

Now was no time for self-doubt. I jammed the bung back in and shoved the barrel back into deep water ... and counted to twenty. Slowly.

Again Lincoln dragged the barrel into the shallows and I un-bunged the hole. Silence. 'I hate ter say this Caspian sar,' Lincoln said. 'But I think you've drowned him.'

'Christ!' I cursed. Get the lid off.'

The barrel was hoisted onto one end and Holly used the fork of the cooper's hammer to prise the lid off. Immediately Hachette's head sprang up like a Jack in the box and he gulped lungfuls of air.

'Well?' I demanded. He said nothing gasping and spluttering. I do think we near drowned the man.

'Well?'

No answer.

'Holly,' I ordered.

'Sar.'

'Nail that bloody lid back.'

'Yessar.' Holly slammed the barrelhead so hard onto Hachette's head I feared she had split his skull.

'No! No!' he squealed piteously. 'It were an accident ... honest it were.'

'What was an accident?'

'I tied 'er up and she were screamin' and screamin' and I thought the whole town would hear 'er so I gagged 'er but it were too tight and she suffocated. It were an accident sar.'

Mad Percy Hachette broke down and cried.

He wept like a baby, bawling uncontrollably. In all my years of police work this is the single most pathetic scene I have had the misfortune to witness. I demanded the contemptible wretch look me in the eye. He refused until Holly took a length of his hair wrenching his head chin high to look at me.

'That little girl was strangled,' I said. 'Asphyxiated by your very own hands.'

'Get him out,' I ordered, my tone hard with loathing.

Lincoln single-handedly extracted the killer like a Frenchman would pluck a snail from its shell. He let the whimpering beast crumble to the ground where he remained in a foetal position sobbing, shaking uncontrollably. I watched in silence, revolted at the animal at my feet and not aware of Holly, until I heard the loud click as the hammer was pulled back on her musket.

'Face me yer bastard,' Holly's voice was guttural. Anger and disgust had altered her judgement. 'Face me I said.' And Holly kicked the man in the ribs.

'Holly,' I said quietly.

'Show me yer face yer firker!'

Gibbering and sobbing Hachette slowly lifted his head to look at Holly who had the muzzle of her pistol one inch from his head. He instantly soiled his britches.

'Holly,' I repeated. 'Don't do this.'

'Say goodbye to this world,' Holly jabbed the muzzle hard against his forehead.

'Hol',' Lincoln swallowed hard. He knew his friend too well. 'No Hol' this ain't the way.'

Holly twitched the barrel one inch off the killer's left ear and fired. At such close range the noise was deafening. The musket ball buried deep in the embankment and Hachette promptly collapsed, fainting into the dirt. Holly was understandably proud of herself.

'Yer didn't really think I would shoot the bastard in cold blood did yer?'

'Holly,' I said sighing with relief. 'Never do that again. Do you understand?'

'Aye Caspian sar.' She used her boot to roll the unconscious prisoner onto his back. 'But we got results, eh?'

'That we did,' I finally smiled.

......

It was early evening by the time we arrived back in Hobart Town. Both Alexander Eddington and Percy Hachette were transported to the watch house in the police cell carriage that I had commissioned earlier in the day. Two soldiers rode in the cart with the prisoners. Four on the outside with the driver. But Alexander Eddington's health appeared to be deteriorating and I ordered the guard to take him to the prison infirmary the moment they arrived at Campbell Street.

As some of the soldiers arrived at the barracks well before us, Captain Maddox, of course, had received the news before our arrival. Solving the Violet Noble killing was one thing, but our failure to catch the elusive Annie Eddington and retrieve the diamond overshadowed that success. Maddox swung back on his chair and hooked his boots onto Fabian's desk.

'The governor expects a full report of this failure of yours Hunter,' he said sourly.

'And I assume the governor would like a full report on how we captured Violet Noble's killer also, *captain*,' I said with contemptuous emphasis on his title. 'Noble being a close acquaintance of the governor and all.'

Maddox harrumphed. 'Do what you must.'

'As for Annie Eddington,' I continued, 'I have ordered every ship be searched and passenger manifests to be checked and cleared before leaving port. There is little more we can do. The woman has the guile of an eel.'

'There's one other thing Hunter,' Maddox said.

'Oh.'

'Miss Villan, Lincoln,' Maddox told the other two. 'I would like to review your reports in the morning.'

And with the wave of the back of his hand Maddox dismissed them both.

I caught Lincoln's eye. 'Wait for me outside if you will,' I said matter-of-factly, softly. Lincoln nodded seriously and stooped below the door mantle.

Maddox righted his chair and sat upright. 'Commander Sedgwick Fribbens of the Norfolk Bay Station has made an official complaint against you.'

'What?'

'You assaulted the man, you struck an officer.'

'In self-defence.'

'That's not what he says.'

'The fool is a liar,' I was furious. 'A liar and a coward.'

'They are strong words Hunter.'

'Holly and Lincoln are my witnesses. They will testify that I was defending myself.'

'You mean your close friends, your colleagues with whom you have a close relationship.'

'Pardon?'

'I heard you arranged to meet Lincoln outside where you were fraternising with your underlings.'

'I am a professional Captain Maddox,' I said angrily. 'And fraternising, as you call it, with my colleagues builds respect in my book. You should try it yourself sometime.'

'Respect!' Maddox eyes narrowed. He clasped his hands before him on the desk and glared. 'I despise you Hunter. You are nothing but a womanising cad.' *He might have had the womanising bit right, but a cad?* 'Sleeping with another man's wife is ... is despicable.'

'You do not know the circumstances.'

'Oh, so you admit it then?'

'As I told you, I was defending myself and I have witnesses to the fact.'

'He has witnesses too Hunter. He has a case against you both legal and moral. You'll be thrown out on the street.'

'Why do you hate me so?'

'I told you why. Now leave.'

Back on Campbell Street, outside the barrack's gate, I flipped the lid on my turnip. It was 8 o'clock. I found Holly and Lincoln waiting across the street in the light of a gas lamp, and told them of my verbal altercation.

'Sod 'im,' Holly spat.

'I would rather not,' I grinned. We all laughed. God only knows, we needed a good laugh.

'When's Fabian returning any'ow?' Lincoln asked.

'I do not know. Soon I hope.' I took a deep breath of fresh air and looked towards Sullivans Cove. 'I think we have earned refreshment. How does the Shades sound?'

'Thought you'd never ask Caspian sar,' Holly's grin was infectious.

The Shades was a small inn beneath the Theatre Royal, also in Campbell Street on the northern outskirts of Wapping. The windowless taproom was ill-lit, smoky, stank of stale grog and seafarers sweat, but it was private. Toffs rarely ventured there, more the steerage class of theatre patrons. Villains loved it here also and tonight I felt like being in the company of villains. Sick and tired was I of prying eyes.

'I should have hit Fribbens harder,' I told Holly and Lincoln when they asked why I was so upset after my confrontation with Maddox.

There was standing room only in the bar beneath the theatre above. A musical was taking place and muffled music and clodhopping dancers on the stage overhead mingled with the chatter and clatter of the packed taproom beneath them. Mandy Machin, a bar wench I knew well, served the other two porters and myself a Madeira wine, after recommending the new stock of Madeira just in off the schooner *Hawk*, recently in from Cape Town.

'Dunno how yer can drink that Caspian sar,' Lincoln pulled a face. He was a porter and ale man through and through.

'Portuguese ain't it Caspian sar?'

'Yes Holly, Madeira's a small island off the northwest coast of Africa. Did you know Madeira was discovered by accident?'

'What, the island?'

'No, the wine,' I tried to keep my glass steady from elbowing patrons. My colleagues looked on with interest. 'A merchant returning to Madeira from the West Indies had an unsold, unopened keg of wine remaining on board,' I told them. 'And when it was opened it was found to be pleasantly and uniquely sweet.' I took a moment to sip my wine. 'And this was the result of the barrelled wine being constantly hot in the equatorial heat.'

'Is that so?' Holly quaffed her porter banging the pewter onto the bar signalling for another. She drew a crown from her purse.

'Put that away Holly. It's my treat tonight.'

I slipped my hand into my frock coat to fetch my purse when I felt the heavy metal discs in my pocket that were unmistakably gold coins, namely the sovereigns and the Bank of England one pound notes in the bottom of my pocket. Dan Wheeler's *bloody* money, the dead man at the Sea o' Graves. I had totally forgotten my ill-gotten gains that I had no intention of keeping, when Lynch Savage's men walked into the victim's lodgings. Now my frock coat pockets have been known to resemble a woman's purse; full of knickknacks like my pocket watch, coin purse, pocketknife, notebook, pencils, handkerchief and boiled sweets of which I am most fond. So the fact that folded bank notes and a few extra coins loose in my pocket were misplaced was understandable. I carefully felt in my pocket, peeling blind, a one pound note from its fold, and finally slid it onto the bar.

'I hate to say this,' Lincoln said, 'but that looks like blood.' The note was soiled somewhat and the dried blood had gone a deep rust colour.

'Oh!' I feigned surprise. 'It does look a little odd. It is from the prison treasury,' I said of the note, suggesting it was a portion of my month's salary.

'We don't care none for bloodstains in 'ere squire,' Mandy Machin cackled, snatching up the note. 'A quid's a quid.'

And indeed it is. A pound note attracts attention, especially in a place like the Shades. I was aware someone watched me across from the adjoining bar.

Holly also noticed. 'Ain't that the bushranger Martin Cash?' she asked me not too subtly.

They say a person can hear their own name mentioned over the din in a noisy room. It was Martin Cash all right, staring with his sad eyes. Some years back, whilst he was a wanted felon pursuing the love of his life, Bessie Clifford, Cash was caught trying to escape Hobart Town for its environs. Unfortunately, in the fray he shot and killed a policeman, Constable Peter Winstanley. For this he was destined to hang, but at the eleventh hour the decision to hang Cash was reconsidered and he was given ten years on Norfolk Island instead. That was back in '44. Now 48 years old, Cash had served his time on Norfolk Island, which was also disbanded as a prison colony last year.

'I thought 'e was on Norfolk,' Lincoln said.

I turned sideways with one elbow on the bar and my back to the retired bushranger in an act of discretion, but my guess is that the man was used to being talked about. 'Norfolk Island is no longer a prison,' I said.

'Oh aye. I forgot.'

'Most of the island's inmates were transferred here to Van Diemen's Land,' I said. 'And Cash there was given his ticket of leave and a position as a gardener at government house gardens.'

I had met Martin Cash once whilst visiting the gardens on official business not long after he arrived back here. Cash recognised me and smiled, raising his tankard slightly, and I saluted back likewise. He signalled the desire to converse with me. Under the watchful eyes of my colleagues, I pushed my way around the bar to meet the man.

'Mr Hunter,' he started in his heavily Irish accented English. 'Tis a pleasure to be meetin' yer once again. I read about yer exploits in the *Gazette* sir. Yer quite the sleuth and god bless yer for it.'

'Thank you Mr Cash ...'

'Martin, please.'

'Thank you Martin. But my guess is you did not simply want to make my acquaintance since we first met.'

'Ah straight to the point. I like that in a man. Yer right o' course. I have some information what I would like to give to yer.'

'Information?'

'Aye sir. Will yer join me in a whiskey?'

If it meant socialising with ex-villains to extract information. 'Why not,' I said. 'Thank you.'

Martin threw a shilling on the counter and it was exchanged for two cheap Irish whiskeys, the type of spirit great for starting fires. Cash then took me by the arm leading me into a dark corner, of which there were many in the Shades.

He raised his glass.

'To pretty maidens,' he said. I humoured his salute and we drank to pretty maidens.

'So what information do you have for me Martin?'

'This Maharaja diamond of which every cove in Hobart Town talks.'

'What of it?'

'Erasmus Peck had an accomplice at Port Arthur yer know.'

'Oh?'

'Aye. 'e were not that smart as to escape Port Arthur Mr Hunter. Not Erasmus Peck. 'e were not as clever as Martin 'ere.'

And Cash congratulated himself by finishing his firewater in one gulp.

'And do we know who this accomplice is?'

'A warder sir.'

'A ... a warder! Are you certain?'

'Aye. Absolutely.'

'All right then, I'll buy. Which warder?'

Cash contemplated his empty glass and smacked his lips theatrically. *Oh well, we were at the theatre.* 'Tell me who and I'll buy you a whole bottle.'

'It's not that. Look. I'm off to New Zealand Mr Hunter. Very soon.' He must have seen the look on my face, as if informing me of yet another escape – the man was after all an accomplished prison escapee. 'Oh worry not squire; I'm doing nothing untoward. I've got me ticket sir.'

'But you cannot leave the colony with only your ticket Martin.'

'I know. That's why I need your help.'

'My help?' *God he is not asking me to aid him in absconding illegally surely.*

'I need your recommendation to get me a conditional pardon Mr Hunter. Then I can sail to New Zealand.'

'So what is so important about New Zealand?'

'Business prospects and ...' the retired bushranger looked at me a moment and managed a wry smile. 'Dare I say it, but I have a love interest.'

Who am I to interfere with someone's love interest? Tell me the warder's name and I will see what I can do.

'Gentleman's agreement?' he said spitting on his right palm and thrusting his hand towards me.

'Gentleman's agreement,' I agreed and did likewise.

Cash grasped my hand and shook firmly before pulling me tight towards him, cheek to cheek.

'Carvel Dwight Mr Hunter,' he whispered in my ear. 'Dwight be a badd'en when I was in Port Arthur back in the forties, an 'e's a badd'en now. I also know the bastard's in Hobart Town as we speak, supposedly on Port Arthur business, transferring prisoners or some likely ruse. But 'e's after that Annie an' he'll kill her if'n he gets to her before you sir.'

'You know Annie Eddington?'

'I know of her, yes.'

I was not certain whether to believe Cash or not but I hardly had a choice.

'Oh shite!' he said. ''ere's trouble.'

I twisted to face the stairs as Solomon Blay the hangman entered. Blay was himself a convicted felon – for counterfeiting the King's coin – but, like Martin Cash, he had also done his time and earned his pardon by accepting the position as Her Majesty's executioner in exchange for his own life, as no one else would do the work. He launched his first victims into the afterlife at the age of 25. He was now forty. Solomon Blay had been publicly vocal about Martin Cash not hanging for the killing of the policeman years back. Now the men were sworn enemies and taunted each other whenever their paths crossed; which was often in the moderately small colony of Hobart Town.

At 5 foot 8 inches tall Solomon Blay was a long-faced sallow man with a rather wide mouth. His blue eyes had seen their fair share of death but he cared not. The hangman stooped below the doorsill and descended into the taproom, removing his weathered top hat, frayed at the seams. Those in his immediate path nudged each other, some went silent, others moved away; for Solomon Blay was not a popular man. He shoved by likeminded drunkards and positioned himself at the bar, demanding gin in a drunken slur.

'He's had a skinful,' I heard the man closest to me say. 'Cos he hung Betty May today and he hasn't hung a woman for a while.'

Blay ignored the people about him. No one wished to speak with him and he certainly did not wish to converse with anyone either. Suddenly he spotted Martin Cash who had stepped into lantern light at the counter opposite Blay. The hangman's recognition of his old foe caused him to leer at Cash, and then he mimed a noose about his own neck, pulling it tight over his head and flopping his tongue loose to one side in a macabre mime of choking.

'Bastard!' Cash spat across the taproom. Blay simply pulled the noose tighter and gagged louder.

'Firkin' bastard.' Cash slammed down his glass and rounded the bar rolling his sleeves and preparing for a scrap. Blay was eight years younger but Cash was stronger.

'Billings! Jasper!' I yelled across the bar. But they were already onto it and closed in on the angry Irish bushranger, restraining him. Blay continued his taunt. Maybe he knew Cash would never make it. I shoved in beside the executioner.

'I advise you to finish that gin and leave sir.'

'He should'a hung for murder Mr 'unter,' Blay's befuddled angry words reached me on drunken spittle. 'I should o' hung that bastard fifteen years ago.'

'Maybe so Mr Blay. But the law is the law and he was acquitted of murder.'

'Murderer!' Blay shouted at Cash who tried to shake free but Holly and Lincoln joined in to help restrain him. 'Look at him,' Blay slurped his gin and his rage dissipated. 'He's all smug like, now. But I'll get the bastard eventually.'

Chapter Eight

Day eighteen. Next morning. Prisoners' Barracks.

We gathered around morning coffee in our humble office with clear heads and in serious moods, to try and solve the remaining murders before some other murderous misdemeanour confronted us. Some weeks were blissfully peaceful, and other weeks, well ... *if it didn't rain it poured,* as my dear mum would say.

I had shared Martin Cash's sentiments about the prison warder Carvel Dwight and we all agreed we would have to have strong evidence against him before we went public. For this reason everyone agreed to keep our intrepid leader, Captain Maddox, in the dark. I ran an eye over a map of Hobart Town and its environs pinned to the wall next to our blackboard.

'Annie Eddington,' I asked of no one in particular. 'Where are you?'

'I hate to say this,' Lincoln said, 'but are you certain she hasn't flown the coop?'

'You would never know,' I said staring at the map. 'But we have the harbour and docks well policed the past few days and the highway north is guarded.'

'Tight as a drum,' Billings acknowledged his extensive network of spies and guards. He was rightly proud of his efforts. All available lawmen were searching for Annie Eddington.

'She could 'ave hiked south and caught a whaler with a dodgy captain,' Holly offered and Lincoln was all nods and smiles and for the first time I noticed their public display of admiration. If I did not know any better I would say they were more than keen on each other.

'It is a possibility I will concede,' I said. 'But I have a strong feeling she is still on the island.' I cast an eye over the black board notes. 'Annie Eddington aside a moment, what have we learned about the beehive tattoo, Jasper?'

Jasper was in the spotlight and looked pleased with himself. He had spent half the previous day searching through the prison records and was certain his time had been of value.

'There be several prisoners what have been recorded with the bee'ive tattoo over the years Caspian sar,' he said proudly holding the floor. 'I noted dozens in fact, since the beginning of the preserved records some forty years since. As for contemporary, well I seen Calhoun's records and that o' Phineas Nibley an' Dan Wheeler. But there was nuthin' to say they was in cahoots with each other.'

'Although they three originated from Manchester did they not?'

'Aye.'

'What's the thing about Manchester and beehives?' Billings asked.

'I believe it represents community, co-operation, commerce,' I said.

'What? Between felons?'

'Not necessarily. The bee is kind of revered as a city mascot in Manchester. But I rather fear our beehives in question are gang related.'

'Angus McRae, the cove what clerks them records,' Jasper said, 'showed me Calhoun's records, and it's written he has an anchor tattooed between his legs also.'

Holly looked horrified. 'You mean on his pecker?'

'Aye.'

'Now that's really got to be painful.' Holly looked at Lincoln who made a suitable face. 'How's it done anyhow?' Holly asked.

'The pricker, that's the tattooist,' I said, 'first traces a design onto the skin. Then he stipples the pattern into the skin.'

'Stipples?'

'Yes. Multiple pinpricks. The skin must be pulled tight you see. Sometimes they use two pins tied together. This pin, or needle, is continuously dipped into China-ink or India-ink and must penetrate the outer layer of skin.'

'Doesn't it bleed?'

'Aye,' said Lincoln who had the tattoo of a swallow on his hand. 'But they use alcohol or piss to wash the blood away.'

'Nice!'

'I knew a cove what practised pricking crusty bread before he attempted the real thing,' Lincoln added.

'Sometimes gunpowder or charcoal is used instead of ink.'

'Like scrimshaw.'

'Exactly,' I said. 'Governor Young once told me they don't discourage prisoners tattooing themselves as it aids identification later, should they get up to further misdemeanours.'

Captain Maddox, from his own perspective, could not have walked into the office at a more inopportune time. There we were chatting amicably and drinking coffee before heading off into a world of conniving, thieving scoundrels, when Maddox singled me out – the lamb for slaughter.

'Your prisoner, the Greek …'

'Alexander Eddington.'

'Yes. Well he's dead.'

'What?'

'He died in the infirmary last night.'

'What … how?'

'If you did what you draw remuneration for Hunter, you would not be in a position to have to ask. I suggest you visit the morgue and find out, if it is not too much to tear you away from the coffee pot.'

Sod him!

Morgue. St Mary's Hospital. Davey Street.

My watch read three-quarters of an hour past eight as I descended the spiral stair to the morgue. Seventy-one-year-old Doctor Ernest Crawley stood over his mortician's slab, his tall slender body backlit by a lantern making him some-what a darkened figure. He held a porcelain saucer in one hand with a cup of tea in the other, little finger out, and I noticed a small matching Spode plate of cream cake sitting on the slab next to the body. The man had always been hard of hearing; however my shadow announced my arrival.

'Good morning Mr Hunter,' Crawley turned to face me. 'You heard of the fate of your prisoner then?'

'Yes, Doctor Crawley.'

'I said you heard then?' he repeated. *Deaf as a bedhead.* I humoured him with a polite nod. It was then that I realised the cadaver on the slab the coroner was contemplating tea over was Alexander Eddington. The corpse was stark naked. *No modesty, especially in death.*

'He looked terribly ill when we arrested him and we afforded him all medical care although he was a felon, but here he is. Do you know the cause of death sir?'

'What was that?'

'I said do you know the cause of death.'

'Lockjaw.' Crawley slurped his tea and I am certain the doctor had no idea of the sound he made. 'Please excuse me Mr Hunter. The tea is hot.'

'Lockjaw eh?'

'That's what I said.'

I was having difficulty with the light in the morgue and fetched another lantern from behind me holding it over the slab. In the fresh light the doctor's pate looked shiny and waxy with his long strands of silky snow-white hair combed across it.

'Lockjaw from what pray tell?' I spoke loudly and articulated.

'From that wound you see.' He drew my attention to a nasty infliction of the left arm. It was badly infected.' Crawley placed the cup and saucer on the slab and twisted the dead man's arm so I could see the exposed wound more clearly. 'If I were to hazard a guess I would say it is a knife wound.'

'Knife wound?'

'That's what *I* said. Like the man has fended off an attacker and was stabbed in the arm. If cleaned properly and dressed at the time the septic would not have set in. It has most likely been dormant for weeks and weeks. Although he has seen a physician at some stage for he has been bled.'

'Oh.'

'Yes. You can see where the bleeding of the vein has occurred there in the crook of the left arm above the wound. Purging of the body's impurities is the most advanced remedy we know, Mr Hunter. Maybe he visited some backyard sawbones on the goldfields.'

'You read my report then?'

'Of course. Bloodletting, or phlebotomy as we professionals call it, stops the blood from stagnating in the body.' Crawley's eyes lingered a moment over the plate of cake. 'Leeches do a damn good job too,' he continued. 'Simply place the little suckers on the wound and away we go eh? Let nature do her business.'

The doctor's long thin fingers wrapped about a slice of cream cake and I had a sudden thought that the raspberry jam leeching through the cream was not jam but the cadaver's blood. I shuddered.

'How rude of me Mr Hunter,' he passed me the plate. 'Would you like some cake?'

'Oh god no!' I said all too adamantly. Crawley looked startled at my over-reaction. 'Cake for breakfast?' I added. 'I could not possibly ... thank you all the same.'

'Very well then.' The doctor shoved the last bite of cake into his mouth while I allowed the lantern light tilt down Eddington's body, when I noticed something extraordinary about the genitals. 'He appears to have no testicles doctor.'

'No what?' he said, mouth full.

'No testicles.' I pointed.

'Oh them. Yes. That is correct. The man has been castrated.'

'No! Castrated? Are you certain?'

'I assure you Mr Hunter, I know a castration when I see it.'

'How?

'What do you mean, how?'

'I mean I know how, but why. Were they diseased?'

'No. It is my guess that the man being Greek was at some stage a Turkish prisoner. The Turks loved to castrate their enemies.'

'That is a probability. Yes.' My thoughts went to Annie. *My husband and I are estranged Caspian.* It suddenly made sense, her blatant infidelity that is. 'Tell me doctor, would that make the man ... ah ... impotent?'

The coroner's old face crumbled into a chuckle. 'If you mean he had no use for his Jolly Roger than using it to relieve himself, then yes.'

Doctor Ernest Crawley looked pleased with himself. He shoved the cake plate towards me once more. One slice remained. 'Last chance,' he said.

'No. All yours sir ... thank you.'

'Very well then.'

I walked briskly up Murray Street turning east into Liverpool Street where I crossed the road to avoid the chatterboxes seated near the windows of Mrs Adkins Tea Rooms; the dining room beneath Mrs Royle Rowley's Photographic Studio as it turns out. I continued along the footpath, masked by horses and carriages, hansom cabs and busy merchant carts with my thoughts shifting from dalliances with Royle to snatched passions with Annie, when I approached Hester James the game-seller. The game-seller stood on the corner of Liverpool Street and Elizabeth Street, holding a ring-neck pheasant by its legs.

He called out his wares. 'Wild duck, brown quail, water-fowl.' All these were assembled at his feet on the cobbled path in an orderly manner. His faithful hound, Bullet, curled next to the baskets, asleep – no doubt exhausted from the morning's hunt.

I knew Hester had just descended from bushland on the northern slopes of Mount Wellington, still wearing his brown chamois jacket with black neckerchief, moleskin britches beneath thigh high leather waders and a wide-brim black felt hat to keep the Antipodean sun from his weathered face. He was clean-shaven except for a neat beard beneath his chin. Behind him were his worldly belongings in a canvas satchel slung against a shop front.

'Mr 'unter squire,' he smiled, pleased to see me.

'Hester.'

'I was wonderin' if'n yer'd pass me by this day. I have some news wha' might be of importance to yer.'

'Oh.' Hester James had always been an asset in my crime-solving arsenal; a fiercely honest man, he worked hard and drank moderately and expected others to do the same. He deplored thieves and villains bent on making a dishonest living. In simple words, he was a rarity, and was always eager to divulge titbits of information he picked up here and there involving malefactors.

He looked about us, keen that our liaison was not being observed and signalled for me to come closer. 'This Salmon Princess,' he said quietly.

'Oh yes.' I was immediately alert.

'Aye, this diamond what yer seek, the stolen maharaja's treasure.'

'Yes.'

''Tis the word 'bout 'obart Town that the rock is bein' fenced.'

'What? Really?'

'Aye.'

'How? By whom?'

'A cove what's not a cove.'

'A woman perchance?' I asked.

'Yer know then?'

'I know Annie Eddington, bounty hunter.'

'Aye, that's 'er. The same what captured One Ear Kearney and Erasmus Peck. The whole town's talkin' 'bout 'er.'

'What's the town saying?'

'That's she's wanted. No vessel can get in or out o' the 'arbour without being searched. The town want her caught Mr 'unter.'

'So do I. But what about the diamond?'

'Well this Annie Eddington ... she's got it, ain't she.'

'I know this Hester,' I sighed. 'Tell me something I do not know.'

The game-seller's eyes brightened. 'Benjamin Raj!'

'Benjamin Raj, Benjamin Raj,' I racked my brain. 'Where have I heard that name before?'

''e's the cove what's been sellin' the new-fangled rubbers to all the whorehouses about town.'

'Of course.' This was the Indian merchant I met at the Sailor's Rest selling vulcanised rubber contraceptives to Bonnie Nettle. It suddenly registered. '*He* is the fence?'

'You're a clever'n ain't yer?' Hester smiled with more than a hint of jovial sarcasm.

'Where can I find this Benjamin Raj?'

'Dunno squire. But what I will tell yer for nuthin' like, 'obart Town ain't London.'

'What about Annie Eddington?'

'Folks say she camps up in them hills,' Hester tipped his head towards the foothills of the mountain. 'Close to town.'

'Thank you Hester. You have been a great help.' I knew the mountain's foothills to be a desolate place and home to runaway prisoners and lawless sawyers who eked an existence out of the bushland.

'Pleasure squire.' The pheasant he held by its legs reappeared inches before my eyes. 'Can I interest yer in supper. Two bob Mr 'unter.'

I fished about in my pocket feeling the heavy round disc of gold I knew to be a half sovereign once belonging to Dan Wheeler. I passed it discreetly to the game-seller. 'Here. It is all yours.'

'Half sov!' he gasped softly. 'Here sir.' He passed me the pheasant by its legs. 'An' 'ere's a pair o' quail as well.'

'Thank you. But that is not necessary Hester.'

'Nonsense. You take 'em all sar. Devil's blood ... a half sov.'

......

Jasper was mighty pleased with himself. He had a match on the boot cast moulded in plaster from the imprint in the mud outside Edwin Piketon's cottage window.

'The boot was made at Port Arthur,' Jasper said proudly.

'And how have you deduced that?' I asked him.

'Jonathon Birch is a cobbler down in Wapping who learnt the trade as a lag at Port Arthur in the boot workshop there. He recognised the stubby nails inserted into the sole – short stubby nails for extra durability. You see, the nails are inserted in a regular pattern; say 12 rows of 2 either side of the sole with 10 rows of 3 between them and 2 rows of 5 at the toe. Other regular cobblers use less nails, like eight rows of two nails each side o' the bridge o' the foot. And the heel has a horseshoe shaped cap. Some, he said, had steel toe caps.'

'And our plaster cast?'

'Has the horseshoe shaped cap, aye.'

'Hmm. Why do the Port Arthur cobblers use more nails?'

'Well, he said on account they 'ave plenty of them, the blacksmiths there make them extra on account it keeps the lads in the chain gangs safer, workin' in the mud like. Especially in winter.'

'Why winter?'

'Well 'e said in winter the iron nails would channel the icy cold to the sockless foot. And whilst they provided grip on muddy ground they were slippery on wet cobbles and the like. But more nails gave better grip in the bushlands.'

'As we know Erasmus Peck had the diamond sar, I also deduce it to be his boot print outside the window.'

'I agree Jasper.'

Holly. 'So who's the other boot belong to?'

'Don't know. But whoever it is, he was wounded by Piketon's knife what we found outside with blood on it.

'Alexander!' I said aloud.

'The Greek?'

'Yes. He died in the infirmary yesterday from a knife would that turned septic. He died of Lockjaw. Is it possible he was at the cottage?'

'Are you sayin' Annie Eddington's husband was at the crime scene also, only for Annie to capture and collect the bounty on Erasmus Peck later, whom we know was also at Piketon's cottage?'

'It looks that way.'

'Hells' blood sar.'

'So, Annie knew of the diamond all along.'

'I don't believe she did,' I said. 'Otherwise she would not have questioned me so. I let her believe Peck's coat had valuable plans sewn into the lining.'

'Plans?'

'Long story, suffice to say she believed me. No ...' I contemplated a moment. 'No, Annie did not know of the diamond at that stage. Alexander had kept that information to himself. They were estranged after all, as she said.'

'Yet partners in crime.'

'Exactly. No honour amongst thieves there. Alexander must have confided to Annie about his involvement after he learnt of me pursuing her to Ballarat.'

Later in the office of Mr Warren Boyles, editor of the *Hobart Town Gazette*, at his residence. Elizabeth Street.

At week's end it was customary for Fabian and myself to have a meeting with Tasmania's governor, Henry Fox Young. The studious and devoted servant to Her Majesty Queen Victoria insisted on updates of law and order under his dominion. However this week, soon after Captain Maddox's audience with the governor, the governor and his wife travelled to the north of the island in his new role as head of the legislative council. This was in addition to his position as governor. Young cherished this role, now unrestrained by orders and harassment from Britain. The *Cessation of Transportation Act* had been passed in '53 and Van Diemen's Land was now to be known as Tasmania, to try and rid the colony of its dark reputation as a prison island. Now the governor travelled the countryside encouraging development and capably carrying out the work of his office. In his absence I was ordered to report to Mr Warren Boyles, editor of the *Hobart Town Gazette*, who was also under instruction from the authorities to publish the details of our latest investigations.

Editor Boyles lived in his modest abode at the rear of his *Gazette* offices in Elizabeth Street, where he also composited and printed his paper. On still days the lane behind Boyles's residence was permeated by smoke from the nearby blacksmith, while over his western border fruit flies molested the greengroceries of Henry Chung. It was late afternoon when I called, and the office closed, but the editor was expecting me.

'Caspian, Caspian,' his hand shot out in greeting and he hauled me through the back door. 'Good to see you lad.' And I knew he meant it. 'I can see it in your eyes, you are fair burdened with news and gossip. In you come. Sit. Sit.'

The kettle was pushed aside upon the stove and the cut glass decanter of Madeira wine appeared with two fine tall stem glasses. On the kitchen table was his notebook and a selection of lead-filled pencils ready to take notes.

Upper-middle-aged Mr Boyles had been a handsome man in his youth, but now he enjoyed the dignity and personable appearance of maturity. He is an intelligent man full of jocularity and wisdom, with a wit as sharp as ripe Stilton. It is always a pleasure to share his company. What he lacked in stature he made up in strength of character; like years-old Chateauneuf-du-Pape-Calcernier – aged in the bottle, full bodied and an absolute delight at the dinner table.

I started with the arrest of Mad Percy Hachette. 'Hachette was indeed a kidnapper,' I told the editor, who I now knew to be a good listener, rarely criticising without due reason. 'Although it was never planned, it was a spontaneous act. He saw Violet alone in the street outside the drapers where her older sister had gone to purchase cotton for their mother, and on the pretext of seeing his newborn puppies Hachette lured seven-year-old Violet Noble away. Hand in hand he led her along the creek where he was certain no one would see him. Fortunately for our investigation ten-year-old Walter and his younger brother Todd saw him. Once he had Violet at his cooperage he bound her and gagged her. His intention was to ransom Violet but the kidnap went terribly wrong.'

'That is so, so sad Caspian. I met Mr Noble once at a Town Hall meeting and I remember him speaking of his love for his daughters and expectations for their futures.'

'There is more. Percy Hachette had a fierce grievance against Noble.'

'Oh?'

'Yes. Billings spent hours in the public records searching through your Hobart Town Gazettes and discovered that Percy Hachette was bankrupted by Gilbert Noble who was at one time his neighbour.

Mr Boyles looked sagely a moment, rubbing his chin through his greying honey coloured beard. 'Yes, I seem to remember printing that.'

'Yes. Hachette was broke, he could not repay his debt to Noble, so Noble had Percy forced off his land. Percy was also married but his wife was committed to the lunatic asylum more than five years ago. That's why Percy took up as cooper at the asylum where he could be close to her, but she died some time ago.'

Mr Boyles shook his head slowly, silently taking notes.

'Billings interviewed Noble's neighbours and discovered that Noble thought Percy Hachette was a threat to his young daughters who played in the vicinity of their land boundaries. The debt was only an excuse to force the man off his land.'

'A threat? As in what? An unhealthy interest?'

'I believe so. Noble caught Percy apparently, watching the girls discreetly, while hidden in bushes. But this was never substantiated.'

'You said everything went terribly wrong. What happened?'

'Hachette tied Violet's gag too tightly and Violet suffocated.'

Warren Boyles listened with his mouth open, incredulous, his eyes moistened.

'This death was unintentional. Hachette hid Violet's body under floorboards of his cottage next to the cooperage, still bound and in a foetal position with her knees up to her chin. Weeks passed but the putrefaction of the body threatened to expose the cooper's crime, so late one night he disposed of the body in the River Derwent. The body was not weighted sufficiently and all it took was the ferrywoman's oar to disentangle the corpse from the tree roots in the river a few feet below.'

'Dear god, how terribly, terribly sad. And the court case?'

'He has pleaded guilty and confessed all I have told you. There will be a hearing and he will be sentenced tomorrow. The man is in solitary, as much for his own protection, as there are prisoners keen to tear his head from his shoulders.'

'I can imagine.'

'Yes. So justice will be swift. He will hang by the end of the week.'

The room grew chilly and Mr Boyles stooped over the modest fire stabbing the coals back to life with an iron poker made from a damaged whaler's harpoon. He tossed two more logs upon the blaze and when he was satisfied they were secure he resettled at the table and filled our glasses.

The editor and myself then sipped our Madeira respectfully; our thoughts of the poor wee lass's unfortunate and unnecessary death fogging our emotions. It was time to move on.

'So then,' Warren Boyles snapped from his own dark reverie, 'you solved the South Hobart Cottage murder ... ah ... the grave digger Edwin Piketon, I do believe.'

'Yes.' I consulted my own notes turning pages back to the front of my notebook. 'Edwin Piketon was murdered by Alexander Manis, a Greek man born to an English woman. Manis arrived in the colonies after the Crimea War ended. As he was Greek he assumed his mother's name of Eddington. Greece, you must understand, used Russia's war with Britain to try and further their own enterprises by occupying Ottoman's lands to the north. But it failed and effectively Greece was an enemy of Britain. I am of the opinion he was captured by the Turks at some stage and castrated.'

Boyles' face distorted into what I could only describe as a wince and I imagined the image of a man losing his testicles flashing before him. 'Castration,' he understood as a well read and educated man, 'is a common punishment by those barbarian Turks I have heard.'

'Indeed.'

'Alexander had a partner Annie. I do believe they were married although they were, I believe, estranged.'

'Because he was castrated?'

'I believe so.'

'Annie? You speak of the bounty hunter Annie Eddington I take it?'

'Yes. So Erasmus Peck, whom Mrs Eddington captured ...'

'She shot him did she not?'

'Defending herself,' I said rather too bluntly.

'She must be a piece of work, this Annie, to cut off a man's head and bag it for a bounty.'

'Yes. Well.' I was lost for words a moment. If only Warren knew the truth.

'But how did Erasmus Peck end up with the diamond if this Manis Greek fellow killed Piketon?'

'It was a rare turn of events that drew two separate, desperate men to Piketon's cottage that fateful morning.'

'A coincidence?'

'Yes. But I must say I was not surprised when I heard of all the talk of a rare and valuable diamond about the colony.'

I told the editor briefly about Ballarat and how I had to chase Annie Eddington and her husband back to Hobart Town once she knew of the diamond's existence and realised she had inadvertently buried it with the headless body.

'News travels fast in this small community,' the editor said. 'Especially news about treasure, it would seem.'

'Exactly. Erasmus Peck was the first at the cottage. The proof being boot prints in the muddy yard outside the kitchen window and the fact he had the diamond when Annie captured him.'

'But she didn't know about the diamond at this stage, right?'

'True. But more about that later. From what I can ascertain Erasmus Peck, who was not a man to be trifled with, tortured Piketon into submission. Under pain of death he capitulated and showed Peck the hidden diamond in its recess carved into a door. Knowing Piketon could not go to the authorities, Peck made his escape with the gem.'

'Leaving Piketon alive?'

'Exactly.'

'So how did he end up dead?'

'Thought you would never ask.' My attempt at humour was lost in all the serious contemplation. 'So, not long after, Piketon has another visitor.'

'The Greek.'

'The Greek Alexander Manis, yes. A neighbour spoke of a stranger in the area with olive skin, or a Mediterranean appearance. Manis was another determined and desperate criminal but at the cottage for a different reason.'

'Oh?'

'Yes, you see Manis was a habitual burglar. Certainly he worked the goldfields but he was also a thief. There were other cottages broken into that day and Manis happened to be in the area. Not realising Piketon was at home, Manis entered his cottage. Now I am of the opinion that Piketon thought Peck had returned and he attacked Manis with a knife. But Manis flies into fury and attacks Piketon with the flat iron sitting on the stovetop. Piketon has fallen onto the stove. Manis has panicked and fled and somehow the offending knife was dropped outside. Now Piketon was still alive, but unconscious. And in this state he was cooked alive.'

'Oh god! So Manis never knew about the diamond?'

'Exactly. He was simply in the wrong place at the wrong time. A petty thief.'

'That's why Annie Eddington knew nothing about the diamond at that time she buried Peck.'

'Yes.'

'And Manis?'

'He died recently. Lockjaw.'

'From the knife wound?'

'Yes.'

'And Edwin Piketon burnt alive. How awful.'

'Yes, the stink was horrendous.'

'So,' the editor contemplated, 'Alexander Manis, or Eddington, returned to the goldfields and when Annie met him back there after capturing the escapee One Ear Kearney and then Erasmus Peck, she was unaware that her husband, had been involved in a killing back in Hobart Town.'

'That's correct.'

'Then you track her down in the goldfields and start asking questions about Peck. Annie in turn makes her own enquiries and learns that the diamond, swallowed in haste, must be in Peck's body where she buried it in a shallow grave back at New Norfolk. Correct?'

'Uh-ha.'

'My god,' the editor whistled. 'You couldn't make this up in a work of fiction. Fascinating. The *Gazette*'s readers will love this.'

I finished my wine and looked at the editor's mantle clock. I was hungry and tired. I made to excuse myself.

'But the diamond Caspian,' Boyles asked me. 'Where is this valuable gemstone, the Salmon Princess?'

I stared at my wine glass a moment, feeling defeated. Finally, reluctantly, I told the editor. 'I fear it is lost Mr Boyles.'

'Lost? How?'

I explained in some detail, the exhumation of Erasmus Peck's headless body at New Norfolk by Annie.

'As I said Caspian, one could not create fiction with such turn of events.

'But,' I said, 'all is not lost. The docks are guarded and the highway to Launceston blockaded. 'We can but live in hope. I will meet with you again, sooner than later I hope, with positive news for your next edition of the *Gazette*.'

'I wish you well then.'

The Prisoners' Barracks. Late afternoon.

At the waterfront, the net around Sullivans Cove was tightening and I was confident we would catch Annie sooner than later. Out on the water, merchant ships, whalers, supply punts and barges, wherries and private yachts were all subject to search. Two Royal Navy vessels, HMS *Dolphin* and HMS *Admiral Benbow* conducted the searches on water, while about the docks soldiers from Anglesea Barracks conducted land searches. And the citizens were not happy with the disruption. Only marauding seagulls had their freedom, circling the ships and swooping for discarded scraps.

Not being certain when I would see Emma Rumball, my housekeeper, again and being in possession of one pheasant and two quail, I ordered one of the guards at the prison gate take the birds to the officers' cookhouse and have them dressed and cooked. The plan being to take enough home for my supper and let the guards and the cook do as they wished with the remainder.

The sun was low in the sky and heavy rain clouds threatened a prematurely darkening evening, while on my stroll home the docks grew miserably black. The key to Blue Whale Cottage's front door was where I left it, hidden under leaves next to the sundial. I unlocked the door, stepping into the darkness of my shuttered abode and was immediately accosted by a familiar odour, or I should say parfum. Although it was only dusk outside the kitchen was dark. I froze. A figure awaited me, seated at the kitchen table.

'Caspian, you're home at last.' I matched the familiar voice with the parfum. Lavender.

'Annie!'

I threw my parcels onto the table and floundered about feeling for my tinderbox. A lantern flame soon exposed the most wanted felon in Hobart Town.

'Jesus Christ Annie ... Mrs Eddington. What are you doing here?'

'Waiting for you,' she said softly. It was then I noticed a Tower pistol lying close at hand on the table before her.

'How did you get in?'

'Your doors might be firmly locked but there's no point if you leave the back window ajar.'

'Mrs Rumball,' I said annoyed.

'Mrs Rumball?' Annie said with a wry smirk. 'You like the married ladies then?'

'Emma Rumball is my housekeeper,' and I added as if I excusing myself. 'Four hours a day, three days a week only.'

'I see.'

Annie's voice sounded weaker than usual. Then I saw the blood.

'You are wounded.'

'I shredded my arm on a branch escaping from that mad dog constable you sent to skitch me.'

'Holly.' I remembered Holly chasing after Annie at New Norfolk.

'If that be her name. She's a wild one.'

I fetched a bottle of Geneva and some clean bandages that Mrs Rumball always kept in the scullery for such an occasion and dressed the wound after dousing it with gin. The injury was not too deep but she had lost some blood.

'Have you heard what happened to Alexander?'

'You have him in prison, yes?'

I suspected her feelings for the man were not as sentimental as most marriages, however I said tactfully, 'He ... he passed Annie.'

'Passed? Passed what?'

'Alexander is dead. I am so sorry.'

'No!' Annie did not seem all that surprised. 'I heard several shots. God, how many times did you shoot him?'

'We didn't. He was wounded by a slingshot.' I went on to explain what actually happened and how he died of lockjaw due to the untreated knife wound Piketon gave him. 'We took him prisoner but he died yesterday in the infirmary.' Annie's face did not betray remorse. 'Annie, you are wanted by the law. I am going to have to fetch the constables.'

She snatched up the pistol with the speed of a cornered rat, pointing the muzzle at my head and cocking the hammer. 'Not going to happen Caspian ... dearest.'

Dearest!

The small black circle of the pistol's bore suddenly looked terrifying.

'Ah Annie ... would you put the pistol down please.'

'Back away. Sit.' She twitched the barrel towards the chair at the furthest end of the table. 'Alexander dead!' The fact seemed to slowly register. 'Well that changes everything.'

'Changes what?'

'I came here to kidnap you in exchange for Alexander's release.'

'Well it is too late for that,' my mind raced. Maybe she did harbour sentiment for the castrated gorilla after all. What to do? I sat. Annie waved the pistol for me to keep my distance.

'You do not sound upset,' I said.

'I told you we were estranged.'

'He was castrated,' I said without thinking.

'How did you know that?'

'The coroner at the morgue told me.' I smartly changed the subject. 'Where is the diamond?' I asked, thinking maybe if she returned the diamond I could let Annie escape somehow. 'You are guilty of the illegal possession of the Salmon Princess, nothing else. Give me the diamond and I will see you have a safe passage free of Tasmania.'

'I told that fool to see a doctor, to have the wound seen to,' she replied, ignoring my offer. 'Stubborn man.'

'Wound? You mean his arm?'

'Yes. That man Piketon stabbed him in the arm.'

'Ah! I guessed as much.'

'You see Alexander paid Piketon a visit at his cottage. He knew the man had hidden the stolen diamond. But he never told me. I only found out about the diamond later. After I buried Erasmus Peck.'

I was not too certain I wanted to hear this. 'So are you telling me, Annie, that you were not in cahoots with Alexander trying to rob Piketon?'

'No. I was in the north of the island hunting One Ear Kearney.'

'I am pleased to hear that.'

'As you well know, I caught the killer, claimed the bounty money and joined Alexander at the goldfields.'

Then I remembered the robbery of the innkeeper's two hundred-guinea prize money at the Mistletoe Hotel.

'Annie, did you rob the Mistletoe Hotel in Melbourne?'

'What, that lecherous philanderer Charles Wright?'

'Yes.'

'No.'

Fair enough. He was a liar and a cheat. I swept that misdemeanour under the rug, although I knew her to be guilty of the theft.

'How did your husband know about Piketon anyhow?' I asked.

'Alexander met an old lag from Port Arthur on the goldfields. He shared his first dig with him. He told Alexander all about Piketon and the diamond. The two found a reasonable amount of gold. One nugget alone fetched four-hundred and fifteen guineas.'

'Lucky.'

'Very. But then when their plot dried up and there seemed no more gold this man disappeared in the middle of the night taking all the cash he and Alexander had hidden on their plot ... it was buried you see.'

'Who was this lag, ex Port Arthur you said?'

'A man called Dan Wheeler ...'

'Dan Wheeler?'

'Yes. You know him?'

'I do. And he died a most horrible death at Browns River.'

'Oh! I know nothing of that.' But Annie's face read otherwise. 'Alexander had a vile temper. He was like a dog with a bone. If someone crossed him, well, look out.'

'What was Alexander like with a sword?'

'If you mean was he a good swordsman then the answer is yes.' Annie thought a moment. 'Come to think of it he always wore a German sword at his side. Won it at cards in Queensland. But he misplaced it recently and would not say where.'

'I know where.'

'Oh!'

'It was discarded at a crime scene.' Now I was certain Alexander was Dan Wheeler's killer. 'Annie ... the Salmon Princess. I know you have it. You must hand it in and I will guarantee you safe passage.'

Before Annie had a chance to answer, the brass knocker on my front door reverberated throughout the cottage. Annie jumped to her feet with her arm outstretched aiming her pistol directly at my face.

'Expecting someone?' she hissed in a low voice.

'No.' I skulked to the window but the shutters were closed.

Another knock rang out then Emma Rumball's voice. 'Caspian. It is me, Emma.'

'Emma Rumball, my housemaid,' I whispered.

'So you do have a housemaid!'

'Only four hours, three days a week.'

'Yes, you said.'

Damn! Why do people begrudge me one of the small luxuries in life?

Annie signalled for me to open the door and be rid of the woman. Another knock. 'Caspian? Are you alright?'

Annie. 'Get rid of her. Now. Or I'll shoot both of you.' Annie alluded to a second pistol, a lady's pocket pistol under her skirts.

I opened the door enough to peer out. 'Emma! What are you doing here at this hour?'

Emma looked at me in expectation. My unsociable behaviour was most untoward. It was then that I noticed a carriage on the street and in the light of the carriage lamp, sitting on the driver's bench was no other than Captain Seabert

Philbrick. The man was grinning like a schoolboy who had just kissed his first girl.

'Captain,' I acknowledged awkwardly, not budging with the door ajar. It was becoming embarrassing for all of us.

'This is a courtesy visit Caspian. Seabert and I are to be married and you are the first to be told, as I will no longer be able to cook and clean for you.'

'M ... married. You! I mean you and the captain.'

'Yes Caspian. Don't look so shocked.'

'But so soon?'

'Youth is not on our side Caspian. We have both buried our loved ones and have been alone too long.'

'And you are to leave town?'

'Yes. Seabert has been promoted and we are being transferred to Port Dalrymple.'

'Oh dear Emma. My apologies I ... ah. Where are my manners? Congratulations.' Emma's head nodded this way and that attempting to pry over my shoulders. 'I would ask you both in for a celebratory drink but ... ah ...'

'You're busy entertaining. I knew it,' Emma's nose twitched as she caught the pleasant aroma of my cooked pheasant and suddenly seemed happy for me. 'I understand. And you do not want a couple of old fossils spoiling your dinner.'

Now I felt even more embarrassed. I winced, bunching up my lips and pinching my face. 'Sorry Emma, you know how it is.'

'Well now you have my news we'll be off. Good luck to you Caspian, it was a pleasure knowing you.'

I closed the door on my dedicated servant, my stomach knotted with awkwardness.

'Housekeeper eh?' Annie said stepping from the scullery.

'Yes. Do you have a problem with that?' I said curtly.

I looked at Annie and now noted for the first time since she surprised me sitting at my table how beautiful she looked. We had been intimate. Why was life so complicated? Annie uncocked the hammer on her pistol.

'This is crazy,' I said. 'I need a drink.'

I took up the half bottle of Geneva and poured two thick-bottomed glasses. An element of trust returned. Annie scooped up her glass and drank the contents in one experienced gulp. I did likewise when I caught Annie staring at my parcels on the table. One leg of my roasted half a pheasant protruded from the cloth sack. The other held cold boiled potatoes and bread. Annie suddenly looked distracted.

'Hungry?' I asked.

'Starving.'

Annie poured more gin and I untied the parcels of food. Suddenly the aromas assaulted our taste buds and we ate in silence.

'The Salmon Princess?' I asked after our fourth shot of Geneva over a tabletop of picked bones and breadcrumbs. Annie sat in silence. Staring at me through glassy gin fuelled eyes. She seemed distant.

'Annie,' I persisted. 'We cannot avoid the inevitable. The diamond? Where is it?'

She stood suddenly pushing back her chair so hard it fell over and I thought she was going for the pistol, when she rounded on me.

'No,' she said in her husky voice. 'We cannot avoid the inevitable.'

I stood as if to defend myself when Annie threw me hard against the wall, pinning me by the shoulders. Her face met mine and we kissed with the fiery passion of newly-weds, our pheasant-greased lips lubricated and wet. We stumbled up the stairs tripping on discarded garments. Tonight, I had all the time in the world but our passion was such that round one was finished in moments.

'Jesus, I've missed that,' Annie gasped rolling from her mount and onto her back.

'And me you, too,' I grunted blithely, misunderstanding her comment, beads of sweat stinging my eyes.

'I mean it,' she said. 'I miss the copulating.'

Copulating? Really?

'That was one of the most unromantic things I've ever heard,' I said, hurt.

'Oh lover boy. Caspian,' she teased. 'You can't tell me that was lovemaking.'

'I ... ah ...' I felt my manhood confronted.

'That was fornicating,' Annie said. 'End of story.'

'Fornicating huh?' I was so on the wrong side of the law right now and I simply did not care. 'I'll show you fornicating!'

I rolled on top of the siren, pinning her shoulders to the bed burying myself deep as she locked her heels behind my back and squealed in girlish ecstasy.

Copulate, fornicate, shagging, whatever Annie wanted to call it, we managed once more before lying exhausted on our backs in a sea of blueish light washing over our sweat glistened bodies from a full moon. We talked for what seemed hours. It must have been near eleven when I again dared broach the subject in hand.

'The Salmon Princess?'

Annie propped on one elbow and swept my fringe back off my forehead in a romantic gesture. 'It is sold Caspian.'

Her face was shadowed, ill-defined, silhouetted by the moonlight. Her eyes obscured for the moment. Did she lie?

'Sold!' I asked.

'Yes. I am meeting my buyer in the morning. Four thousand guineas.'

'F ... four thousand guineas!' I decided to humour Annie. 'But I have heard valuations at more than twice that figure.'

'True. But it is hardly a legitimate sale Caspian. I will live extremely comfortably on four thousand guineas.'

'I would have to agree. So, this fence ...'

'Fence?'

'Buyer. Who is he?'

'Or she?' Annie feigned a yawn. She was retreating back into her shell, clearly she had said more than she intended.

'It is a 'he' I would imagine,' I said, now looking Annie in the eye. 'And maybe an Indian business man who intends to make a large profit taking the gemstone back to its rightful owner in India.'

Annie was clearly taken aback by this comment. She changed the subject.

'So as I will have no charges to face, as I will not be in possession of this diamond, you will see that I am safely free to leave on the *Albatross*, will you not?'

So she is here to use me. The fox. 'The *Albatross*?' I asked.

'Yes. It's leaving tomorrow noon for Sydney.'

I knew *Albatross* to be a merchant ship keen to leave port, as were many vessels held up by Annie's actions.

'Annie. Why are you telling me this? You know I am a lawman.'

Annie leant over and kissed me once more, a slow passionate kiss.

'I need to clear the harbour without fuss. I need your help and I am offering you five hundred guineas to see me safely away.'

'You are bribing me!'

'In a nutshell. Yes.'

This was the moment I waited for. I allowed a suitable period of time pass as I contemplated five hundred guineas. 'And how pray tell is that going to happen?'

'I will sell the diamond in the morning. You will accompany me, watching from a distance. Then the moment the exchange has taken place, the moment I am safely away, you arrest the dealer, retrieve the diamond and be the town hero. We meet shortly thereafter and I pay you from the sale money. Then you clear my passage and I leave for Sydney.'

'Sounds fair enough to me,' I said, trusting I did not sound too obliging. Then added. 'I want to see the diamond ... the Salmon Princes.'

'It is hidden like I told you.'

'I still want to see it. How do I know you aren't fabricating this story to escape justice?' Annie was silent a long moment. 'Well?' I insisted.

Annie leant from the bed taking her brass powder flask from her hunter's belt. She shoved alongside me once more and twisted the cap free. A dusting of gunpowder sprinkled the bed as she tipped the rare gem into the cusp of her hand.

'There.'

I was stunned.

The Salmon Princess diamond lay before me. I never thought I would ever handle the prized gemstone. And it *was* truly the size of a quail egg. In the light of the moon its rare, exquisite salmon pinkness sparkled with the blue hue of the night. I would like to have seen the diamond in daylight.

'It is beautiful,' I whispered with reverence. 'Simply beautiful.' I made to pick it up but Annie clenched her fingers about the gemstone before slipping it back in the powder horn and recapping the flask.

Annie drew her face closer, running her tongue inside my ear. Heaven forbid the woman was insatiable. She slid the powder horn under my pillow before pressing herself hard against me once more. The coarse curls of her mons tickling, teasing. We made love, fornicating a third time. Exhausted, sated, I rolled onto my side.

'What time tomorrow?'

'What?' Annie's mind had been elsewhere.'

'What time is your rendezvous tomorrow?'

'Oh, nine o'clock of the morning.'

'Where?'

'In the cemetery near the hospital.'

I leant on one elbow and fixed Annie with a stare. 'You aren't lying to me, are you?'

'Caspian! How could you think that? No! You clear my passage and I pay you five hundred guineas. You get to be the hero arresting the fence and rescue the diamond to boot.'

'Fancy a drink?'

'What?'

'Fancy a drink. To celebrate like?'

'Yes. Let's drink to us, me and you. Partners.'

Partners all right. Partners in crime!

I felt my way down the narrow attic room stairs to the kitchen swamped in darkness and apprehension. Here I fetched the remaining Geneva and our two glasses from the sideboard. I then felt about in the dresser drawer where I hid the Tower pistol and Annie's pocket pistol, collecting in their place a set of iron hand-cuffs that I kept for such an occasion.

On my return I saw Annie's silhouetted figure sitting up in bed in anticipation of a dram before we slept. She looked shapely in the moonlight; she was truly a most liberated and seductive woman. I poured two gins, passing one to Annie while I stood at the bedside.

'Here's to us,' I saluted.

'Here's to us.'

We drank in one draft.

Then I struck fast. I cuffed her left wrist and snapped the link, twisting the key in the lock with skilled practice. I threw the key into a dark corner. Annie was caught totally off guard.

'What the!'

She raised her arm and mine raised with her. We were cuffed securely together. 'What have you done?' Any immediate thoughts of bondage – unorthodox fornicating – dissipated smartly as the realisation she had been duped occurred to her.

'Unlock this immediately!' she shouted.

'Sorry Annie, but you have slipped away in the middle of the night twice too often.'

'We had a deal.'

'Yes. And I intend to keep my end of the bargain.'

'But I have shown you the diamond. You promised to work with me on this. You ...'

'Sorry Annie. But I' am not taking any risks.'
'Bastard!'
'Maybe ... but ...'
'Bastard!'

Chapter Nine

Day nineteen

Sleeping soundly whilst handcuffed to another in a narrow bed is not an easy task. Neither of us slept well. Annie's attempts to seduce me at dawn in exchange for her release were resisted. I locked her in my bedroom to wash and dress in a suit of my own clothes – it would be best, I thought, if she masqueraded as a man – before allowing her downstairs where we breakfasted on cold pheasant, stale bread and hot tea. Annie was quick to note I had removed the keys from both the front and back doors and her pistols were nowhere to be seen.

'You must trust me Caspian. I have no desire to cheat you.'

'Your past record is not one of trust,' I answered.

'I understand. But all the same all I want is to be free of this island. I'm not a bad person Caspian.'

I could argue that. She was not a mindless killer, well not wanton murderer that is, but she was a thief no less. But I refused to be drawn into such a debate. Silence reigned. I sipped my hot tea uncaring I was slurping noisily; a habit of bachelorhood.

'So,' Annie broke the silence. 'What's the plan?'

Truth be known I had had plenty of time to think during the night. 'The plan?'

'Yes ... you do have a plan I take it.'

'Yes, well. What time does *Albatross* sail?' I asked.

'It's scheduled to depart at ten o'clock.'

'This morning?'

'Yes.'

'So the soldiers will be on board for a clearance an hour before departure. I will see you on board dressed the way you are, as you are to masquerade as a male passenger. I will do the talking. You will act as an acquaintance of the barracks administration ... ah ... a clerk maybe.'

My real plan, of course, was to arrest both Annie and Benjamin Raj the condom salesman and jewel fence, the moment the exchange took place in the cemetery. Unfortunately I had no choice but to do this alone. There was no way I could summon assistance without drawing attention to Annie. And my only companion was my double-barrelled Yale, loaded and hidden within the deep pockets of my frock coat.

We stepped from Blue Whale cottage at half the hour before nine o'clock. Annie played the role perfectly, dressed in a suit of my clothes, with her short hair poked under a felt topper. She carried a leather satchel, having transferred her meagre belongings in her carpetbag, excluding her pistols of course.

Now. My plan ...

Naturally I had no intention of taking Annie's bribe. However I would forge on with that notion, all the better to trap the minx. She would exchange the diamond for four thousand guineas in one hundred pound notes payable on the Bank of England. She would then leave the cemetery via the western gate and await me in the parlour of the Custom's House Hotel where I would personally escort her, as per my guarantee for her safe passage, on board *Albatross.*

That was the plan ... but ...

We arrived at the cemetery fifteen minutes early, having walked from my cottage along St Georges Terrace to Sandy Bay Road. Annie walked ahead one hundred yards, strolling with a manly gait, holding her satchel and armed with an old cane of mine. I watched her walk down Gladstone Street and as discussed, Annie took the narrow lane behind four neat stone cottages that backed onto the cemetery. At the lane I dissolved into bushes and as discreetly as possible, I watched Annie negotiate the tombstones towards Davey Street at the north of the cemetery. As expected this hour of the day, the graveyard was deserted, except for a yardman raking leaves into piles at various positions throughout the cemetery. Several of these piles smouldered away as the autumn leaves were being incinerated. Annie stopped at her pre-arranged meeting place. Any one observing her would be under the illusion she studied the inscriptions on various headstones. The yardman looked momentarily towards the *gentleman* in the top hat and suit, but soon lost interest.

There was no sign of Benjamin Raj. I flipped the lid on my silver turnip; ten minutes past the hour. Annie looked anxious, but it was difficult to see from where I was hiding eighty yards away. Artfully, I crept closer; confident my actions were masked by the smoke of a nearby fire. If Annie noticed she certainly showed no sign.

My watch now read twenty minutes past. I grew anxious.

Fearing the worst I was considering arresting Annie and securing the diamond, when the figure of a tall, dark-skinned man wearing an angrakha kurta tunic, a turban and brightly coloured sashes entered the cemetery from the hospital's entrance to the east. Benjamin Raj!

Annie was not lying after all.

Raj took a path parallel to Annie's, surveying the surroundings. I kept my head low. The yardman passed close by me teasing the nearest fire into life, but finally made his exit.

At first Raj was circumspect, after all he was not expecting Annie to be dressed as a man. But when he confirmed her identity and was satisfied they were alone he approached. I dared observe them as they exchanged a brief conversation. But Raj looked nervous, alert. His head pivoted this way and that. He was anxious to make the swap. I watched as Annie took the gunpowder flask from her pocket and tip the diamond into the palm of her hand. Raj relaxed a little. The rare gem had a hypnotic effect. He quickly inspected the diamond and placed it back in the flask. His hand slipped behind his tunic and he passed Annie a tight roll. Annie took a cursory look at the money but surprisingly she did not count it. The exchange took place. Their farewell greetings drifted to me across the silent graveyard and, as we had discussed, Annie made her exit towards the west gate.

Excellent.

All was going to plan.

The plan ...

As soon as I arrested Raj and delivered him to the watch house in nearby Macquarie Street, I would rendezvous with Annie at the Custom's House Hotel and take *her* into custody. This I was not looking forward to but, that is the life of the law enforcer.

I took a deep breath and waited.

Benjamin Raj walked in my direction.

This is all too easy, I thought, silently cranking back both hammers on my trusty double barrel Yale. I stepped from the bushes.

'Put your hands where I can see them Raj.'

The man was clearly taken by surprise. 'What is the meaning of this?'

'I am arresting you in the name of the Queen.' I flashed my brass badge pinned on the inside lapel of my coat.

'Mr Hunter isn't it? I met you at the Sailor's Rest.'

'Yes. Now put those hands where I can see them.'

'But ...'

'I will not ask a second time, Benjamin Raj,' I said in a low voice pointing the Yale directly at his chest. 'Now hand me that diamond thank you.'

'D ... Diamond. What diamond?'

'The Salmon Princess Raj. You know only too well what I mean.'

'Oh!' Raj slipped his hand into his tunic.

'Easy!' I warned. Raj extracted the powder flask. He unscrewed the cap and tipped the diamond into his hand. 'You mean this diamond.'

Everything happened so quickly.

'Here, catch.' And Raj threw the gunpowder flask into the fire at my side. The explosion was instant. I was thrown to the ground, both barrels of my pistol discharging. I heard a cry in shock or pain. I must have wounded the man but clearly not seriously, as Raj ran. I stumbled awkwardly to my feet, disorientated by the explosion. My ears were ringing and I felt faint. Immediately I heard angry yelling. It was the gardener. I turned towards the gate only to catch a fleeting glimpse of Raj escaping, chased by the exotic and colourful textiles of his flowing robe and sashes.

Angry with myself. Angry with Annie, I hurried to the Custom's House Hotel five minutes distant. Surprise, surprise. Annie was not in the parlour. She had not been seen there either; as Annie Eddington or as a gentleman in top hat and frock coat, albeit sporting a fine figure.

I had been duped. Shafted good and proper, as Holly would have said. I stepped from the hotel onto the docks. The harbour, the wharves, the cove was a scene of activity and commerce. There must have been two dozen ships within view and a thousand plus souls each with his or her own busy agenda. Annie could be anywhere. Raj could be anywhere. I had no choice but to report to the barracks and admit my defeat.

My story was received with some interest back at Campbell Street. Some interest, that is, from Jasper, Holly and Billings. They did not judge me for the fool I had been. Thankfully Captain Maddox was nowhere to be seen.

'I had no choice but to go it alone,' I reiterated to my colleagues.

'We understand Caspian sar,' Holly put a hand on my shoulder.

'Jesus Christ!' I blasphemed. Annie and a slippery Indian condom salesman had duped me.

At that moment Lincoln returned from the harbour. 'I hate to say this Caspian sar, but I just got word from the docks that Annie Eddington never booked a berth to sail on the *Albatross* for Sydney.'

'She would have used a different name.'

'No sar, no one of her description.'

'Why does that not surprise me?' I said sullenly.

'It gets better sar.'

'Oh?'

'The *Swift* sailed for New Zealand at ten o'clock.'

'The *Swift*?'

'Aye. She be a yacht an' she be chartered, private like. Chartered by a Mr Charles Wright.'

'Charles Wright?'

'That's wha' I said.'

'That's the publican of the Mistletoe Hotel in Mackenzie Street Melbourne.'

'So, what's that got to do with the price of eggs?' Holly frowned.

'It's a long story Hol, suffice to say I am certain Annie was on that yacht for New Zealand.' *Charles Wright,* I mulled over in my head. Cheeky minx, she used the publican's name and I gave her the suit and my best top hat disguise to pull it off. Damn.

'Then how did the *Swift* slip away so easily?' I wanted to know.

'The guards would have thought her a river craft sailing down river only.'

'Jesus!'

'Yes, Jesus.'

'That's the last we'll see of her then.'

'Aye.'

'Come then,' I spoke to the team. 'We must catch Benjamin Raj. The blockade is still in place and all ships must be cleared before leaving port. He must be desperate to leave and if we are smart enough we will thwart his plan.' I had an immediate thought. 'And I suspect I wounded the man.'

'Wounded 'im sar?'

'Yes, I will explain later.'

Three hours later. Prisoners' Barracks, Campbell Street.

Through no effort on my part I finally had Benjamin Raj where I wanted him. And it was Raj himself who fell into his own trap.

It eventuated that Benjamin Raj *was* wounded when my Yale accidentally discharged; a minor wound to the hip, as it happened. But Raj was terrified of infection, and rightly so. Unbeknown to the police department, Raj was acquainted with the Royal Navy surgeon on HMS *Admiral Benbow*, a navy frigate moored in the harbour. Apparently he had sold the surgeon, Lieutenant Gilchrist, a consignment of his new vulcanised rubber condoms, ostensibly to be handed out to the young officers on board. There is nothing worse than a pandemic of syphilis on board a navy vessel in this modern age. Now, Gilchrist, like so many other opportunists with rank on a Royal Navy ship, was not opposed to earning an extra guinea or two. So when Raj came to him for medical attention – a suspicious bullet wound no less – he obliged. For a small fee, you must understand.

But being a creature of spontaneity Raj saw an opportunity whilst on board the *Admiral Benbow*. You see, the surgeon dressed Raj's wound below decks in the surgeon's cabin. Now bandaged, Raj was left to his own devises to vacate the unmanned ship – only a skeleton crew remained on board as all available hands were searching for Annie Eddington.

Benjamin Raj now saw an opportunity, and took it. A dark-skinned, heavily-accented Indian fugitive, dressed garishly in traditional clothing, was always going to stand out amongst a tight community of Caucasians. So Raj, in his new role as fugitive, was not averse to rummaging through an officer's locker on his way to above decks. Unfortunately he chose the cabin of Lieutenant Richard Wildflower, who happened to be one of the few officers remaining on board this day. And when Wildflower chanced upon Raj mounting the companionway and dressed in the lieutenant's private civilian attire ... Well, he was incensed.

We, that is Holly, Jasper, Lincoln and I, finally caught up with Raj after his arrest, where he was locked in the watch house cells on Davey Street after being transferred there from the navy brig aboard *Admiral Benbow*

'Search him,' I ordered. Benjamin Raj looked a sorry sight. One eye was closed and black where he had cushioned a right hook from the angry Lieutenant Wildflower. However, Raj appeared to accept his fate, although the question of the whereabouts of the Salmon Princess was avoided the moment I broached the ever-important question.

'I hate to tell yer this Caspian sar,' Lincoln said. 'But it ain't in his pockets like.'

'Search him again.'

Raj remained at attention in his cell and did not resist my request.

'Nothin',' Jasper eventually muttered, frustrated at the futile search.

Holly pushed Jasper aside. 'Argh! Give me a go.'

After watching Holly pat the man's pockets in a thorough, yet failed search, I ordered the felon to disrobe.

'Remove your clothes Mr Raj, if you please.'

Raj feigned horror. 'My clothes? I have nothing to hide sir. I told you, the diamond was lost in my haste to escape you Mr Hunter. You must believe me. The jewel is lost. Dropped somewhere.'

'Not likely,' I said. 'Remove your clothes.'

'But Mr Hunter sir, I ...'

'The man said disrobe,' Holly grew more impatient.

She planted her boots firmly and hooked back the flap of her smock revealing her Tower pistol wedged behind the belt holding up her britches. Raj removed his angrakha kurta – having been forced to redress in his traditional clothes on capture. Jasper took the attire, along with silk sashes and his turban, searching its creases once more. Nothing. Holly tugged at his under garment, which was removed without incident. Nothing.

'Britches,' I said of his traditional churidar.

'Britches?' Raj looked coy.

'Aye,' Holly stood firm, 'Britches. Remove yer britches.'

It was difficult to tell whether Raj was incensed or intimidated. He untied the churidar and the loose-fitting britches dropped to the flagstones. Jasper and Holly searched the abandoned garment. Nothing. I stared at Raj, naked as the day he was born except for his Indian cloth napkin protecting his private parts.

'Remove the napkin,' I insisted.

'I ... I ... ah ... Mr Hunter, this is too much.' Raj's face was one of sheer horror and humiliation. He snapped his head to Holly.

'Holly,' I said. 'Leave us be if you please.'

'Sar?'

'Leave us be.'

'But Caspian sar I ...'

'Holly. Kindly allow Mr Raj some modesty. Now will you leave ... please.'

Holly was not happy. She took her police work seriously, but as much as she thought she was one of the lads, she was still a woman. Holly grumbled and sauntered away. 'I'll be just outside if'n yer want me Caspian sar,' she said in a final bid.

'Mr Raj, I will not ask you again. Either remove your napkin yourself or these gentleman will do it for you.'

I must concede at this stage I was anxious. If the Salmon Princess was not concealed within the folds of his napkin I had only one remaining place to inspect, and I had disturbing visions of the tall Indian condom salesman struggling as we forced him to hold his ankles. But the man's expression was now one of surrender. Deftly he slipped the corner of the napkin tucked at his hip, careful to lift the cloth over his wounded hip. The cotton shroud unfolded and dropped about his ankles.

We all gasped.

'Goodness!' I grinned.

A grin of both surprise and what I suspected was finally success. I say *suspected* of success for the reason I still had no clear vision of the diamond. But what we all stared at in shocked admiration, admiration for the sheer ingenuity of the act, was the man's generous John Thomas cosy within one of Benjamin Raj's vulcanised condom's. It was tied securely at the base of Raj's manhood and weighted at the enclosed end by an anomaly the size of a quail egg.

We lawmen stood speechless a moment. 'Well well,' I finally said.

'Jesus Christ!' Holly gasped from the corridor, where the cell door remained ajar.

I was naturally elated and could not wait to dictate the incredible turn of events to Mr Warren Boyles the *Hobart Town Gazette* editor. But despite our success there would be no respite this day. Captain Maddox had requested we meet at the office … immediately.

Moments after our success with Benjamin Raj a guard was sent to the cells to fetch us. We were informed the prison superintendent, Mr Simeon Mead, wanted to see us immediately in the administration office. As for Captain Bradley Maddox, that man and myself would never see eye to eye.

Maddox hated my very existence and that was the end of it. For my part I did not so much hate the man, but I did wish him ill somehow. I was only human after all, and especially after the way he treated me.

My chance came shortly after I arrived at the prison for our appointment with the prison superintendent. Maddox scowled at my arrival in the cramped office, rolling his eyes contemptuously in my direction. He said nothing as he sat alone, ignorant of our victory.

And for the moment I decided to keep it that way.

Once all were present the captain bounced to his feet and ordered us follow. Serious business was a foot by all measures. Maddox lead the way down the stairs, I was last out the door and noted a drop in temperature. Rain was in the air, maybe even snow on the mountain.

Maddox paused, looking at the sky before ordering Holly, 'Fetch my coat from the office.'

Holly rolled her eyes and made to return upstairs when I had a spontaneous thought.

'I'll fetch it,' I said.

After all I was the last out the door. I hurried back to Maddox's desk where his swallowtail coat hung neatly on an iron hook, thought of the repercussions of what I was about to do, dissolved all doubts and did my business. Catching up with the others in the courtyard I passed the coat to Holly as we followed our stalwart leader across the flagstones. He snatched the garment throwing it over his shoulders and hurried to be at his master's side.

To my right a figure caught my attention on the balcony of the superintendent's residence ... Elizabeth Mead.

I sighed heavily. With all the activity in my life of late I had endeavoured to put the question of my apparent fatherhood aside. Now here she was, watching my progress as I crossed the flagstones of the prison yard, *off to meet daddy*; another man I did not see eye to eye with.

And she blew me a kiss.

Superintendent Simeon Mead waited at the entrance to the officers' kitchen. He cupped his hands behind his back while he puffed at his florin Havana like it was a farthing cheroot. Wearing a tweed swallowtail coat and pipe stack top hat he greeted us with a formal frown. Instantly a brief break in the clouds streaked midday sun down upon us, which being low in the winter sky spot lit Mead with a bright light. With this temporary sun backlighting the superintendent, along with the thick cigar smoke swirling about him, reminded me of an actor playing a scene in an Edgar Allan Poe stage play.

'Captain Maddox,' Mead nodded civilly to the captain.

'Sir,' Maddox acknowledged his superior and Mead cast an eye over Lincoln, Billings and Jasper.

'Gentlemen,' he addressed the crew before singling out Holly. 'Miss Villan.' There was a notable pause. 'Hunter,' he acknowledged begrudgingly.

'Mr Mead,' I reciprocated, holding the man's eye a moment. *How much did he know about his daughter Elizabeth and myself?*

We followed Mead into the officers' kitchen. There were only two windows, both well above head height and housed in stone walls rendered with plaster painted with white wash. At least a log fire warmed the mood.

Captain Bradley Maddox stood at the superintendent's side with a confident smirk. The smirk of a conspirator. A subtle smirk I felt like swiping with a hard slap. Jasper, Holly, Lincoln and Billings shuffled into line next to me.

'Mr Winter returns to duty on the morrow,' Mead said matter-of-factly. This was good news. Good news indeed, and met with delighted murmurs.

'Jolly good sir,' Billings was the first to speak. 'May we ask why he was off duty sir? Was he poorly?'

Simeon Mead pushed out his chest, his signature of authority, and chose his words carefully. 'It appears your colleague Mr Winter has been living a lie.'

'A lie sir?'

'Yes. You see Mr Winter's wife, Sally Winter has been residing at Parramatta the past nine years.'

'Parramatta?'

'Nine years!'

'Yes. She deserted Fabian to join the Irish order of Catholic nuns, the Sisters of Charity, who started their order in New South Wales back in '38. Ostensibly to administer to women convicts in the Female Factory in Parramatta.'

I was incredulous. 'Nine years ago?'

'Yes. Then recently Fabian received word to say Sally had died at the convent. Heart failure apparently.'

'But she was not that old.'

'Thirty years of age, he said. Mr Winter confided in me that he felt ashamed. He felt guilty, that he had let her down. And ashamed that he had never acknowledged the fact to his peers ... namely you lot.'

'So all this time he has lived a lie.'

'Yes, it appears so. Technically he was not married like he said: the faithful wife waiting patiently at home and all that rubbish.'

Hence the actions of a philanderer, I thought to myself.

'Well that answers the question, why we never met the woman ... his wife that is.' Billing said.

'But all is well,' Mead continued. 'Mr Winter returns on the morrow. It was he who instigated this meeting, to tell you all, like.' Mead tossed his spent cigar into the fire. 'He resumes duties at eight, ante meridiem. Now, I expect you all have work to do so ...'

'While we are about it,' Maddox interrupted, 'would you kindly explain your relationship with the fugitive Annie Eddington, Hunter.' It appeared he had been waiting for his moment and this meeting was perfect timing. 'You followed the woman to the goldfields at great expense to the crown, only to let the woman slip through your fingers.' Maddox turned to the superintendent. 'I have reason to believe Hunter here has been having a ... a relationship with the woman.'

'A relationship?' Mead's mouth dropped open. I sensed the man had an immediate vision of his own daughter scantily clad in my lustful embrace.

'Yes superintendent,' Maddox shared a dark smile with the room. 'And now she appears to have escaped, again.'

'Is this true Hunter?' Mead asked.

'Explain your relationship with this criminal to the superintendent,' Maddox spat venom.

'My private life is none of your concern, captain,' I said angrily.

'Then it is true,' Mead face darkened. 'You have had a liaison with this known criminal?'

'Sleeping with the enemy I think it is called.'

'Damn you Maddox,' I stepped forward but Billings and Lincoln stepped ahead, restraining me before I assaulted the captain.

'Mr Hunter,' Mead shouted. 'Restrain yourself sir.'

I stepped back and took a deep breath. This man Maddox, if he could be called a man at all, was not worth losing my position over. And Mead knew only too well that I had spent days in the lockup on another occasion for an alleged indiscretion that once again I did not commit.

But I had the ace up my sleeve. Or I should say Billings had the ace in the palm of his hand. As we had previously schemed, Billings was waiting for this moment also. It was time. He turned for instruction and I gave him the nod.

'My time with Annie Eddington was clandestine,' I told the superintendent. 'Covert Mr Mead. I liaised with her to gain her confidence, to extract from her the information that has led to yet another very successful assignment on the part of my colleagues here; these true honest hard working and dedicated law men.'

Holly cleared her throat.

'And a law *woman*. Yes Mr Mead may I present the Salmon Princess.'

Billing stepped forward and opened his hand to reveal the huge pink diamond. Mead gasped. Maddox looked quite ill. Even in the dull afternoon light, the flames of the fire and a lone lantern, the diamond's interior sparkled, white and pink flashes of fluorescent fire. It looked stunning.

'I am speechless Hunter,' Mead conceded. 'Speechless.'

'Secured by myself and my colleagues,' I went on to rub salt into Maddox's wound. 'No thanks to Captain Maddox there.'

'Y ... you did not tell me Hunter,' Maddox started. 'You had a duty to tell me ... you ... what were your intentions?' The captain grew instantly defensive. 'That stone is priceless, it should have been handed over the moment you took possession of it.'

'It is not priceless Maddox,' I said, omitting the man's rank. 'It could be bought for around eight to ten thousand guineas I have been informed.'

Mead reached out and took the stone from Billings who, quite frankly, was glad to be free of it. The superintendent held it a moment, savouring the honour, his voice reverent.

'Guard,' he called for soldiers. Three prison guards immediately surrounded him. 'Take this to my residence and wait for me in my parlour. Mrs Frances will accommodate you,' he said of his housekeeper. 'And guard it with your life. I will be there shortly.'

Maddox was a dog with a bone. A drowning man clutching at straws. If we were not arch-enemies before we were now. 'I would like you to explain why the secrecy. Why did you take it upon yourself to hide the diamond from me Hunter? I suspect mischief afoot.'

'You scoundrel. *You* accuse *me* of dishonesty.' It was time for the coup de grâce. '*You* of all people accuse *me* of deceit. At least I am free from corruption.'

'What are you implying?' Maddox screeched. 'How dare you!'

'Oh!'

'Corruption?' Superintendent Mead coughed. 'That is a serious allegation Mr Hunter. Explain yourself.'

'Ask Captain Maddox to explain himself sir, explain why he has blood-stained Bank of England pound notes in his pocket.'

Maddox jaw dropped to his chest. The man was incredulous.

'Why you scoundrel,' he roared. 'You insolent villain. I should have you whipped.'

'Why, I can see the evidence from here,' I shot a winning smile and pointed to the bare corner of a quid note poking from the captain's pocket.

'Captain,' Superintendent Mead alluded also to the telling triangle of the corner of a banknote. Maddox gasped. If it were not so serious I could have laughed out loud. He deftly slipped the two one pound notes from his pocket like they had been in the possession of a leper.

'I ... I ... I ... know nothing about these.' He looked to the superintendent who clearly had doubts about the captain's credibility. 'I've never see them before.' And then the anger returned and he spun to face me. 'I have been framed Mr Mead, set up.'

'They *are* blood stained are they not? Mead noted. 'You'll need to explain yourself captain. This does not look good for you sir.'

'Hunter put them there!' Maddox screamed.

'I beg your pardon Captain Maddox,' I feigned horror. 'How dare you try and pass the blame of your nefarious activities onto me.'

'Nefarious!'

'Yes nefarious. How dare you I say.'

'How did you know they were there Mr Hunter?' Mead asked me.

'I only noted them the moment Holly fetched the captain's coat from the office.' Holly fetched me a sly wink.

'Someone is trying to falsely incriminate me,' Maddox had reddened from anger not guilt, but it only helped hang the man as far as I was concerned.

'Then I declare this meeting concluded,' the prison superintendent said, 'until we get to the bottom of this matter.'

'That was a rotten trick Caspian sar,' Holly grinned at me as we ascended back to our office. 'A rotten trick indeed. But a good'en.'

'Thank you Holly. At least it will keep the mongrel on his toes awhile.'

'What if'n 'e gets arrested sar? Then what?'

'Oh it's flimsy evidence Holly. And it would never stick in the courtroom of course, as far as the law was concerned anyone could have planted those notes in the man's pocket. But mud sticks as they say.'

And the mud on Captain Bradley Maddox was thick.

Chapter Ten

Day twenty

It was to be a triple hanging in the open before the prisoners. Mead was desperate to set an example. The temporary gallows were erected at the southern end of the prisoners' barracks yard near the solitary cells. The condemned men would hang facing a brick wall south. Over a hundred convicts, men on hard labour and in irons, were made to attend. *A deterrent,* the superintendent demanded. The prisoners were led in a procession between four javelin-men with halberds on their shoulders and the sheriff, gaol officials and the clergy representing each man's faith. Prayers continued as the prisoners climbed the steps to the gallows, with the prisoners responding to prayers in the same low tone as the religious incantations.

Solomon Blay the executioner stood on the scaffold waiting. He was one hangman who refused to mask his face to the condemned or the witnesses. He saw each hanging as his duty and fiercely protected his reputation. He caught my eye amongst the witnesses below – Fabian included – and eyeballed me with cold dark eyes, but did not acknowledge my existence.

I have witnessed many executions and will never be used to it. Each prisoner kissed his rope before it was pulled over his head and tightened about the neck. Solomon Blay pinioned each prisoner behind his back by the wrists. Cotton hoods were placed over each prisoner's head.

More prayers were read aloud.

The hangman pulled hard on the lever.

The trapdoor dropped.

The condemned fell.

Two men died instantly as their vertebra shattered when their necks snapped. But cooper Percy Hachette heaved, kicking his feet violently, choking to death, as his rope was strangling him and had not taken his life outright. To me it seemed apparent that Solomon Blay had deliberately given Hachette a short rope. This meant he would drop only a short distance causing him to choke rather than die instantly. The chord binding Hachette's wrists came loose and the man grabbed at the noose about his neck. Solomon Bray was indifferent. He tugged at the rope. The prisoner held the noose. Blay booted his hands away from the rope. Each time the condemned man tried to grab the noose the hangman kicked his hands free. This continued for several long minutes. The sight was pathetic. Blay held the rope with one hand and placed a foot onto the dying man's shoulders weighting him further until slowly the wretched prisoner quivered, twitched and choked to death. It was a blundered execution. Horrific.

We all left in silence.

Hachette's body, as was usual with such criminals, was taken away to be atomised; that is, to be dissected and studied. A plaster death mask was made of his head and a phrenologist inspected his brain. Finally Mad Percy Hachette's remains were dumped into an unmarked grave in unconsecrated grounds and Solomon Blay would get to keep his clothes for resale, a perk of the employment.

There is nothing like a good hanging to give an honest lawman a thirst. We met at Waterman's Dock – Fabian, Jasper, Billings, Holly and Lantern Jaw Lincoln. It was early evening. However Hobart Town's waterfront was vibrant. The port was extra busy and the inns doing a roaring trade with the blockade lifted. Life was good. Maddox had left town in shame and Fabian apologised for his deceit, for which none of us held a grudge. We were a team once more, and god help anyone who would come between us. And as a team we all agreed on Bonnie Nettle's Sailor's Rest. Tonight she was presenting a new troupe of musicians. A four-piece Irish quartet with a fiddler, a drummer playing a skin tray called a bodhran, one on cymbals and a feisty red-headed singer called Maggie. The troupe called themselves the Dead Maggies. We strolled towards the music spilling out onto the street when an unwelcome sight offended my eye. The self-appointed Reverend Ashley Andrus Alcock was perched on a barrel preaching his one-sided views on religion.

'And the Lord said ...' I heard the man rant.

'Did not Bonnie warn that mongrel about preaching outside her inn?' Holly muttered in disgust.

'Aye,' Fabian scowled. 'That she did Hol.'

I stepped away from my colleagues into the shadows and found two suitable lags with enough rum under their belt to take up my offer. I slipped them a pound note each – blood money one could say, as murdered Dan Wheeler's blood-stained each note I had pocketed at the Sea o' Graves.

'Ahoy there,' Fabian whistled to me. 'Are yer joinin' us or not?' he called out as my peers were about to step into the Sailor's Rest.

'Absolutely,' I said, grinning away. 'Just one moment, watch this.'

As my colleagues watched on, the two ruffians, each a pound richer, strolled over to the gospel menace, hooked an arm each, hoisted him from his perch and, dragging him kicking and screaming across the dock, they heaved him into the dark reaches of a freezing harbour.

Ah yes, it would end as it started. Unpleasantly.

Epilogue

On his return to Hobart Town I spoke with the governor, Henry Fox Young, regarding the issuing of a conditional pardon for Martin Cash. He did not hesitate.

'It would be best he left this island anyway Caspian,' he said. 'After that dreadful botched hanging of Hachette last week I think Solomon Blay needs to concentrate on his craft and not be interrupted by harbouring hatred for enemies like Cash. He can sail to New Zealand on a conditional pardon. But he is not to return to England.'

At the same meeting the governor signed a warrant for the arrest of Port Arthur warder Carvel Dwight for aiding and abetting Erasmus Peck's escape from the penal settlement and in conspiracy to steal the Salmon Princess. It was Dwight, you must understand, who saw Peck transferred to the abattoir where he managed his escape under the cartload of sheep carcasses. I took great pleasure in personally arresting the man at Port Arthur where he was taken back to Hobart Town in irons. Oh, to hear the jeers and abuse from the old lags when they heard the news, and I could not help it but to sympathise with the man, for his time in servitude would be fraught with danger from prisoners bent on revenge for the unforgiving ex-warder.

On the same visit to Tasman Peninsula I made my peace with Lieutenant Sedgwick Fribbens, commander at the Norfolk Station and convict railway. He in turn had made his peace with Petula, his estranged wife, who had sent him a letter. She now resided with her brother in Moreton Bay in Queensland. The lieutenant and I compromised; we apologised to each other and agreed to let bygones be bygones. He dropped any charges against me as he certainly did not wish for more negative publicity than he already had. We dined together on this last visit – while Dwight sat in the lockup – and this meeting gave the man some face in the eyes of his colleagues at the station. *All's well that ends well,* as my dear old mother would say.

The only other noose about my neck was fatherhood. I had a son. One part of me thought: *well lad, you are over thirty and it is about time you settled down. A wife and child, how difficult could that really be? Return home after a tough day chasing villains to a cosy cottage and a hot meal and the embrace of a loving woman.*

Argh!

It frightened me. I think the other part of me was right. There are a few more voyages in you yet old boy. I had a vision of Elizabeth blowing me a kiss from her father's balcony. There is no way to sweep this situation under the mat. My mind fogged, when …

'Caspian dearest, there you are. I've been looking all over for you.'

'Elizabeth! What a surprise.' Notice I did not say, *What a nice surprise?*

I should remind the reader here that Miss Mead had a narrow escape from death two years past. Drawing as little attention to themselves as possible, a community of Chinamen had settled north of Launceston at a place called Brandy Creek, where gold had been discovered. However it was not enough to start a gold rush. With much of the precious ore being deep underground, it proved difficult to extract.

Prior to Brandy Creek the only Chinamen I had had experience with were Chinese sailors who settled in Limehouse in East London, where for fifty years their community had grown and was now known as Chinatown. Their race was one of colour, both in appearance and behaviour. Most wore their long hair in a queue, or a pigtail as we call them, with circular caps on their heads usually made of silk. They wore a double-breasted coat to the waist fastened down the chest and belly by wooden buttons, like pegs. The coat sleeves were loose to the wrist and they all wore what I would call loose pantaloons, with slippers on their feet.

This community were all men, having left their families back in China while they hopefully made their fortunes. And men away from home craved the company of women and in particular Caucasian women. Their other vice was opium and an entrepreneur standover man, a vicious Triad named Chung Fang, took advantage of the situation.

Early one afternoon in Hobart Town, in broad daylight, Elizabeth Mead was at the wrong place at the wrong time. She was kidnapped and smuggled to Brandy Creek where she was coerced into a situation involving laudanum and then smoking opium and finally she was forced to lie with the Chinese miners.

Now as difficult as this is to believe, I was suspect number one when Elizabeth disappeared without a trace. Superintendent Mead was bent of revenge after catching me in a compromising position with his precious daughter, and in his own home. I was arrested and imprisoned at the prisoners' barracks. But I escaped and with the help of Fabian we tracked Elizabeth to Brandy Creek, finally saving her life. That adventure alone is another chronicle in my amazing life, suffice to say my reward was freedom and a begrudging nod from the superintendent.

Shamed at what happened, Elizabeth sailed for England and became nothing but a memory until ...

'Elizabeth! What a surprise.' I sensed trouble and had difficulty hiding my thoughts. She hurried to me, standing before me in the centre of the prison courtyard. She took both my hands in hers to the surprise of the guards. 'I've been looking all over for you dearest. I have not seen you this past two weeks.'

'I have been extremely busy Elizabeth. I have been to the goldfields.'

'Yes, Daddy told me. But you have been back some time now and ...'

'Look Elizabeth,' I said rather curtly. 'What do you want?'

'Want? Oh Caspian, you don't know my dearest?'

Dearest!

I ground my teeth.

'Elizabeth, it is late,' I said, clearly unenthusiastic about our meeting and attempting to shake my hands free. 'I was just on my way home.'

She held my hands firmly. 'Then I shall accompany you.'

'Accompany me! Ah ... no.'

'No!'

'No Elizabeth. I wish to have an early night. Alone.'

'Oh ... then I must ask, have you made up your mind Caspian?'

'Made up my mind? About what?'

'About asking Daddy for my hand in marriage.'

Now I managed to shake my hands free. 'What on earth are you talking about?'

Elizabeth's chalk white face plunged into despair. Her blue eyes welled with tears. 'But you said ... you promised ...'

'I did nothing of the sort.'

'But we have a child,' she wailed.

Now this did capture the guard's attention.

Elizabeth looked to her gathering audience; mainly three guards, Sergeant Clincher the gatekeeper and a washer-woman who wandered into the yard keen to see what was afoot.

'We have a wee boy,' Elizabeth now yelled for all to hear. 'And his name is Caspian!'

I heard the washerwoman suck in a lungful of air and shot her a scowl before she hurried away; best be quick while the gossip's fresh.

'Daddy will sue you for breach of promise.'

Now I was angry. This was a threat. I took a deep breath in, to calm myself, to stop saying something I would regret, and especially in front of witnesses.

'Elizabeth,' I said calmly, quietly. 'I have not even met this wee boy.'

'Of course, how silly of me.' Elizabeth's attitude had made a complete turn-a-round. 'Come.'

She took my hand and started for the superintendent's house.

'Where are we going?'

'Mirabelle the wet nurse has little Caspian upstairs. Come, you must meet your son.' I held back. 'If you are concerned about Daddy he is at the Royal Society meeting. He will not return home before nine.'

I had no choice. I felt cornered. Trapped. Yet I had a commitment. I followed Elizabeth through the iron gate leading through the rose garden to the superintendent's front door and felt as vulnerable and exposed as the rose bushes; bare and thorny from their winter pruning. I had been shot at, attacked, vilified, abused and survived with flying colours. But now I was to meet Caspian the younger. I was terrified.

I had not entered this residence, on prison grounds, since I was invited inside the first time with Elizabeth two years since. Not much had changed. Elizabeth hitched her skirts and hurried up the wide staircase to the first floor. I followed her to her bedroom at the rear of the house. She looked to me before entering, her own expression one of trepidation. Placing a finger to her lips for silence she motioned for me to wait in the passage a moment before disappearing inside. Seconds later the wet nurse, a plain-looking woman in her late twenties I imagined, with large rounded breasts, passed me in the doorway. She stopped briefly and looked me up and down before hurrying away. She said nothing.

'Come on then,' Elizabeth said in a loud whisper. 'In you come dearest.'

I trod carefully, walking to a large barrel crib on rockers. I could hear the wee lad blowing bubbles as he lay waiting to meet his daddy. Stealthily I peered into the cot.

Jesus!

My mouth dropped open.

Jesus Christ!

'Isn't he the cutest little boy ever?' Elizabeth said, with both hands clasped before her mouth, now curled in a huge smile.

I was speechless. I mean ... I was truly speechless. Words would not form within me. Little Caspian, a handsome baby boy who by all accounts was a healthy thirteen months old, had black silky strait hair, purplish-black sloe eyes and enough darkening of the skin to indicate to me that this child was a half-caste Chinese. For all I knew he could be a product of the infamous Triad Chung Fang himself. Little Caspian looked up at me giggling and kicking his legs before blowing me another mouthful of bubbles.

Elizabeth was shocked at my reaction. 'Well?'

'Well what?'

'Well what do you think of your little boy? Isn't he the most adorable little thing ever?'

'Oh he is adorable, a winsome wee boy if I ever saw one.'

'Here, I'll pick him up for you so you can have a cuddle.'

'No!'

Elizabeth froze with shock.

'I mean ... no Elizabeth. Leave him be. He's happy where he is.'

'But would you not like to hold your son?'

'Elizabeth ... I ...'

'Here.' She leant into the cot.

'Leave him Elizabeth.'

'But why?'

'Elizabeth, that is not my child.'

I stepped back, floundering in mixed emotions.

'What a terrible thing to say. Caspian you and I ... we ...'

'We did not make that child Elizabeth. Look at him. He is distinctly the product of a liaison between you and ...'

'How dare you.'

I wanted to say the baby looked so oriental he may as well of had a dragon tattooed on his forehead. But it was then I realised Elizabeth was living in denial. Drugged, stupefied on opium while captive that short time at Brandy Creek, she had been violated.

Without warning, the bedroom door opened and in walked Superintendent Simeon Mead. The wet nurse followed.

'Mr Mead,' I said feeling suddenly more awkward. 'I ... Elizabeth invited me to see the child. Her child.'

'Your child,' Elizabeth said angrily.

The superintendent stood silently in the doorway. He looked forlorn and exhausted.

'I will be leaving immediately sir.' I made for the doorway but the large man did not budge. He held his position while the wet nurse attended to the baby.

'Sit Caspian,' Mead said in deep yet soft voice.

'Sit?'

'Yes, sit.'

Keeping an eye on the superintendent I backed into a chair. Meanwhile the wet nurse plucked little Caspian from the cot and, at her father's bidding, Elizabeth left the room. The wet nurse followed. Mead sat on the end of Elizabeth's bed.

'Look I am sorry sir,' I blabbed. 'Elizabeth told me you were at a meeting and she really wanted me to see the baby and ...'

'Look Hunter, Caspian,' Mead cut in. 'Any fool can see that child is not yours. Clearly he is a Chinaman's bastard.' Well that was a good start I thought, all things considered. 'And I think you are clever enough to understand that Elizabeth is a little unstable.'

I nodded sagely.

'Truth is she returned from London with the child. I had not a clue. There was no mention in her letters. Now I must endure the embarrassment, the gossip, the stares. It has not been easy since her mother died. God only knows I have tried. Now this.' Simeon Mead stood and walked to the window looking out to Melville Street at the rear of the prison. 'She is a good lass all the same. Do you agree?'

I could hardly say otherwise. 'Y-yes. Yes indeed sir.'

'And I am convinced she will make a fine wife for some lucky man.'

'Yes sir, I have no doubt.'

'So what do you say?'

'Pardon?'

'You Mr Hunter. I would be honoured to have you for a son-in-law.'

'No! I mean no sir, I am not your man.'

'I will see you promoted and that your remuneration is quadrupled.'

'Quad ... quadrupled. I ... sorry sir I cannot.'

'Jesus Christ man,' he twisted from the view out the window to stare me down. 'Why not?'

'I ... I ah ... I am betrothed sir,' I floundered. 'To a woman.'

'A woman.'

'Yes sir. A woman back in Birmingham.'

'I had no idea. Why have I not heard of this before?'

'Well as you know sir my contract is for five years.' This much was true. 'And I plan to return to England in two-and-a-half-years' time,' I lied, 'to marry her ... this woman.'

'Oh. And what is this woman's name?'

'Mary.'

'Mary.

'Yes sir. Mary.'

'Mary who?'

Now I really floundered. He did not believe a word I said. 'Mary Smith.'

I whipped my fob watch from my pocket and flipped open the lid.

'Goodness gracious me sir, it's that time already. If you will excuse me Mr Mead I must be off.'

And without a further moment wasted, I took leave, scurried down the stairs and hurried back through the guard line of thorny rose bushes.

I never looked back.

And my relationship with the superintendent would remain unchanged.

The End

Compared to most colonised countries like the United States, Tasmania's history is relatively young. Tasmania celebrated its bi-centennial less than twenty years ago. But in that *short* time some fascinating stories have arisen.

And whilst Caspian Hunter is a man of fiction, there are real characters from Van Diemen's Land woven into the fabric of this yarn. Real people who stand alone, forced to deal with extraordinary difficulties in their lifetimes.

Characters such as Solomon Blay the hangman and Martin Cash the bushranger.

Martin Cash was one of Van Diemen's Lands most complex bushrangers. Born in 1810 in the town of Enniscorthy, County Wexford, Ireland, he was overindulged by extravagant parents who had inherited wealth. In his autobiography Cash writes poorly of his father who was an indolent spendthrift who neglected his two sons' upbringing, whilst spoilt by his mother who pampered him with money whenever he asked. At the *ripe old age* of seventeen Martin Cash was transported as a convicted felon to Botany Bay. By his own admission, jealousy had taken possession of him, and he had fired his musket through the window of his mistress' house hitting a rival suitor in the shoulder. In New South Wales he managed to keep a clean slate and was eventually given his ticket-of-leave (document of parole). He was now free to journey to Van Diemen's Land with his new sweetheart Bessie Clifford. But by 1839 he was in trouble again, convicted of larceny and sentenced to seven years.

He escaped custody three times, and each time he was recaptured he was returned to Port Arthur, Van Diemen's Land's notorious prison for re-offenders. These events occurred in the years 1833-1877. Following each escape more time was added to his sentence. However Cash escaped from Port Arthur one last time, absconding from a work gang, he swam across shark-infested waters at Eaglehawk Neck (where an isthmus joins Tasman Peninsula to the main island) with two other convicts, Kavanagh and Jones. Stripping off, they had bundled their clothes together for the crossing; however all lost their attire in a strong tide. Now naked, they trekked overland until they found a road gang's hut where they stole clothes. The three became a gang of bushrangers (highwaymen) robbing inns and the better-off settlers' remote farms. Over time they earned the reputation as gentlemen bushrangers as they did not use unnecessary violence.

All the while Martin Cash's lover lived in a cottage in Hobart Town. But eventually Cash heard rumours that another man was in her life. Jealousy enraged the thirty-three-year-old and he risked visiting the settlement. In Brisbane Street, not all that far from the prisoners' barracks, an argument erupted between Bessie and Martin. A very rowdy argument, as it unfortunately turned out, and on the street in full public view. The police arrived. Martin was pursued and in attempting to escape he shot and wounded a policeman, Constable

Peter Winstanley, who died in hospital two days later. He was found guilty of murder and sentenced to death by hanging in a time when capital punishment was served to many for much lesser crimes. However at the eleventh hour he received a reprieve that saw him transported for life from Van Diemen's Land to Norfolk Island, a remote and notorious prison island in the Pacific Ocean. (1000 miles from Sydney)

Good behaviour finally paid off and nine years later, in March 1854, Cash was given permission to marry Mary Bennett, another convict, and with his new ticket-of-leave he finally returned to Van Diemen's Land (Now re-named Tasmania) when Norfolk Island was closed. (The Cessation of Transportation Bill was passed in 1853 and the last convict ship, the St Vincent, arrived on the 26th of May 1853)

Martin Cash received a conditional pardon in May 1856 and travelled to New Zealand with his wife and their only son, also named Martin. Martin Cash returned to Tasmania and died in his bed in 1877 – the only bushranger to die of natural causes as a free man.

Solomon Blay the hangman was never happy about these events. He forever wanted to hang Cash.

Solomon Blay was born in in the village of St Aldate's near Oxford six years later than Cash and would outlive him by twenty years. Unlike Cash he was born into poverty. Under such circumstances crime was widespread and for many families like the Blays stealing was the only way to feed the family. Under such terrible conditions it was inevitable Solomon's father, Joseph, would eventually be caught. He received 14 years' transportation for stealing two coats. About the same time sixteen-year-old Solomon was caught stealing onions. History has recorded the leniency of an understanding magistrate:

> *Young man, you have been found guilty of a crime, for which in years gone by your life would have been forfeited; and even now, there are many who are passing their lives in hopeless servitude, for smaller offences. I hope your first departure you have made from the path of honesty, and in the trust that your escape may make you in future a worthier member of society, I pass upon you the nominal punishment of four months' imprisonment.*

Indeed, for the times Solomon Blay was a most fortunate lad. However one year later he was found in possession of one sack of potatoes taken from a local field and was sentence to one-year's gaol with hard labour. Included in the sentence the magistrate ordered Solomon serve three separate spells of a fortnight each in solitary confinement. This left Blay with a deep resentment of society. Solomon left prison bitter and cunning. By 1836 Solomon Blay was back in prison for the far more serious crime of forging the King's coin. He received fourteen years' transportation. After four months of misery waiting on board the prison hulks (with hard labour ashore included) Blay was finally transported to Van Diemen's Land with 253 other lost souls, on board the convict ship HM *Sarah*.

Sarah anchored in Sullivans Cove, Hobart Town on March 29th 1837. Solomon had turned twenty-one on the voyage. Once ashore he was written up in the roster.

Solomon Blay. Convict No.2598

Trade. Boatman.

Height. 5ft8 3/4inches.

Age.21

Complexion. Sallow.
Head. Large, long.
Visage. Long.
Hair. Dark brown.
Eyes. Blue.
Nose. Medium length.
Mouth. Rather wide.
Remarks. Deeply pock-pitted, small lump under right
  eye.

He was now the property of the British colony.

Interestingly convicts were encouraged to have tattoos for, in an era before photography, a tattoo helped identify the prisoner.

Blay maintained a reasonable record. He was by no means a model prisoner but not many were. By 1840 his application to become the Hangman of Hobart Town was approved by Lieutenant Governor John Franklin, the same Franklin who would vanish in the Arctic searching for the Northwest Passage. With four years of his sentence remaining, he would still be kept in prison but with a monthly salary of seven pounds one shilling and seven pence. He would also see a reduced sentence, but the price to pay was to become the most hated man in the colony.

Blay was angered by Martin Cash's reprieve from the death penalty and the fact that he did not hang Cash annoyed him all his life. And Hobart Town was a small community, and both men liked a drink, so their paths would often cross in the inns and taverns. On these occasions Cash took great pleasure in taunting Blay for the fact he had escaped the hangman.

Blay hanged over 200 felons in a long career ceasing in 1891 and he went on to outlive Cash by twenty years, dying in 1897.

Van Diemen's Land. A short history.

Until the dawn of the nineteenth century the island of Tasmania, then known to the European world as Van Diemen' s Land, was a forgotten land, a land roamed by tribes of aborigines living in harmony with nature. It was estimated somewhere between 3,000 to 15,000 Palawa natives called the island home at the time of European settlement in 1803. Appallingly, that was about to change.

These people had crossed into Tasmania some 40,000 years ago. Archaeological evidence excavated in the South-West's Warren Cave in 1990 has been dated to 34,000 years, making Tasmanian Aborigines the world's southern-most population during the Pleistocene epoch.

Tasmania was connected to the mainland by a land bridge during the last glacial period but sea level rise following the last ice age, some 8000 years ago, separated these aborigines from their mainland counterparts.

The first recorded European visitor is Abel Jansoon Tasman, a Dutch seafarer and merchant in the service of the Dutch East India Company, who is credited as the first known explorer to reach the southern islands, including New Zealand, in two separate voyages, 1642 and 1644. Tasman named the island Van Diemen's Land after the governor of the Dutch East Indies. Interestingly the expedition did not encounter any aborigines when they landed.

However a French exploratory expedition, under Marion Dufresne, did encounter the aborigines the day he rowed ashore in 1772. At first they were friendly. It was only when a second longboat was dispatched to join him on the beach that the natives grew anxious and responded by throwing stones and spears. Musket shots were fired and regrettably one native was killed and several wounded. It would be twenty years later before another European ship explored the region.

The French returned almost a generation later and animosities were either forgotten, or forgiven. Bruni d'Entrecasteaux's visit in 1792-3 and Nicolas Baudin in 1802 both enjoyed friendly encounters.

Meanwhile from the 1790s the northern most tribes on Van Diemen's Land encountered the sealers, a violent and determined group of piratical characters making a living by trading in sealskins captured from the Bass Strait Islands. Many of these men were escaped convicts from Port Jackson or whalers who had abandoned ship for a castaway lifestyle. Their treatment of aboriginal women was abhorrent; kidnapping them for their sealing skills and forcing them to gratify their 'companionship' urges. Many were kept tied up and treated like dogs. Many of the Aboriginal men were murdered by sealers.

British settlement and domination was not far off.

In December 1798, ten years after the first fleet arrived to settle New South Wales, Mathew Flinders and George Bass sailed to Van Diemen's Land's Frederick Henry Bay in their little colonial sloop *Norfolk*. They circumnavigated the southern lands proving it was an island by exploring the strait between the mainland and Tasmania, which now bears the name, Bass Strait. In the southern estuary, now known as the River Derwent, they sailed parallel along the seven-mile beach coastline believing the bay to be the one Abel Tasman chartered as Frederick Henry Bay, 156 years earlier in 1642. They did not, however, come ashore.

Four years later the wily French were prowling about the Pacific once more, spying on the British colony on behalf of Napoleon. The expedition of the French explorer, forty-eight-year-old Captain Nicolas Baudin, sailed into New South Wales' Port Jackson on board *Geographe* and *Naturaliste* in the summer of 1802. Like true gentlemen officers, the British entertained their enemy in Sydney Cove. Many of Baudin's crew suffered scurvy and were permitted recuperation time in the NSW sun, whilst the officers were entertained at government house. But over roast wallaby, Madeira wine and rum the French bragged about erecting the tricolour on Van Diemen's Land shores, while recently there. (It is rumoured they imbibed too much of their host's hospitality)

They told of discovering Pittwater with its good anchorage, rich black soil, tall timbers, white freestone for building material and an endless source of fresh water. Why even Napoleon was keen to have a settlement here, they declared. After dinner this night the French officers showed off charts of Van Diemen's Land with areas coloured in gold and red denoting the proposed French settlements.

Among Baudin's crew a young Louis Freycinet and Francois Peron had gone ashore in what is now known as Freycinet Peninsula, ostensibly to collect flowers and insect specimens. While there they planted a small provider garden of their own. Clearly, they planned to return or at least leave a food source for future expeditions.

When the gout-pained NSW governor, Philip Gidley King, heard of this French boast he was furious and his response immediate. The southern island must be colonised and staked British for George III before the French did likewise for their rogue emperor, Napoleon. Before the French even sailed out of Port Jackson, King sent a young lieutenant, Charles Robbins, in the small schooner *Cumberland* to seize King Island for King George 111, under the French noses. To make a statement, Robbins claimed Port Philip next.

I don't think Tasmanians today realise just how close we were to being a French colony. We might all be speaking the French language and eating our daily baguettes. The local snails would probably taste alright too if we gave them a chance. Baudin's officers also sang the praises of the north coast of Van Diemen's Land, claiming the rich bounty of what would be Port Dalrymple, George Town and Launces-ton.

But with France's economy struggling through what would come to be known as the Napoleonic Wars, the French sailed for Europe and eventually Colonel Paterson was dis-patched south where he settled this northern coast.

Tasmania could also very well have been Dutch for that matter. Abel Tasman anchored *Heemskerk* and *Zeehaen* off-shore near Hobart on 1 December 1642. But the surf was up at Seven Mile Beach and the Dutch could not land, causing Tasman to send a strong swimmer, Master Carpenter Pieter Jacobsz, ashore to plant the flag of the Prince Frederik Hen-drik, as a token gesture of Dutch possession. Endearingly, today Tasmania bears the man's name.

Hobart Town finally settled.

To blight the French further, Governor King sent a young, albeit foolish, Lieutenant John Bowen to the Derwent estuary to claim southern Van Diemen's Land for King George III, arriving on board *Lady Nelson* and the whaler *Albion*, on 12 September 1803. He unwisely chose to settle on a marshy landing on the river's eastern shore.

Months later on 11 February 1804 Lieutenant Colonel David Collins was sent by King to join Bowen and establish a permanent settlement. He sailed aboard the grossly over-crowded 481-ton convict transport *Ocean*, captained by Captain John Mertho. Accompanying him was his chaplain, the Reverend Robert Knopwood, Lieutenant Edward Lord with 25 Royal Marines and 178 prisoners from Port Phillip.

Previously Collins had abandoned Port Phillip in Victoria declaring the settlement as an unsuitable, sandy waterless wasteland. It's now called Melbourne.

On arrival in the estuary Collins was impressed with Pipeclay Lagoon and Pittwater on the eastern shore of the wide River Derwent. But this is well south of Bowen's chosen site, which Collins had yet to inspect.

Knopwood was also impressed, writing glowing reports also in his diary where he noted the reedy shores abounded in the game precious to him as a sportsman and a lover of good living:

> *'We see a great number of wild fowl and one emu,'* he wrote. *'Quails, bronze-wing pigeons and parrots. At 4 we returned to the party we left and got a great quantity of oysters. It appeared to me that the natives were much better supplied with fresh fish and birds than those at Port Phillip. Near the first lagoon which was*

large, more than 12 or 14 miles round, was a quantity of flax and very fine, ducks and teal, and I think woodcock was flushed.'

That was written the morning after they landed at Bowen Bay. The next day they encountered their first natives. A party of 17 appeared.

Knopwood wrote: *'They were well made, entirely naked; some of them had war weapons; they had a small boy with them about seven years old, and did not appear to flee from them.'*

But innocence was lost that day. Tragedy awaited these tall brown hunters with their ochre matted hair, carrying long thin spears accompanied by their women wearing gleaming necklaces of shell and carrying woven baskets and stone hand axes. The sight of the tribe passing by on their way to find fresh hunting grounds panicked an ignorant Lieutenant Moore and his charge of uneducated marines. They fired a carronade loaded with canister shot into the tribe. It is not recorded exactly in the history books but there would have been many aborigines wounded, if not fatalities.

Collins was rowed ashore at ten o'clock on the morning of 16 February and inspected Bowen's new settlement, basically a few tents. He was not happy. What he saw was a desolate repeat of Port Phillip Bay, from where he had just sailed; a land of marsh and brackish water; a miserable trickle only, could be gathered as soakage, through the sands and into their sunken water barrels.

The next morning Collins, Reverend Knopwood, Collins' kinsman William Collins, two marine guards and a rowing crew, journeyed down river in search of a better location to start a settlement. En route several points and landmarks were charted and named, with Collins naming Sullivans Cove himself, after the Permanent Under Secretary to the Colonies, John Sullivan.

The natural and deep harbour was surrounded by tall timber growing back into the rolling foothills of a mountain they referred to as Table Mountain, due to its resemblance to the mountain at Cape Town. This would be renamed Mount Wellington in honour of the famous Duke of Wellington, some years after he defeated Napoleon at Waterloo in 1815. Now in the 21st century Mount Wellington shares its name with the aboriginal name, kunanyi.

The area appeared unsettled by the indigenous people. There were streams running east through the mountain forests of eucalypt and the tea-tree forests closer to the shore. Here the water filtered through reeds where bird life was prolific. The location for a settlement was idyllic.

Idyllic for the moment. It would not be too long before these fresh water rivulets ran with cholera and other pestilences of 'civilisation'.

The main stream poured into the harbour either side of a rocky outcrop, a sparsely timbered islet, which, at low tide, was linked to the shore by an isthmus, or a bar of sand.

Collins made a short walk that day into the woods with Knopwood, and immediately recognised the area as suitable for the new settlement. The water ran deep and swift through the forest and was clear, cool and sweet in the height of summer. Timber and stone, lime and clay were all there in abundance. The soil was black and rich and ideal for corn, which Collins preferred to grow. The islet, he named Hunter Island, would prove ideal for unloading stores and also protection of their precious supplies.

(Captain John Hunter was Second Captain of the First Fleet and governor of New South Wales from 1795 until 1800)

'The Lieut.-Governor, Collins and myself went to examine a plain on the S.W. side of the river, the plain extensive and continual run of water which is excellent, it comes from a lofty mountain, most resembling the Table Mountain at the Cape of Good Hope, the land is good, and the trees very excellent, the plain is well calculated in every degree for settlement.'

Bowen must have felt supremely inadequate. He had arrived on the 12th of September. What on earth had he been doing for five months, swatting mosquitoes in the swamplands of a land now called Bowen's Park?

Within weeks a village of wattle and daub dwellings sprung up at Sullivans Cove, and a government 'house' was erected, mostly of canvas at this early stage, on the site now known as Franklin Square.

In 1807 the population swelled somewhat as the penal colony of Norfolk Island was abandoned and its residents sent to Hobart Town, as the new settlement was now referred. Unfortunately, soon they all faced famine. Some corn and small gardens grew to supplement the meagre and rotting rations sent from Sydney Cove, like two-year-old salted pork and beef. Rice brought from India however was a staple.

Hunting parties were sent into the bush, with fowling piece, powder and shot making kangaroo reasonably plenti-

ful in the diet. Even convicts were sent, armed, into the bushland to hunt. Many absconded, befriending aborigines where
possible. But the reckless shooting of natives at Risdon must
have made the natives wary.

Collins settled the Norfolk Islanders a few miles north of
Hobart Town, at a place they called New Town. Here the soil
was fertile and the more industrious made a go of it.

Eventually, as the decade progressed, younger convicts
were sent to replace the 'old men' Collins had brought with
him in 1804. However, these younger men, while stronger
and fitter, were a dangerous breed to be watched at all times.
Cheap rum from India did not help stabilise the colony.

In those early years government house grew to a three-
room residence. Its walls were one brick thick, the roof was
leaky, but it was not draughty in calm weather or damp on
rainless days. Reverend Knopwood, chaplain to the young
settlement, was better housed on Cottage Green, Battery
Point, where he had a pleasant garden of fruits and potted
herbs. Collins and Knopwood remained close friends and
dined together regularly, often entertaining the masters of
visiting ships.

Except for the facts that the population was outnumbered
by convicted felons – many of them marauding bushrangers
– resentful natives and general corruption amongst the constabulary, Hobart Town was shaping nicely ...

Until the infamous Rum Rebellion of New South Wales.

Sydney Cove was becoming a maverick settlement. Disorder was the order of the day and the straw that broke the
camel's back was the installation of Captain Bligh as governor to replace Philip Gidley King. Yes. The Captain Bligh of

the *Mutiny on the Bounty* fame. The British Government appointed Bligh on the strength of his reputation as being a tough leader. Unfortunately his strict demeanour only replicated the situation on *Bounty* and the rebellion – known as the Rum Rebellion – became the only successful armed takeover of any government in Australian history. The New South Wales Corps, under leadership of Major George Johnson and John Macarthur, deposed the Governor of New South Wales, William Bligh. The military ruled the colony until the arrival from Britain of Major-General Lachlan Macquarie as the new governor in 1810.

The reason I mention this is that the Rum Rebellion had a ripple effect down in Hobart Town.

Bligh, you must understand, was put aboard *Porpoise*, to be sent back to England. But breaking his word as a gentleman, he ordered his ship sail to Hobart Town, much to the embarrassment of David Collins. Collins humoured Bligh with the intention of placing him under arrest and returning him to Sydney Cove. However the wily fifty-six-year-old sea captain, once master of the *Bounty*, saw through Collins's ruse and once again escaped on *Porpoise* before Collins could arrest him. But not before threatening to blow Hobart Town into the Derwent. Had the great mariner, who had once served under the famed Captain Cook, lost his marbles?

Bligh waited out his time anchored in Norfolk Bay on Tasman's Peninsula, continuing to be a thorn in Collins side. Collins, by decree of proclamation, made it an illegal offence to aid or supply Bligh. All the same Bligh waited out the year before returning to Sydney Cove, arriving January 1810. Before the new governor Lachlan Macquarie, Bligh demanded Collins be court-martialled. Unfortunately David Collins,

Hobart Town's founder, collapsed and died suddenly on 24 March 1810.

Shamefully, to this day, David Collins body lies in an unmarked plot somewhere beneath St David's Park.

The settlement's first warehouses were built in the early 1820s on Hunter Island. The narrow isthmus offered security from theft by the aborigines and convicts.

A decade later another group of warehouses was constructed on the opposite side of Sullivans Cove. Collins named Sullivans Cove after John Sullivan, the Under Secretary at the Colonial Office. These later warehouses now make up Salamanca Place, which was originally called New Wharf; probably named by the same creatively minded committee, which named the old wharf on Hunter Island, Old Wharf. I personally prefer the name Old Wharf; it has more charm I feel than Hunter Street. Salamanca Place was named after a town in Spain, which was captured by the famed Duke of Wellington during the Peninsula Wars of 1812.

The indigenous Mouheneener people of the land had little choice but to move on and the aboriginal name for the area has been lost to history.

Now Hobart is a thriving capital city and in recent years has become a tourist Mecca.

About The Author

Craig Godfrey

After decades in the hospitality industry and the best part of forty years since opening the Drunken Admiral Seafood Restaurant Craig hung up the apron to leave family at the helm and indulge in his other passion, writing fiction.

Craig is currently writing the seventh book in a series called Shadow Hunter involving Caspian Hunter who travels to Van Diemen's Land in 1855 from Birmingham to take position as second in charge of Hobart Town's fledgling police department. His adventures around the waterfront inns are boundless.

Another contemporary series, with number five recently completed, involves the chef of a Hobart waterfront restaurant called the Hook, Line and Sinker. Along with his partner, assistant curator at the Tasmanian Museum, they find themselves in continuous trouble whether it be solving the disappearance of rare art works on Tasmania's west coast, caught in hand glider dog fights over the Caribbean Sea, lost in the myriad of tunnels under the battlefields of Flanders or imprisoned by antiquity thieves in Venice.

Other action adventure novels are either set in 1830s Van Diemen's Land, 1940s Tasmanian wilderness and a murder investigation set in Sydney and Darwin in 1974.

Craig was born in Hobart in 1952 and travelled extensively giving him the experiences and escapades he so enjoys putting into print. This includes working as a chef for a restaurant owned by Sydney underbelly figures in the early 70s and cooking in Darwin when cyclone Tracy destroyed the city. Life has been busy and interesting to say the least.

In the 90s Craig independently shot two feature films, a murder mystery set in Southern Tasmania which aired on television and a splatter comedy still available online. He wrote, produced and directed both.

Having led a 'normal' life of work and duty Craig Godfrey decided to follow his real passion of writing fiction. And with Tasmania's fascinating past he has plenty to write about.

Using Tasmania's history as a blank canvas Craig loves nothing more than to weave adventure, mystery and mayhem involving colourful characters from all walks of life. He has published 18 previous titles.

BELLERAPHON'S

CHAMPION

BY

JOHN DANIELSKI

Deep within each man, lies the secret knowledge of whether he is a stalwart or a coward. Three years an un-blooded Royal Marine, 1st Lieutenant Thomas Pennywhistle will finally "meet the lion," protecting HMS Bellerophon at the Battle of Trafalgar.

Not only will Pennywhistle be responsible for the lives of 72 marines aboard Bellerophon but their direction will fall entirely on his shoulders since his fellow Marine officers consist of a boy, a card shark, and a dying consumptive. If he has what it takes to command, it will take everything he's got.

In the course of battle, he will encounter marvels and terrors; from valiant foes to women performing miracles, from the skill of acrobats to the luck of the ship's cat, from a dead man still full of fight to a coward who has none. He and his marines will meet enemy élan will with trained volleys and disciplined bayonets. Most of all, he will meet himself; discovering just how dark his true nature really is.

Europe will be changed forever by Trafalgar, and so will Pennywhistle.

PENMORE PRESS
www.penmorepress.com

THE BENDS
BY
LEAH DEVLIN

Maggie May has only weeks until graduation when Edward Gripp, a wealthy benefactor and the architect of Maggie's art college, goes missing from a campus Halloween party. Bill Bleach, the gawkish young detective assigned to the case, discovers a mysterious labyrinth within the walls of the art college where it appears Gripp spied on the activities of the faculty and students. When Gripp's mutilated body is found and a gorgeous art professor is also slain, panic spreads through art college. No one escapes Bleach's scrutiny, from the party's most distinguished guests to the terrified art students. But his investigation is complicated when he finds himself attracted to Maggie, whose dark and troubled past makes her a prime suspect. Bleach fights to stay focused, determined to untangle the web of lies and stop a devious serial killer from striking again.

Leah Devlin is rapidly establishing herself as a writer of modern day mystery-thrillers. This story is as tight as a piano wire. Life at a seaside town in New England is full of treacherous undercurrents and peril, as residents are threatened by a menace from a thousand years ago. Murder, romance and deceit are a potent mix in this gripping novel, which I didn't want to put down.—James Boschert, author of the Talon Series and *Force 12 in German Bight*

PENMORE PRESS
www.penmorepress.com

WHAT HAMLET SAID
BY
TERRY MORT

Hollywood in the Thirties: Nazi saboteurs, gangsters running gambling ships, British spies and diplomats, FBI agents, starlets looking for the big break, cheap hustlers on the fringes of the law, local cops – some are friends and some are adversaries, but all are involved somehow with Riley Fitzhugh, a private eye who's wondering whether the death of an English aristocrat really was an accident.

PENMORE PRESS
www.penmorepress.com

Penmore Press

Challenging, Intriguing, Adventurous, Historical and Imaginative

www.penmorepress.com